IMPOSSIBLE SAINTS

SAINTS

CLARISSA HARWOOD

PEGASUS BOOKS
NEW YORK LONDON

In memory of Mom,
who believed
and Rob,
who remembered

IMPOSSIBLE SAINTS

Pegasus Books Ltd
148 West 37th Street, 13th Floor
New York, NY 10018

Copyright © 2018 by Clarissa Harwood

First Pegasus Books hardcover edition January 2018

Interior design by Sabrina Plomitallo-González, Pegasus Books

ISBN: 978-1-68177-624-8

10 9 8 7 6 5 4 3 2 1

Printed in the United States of America
Distributed by W. W. Norton & Company, Inc.

1

"Mr. Stelling," she said . . . "couldn't I do Euclid, and all Tom's lessons, if you were to teach me instead of him?"

"No; you couldn't," said Tom, indignantly. "Girls can't do Euclid; can they, sir?"

"They can pick up a little of everything, I dare say," said Mr. Stelling. "They've a great deal of superficial cleverness; but they couldn't go far into anything. They're quick and shallow."

—George Eliot, *The Mill on the Floss*

INGLEFORD, SURREY: JUNE 1907

The day her pupil's father threw Lilia Brooke's copy of Homer's *Odyssey* across the schoolroom was the day she knew she'd have to leave Ingleford. Given time, she could forgive most offenses, but all bets were off if violence was done to her favorite book.

She didn't usually bring the book to school. It was beautifully bound in dark green leather and too sacred to risk among her pupils, most of whom treated their books with a troubling lack of respect. But Anna Martin, Lilia's cleverest pupil, had no copy of her own, and Lilia knew she could trust Anna with hers.

The day in question was ordinary, even dull, until Anna's father burst into the schoolroom. Lilia had assigned an arithmetic problem to the younger girls and reading to the older ones. Then she invited Anna to sit with her at her own desk so she could help with her pupil's translation of Homer.

Anna had just whispered a question about the proper translation of περιπέλομαι and Lilia turned to look at the word in context of the passage when the door was flung open and Mr. Martin—all six feet and eighteen stone of him—strode towards Lilia's desk.

At Lilia's other side, Anna shrank back, her face white.

Lilia shot to her feet, standing between Anna and her father, and demanded, "What is the meaning of this, Mr. Martin? We're in the middle of a lesson."

"Is that what you call it?" A stonemason, he was wearing his work smock, and as he moved, the dust of his trade settled on the floor and the front-row desks. The first-form pupils stared at him open-mouthed.

"Come, Anna," he ordered. "We're going home."

Anna rose hesitantly, looking from her teacher to her father.

"Anna hasn't finished her lessons," Lilia said firmly. "She'll go home later."

Mr. Martin took a step closer—close enough for her to smell the sour reek of his breath—but she stood her ground. She was tall, though slender, no match for this huge man if he chose to be violent. But surely he wouldn't shove or strike her in front of her pupils.

Instead of touching her, Mr. Martin snatched the Homer from the desk beside them and said, "This again? Just as I thought—you didn't listen when I said no more Greek and Latin gibberish for Anna. She's done with school."

He then committed the unpardonable sin, flinging the *Odyssey* across the room with such force that it crashed against the wall. Some pages came loose, gracefully weaving through the air like dead leaves before coming to rest on the floor.

"How dare you?" Lilia cried, torn between wanting to save the book and wanting to scratch the man's eyes out. "You have no right—"

"She's my daughter, and I have the right to take her out of school. Anna, come!"

Anna, head bowed, went to her father, and he pushed her ahead of him towards the door.

Lilia moved quickly. She reached the door first, barring the way out with her body.

"You don't understand how intelligent your daughter is," Lilia said. "She can do anything, learn anything. Be anything."

"She's going to be a wife and mother. And a wife and mother doesn't need to know Latin and Greek."

Lilia didn't move. "Don't you care what Anna wants?"

"What Anna wants!" He snorted. "She wouldn't want all this learning if you hadn't put ideas in her head. You're a menace to these girls, making them unhappy with their lot. Get out of my way!"

Lilia had no intention of obeying him, and he moved as if to push her aside, but at that moment, the headmaster appeared in the doorway just behind her. He was as tall as Mr. Martin, though not as solidly built. He also happened to be Lilia's father.

"What's the trouble here?" Mr. Brooke inquired.

"I'm taking my daughter out of school," Mr. Martin said, "but *your* daughter is in my way. If you don't remove her, I will."

"Remove yourself!" Lilia snapped. "Then all will be well."

"Let's go to my office and discuss this calmly," her father said. "I'm sure it's merely a misunderstanding."

Every conflict was a misunderstanding from her father's point of view. He wasn't a stupid man, so he was either willfully blind to true differences of opinion or using the word *misunderstanding* as a strategy to pacify people. But he had used it too many times with Lilia and her siblings for it to work on them any longer.

Apparently it wasn't working on Mr. Martin, either, for he said, "There's nothing to talk about. If you don't do something about this harpy you call your daughter, you'll be hearing from the school trustees."

Before Lilia or her father could say another word, Mr. Martin pushed past them, dragging Anna after him, and left the building. Behind her, Lilia could hear her pupils whispering excitedly.

"Papa, how could you let him do that?" Lilia said in an undertone. "Not only the way he spoke to me, but abusing Anna in such a way—"

"Let's talk in my office," her father said firmly. "Will you ask one of the older girls to watch the class?"

She clenched her jaw to prevent herself from further protest and returned to the classroom. After asking her most responsible pupil to supervise, Lilia picked up her fallen Homer, carefully smoothing the creased pages and gathering up the loose ones, and left the room.

She and her father made their way to his office in silence. It was a small room at the back of the building, with papers and books stacked on every available surface, including the two chairs.

Lilia moved books from a chair to her father's desk and sat down, gripping her Homer as if it had protective powers. Her father took the papers from his own chair, set them on the floor, and sat opposite her.

"I know how difficult this is for you," he began, "and how much you care about Anna's education, but it doesn't help your case to exaggerate."

"What do you mean?"

"You said Mr. Martin is abusing Anna. There's no evidence to suggest such a thing."

"Refusing her a proper education is abuse, as far as I'm concerned. But he's rough with her, too—didn't you see the way he forced her out of the classroom?"

Her father sighed and rubbed his temples with his index fingers. "I thought you stopped Anna's Greek and Latin lessons when Mr. Martin complained weeks ago."

"I didn't promise to stop them. Besides, Anna wanted to continue."

He looked skeptical. "You didn't push her?"

"No. Do you think I'm some sort of tyrant?"

"No, Lilia, but you're very persuasive and very determined, and sometimes your passion for educating these girls carries you away."

She stared down at her lap and said as calmly as she could manage, "I can't bear the thought of someone with Anna's brain becoming a farm laborer's wife and having ten children."

"What if she's content with that?"

"How could she be?" cried Lilia, angry all over again.

Her father gave her a wry look. "We shouldn't have sent you to Girton College. Though perhaps it doesn't matter—you've never suited Ingleford's simple village school."

"Am I being sacked?"

He looked at her as if he had no idea what to do with her.

Lilia stared at this man who was both her employer and her father. Their resemblance—both tall and thin, with unruly dark hair—didn't extend to their temperament. He was phlegmatic, a peacemaker in situations that Lilia thought called for open war. If he had been only her employer and not her father, she would have fought harder against the injustice she believed was being done to poor Anna.

"You haven't been teaching here very long," he said, "but I've had to defend your unconventional ideas and teaching methods more times than I care to count. And you haven't been willing to change them."

Lilia couldn't deny this.

"This isn't the place for you," he said gently. "I'm sorry, little twig."

The pet name brought tears to her eyes. She blinked them away, concentrating on the bookshelf behind her father's head. She was surprised by the stab of sadness she felt: after all, she had been feeling as trapped in this school as if it were a prison, and now she was free.

"Very well," she said. "Shall I go back to the classroom?"

"You may go home for the rest of the day. No doubt your mother could use your help."

But Lilia didn't go home. Going home before the end of the school day would mean unavoidable hysterics from her mother, who would want to exaggerate every detail of the trouble Lilia had caused for the family. She wasn't ready for that, not with her own emotions so close to the surface. Instead, she went to a place she considered her second home, to see her Aunt Bianca and Uncle James.

Bianca and James weren't really her aunt and uncle, nor were they properly married. Uncle James was the village physician and a childhood friend of Lilia's father, but her family had always treated him as one of their own. When Bianca had left her husband twelve years earlier to live with James, he had lost most of his patients to the physician in the neighboring village. He'd lost some friends, too, but Lilia's family hadn't deserted him. Lilia would have loved Bianca and James even if they hadn't caused a scandal in the village, but the scandal cemented her adoration. It gave her a cause to fight for: a man and woman didn't need an outdated custom like marriage to prove their commitment to each other.

Lilia burst into James and Bianca's small house unceremoniously, as she always did, and startled Bianca, who was in the tiny front parlor doing needlework. Bianca was in her mid-forties and was still beautiful—so beautiful that people often turned around in the street to stare at her. She was all lush curves, with masses of red-gold hair and green eyes. Uncle James hadn't had a chance.

Lilia thought their story was wildly romantic. They'd both been very young when they'd fallen in love and had parted without either of them knowing Bianca was pregnant with his child. She'd moved to London and married Philip Harris, who had loved and raised the child as his own. But when the boy was fifteen, Bianca had left Philip and returned to James and Ingleford, where she'd been ever since.

"Lilia, whatever is the matter?" Bianca exclaimed, setting aside her needlework.

"Mr. Martin has taken Anna out of school," Lilia said, sitting in the chair beside her aunt's.

"Oh dear. Is it because you didn't stop teaching her Latin and Greek?"

"Yes. But she could have gone on to college, maybe Girton. She could have made an independent life for herself, instead of being stuck in this horrid village forever."

"Like you?"

Lilia blinked. "I went to Girton."

"I know. But you're back, 'stuck in this horrid village,' aren't you? Why do you stay here?"

"You know why." Lilia sighed and stared past her aunt and out the window. The trees were lush with summer leaves and a chaffinch was hopping about on the grass.

"You're what, four-and-twenty now?" When Lilia nodded, Bianca continued, "More than old enough to make your own decisions. And your mother doesn't need your help with your siblings anymore. Even Emily is nearly grown up."

"A friend of mine from Girton has cofounded a girls' school in London. She's invited me to live with her and teach at her school."

"Do you want to?"

Lilia nodded. She couldn't possibly express how badly she wanted to move to the city. "But Mama wants me to stay. She'll disown me if I go to London."

"Is she worried for your safety?"

"She says so, but I know she's more worried for the city's safety."

Lilia and her aunt locked eyes, then burst out laughing.

Becoming serious again, Bianca said, "She's hard upon you, Lilia, I know, but she's only worried that you won't be accepted in polite society, that you'll be an outcast like me. Not that you'll do what I've done, of course"—a faint blush colored her cheeks—"but you're so outspoken about women's rights—"

"City people won't find my ideas as shocking as the villagers here do."

"I'm not sure about that. Your ideas may be too advanced even for London."

Lilia shrugged. "I wouldn't mind being an outcast if I were free to live and work as I choose."

"You're stronger than I am. But your mother minds. Very much."

Lilia wasn't afraid of her mother, but she was afraid of what happened when she and her mother argued. "Will you talk to her with me?"

"Certainly. And your mother might feel better about your moving to London if Paul knows you're there. He can keep an eye on you. You'll see him, won't you?"

Lilia hesitated. Paul was Bianca and James's son, but Lilia hardly knew him. She did have fond memories of the summer she'd spent at the Harrises' London home, when Bianca was still with Philip. Paul was three years older than Lilia and had been a shy, awkward adolescent, very different from Lilia's boisterous younger brothers. But he was a brilliant scholar and the person to whom she owed her first lessons in Latin and Greek. Even at twelve, she'd been persuasive, or perhaps just annoying. In any case, she'd pestered him until he'd given in.

Despite this positive experience, there were two counts against Paul from Lilia's perspective. First was his refusal to visit his mother in the twelve years since she'd been living with James in Ingleford. Second, he was a clergyman. And not just any clergyman, but a canon at St. John's Cathedral. Lilia found

Christianity faintly repugnant and its ministers decidedly so. The virtues Paul possessed as a child would have almost certainly been crushed by his choice of profession.

Nevertheless, it was only fair to see the man if it pleased her aunt, since Bianca had been Lilia's advocate in so many ways. It was largely due to her influence that Lilia's parents had sent her to Girton. When she was twelve, Lilia had rebelled against her parents for sending her brothers to school while keeping her at home by running away to London, in hopes of being allowed to live with Bianca and Philip. Bianca had convinced the Brookes that if they promised Lilia that she could attend Girton when she was old enough, she would be easier to manage. Lilia had struggled valiantly, if not always successfully, to comply with her side of the bargain.

Another reason to see Paul was Lilia's precious *Odyssey*, which had been a gift from him as a reward for her hard work as his pupil. Surely any adolescent boy who had given such a gift wouldn't grow up to be a bad man.

2

Ah, but a man's reach should exceed his grasp,
Or what's a heaven for?

—Robert Browning, "Andrea del Sarto"

LONDON: JULY 1907

Paul Harris was alone in the sacristy, removing his vestments and feeling nostalgic. It had been exactly two years ago today that he was installed as a canon at the cathedral. He remembered how nervous he had been the first Sunday he had celebrated the Eucharist. He'd worried that he would stumble over his words or read the wrong prayers. He'd worried that he would drop the Body or Blood of Christ on the floor. He'd worried that he would miss a cue or look undignified at the altar. But none of those things had happened, then or since.

Except for one notable exception, the cathedral clergy had welcomed him warmly and made no disparaging comments about his youth. He had been only five-and-twenty when he became a canon, and even now he was young for a cathedral clergyman. His dream of becoming the youngest dean in the history of the cathedral was surely not out of the realm of possibility.

Paul's musings were interrupted by the notable exception himself, Thomas Cross. Cross poked his head into the sacristy and said, "There you are, Harris. Are you coming?"

"I beg your pardon?"

"Johnson and I are going to visit the prison inmates. It would do you good to come with us." Cross was four or five years older than Paul and hadn't held his own canonry for more than a few years, but he treated Paul like a stupid younger brother who was in constant need of advice.

"I can't," Paul said. "I'm otherwise engaged." He had no intention of canceling a long-awaited luncheon with his friend Stephen Elliott, whose visits to London were rare.

Cross raised one eyebrow. He was darkly handsome, in a pantherlike way—sleek, muscular, and, Paul fancied, ready to spring upon his prey and sink in his gleaming fangs in one quick motion.

"Is that so?" Cross said. Quoting from his own sermon that morning, he added, "'I was a stranger, and ye took me not in: naked, and ye clothed me not: sick, and in prison, and ye visited me not.'"

"As I said, I have other plans," Paul replied evenly, turning to put away the richly embroidered stole he'd been wearing.

"Very well." Cross turned to leave. "Enjoy your solitary religion."

His solitary religion! It was a common taunt from Cross, but it made Paul's blood boil all the same.

Paul flung himself out the opposite door, which led to a private courtyard at the side of the cathedral. He paced back and forth, taking deep breaths, until he could assume his calm public mask again. But as he made his way to the front entrance of the cathedral where his friend Stephen was waiting, he was still struggling to keep his temper.

Stephen greeted him cheerfully and said, "You did a fine job with the Eucharist."

"Thank you."

"What do you say to a walk before we eat?" Stephen said. "It's a beautiful day."

Paul agreed, and the two men headed down the street, Stephen adjusting his pace to match Paul's quicker one. They had met as students at Oxford, and Stephen was now the vicar of Stretham, a village fifty miles from London.

As soon as they were a safe distance from the cathedral, Paul exclaimed, "He ought to be ashamed to call himself a clergyman!"

This violent outburst didn't mystify Stephen, who said placidly, "Ah, Thomas Cross is at his tricks again?"

"Yes."

"What did he do this time?"

Paul related his exchange with Cross, adding, "He loves to make a public display of his so-called faith in action and to criticize me for spending too much time in private study and prayer. I'll be preaching in a few weeks and I'm sorely tempted to include a few of my thoughts on his 'faith in action.'"

"Harris, don't do it. You'll only lower yourself by entering a contest of dueling sermons with him."

Paul sighed. "I know, but the temptation is strong. What would you do in my place?"

"I'd be far too lazy to do anything at all," Stephen said. "Besides, his actions are motivated by jealousy. Not only are you his intellectual superior, but you also have the ear of the bishop. If you could ignore his attempts to provoke you—or better yet, kill the man with kindness—I'm sure he'll tire of the game and leave you alone."

"If I had your temperament, Elliott, it would be easily done. But I'm too susceptible to his provocations. He loves to twist my words to make my position on any subject seem ridiculous. And he loves to contradict me. If I were to say there are three persons in the Trinity, I should not be surprised to hear him insist on four."

Stephen laughed.

Paul noticed that his friend was short of breath. "Shall we sit down?" Paul said. They had just entered Regent's Park, and they made their way to the nearest bench. They sat, enjoying the cool breeze and the birdsongs in the trees above them.

"There are times when I think Cross is right, for all his distortions of my weaknesses," Paul went on. "I find pastoral duties difficult. Although I do visit parishioners, I can't help wishing I were alone, writing in my study, or even preaching from the safety of the pulpit. I don't understand so many of my fellow men. I wish to help them, but I don't know how."

"We all have our weaknesses," Stephen said, "and the best we can do is struggle to overcome them. I half wish I had a Thomas Cross to make me more aware of mine. Mark my words, Harris, he'll make you a better man. As our Lord himself said, 'Take up your Cross, and follow me.' Ha-ha!"

Paul smiled wryly and shook his head. "I don't see how that man will do anything to improve my character."

He changed the subject, asking Stephen about his life, and Stephen regaled him with tales of eccentric parishioners, rodents in the church pantry, and his unrequited love for the village squire's daughter, Rosamond. By the end of the afternoon, thanks to Stephen's calming influence, Paul's mood had brightened considerably.

❧

Monday was a precious day of solitude and a respite from Paul's duties at the cathedral. He spent the morning and most of the afternoon working on his book, tentatively entitled *Anglo-Catholicism in the Nineteenth Century*.

He had just finished his tea when his housekeeper, Mrs. Rigby, appeared in the open doorway of the study. Mrs. Rigby had come with the house, which had always been occupied by cathedral clergymen. The cathedral's proximity to the house and its small but richly furnished rooms would have made the house irresistible to any unmarried priest with the means to afford its rent. Paul had such means, and he made no objection to the landlord's requirement that Mrs. Rigby and the house not be separated.

"Canon Harris, there is a Miss Brooke at the door asking to see you. She claims to be a family friend." Mrs. Rigby was a stately woman with steel-gray hair and a forbidding aspect, and she uttered the word *claims* with particular emphasis.

His head was filled with the intricacies of connecting Anglicanism to its Catholic roots, and Paul at first had no idea who Miss Brooke might be. Then he realized she must be Lilia Brooke from Ingleford. When he thought of Lilia, it was never as a family friend, only as a wild little genius girl from a part of his past he'd rather forget.

"Oh, I see," he said. "Show her in, please."

A few minutes later, Lilia entered the room and Paul rose to greet her. She was tall for a woman; they stood nearly eye to eye.

Paul's first impression of her was in fragments. She wore the businesslike dress of the New Woman, a long, slim black skirt and white linen blouse. Stray wisps of dark hair escaped from under her shabby straw hat. Her lips were perfect—full, yet finely cut. He was struck by the incongruity of such a beautiful mouth on a young woman who clearly took no pains with her appearance.

She shook his hand firmly, like a man. "I'm sorry to drop in on you unannounced," she said, "but I've been meaning to visit for ages."

"It's no trouble," he said with a smile. "I'm glad to see you."

Lilia turned away suddenly, as if he weren't there, and went to the bookshelves. She swept her fingers along the spines of the books, then let them rest on the polished wood of Paul's desk. When she met his gaze again, she said, "This is a beautiful room."

"Thank you." He offered her one of the chairs in front of his desk and pulled up another for himself. "Congratulations on your achievements at Girton. My mother wrote that you ranked above the Senior Classic in the classical tripos. First Philippa Fawcett in the mathematical tripos, and now you. You'll change the way universities treat women."

Lilia gave him a guarded look, as if he had spouted some frivolous gallantry. He noticed her eyes resting on his clerical collar.

"Thank you, but I don't think that will happen soon," she said. "Until Oxford and Cambridge award degrees to women, we won't be taken seriously. It's too easy to dismiss women's achievements as the exceptions that prove the rule. Why should it be shocking or sensational for a woman to rank above the senior wrangler in anything?"

"Change doesn't happen quickly," he said, surprised by her forcefulness.

"It won't happen at all if people don't act. I have no patience for those who propose theories for reform without putting them into practice."

"You're just as frightening now as you were twelve years ago."

"Was I frightening?" Lilia gave him a curious look. Her eyes were an unusual dark blue, the color of the sky during an electrical storm.

"Don't you remember the first time we met in Ingleford? You were playing Jeanne d'Arc and your siblings were the French army. I tried to save your little sister from the battle—she couldn't have been more than two or three—but then you were angry because she was the Dauphin of France and I was interfering. And then your dog pushed me to the ground and muddied my shirt."

She laughed. "I do remember now. Was it really so traumatic for you?"

"Of course. You forget I had no siblings and lived a quiet life. It was a great shock to meet such boisterous, active children."

"We were just playing." Once again her manner changed. In a voice that was both serious and warm, she said, "I don't think I ever thanked you for the trouble you took to teach me the ancient languages. That summer I spent in London with your family was the best one of my childhood."

Paul couldn't keep up with the quicksilver shifts in her manner. It was like trying to catch a wildly thrashing fish, only to have it repeatedly slip out of one's grasp.

"So what am I to call you now?" she went on. "The Very Honorable Reverend Father Canon or something just as ridiculous?" She smiled at him in such a way that he couldn't take offense.

"Call me Paul, as you used to."

She contemplated him. "You surprise me. You're not what I expected."

"What did you expect?"

"A humorless, stuffy, pedantic bore." She hesitated, then added, "Excuse my plain speaking."

"I'm relieved I don't meet your expectations," he said. "Were they based on my association with the church?"

"Yes, partly, but you were rather stuffy when you were fifteen. I didn't think there was much hope for you."

"I was shy around other children, especially girls. It was easier to speak to you in Greek and Latin about books than in English about . . . anything else."

She gave him an arch look. "You speak English very well now."

He laughed. "Are your siblings well?" Since he had met them only once, he couldn't remember which of her four brothers was which, and he remembered her sister, Emily, only as the toddler Dauphin of France.

"Yes, indeed. Harry went into the navy and has just been commissioned as a lieutenant. Edward is a sculptor. John and David are at Rugby, enjoying the games far more than their lessons, and Emily's only fourteen, so she's still at home. She has the sweetest disposition of the lot of us." She beamed with pride, adding, "You really ought to come to Ingleford for a visit when everyone is home for the holidays."

Paul frowned. He had avoided the place for twelve years as if it were the portal to Hell itself, and he saw no reason to change his mind now. "I'm afraid that's not possible."

The best summer of Lilia's childhood had been the worst one of his. While he had enjoyed tutoring Lilia in Latin and Greek, the summer had ended with his mother leaving him and his father to live with James Anbrey. James might have been Paul's natural father, but he was also the destroyer of the only family Paul had ever known.

Lilia must have been thinking of the events of that summer, too, for after a brief pause she asked, "How is your father? Mr. Harris, I mean."

"He is well," Paul said. It was a polite falsehood designed to protect Philip Harris, who had aged prematurely after his wife left him. He was quieter, more guarded, no longer gregarious, though he brightened whenever Paul was with him. Philip hadn't granted Bianca the divorce she had asked for, but he never spoke ill of her or James. Paul considered Philip a saint, not only for this restraint, but also for having married a fallen woman in the first place and loving her baby son as his own.

"Are you a Papist, then?" Lilia asked.

The non sequitur confused him. Had she seen through his falsehood about his father being well, and had it prompted her to express anti-Catholic sentiments? But then he saw that she was looking at his bookshelf and realized she was merely changing the subject.

"Not exactly. I prefer the term *Anglo-Catholic*," he said. "What gave me away?"

"One of our family friends in Ingleford was a Dissenter and he taught us to recognize the signs. John Henry Newman's *Pro Vita Sua* sits in the place of honor on your bookshelf, you're clean-shaven, and you're wearing the clerical collar and cassock, even though you're at home. I don't see the Mark of the Beast waistcoat, though, so perhaps you're not completely lost to Romish practices." She sat back with a smile, clearly proud of herself.

"I'm impressed," he said, and so he was. "I would never have pictured you as a Dissenter, though."

"Oh, I'm not, I assure you. As happy as I am to dissent from almost anything, I'm not one of that party. I can't stomach Puritanism in any form. The last time I attended my family's church, the curate preached such nonsense about the proper role of women that I left in the middle of his sermon. I haven't returned to any church since."

"Are you an atheist?"

"I consider myself agnostic. Being an atheist would require far too much effort. If there is a God, I'm quite sure He is as content not to believe in me as I am not to believe in Him."

"I see."

"Have I shocked you?"

"Not at all. I am of Tennyson's opinion that 'there lives more faith in honest doubt than in half the creeds.'"

"That's generous of you," she acknowledged. "You've also cleverly found out my weakness: how can I dissent from anything when my opinions are met with such kind responses?"

He smiled. "You've said nothing about your life. What are you doing in London?"

"I'm about to begin teaching at a school my friend Harriet Firth helped to found. We went to Girton together and talked a great deal about reforming girls' education. We share the same vision of creating a nation of self-respecting women who have no doubts about their equality with men."

"That seems a noble goal. What sort of curriculum does the school have?"

"It's a small school, with only three teachers, but their curriculum is equal to that of the best boys' schools. Harriet's friend Miss Chapman teaches history, art, and literature; Harriet teaches science and mathematics; and I'll teach Greek and Latin, of course."

"There are already a great many private girls' schools in London. Has your friend had trouble finding students?"

"Not at all. Harriet is a member of the National Union of Women's Suffrage Societies, and most of the pupils are daughters of their members."

"I see." Some of his parishioners were members of the NUWSS, but Paul knew very little about the society.

Lilia leaned forward and said, very seriously, "May I ask a favor of you?"

"Of course."

"If my mother writes to you to ask about me, could you tell her we see each other every week?"

He frowned. "Do you mean you want me to lie for you?"

"Well, not exactly." She bit her lip, looking uncomfortable. "My mother is upset about my move to London. She thinks I'll run wild and get into constant scrapes, as if I'm still a child. Your mother convinced her that if you'll watch out for me, I'll be fine. But I think it's ridiculous to have to report to a man, respectable family friend or not, about my activities. I don't want to put you in a difficult position, though. It's not really the thing for a clergyman to lie. Not on purpose, anyway."

He tried to hide a smile. "Not really. But I'd be delighted to have such a commission. We could have short weekly meetings and I could send honest reports to my mother, which she could then pass on to yours, assuring her of your well-being."

"I suppose we could try it," she said, looking doubtful. Then she glanced at the clock on the mantel and jumped to her feet. "I had no idea it was so late. I must go at once—I promised to meet a friend. She'll be cross with me; I've been late the last two times we've met."

Paul rose also. "Thank you for coming. May I visit you, or do you prefer to come here?"

"Of course you may! Have you a paper and pen? I'll write down my address." He produced the requested implements and she wrote quickly, pausing once to look up at him. "I didn't mean to suggest I wouldn't enjoy your company. I'd be ever so glad to see you again."

Paul found the suddenly uncertain look in her eyes and girlish effusiveness endearing. "The Archbishop of Canterbury himself couldn't keep me away," he said.

She smiled, then raised her hand in farewell and left.

As glad as he was to have seen her, Paul was unsettled by Lilia's visit. He saw nothing wrong with women's well-established positions as lovely, gentle creatures whose main purposes were to support and comfort the men and children in their lives, and it seemed to him that women were generally happy with these roles. But, clearly, Lilia was a different sort of woman. Still, he was disappointed by how utterly conventional she was in her unconventionality: he could identify the signs of the Girton-educated New Woman in her just as easily as she had identified his Anglo-Catholicism.

He thought of the first time he had seen her, as a twelve-year-old Jeanne d'Arc with her ill-assorted French army. Perhaps that was the problem. She could never live up to that first impression. A Jeanne d'Arc who grew up to be a schoolmistress instead of dying a triumphant martyr at the stake was bound to be a disappointment.

3

"You're too fond of your own ways."

"Yes, I think I'm very fond of them. But I always want to know the things one shouldn't do."

"So as to do them?" asked her aunt.

"So as to choose," said Isabel.

—Henry James, *The Portrait of a Lady*

Lilia made her way to the podium, feeling more anxious than she had expected. She was used to speaking before an audience: after all, she had made many speeches in college and in front of her pupils in Ingleford, not to mention the impromptu speeches she had subjected her siblings to throughout her childhood. She was used to bored, even hostile, audiences.

But this was different. It was her first official, invited speech. Harriet had introduced her to Lady Fernham, an influential member of the National Union of Women's Suffrage Societies who had also provided most of the capital for Harriet's school. After talking to Lilia about her ideas for reforming girls' education, Lady Fernham had been sufficiently impressed to arrange the speaking engagement, and Lilia didn't want to let her or the NUWSS down.

Before she started to speak, she took a deep breath and paused to survey her audience. It was mainly women, but there were a few men, too. The small public hall they were in was full. There weren't enough seats for everyone, so some people had to stand at the back.

She began her speech with examples of the ways a poor education limited a girl's prospects in life. After the first few minutes, her anxiety fell away and was replaced by a surge of excitement. Everyone was listening intently, waiting for her next words in expectant silence. Especially enthralled was a girl sitting beside Lady Fernham in the front row who looked hardly old enough to be out of the schoolroom herself. Her delicate, ethereal frame reminded Lilia of Anna Martin, but something about her dark, mournful eyes suggested she was older than she looked. She seemed ill at ease in her fashionable burgundy silk gown.

Lilia went on to discuss the importance of women's suffrage in relation to education reform. "Isn't it time to treat girls like rational human beings instead of empty-headed dolls? Isn't it time to teach them to ask for what they want directly instead of putting them in positions in which they must manipulate and flatter? We can do none of this without the vote."

Several audience members nodded and smiled.

I was born to do this. The thought buoyed Lilia as she continued her speech, words flowing from her as if she had rehearsed dozens of times. In fact, she had only briefly looked at her notes beforehand. Now, she said things that hadn't even occurred to her when she was planning the speech.

"Our struggle is great, but do not be discouraged. Do not think, 'What good can I, one little woman, do for the mighty cause of womankind?' Do not wait for others to act because you are afraid. Do what you can in your corner of the world and know that a great army of women acts with you. No fight men have ever embarked upon is more noble than this."

The sad-eyed girl's eyes lit up as Lilia spoke, and she spoke as if to her alone. She concluded by saying, "Let me leave you with some words, slightly amended, from Shakespeare's *Henry the Fifth*:

> She which hath no stomach to this fight,
> Let her depart; her passport shall be made
> And crowns for convoy put into her purse.
> We would not die in that woman's company
> That fears her fellowship to die with us."

The audience's applause was gratifyingly loud and long, and it continued as Lilia left the podium and made her way back to her seat beside Harriet. People who didn't know Harriet were often intimidated by her: despite her small, rotund figure, she had piercing gray eyes and a face that was stern in repose.

"Good work!" she whispered. "Using King Henry's Saint Crispin's Day speech was a brilliant touch."

"Thank you. Harriet, do you know that girl beside Lady Fernham?"

"That's her boarder, Ellen Wells. I'll tell you about her later."

When the meeting was over, Lilia rose from her seat and was instantly surrounded by several women who congratulated her enthusiastically on her speech. She accepted their compliments with pleasure, then turned to Lady Fernham and her companion, who were waiting to speak with her.

Lady Fernham, an attractive middle-aged woman, made the necessary introductions. Miss Wells, even more fragile-looking at close range, murmured something that could have been "How do you do?" but she spoke so quietly that it was nearly inaudible.

"You're an inspiring speaker, Miss Brooke," said Lady Fernham. "It's a pity women can't be members of Parliament, for I should like to see you in a position where you could influence the decision makers in our country more directly." Lady Fernham's husband was an MP, and Harriet had told Lilia that Lady Fernham was the driving force behind many of Lord Fernham's political decisions.

"Thank you."

"You make us believe we'll get the vote soon," Miss Wells said, a little louder this time, but Lilia still had to lean closer to hear her.

"It depends on how hard we're willing to fight for it," Lilia replied.

"Indeed." Lady Fernham studied her thoughtfully. "I hope the other NUWSS members will apply what you said about direct action to themselves. We are too ladylike sometimes, too willing to wait patiently. We could use more young women like you, women who are willing to act—even fight, if necessary. You'll be a good model for my daughters. I'm glad you'll be teaching them."

"Thank you. I'm very much looking forward to meeting them."

Lady Fernham was called away to talk to another woman, and as she turned to leave, Lilia felt a timid hand on her arm. It was little Miss Wells.

"I beg your pardon, Miss Brooke," the girl said, speaking so softly once again that Lilia had to bow her head to hear her. "I wanted to thank you for your speech. Your words gave me courage."

"I'm very glad to hear it," Lilia said.

"I was wondering," Miss Wells said slowly, "if you might be willing to come with me to visit a friend of mine. She's in difficult circumstances, and if you would talk to her, I think she'd be greatly encouraged."

"Of course. Where does your friend live?"

Miss Wells hesitated before replying, "At the Whitechapel House of Mercy."

"Oh. A penitentiary?" Lilia guessed from the name that the place was one of the charitable institutions that housed so-called fallen women.

"Yes." The girl blushed and looked away. "If you consider it a charity visit, there would be no danger to your reputation—"

"Miss Wells, I'm not in the least concerned about my reputation," Lilia interrupted. "I've never visited a penitentiary before, but I assure you I have nothing but sympathy for the women there. I'd be glad to see your friend."

"Thank you so much." Miss Wells smiled tearfully, in a way that made Lilia feel like a princess scattering largesse to the populace.

Harriet and Lilia had much to talk about during the long walk back to Harriet's house once they left the meeting hall. First, Harriet told Lilia what she knew of Ellen Wells's background. Ellen was eighteen years old and had until recently been an inmate at the Whitechapel House of Mercy. Unlike most of the other inmates, Ellen had been reasonably well educated by her father, a widower who had been a poor country parson. She had no other family, and her father died when she was sixteen, leaving Ellen penniless. She came to London and fell into the clutches of a young wastrel, who took advantage of her and then abandoned her. She found herself on the streets and became a prostitute. A few months later, she was arrested and recommended by a justice of the peace to go to the penitentiary. Lady Fernham, in the course of her charity work, met Ellen there and took her in when she was released.

"If girls were better educated, fewer of them would become prostitutes," Lilia said in response to this story. "Even for the middle classes, the useless accomplishments that pass for education only train women to please men and to exchange their bodies for a man's economic support."

"You sound like Mary Wollstonecraft," Harriet observed with a smile.

"That's just it, Harriet. Doesn't it bother you that we're still making the same arguments she made more than a hundred years ago, and so little has changed?"

"Of course it does. But I don't know what to do about it. At least we're trying to improve girls' education with our school, though it seems a small thing sometimes."

Harriet's parents had died shortly after she was born, and she had been raised by her grandfather, who had encouraged her independence. He'd died when Harriet was two-and-twenty, leaving her his London house and a small inheritance, most of which she had used to start the school.

"I don't mean to be discouraging," Lilia said. "The school is a noble venture, and I'm grateful for the opportunity you and Lady Fernham are giving me to teach there. Not to mention allowing me to live with you."

"You're helping me, as well. There was no other candidate who shared our ideals and was suitable for the position. And I confess, I get lonely sometimes, so a housemate will suit me perfectly. We orphan spinsters need company, you know!"

❧

A few days later, Lilia received a visit from Paul. Having seen his spotless, beautifully furnished house, she felt self-conscious about the state of the private sitting room Harriet had offered her. It wasn't Harriet's fault, although her severe utilitarianism coexisted uneasily with the heavy, dark, mid-century furniture and draperies and her grandfather's extensive collection of antique pipes, which were mounted on the walls in this room and the main parlor. Harriet had cleared out the spare bedroom and sitting room for Lilia, but the pipes were fastened so firmly to the walls that she had given up trying to remove them.

The bigger issue was that Lilia had only to spend a few days in any room before it became overpopulated with books and papers. No matter how hard she tried to organize them, they were always spilling onto every available surface. And when Harriet's maid, Lizzie, showed Paul into the sitting room, the papers were in a worse state than usual and there was nowhere for him to sit.

"I'm sorry, miss," Lizzie said. "I would have shown Canon Harris into the parlor, but Miss Firth has two callers there already."

"If this is a bad time, I can return another day," Paul said.

"No, it's fine. Just give me a moment." Lilia moved a stack of papers from a sturdy wooden chair and another from the sofa, then handed them to Lizzie with a whispered instruction to deposit them wherever there was space in Lilia's bedroom.

Before Lizzie left the room, she whispered, "Are you all right, miss?"

"Yes. Why wouldn't I be?"

"We've never had a member of the clergy here before. I thought you might be ill."

Stifling a laugh, Lilia said, "He's a friend. Please bring us tea when you have a moment."

Once the maid left, Lilia said to Paul, "Poor Lizzie seems to think I'm near death and you've arrived to perform the last rites—or is that something only Catholics do? You must think this is a truly wicked house."

"I think nothing of the kind," Paul said with a smile. "People tend to react to my presence in strange ways. In any case, you look perfectly healthy, so that ought to set her mind at ease."

Lilia invited him to sit, and he looked at his two choices: the lumpy sofa, dangerous with loose springs, or the plain, straight-backed wooden chair.

"I recommend the chair," Lilia said, noting his indecision. "The sofa takes some getting used to."

He took her advice and, as he sat, gave her a kind look. She wondered if that was his standard look for poor or untidy parishioners.

"If you weren't in costume, people wouldn't react to you so strangely," Lilia said, her self-consciousness making her sound more confrontational than she intended. "Why do you wear it when you're not on duty?"

"I might ask you the same question."

She eased herself carefully onto the sofa. "What do you mean?"

"You're wearing a costume also, what I believe is called 'rational dress.' Why do you wear it?"

Lilia looked down at her ordinary clothing—a white blouse and black skirt. Although she didn't wear the corseted, fussy clothing that was the mark of the fashionable woman, her apparel was far from the extremes of rational dress, such as knickerbockers, or even a divided skirt.

"I don't think our clothing is comparable," she said. "I wear this because it doesn't restrict my movements, the way so many women's clothes do. I don't believe it's healthy to wear corsets or twenty pounds of undergarments, and I don't consider myself an ornament for men to look at, so I dress to suit myself. And you?"

"I suppose I consider myself always 'on duty,' as you put it, and the purpose of my clothing is the opposite of yours. Rather than releasing myself from restrictions, I choose to restrict myself, to set myself apart from the layman."

Lilia couldn't resist an attempt to shock him. "Ah, but the restrictions you speak of are symbolical. I assume you're not wearing twenty pounds of undergarments."

If he was offended, he didn't show it. "Indeed, I am not," he said. "No man has the strength to bear such weight."

She laughed and began to relax. "I do see similarities between us. We both use our clothing as a public, even political, statement. And I heartily approve of restrictions on men. You've been allowed to act too freely for centuries."

With a wry smile, Paul asked, "Would you have us all become monks and exercise complete self-denial?"

"No, I wouldn't go that far. Even a man shouldn't restrict himself too much lest his natural passions overwhelm him."

"I do believe in self-denial," he said gravely, "but only to a point. One must balance command of oneself with an acknowledgment of one's God-given human desires."

"I think self-denial is good for men, but not for women. Men must catch up to women in that respect; we've been taught nothing but self-denial since childhood. I stand with Mary Wollstonecraft in asserting, 'till men are more chaste, women will be immodest.'" Lilia fell silent, thinking of her conversation with Harriet about prostitutes and their clients.

Looking thoughtful, Paul replied, "You're probably right."

"Do you mind if I smoke?" she asked a moment later. Paul glanced at the pipes mounted on the wall and she added, "Not those—they're from Harriet's grandfather's collection. I prefer cigarettes."

"Do as you please," he said. But as he watched her light a cigarette and put it to her lips, he seemed disconcerted. Perhaps he had never seen a woman smoke before. She was pleased she had succeeded in shocking him.

"I read somewhere that it isn't polite to smoke in the presence of a clergyman," Lilia mused. "The advice was for men, though, so I hope I'm exempt."

"You don't seem the sort of woman who worries about polite behavior."

"That's true. I'm content to rely on my own mind and conscience to avoid giving undue offense to others. You probably think me one of the wicked who does 'that which is right in his own eyes.'" She was pleased with herself for having used a phrase from the Bible against him.

"Would you like me to think that?"

"Of course not," she said, impatient with what she perceived as a patronizing tone. "But you'll think it, nevertheless. I can see you've placed me in the category of the fast, modern woman, and there I'll stay until I can prove to you I'm a real person."

"It seems to me you've taken pains to put yourself in that category.

Besides, haven't you categorized me just as quickly? Don't you see me as a dull clergyman who is out of touch with the world, mired in outdated traditions and rituals?"

She hadn't expected him to challenge her in such a direct way. He wasn't as warm or accommodating as he had been when she had visited him, but she was glad of it. Here was someone worth sparring with, if only verbally, and there was nothing Lilia liked better than a lively debate. On the other hand, she didn't wish to go over the same ground repeatedly, especially if it involved having to defend her way of life.

She held her cigarette out beside her to keep the smoke away from him and leaned forward, meeting his eyes. "Paul, if we're going to be friends, we must speak plainly. If we can't overcome the prejudices we have against our respective ways of life, we must at least acknowledge that they are prejudices. I like you, but I don't like the church or the vengeful, punishing God it seems to promote. However, I'll respect your beliefs if you'll respect mine." She paused and gave him a tiny smile. "And in spite of your clerical garb, I believe there's some good in you."

She was rewarded for her forthrightness—or perhaps for her attempt at humor—with one of his dazzling smiles.

"I hope so, Lilia," he said. "I'll admit to my prejudice against the modern woman, but I must say I'm interested in what this particular modern woman will do with her life. I'm not as accustomed to plain speaking as you are, but I'll do my best. I admire your frankness very much."

"Well, that's settled. Now that we're officially friends, we must learn more about each other's lives. Tell me what you do when you're not busy with your parish duties."

Lizzie came in with the tea tray and left again with a curious sidelong glance at Paul. Lilia poured the tea as Paul told her about the book he was writing on Anglo-Catholicism and his regular visits to Philip Harris.

Lilia had to remind herself that from Paul's perspective, Philip was more his father than James was.

Paul asked Lilia what she did with her time, and she told him about preparing to teach her new pupils at Harriet's school and about the successful speech she had given at the NUWSS meeting. She also mentioned her plan to visit the Whitechapel House of Mercy.

"Whitechapel!" Paul exclaimed, nearly upsetting his cup of tea. "Surely you don't go there unaccompanied?"

She eyed him appraisingly. "I haven't yet visited the penitentiary, but I intend to go next week with Miss Wells."

Paul appeared to be struggling to keep his chivalrous impulses under control. "It's not safe for two ladies to go to that part of the East End alone. May I accompany you?"

"Certainly not. I'm confident I can protect Miss Wells and myself from danger, but to have the added burden of protecting you also . . . that's too much responsibility for one woman to bear." She sat back and put her cigarette to her lips again, regarding him from beneath half-closed eyelids.

"Lilia, be serious. You needn't try to prove to me you can take care of yourself. It's abundantly clear that you can. But plunging into a dangerous situation just to prove you can do it is another matter entirely. And I daresay I know London better than you do. You ought to take my advice."

"How well do you know Whitechapel?"

He hesitated.

"Have you ever been there?" she pressed.

"No," he admitted, "but I don't need to go to Hell to know I don't want to spend time there."

She laughed. "That's a terrible analogy."

"Don't you think you could better achieve your ends by adding a little prudence to your fearlessness?"

"You sound like my mother." She tapped her foot impatiently. "Why is it that men's courage is called bravery but women's courage is called recklessness—or, even worse, foolishness? If I were a man, would you urge me to be prudent?"

"I certainly would," he said firmly. "Not everything is a question of sex."

"That's where you're wrong. Everything is a question of sex, but because you're a man, you don't see it."

"I give up." He did indeed look appropriately defeated. "You're clearly determined to see me as the misguided knight wanting to protect a lady who needs no protection."

"Isn't that the truth?"

"Perhaps, in part. But couldn't I simply be a friend and supporter who would like to learn more about your work?"

"I don't know. There's too much of the medieval knight about you, Paul." She set down her cigarette and took a sip of tea. "I deeply regret telling you about the agreement I made with my mother about your keeping an eye on me, since your relish for the role is only too apparent. 'Friend and supporter'? Perhaps, but I'll have to reserve judgment on that until I've seen more evidence. It's all very well to talk about it, but can you act the part?"

"I can and I will," Paul assured her.

"Very well. Then you may accompany us to the penitentiary, as long as Miss Wells has no objection. I'll be watching you, though, and you'd do well to keep in mind that this is a trial period." She softened her severe tone with a smile.

"I understand. No chivalry. Ordinary politeness may be allowed, I hope?"

"Certainly. Let us shake hands upon it."

And they did.

4

We talk of "fallen women;" but for the far greater number there is
no fall. . . . They are starving, and they sell themselves for food.
        —Anna Brownell Jameson, "Sisters of Charity"

A week later, a small group set out for the Whitechapel House of
Mercy. In addition to Paul, Lilia, and Ellen Wells, Lilia's friend
Harriet Firth joined the party. The group had decided to meet at King's
Cross station, a central location for everyone, and take the underground
railway to Whitechapel.

On the way there, Paul remained in the background, feeling out of his
element. Harriet was a solid little woman with a humorless stare, in some
ways even more formidable than Lilia. After the introductions were made,
she looked at him as if she were calculating what price he would fetch if
he were sold to a museum. She and Lilia then proceeded to discuss people
and ideas surrounding women's suffrage that Paul knew nothing about. The
ethereal Ellen was the opposite of Harriet in both appearance and manner,

and her eyes had widened upon seeing Paul, as if she were afraid he would eat her. She said nothing at all.

When this ill-assorted party finally stood before the stark gray stone walls of the penitentiary, Paul began to have serious misgivings. What, exactly, he asked himself, was he doing there? His desire to protect Lilia, which had evidently been as transparent to her as it was to him, seemed laughable now, considering that the East End held few terrors in the daylight, unless one were afraid of grime and a few beggars. But the other motive he had for this trip, which he hadn't shared with her, was to prove Thomas Cross wrong about Paul's "solitary religion." Doing charitable work was something Paul could accomplish just as well as—perhaps better than—Cross could. Thus, Paul stood outside the penitentiary gates, only too aware of his mixed motives and suddenly wishing he hadn't come.

There was little time for internal debate. The group was admitted and ushered into a waiting room of sorts, a room with no windows, only a gas light that produced a greasy, dim glow. A few minutes later, the matron—a tall uniformed woman—entered and said brusquely, "I understood that only two people were visiting Mary Braddock today."

"That was our plan, but we hope you'll allow two more," Ellen interposed in a surprisingly clear voice. It was the first time Paul had heard her speak.

"We don't commonly allow former inmates to visit our current ones, Miss Wells, but Lady Fernham tells me you're a credit to our House of Mercy and will be a positive influence on the other girls. Mary has certainly caused a good deal of trouble." The matron's eyes passed quickly and dismissively over Lilia and Harriet, then came back to rest on Paul. "And a clergyman is always welcome here."

As the matron led the group back through the door through which she had entered, Lilia whispered to Paul, "It seems you're a useful accoutrement when one wishes to gain admittance to heavily guarded places. I won't put up such a fight next time."

"I've never been called an accoutrement before," he said, "but I do hope to be useful."

The brief moment of levity dissipated when they entered the room in which Mary Braddock sat at a large table. Aside from the table and four chairs, there was no other furniture, and once again, the dim light and stark stone walls seemed to forbid any feeling but gloom. The young woman's face, despite brightening upon seeing Ellen, was haggard and pale. She wore a mob cap and a simple gray dress with an apron.

Paul had entertained two incompatible expectations of these women—the romantic, sorrowful, lovely unfortunates of Pre-Raphaelite paintings on the one hand, and the gaudy, brash, painted courtesans of legend on the other. Neither expectation was realized. What surprised Paul most was how ordinary and young Mary looked. She couldn't have been older than seventeen, yet her face was sober and intelligent, reminding him of his father's upper servants. Was this one of the wicked, abandoned creatures that many of his colleagues spoke out against from the pulpit?

Since there were only four chairs, Paul offered to stand, both to be chivalrous and to better observe the group. Ellen took the chair beside Mary, and Lilia and Harriet sat opposite them at the table. After exchanging a few words with Ellen, Mary described daily life at the penitentiary for the benefit of the other visitors.

"We get up at half past five, do laundry at six, have prayers at seven, breakfast at eight. Then laundry again at nine," Mary recited. Her voice was flat and unnaturally loud, as if she'd been told too many times to repeat herself. She continued to account for every hour of her days, ending with, "Bible reading at nine and bedtime at ten."

Paul was struck by the regimented nature of the inmates' lives. It seemed that penitentiary life was modeled on an efficiently run, pious middle-class home.

"Is laundry the only type of work you do here, Mary?" Lilia asked.

"Mostly. Some of us work at sewing, too," she replied. "But I've done neither since I was in solitary."

"Solitary confinement?" Lilia echoed. "How long were you there?"

Mary shrugged. "I think it was three days."

"Why did they put you there?"

"For insolence, Matron called it." The girl glanced at Paul, then back to Lilia. "The chaplain called me a wicked girl and said I ought to admit I'm a sinner. I said I wasn't no more a sinner than he was, and they popped me into solitary before I could take another breath. Matron said I wouldn't be comin' out 'til I said I was a sinner, and I tried to see their way o' thinkin'—I tried and tried, but it didn't make sense to me.

"It was right dark and quiet in that cell and after a time I didn't care what I said—I just wanted to get out. So I said I was a sinner, and they let me out. But I don't believe it no more'n I did before. There ain't no sin in a poor girl keepin' herself alive any way she can." She looked at Paul again, this time with a flicker of fear in her eyes. "You won't tell the matron what I said, will you, Rev'rend? I don't want to go back to that cell."

Paul was horrified almost to the point of speechlessness. After a pause, he managed to say, "I promise I won't repeat a word."

He looked at Lilia, who was clearly both shocked and angry. Lilia turned to Ellen and said, "I thought women enter the penitentiary voluntarily and can leave whenever they wish. Was I mistaken?"

"Nobody is forced to come here," Ellen explained, "but once in, it's difficult to leave. One girl who asked to leave before she was due to be discharged was put in solitary for a week to 'think about her decision.' When she got out of solitary, she decided to stay. It's not like that for everyone, of course. If the girls obey the rules and appear to be sorry for what they've done in the past, they're treated well."

Lilia turned back to Mary. "You've been badly used indeed. What I suggest you do for now is tell the matron and the other staff whatever they want to hear until you're discharged. Then you'll be free to do as you like."

"A girl can't do as she likes without money and a place to live, miss."

"Yes, of course, you're right. I assume you're being trained for domestic service—is that what the laundry work and sewing is for?"

Mary nodded.

Lilia continued, "That should be of some practical use to you. And Miss Wells and Miss Firth and I belong to a community of women that can help you find employment. I'll write down my address so you can come to see me when you've been discharged. I'll be glad to help you." Lilia reached out her hand across the table and Mary took it, staring at Lilia as if she were an angel.

"I'm very sorry for what you've suffered here," Lilia said.

Mary made a swipe at her eyes and said in a choked voice, "Thank you, miss."

Harriet asked whether inmates had the freedom to refuse to attend prayers or chapel services. The answer was no. Paul listened in silence, knowing himself, at least in his professional capacity, to be the enemy.

When the matron reappeared to show the visitors the way out, Lilia turned to Paul with a determined look and said in an undertone, "I must see the solitary confinement cells."

He nodded. As the group made their way back down the dark corridor, he fell into step with the matron. "Would it be possible to have a tour of the penitentiary?"

"Certainly, Canon Harris. I'll show you around myself."

The solitary confinement cells were at the back of the building, and the matron, proud of the cells' apparent ability to turn even the hardest heart to repentance, allowed the group to look into an unoccupied one. The cell was so small that an average-sized woman couldn't stand upright or lie down at full length in it, although there was a tiny cot for that purpose. It was devoid of light and warmth and had an offensive, damp smell. Horror seized Paul for the second time.

When the foursome left the penitentiary and headed down the street, Lilia exclaimed, "I never would have believed such barbaric practices existed if I hadn't seen them with my own eyes! Are we living in the twentieth century or the fourteenth? What good does it do to imprison these poor girls in such a place—a place that claims to reform and make respectable women out of fallen ones? They're better off on the streets!"

"The House of Mercy did some good for me," Ellen said quietly. "It gave me food and shelter when I had none, and some useful training as a servant, but it's harder for the high-spirited girls." She paused. "I'd never seen one of those cells before, though. I confess it gave me chills."

"And such harsh punishment for minor offenses is shocking," Harriet added. "Correct me if I'm wrong, Canon Harris, but I believe the Bible teaches that we're all sinners—even clergymen—so poor Mary said nothing but the truth."

"You're quite right, Miss Firth," Paul said gravely.

"And where are the men responsible for these women's plights?" Lilia went on furiously, flinging out her arms and nearly knocking over a passing newsboy. "Where are the penitentiaries for them? What consequences do they experience?"

"I think—" Paul began.

"I'll tell you where they are," she continued as the group stepped forward to cross a busy street. "They're in their comfortable homes, enjoying their wealth and their respectable wives. They're probably in high positions in the church and the government. If I met one of them now, I'd—"

Paul caught Lilia's arm and pulled her out of the way of a motorcar that was bearing down upon them. Breathlessly she turned to face him, the full brilliance of her outrage in her eyes.

"I'm not one of those men," he reminded her.

"Of course you're not." She blinked and looked from Paul to Ellen and Harriet, who were safely on the curb and watching her with interest. "Forgive me. I get carried away sometimes."

"There's nothing to forgive. But I do think you need protection if you're going to get carried away on the street and not watch out for traffic."

Harriet and Ellen safely crossed the street together, and Paul and Lilia followed. She took his arm as they walked and slowed her pace.

"Now that I know innocent women are being treated so harshly," she said in a calmer tone, "I must do something."

"Not all the women in penitentiaries were seduced," he pointed out.

"No, some of them chose to be prostitutes because it was the wisest economic decision they could make. I can't say I blame them—again, from a purely practical point of view."

It was jarring to hear her use the word *prostitutes*, but he rallied. "I can't argue with your logic, but focusing on these ugly realities alone is surely discouraging. Would you deny yourself the pleasure of gazing upon a flower in full bloom in order to save one that's trodden in the mud?"

"A flower in full bloom doesn't need me," she said, looking at him with serious eyes.

"But perhaps *you* need it."

"Perhaps, but only when I'm old and my work is done," she said dryly. "Then I'll luxuriate in all the hedonistic pleasures you seem to think I need!"

"You're ridiculous," he said, smiling. "If looking at a flower is a hedonistic pleasure, then I'm a hopeless voluptuary."

"Are you? What other pleasures do you allow yourself to indulge in?"

"Let me think—there are so many. I admire beauty wherever I find it; I love art, poetry, music . . . there's really no end to the pleasure I find in such things."

"I'm shocked!" she exclaimed. "It seems to me I'd be the better priest."

"I agree with you. You exercise self-denial and take action to do good for others, but I am constantly distracted by these self-indulgent pleasures."

"Now *you're* being ridiculous," Lilia objected.

"I do understand why you're angry about the penitentiary," he said. "It's the Contagious Diseases Acts all over again, women treated like criminals while the men who are responsible for the true problems go free."

In order to halt the spread of venereal disease, the acts had allowed the police to detain and inspect any woman who was suspected of being a prostitute. Her middle-class clients—and accusers—were never so much as questioned.

"That's exactly it!" Lilia exclaimed. "It's another example of addressing the symptoms of a social problem instead of the cause. And so many of the supposed solutions ultimately harm women, while having no effect on men. Why, for example, won't people consider addressing overcrowding in the slums by providing the women there with contraception?"

Contraception was a word Paul had never heard from the lips of a respectable unmarried woman. He associated it with prostitution, as most people did, and though Lilia had already shown that she knew more about these things than a well-brought-up young lady should, he couldn't help being taken aback.

When he didn't reply, Lilia looked up into his face and said, "I've shocked you."

"No, not exactly. I just . . ." He floundered for a moment, then decided she was probably just repeating a theory she had learned about at Girton College. "It's not something I've given much thought to."

"Well, you ought to. Everyone ought to."

He was saved from having to reply by Harriet calling to them from the other side of the street. Paul and Lilia had been so engrossed in their conversation that they had walked in the wrong direction.

～

Lilia sat facing her pupil Amy Hightower at the large table in the middle of her schoolroom. Lessons were over for the day, but she had asked Amy to stay behind. From Lilia's first day as a teacher at the Fernham Preparatory School for Girls, she had sensed that Amy would be a thorn in her side. Now, two weeks later, she saw no reason to change her mind.

"Amy, do you know why I want to talk to you?"

The pretty fifteen-year-old shrugged, her cupid's-bow mouth flattening into a frown. Despite her habitually blank expression, she was clever. Not as clever as Anna Martin, but clever enough to attend university and make something of herself if she wanted to.

"You haven't done the work I assigned yesterday, or the day before that," Lilia said. "And the Horace translation you showed me at the beginning of the week was very poor. I know you can do better."

"I haven't had time," the girl said sullenly. "I had to go to the shops with Mama nearly every day. We're having a big family party in a few days."

"That doesn't explain why you're not doing the work during your lessons."

Amy twisted a glossy auburn curl around her finger and stared across the room. "I don't understand why it's so important to learn Latin."

"Then you haven't been listening to me. Latin is the foundation of Western civilization. It's at the root of every discipline, as well as the English language. It trains one's mind—" She broke off, seeing her pupil's bored expression. "Don't you want the same opportunities that boys your age have?"

"No."

Lilia had expected reluctance but not outright denial. She stared at the girl, who separated a thick strand of hair into three sections and began to plait it.

"Amy, stop playing with your hair."

The girl obeyed with a toss of her head and a stony look.

"Your mother wants those opportunities for you, even if you don't. She wouldn't have enrolled you in this school otherwise."

"She just wants me to be able to teach my sons, when I have them."

Puzzled, Lilia said, "Why do you say that?"

"She wrote that thing . . . oh, what's it called? For the NUWSS. About public-spirited sons."

Lilia recognized the reference to a handbill Mrs. Hightower had written that listed reasons to support women's suffrage, including Lilia's least favorite reason: *Because public-spirited mothers make public-spirited sons.* She found it baffling that someone as active in the women's suffrage movement as Mrs. Hightower would focus on sons and ignore daughters.

"That may be so," Lilia said, "but you won't be able to teach anyone if you don't learn it yourself first. Now, will you improve your performance, or must I speak with your mother?"

Amy grudgingly promised to improve, and Lilia let her go.

Alone in the room, Lilia removed her little round spectacles, which she wore only at the school—she thought they gave her a necessary air of gravitas—and stared at the portrait of Mary Wollstonecraft on the opposite wall. The walls of her schoolroom in Ingleford had been covered with maps and charts, but at the new school Lilia had decided to put up portraits of admirable women, in hopes of inspiring her pupils.

"What would you do with Amy?" she said. Mary Wollstonecraft returned her gaze serenely, keeping her wisdom to herself.

A moment later, someone knocked softly on the half-open door. It was Ellen Wells.

"Are you busy?" she asked.

"Not at all. How nice to see you. Please, come in."

Ellen hesitated in the doorway, looking nervous.

Lilia repeated her invitation and patted the chair beside hers. Ellen came in and sat. In response to Lilia's quizzical look, she said, "I don't like schoolrooms. They remind me of a schoolmistress who used to hit my shoulder with her cane whenever she thought I wasn't paying attention."

"We don't do that here. Though I can't say I've found a better method of making my pupils pay attention."

Ellen looked shocked. "They don't pay attention? Not even to you?"

Lilia laughed. "You overestimate my ability to captivate listeners."

"You're the best speaker I've ever heard, Miss Brooke."

"Thank you, but please call me Lilia."

She had invited Ellen repeatedly to use her Christian name, but Ellen seemed to consider Lilia so far above her that she couldn't bring herself to do it. There were a few young women like her in the NUWSS who had latched on to Lilia with an almost religious devotion. It was immensely flattering to be a mentor to these women when she herself was only four-and-twenty, but Lilia didn't want to be idealized.

"I'll try," Ellen said.

"I certainly would have paid attention if I'd had an education like this," Lilia said, her mind still on her conversation with Amy. "When I was in school, all I learned were the rudiments of reading, writing, and arithmetic."

Ellen looked surprised. "Then how did you learn enough to be admitted to Girton?"

"I did what I could on my own. Paul helped me, too."

"Canon Harris?"

"I spent a summer with his family in London when I was twelve, and he began teaching me Greek and Latin. When I went back to Ingleford and he returned to Eton, we exchanged letters. He sent me copies of his lessons and corrected my mistakes. I may be the only woman in Britain with an education from one of the best public boys' schools."

Ellen smiled.

"It's all very well to make speeches," Lilia continued, "but I think we must do more if we want to get the vote in our lifetime."

"What do you think we ought to do?"

"Have you heard of the Women's Social and Political Union?" Lilia asked.

"Yes."

"How did you hear about it?"

"Lady Fernham has mentioned it, and I've read about it in the newspapers."

"Exactly." Lilia rose and began pacing back and forth at the front of the room. "The NUWSS was formed ten years ago, but the general public is only barely aware of its existence. Most people have heard of the WSPU, even though it's a newer organization."

The Women's Social and Political Union, led by Emmeline Pankhurst, had been in the newspapers as of late because two of its members had interrupted speakers at a Liberal meeting to ask when the speakers would support women's suffrage. When the men ignored them, the two women demanded that their question be answered and were promptly arrested for disturbing the peace.

Ellen's eyes followed Lilia's movements back and forth as if she were watching a game of lawn tennis.

"Unlike the NUWSS," Lilia went on, "the WSPU sees the need for dramatic action, even for breaking the law. And those women who went to the Liberal meeting merely refused to be ignored. They didn't hurt anyone, but they were arrested and put in jail regardless!"

"But being arrested must be terrible," Ellen put in. "Wouldn't you be afraid to go to prison?"

"Probably. But a little fear wouldn't hurt me, and it would be worth being frightened and uncomfortable, to be arrested for such a noble cause. Just think how many great women in history were imprisoned for their beliefs—Perpetua, Lady Jane Grey, Jeanne d'Arc!" Lilia pointed to the portrait of an armored Jeanne d'Arc on the wall opposite Mary Wollstonecraft.

"We need to show the world we're serious about getting the vote," Lilia said. "It's time to do something to force a crisis. And there's power in the press, too. If our actions are reported in the newspapers, the public will take notice and put pressure on the members of Parliament to listen to us."

"Do you think it would help people like Mary Braddock if we did those things?"

"Of course." Lilia returned to her seat beside Ellen and said urgently, "Right now, men have all the power, and we must depend on them to protect the interests of women. We know how well that has worked so far in places such as the Whitechapel House of Mercy. But when women have the vote, we'll be able to ensure that women like Mary are supported rather than punished."

"I see," Ellen said, her eyes glowing. "Whatever you think we ought to do, I'll do it, Miss Brooke."

5

Yet still from Nuneham wood there comes that thrilling melody
So sad, that one might think a human heart
    Brake in each separate note, a quality
Which music sometimes has, being the Art
    Which is most nigh to tears and memory
          —Oscar Wilde, "The Burden of Itys"

August 1907

Paul didn't write to his mother every week to report on Lilia's well-being, but it turned out to be no trouble at all to see Lilia that often. They both loved to walk, so they spent most of their time together going for long strolls through the city. When he could, Paul also attended NUWSS meetings, especially if Lilia was speaking. More accurately, he lurked at the edges of the crowd. He still didn't understand why the vote was so important, as opposed to more practical reforms that improved women's lives, but he admired Lilia's confident, eloquent speeches. Indeed, few audience members seemed immune to the power of her passionate appeals to their sympathy and sense of justice. Paul often watched the other audience members' faces while Lilia spoke—some of the women, especially the younger ones, held so rapt they almost appeared to be in trances. The older women and the few men present were also attentive, but sometimes they would frown or shake their heads.

After these meetings, Paul rarely had a chance to speak more than a few words to Lilia, as Lady Fernham would invariably rush her off to meet some important person. Paul seemed to have made an instant enemy of Lady Fernham without trying. Upon their first meeting, she had greeted him pleasantly enough, but the look in her eyes told him he was an obstruction, though what he was obstructing remained unclear.

After one particularly long meeting, Paul was pleased to see Lilia approaching him alone, her usual entourage nowhere in sight. But his pleasure turned to concern when he saw how exhausted she looked.

"You're worn out," he said. "When was the last time you took a few hours to rest?"

"I don't remember. Oh, don't scold me, Paul—I'll let you hail us a cab if you can forgo the lecture just this once."

He was surprised by this concession, since she always insisted on walking home. She had what she called an "ideological opposition" to hansom cabs. But they walked together to the nearest cab stand and once inside the cab, Lilia removed her hat and settled back against the upholstered seat with a sigh. Closing her eyes, she said, "Don't think this will become a habit. I'm far too proud to use this method of transportation on a regular basis. Besides, a lady's reputation is sullied if she is seen taking a cab too often, isn't it?"

"Not if she's accompanied by a respectable clergyman," he said lightly. His concern for her exhausted state made it difficult to listen to her banter.

"I'm starting to become suspicious of your motives for becoming a priest. Your position is too convenient an excuse for breaking rules that ordinary people must abide by."

"Perhaps, but I must always cope with laypeople's preconceived ideas of me. They can't look past the cassock and collar." He hesitated. "I don't want to talk about myself. I want to know when you're going to slow down."

She gave him a suspicious look. "Paul, you're breaking our agreement. I'm in a cab and you promised not to lecture me. Besides, you know how busy I am with my new teaching position. It's all I can do to keep up with that as well as my suffrage work."

"Yes, I know." He wanted to say more, but he knew she would protest vehemently, especially if it sounded at all like a lecture. Then a thought struck him. "Lilia, will you come with me to my father's house for dinner on Friday? He has invited his sister and her family, too, and he loves to have additional guests. It would be a well-deserved respite from your work. What do you think?"

"I don't know," she murmured sleepily. "If it's the sort of social occasion that requires me to behave respectably, I can't agree it will be relaxing."

"These people will require no amazing feats of decorum from you. You may be yourself—though you had better refrain from smoking."

"So you would deny me my only vice? Never!"

"I can't talk to you when you're in such a contrary mood. You may consider yourself invited, and you can tell me your answer when you can converse like a sensible girl."

"You're just as contrary. You have a frustrating way of being kind and patronizing at the same time."

Paul sighed and closed his eyes, listening to the carriage wheels rattling on the cobbled street. After a few minutes, he was about to speak again, but he saw that Lilia's eyes were closed and her breathing deep and regular. How tired she must have been to fall asleep in the jolting, noisy cab!

He took advantage of the rare opportunity to study her face, noticing how long and dark her eyelashes were against her pale skin and marveling at the perfect curve and definition of her lips. It occurred to him for the first time that what seemed to be her lack of attention to her appearance might be a deliberate attempt to downplay her beauty. Asleep, she was even more appealing; she looked young and defenseless, unlike her usual confident, even imposing, public self. He felt a rush of tenderness, followed by a complicated mixture of new feelings that forced him to look away abruptly.

Paul didn't want to feel anything more than friendly regard for Lilia, and he wondered if he was spending too much time with her, if she was becoming too important to him. He didn't belong in her world, and she certainly didn't belong in his. Having few friends, he tended to cling intensely to those who entered the inner court of his heart, and Lilia had certainly found her way in. But her presence there didn't have a calming effect like his father's or Stephen Elliott's. She was disruptive and unpredictable, even untrustworthy, as her manner of entry was by stealth instead of by official permission.

Paul didn't look at her again until the cab came to a halt at the house she shared with Harriet. Fortunately, the abrupt jolt awakened her without his having to do so, and she sat up, momentarily disoriented.

"Oh, did I fall asleep? I'm sorry," she said, rubbing her eyes like a child.

"There's no need to apologize. You were tired."

Paul alighted from the cab and reached out to help Lilia down. Still dazed and sleepy, she stumbled a little as her feet touched the ground, and Paul slipped an arm around her waist to steady her. The brief but close contact with her body stunned him, as if he had ventured too close to an open flame. He backed away to a safer distance and bid her a hasty farewell.

～

That Friday evening, Lilia stood in the front hall of Philip Harris's house, Paul's childhood home. It was even more imposing and luxurious than she remembered. Twelve years earlier she had stood in the same spot, awed by the sweeping staircase with its carved mahogany banister, the polished floors, and the high ceiling where a massive chandelier hung. The Harrises had seemed like royalty to her child-self, no doubt partly because of the beggar disguise she'd employed. She had been upset with her parents' refusal to give her the same education her brothers had, and it had seemed a good idea to run away and live with the Harrises. Naturally, her parents had not been pleased with their twelve-year-old daughter's deception or her adventurous escape to London, but they had allowed her to stay for the summer. She hadn't realized then that the disparity between her family and Paul's had more to do with money than status. Philip Harris had made a fortune in trade and had only one child to support, whereas Lilia's father liked to jest that his six children were his fortune.

The beggar-girl feeling washed over Lilia again and she wished she had borrowed—or stolen—a new dress for the occasion. She was wearing her best dress, a softly draped blue silk tea gown with a high waist, but it wasn't new. Lizzie, who paid attention to these things, had warned her it was at least five years out of fashion.

Lilia's discomfort lasted only as long as it took for Philip Harris to turn from greeting his other guests and approach her with a warm smile. She remembered him as an energetic, gregarious man, and if it weren't for his smile, she wouldn't have recognized him at all. He couldn't have been more than five-and-fifty, but his hair was white, his face deeply lined, and the promise of stoutness in his earlier years had been amply fulfilled.

"Miss Brooke, what a pleasure to see you again," Philip said, taking her hand. "When Paul told me the two of you had renewed your acquaintance, I was glad to hear it."

"Thank you. It's lovely to see you again, too." Lilia had wondered if her connection to James Anbrey would trouble Philip, but it was clear that anyone Paul approved of was a friend of Philip's.

Paul himself appeared at Philip's elbow and greeted Lilia with what seemed to her less than his usual warmth, but perhaps it only seemed so in the wake of his father's hearty welcome. Philip's sister, Mrs. Ross, was far more interesting than her husband and two daughters, whom Lilia dismissed at once as dull and conventional. One other guest was present, a friend of the Misses Ross named Grace Cavendish. Miss Cavendish was so beautiful that nobody would have noticed if she were stupid—though that remained to be seen. She was a perfect English rose, blue-eyed and golden-haired, with a creamy pink-and-white complexion.

Dinner was a lavish affair, six courses with two menservants in attendance. Lilia was glad to be seated next to Mrs. Ross, who served as Lilia's example for choosing the correct cutlery to use for each dish, and whose sharp eye and lively wit marked her as a kindred spirit.

Philip and Mr. Ross began the meal with a tedious conversation about a large dry goods company taking over a smaller one, but it turned into a more promising discussion of evolution and progress.

"I'm starting to feel decidedly old-fashioned when I say I believe in progress," Mr. Ross said, fingering the monocle attached to his waistcoat with the air of a world-weary traveler. "These days, it seems people prefer to worry about the future than adapt to their environment. To my mind, adaptation to new methods in business, as well as to new ideas in society, is the only way to survive."

"There's merit in old methods, as well," Philip replied. "I suppose my own Darwinism is restricted to the idea of competition. If old methods can stand up to competition, why not use them?"

Lilia felt a pang of pity, quick to see the irony in Philip's advocacy of competition. Although he had been successful in business, he was the loser in matters of the heart.

"All this talk of competition and survival chills my blood," Mrs. Ross said, setting down her fish fork. "It's all very well in business, I suppose, but in other spheres I'm against it. I can't help feeling sorry for the poor creatures who are proclaimed 'unfit' or unable to adapt to the conditions of modern life. What do you think of Darwinism, Miss Brooke?"

"I find Darwin's theory of survival of the fittest compelling," Lilia said, "and I'm all for competition and progress, as long as the fittest also use their moral sense to help their fellow creatures."

"What of his belief that men are descended from monkeys? Do you find that theory compelling also?" This came from Paul, who was sitting two places away and across the table from her.

Lilia couldn't resist. "There's no doubt in my mind that men are descended from monkeys. But women owe their origin to a different source."

Mrs. Ross burst out laughing and Philip chuckled, too. Mr. Ross, his daughters, and Miss Cavendish looked shocked. Paul's face was impassive but for a twitch at the corner of his mouth.

"Miss Brooke is being satirical," proclaimed Miss Cavendish gravely. "I can't think of men or women as animals. Our souls are the best parts of us, and Mr. Darwin's theory would deny their existence. Don't you agree, Canon Harris?" She turned to Paul with a charming look of appeal that Lilia found irritating.

Before Paul could reply, Mr. Ross broke in. "Perhaps Miss Brooke meant to say that men are merely human creatures, whereas women have a kind of divinity, a spiritual superiority that makes them the perfect guardians of the home."

This was precisely what Lilia had *not* meant to say. If she hadn't felt constrained by her role as Paul's invited guest, she would have plunged headlong into a debate. After a tiny pause, during which she mustered all her self-control, she replied, "I don't believe in any such spiritual superiority. Women are no more angels—or devils—than men are. Many women are unhappy with the pedestals men have placed us on. They isolate us from the rest of the world and give us vertigo."

"I must respectfully disagree with you, Miss Brooke," Grace Cavendish said in her clear, sweet voice. "I see no harm in men's placing us on such pedestals. Surely you can't object to being treated with respect, even to being viewed as the superior sex."

"I do object to it very much," Lilia replied. "Are women to be content with such vain flattery? The only respect I wish for is to be treated like a thinking, reasoning human being, instead of a vacuous ornament." She had said more than she'd intended and she glanced at Paul, alarmed by his still-impassive face. Was he regretting having invited her?

It was clear what Miss Cavendish was thinking. She gazed at Lilia with the tranquil mien of a woman in complete control of her emotions, and her slight smile implied that Lilia's passionate speech proved she wasn't a thinking, reasoning human being.

Mr. Ross added to Lilia's annoyance by raising his monocle to his left eye and examining her as if she were a species of insect he had never seen before. "Ah, you're one of those . . ." He searched for the correct label, but gave up. "What do you call yourselves?"

Lilia raised one eyebrow. "Women?" she said dryly. She could hardly intensify whatever trouble she had caused, and she was unable to stop herself. At the same time, she could no longer look in Paul's direction, so sure was she that he must have disapproved of her treatment of his relations.

Mrs. Ross stepped in to rescue Lilia. "I think my husband wishes to know if you're active in the women's movement."

"Yes, I am."

"Bluestocking!" roared Mr. Ross, dropping his monocle and making everyone jump. "That's the word I wanted!"

"Now really, Mr. Ross," said his wife dismissively, "nobody uses that old-fashioned word anymore. I agree with Miss Brooke's view of women, and I don't think we're so different from you men as you would have us believe. Only children need protection. An adult woman doesn't, except perhaps when she is threatened with physical harm. Why shouldn't women have the same opportunities as men in the world?"

A look of alarm crossed Mr. Ross's face. "Now, my dear, that would never do. Just think of the practical difficulties in the workplace alone. Surely you don't suggest that women should do the work that men rely upon to support their families?"

"I would never utter such blasphemy," Mrs. Ross said, with more than a hint of mockery in her voice.

"And think of the damaging effects of regular public employment upon women's more delicate constitutions," Mr. Ross continued.

This was too much for Lilia, who nearly knocked a plate of lamb cutlets out of the hands of the manservant at her shoulder as she once again entered the fray. "As a Darwinist, Mr. Ross, surely you would consider allowing women to prove themselves unfit for such employment before declaring them to be so. Where is the harm in allowing women to compete with men for employment? If they are too weak to bear it, they would naturally yield to those men—or women—who are better adapted to survive."

"Ahem. Well, I'll have to think about that," Mr. Ross said, apparently unaware of his ignominious defeat. His wife seemed well aware of it and didn't try to hide her pleasure.

"I have no doubt *you* are well adapted to survive almost anything, Miss Brooke," Philip said, clearly meaning to be gallant.

As the next course was served, the conversation turned to less incendiary topics, and Lilia was relieved that she was no longer the focus of attention. She listened to the Misses Ross describe, in excruciating detail, a dance they had attended the previous week. She listened to Philip's boasts about

Paul's accomplishments and to Paul's good-humored evasions of them. And she listened to Miss Cavendish speak eloquently on the topic of Anglo-Catholicism. Not only was Miss Cavendish's mind expanded by the intellectual richness of the sermons in Anglo-Catholic churches, but her soul was also uplifted, even transported, by the music and liturgy.

During this discourse, Lilia was forced to make a Herculean effort to keep her eyebrows in their usual position. Paul seemed delighted by Miss Cavendish's knowledge of his favorite subject, and Lilia was forced to consider the possibility that Miss Cavendish's beauty had blinded him to her obvious ploy to attract his interest.

Lilia believed that most men became stupid in the presence of a beautiful woman, but she'd expected Paul to have more sense. It was worrisome to think he might have the same desires of any ordinary man, that he might even marry someday. Lilia had never considered the possibility before, and Paul couldn't help but fall in her estimation because of it. Given that he was a devotee of the very Catholic, very celibate John Henry Newman, Lilia had assumed he was as strongly averse to marriage as she was, though he had never said so. What if he should marry a woman she didn't like, or who didn't like her? It would mean the end of their friendship, and she would not take such a loss lightly.

After dinner, Lilia grudgingly followed the other women into the drawing room, leaving the men at the table to converse upon presumably more important masculine subjects. Once seated on an overstuffed sofa, Lilia cast a glance like that of Lot's wife over her shoulder, knowing the men were probably smoking and feeling she'd made a great sacrifice by promising Paul that she wouldn't. A cigarette would have been just the thing to calm her nerves in the face of her worries about Paul, the incessant frivolities from the Misses Ross, and the calm superiority of Grace Cavendish, who, despite her rejection of Darwinism, clearly knew herself to be the fittest of her sex.

The men didn't remain long in the dining room. But Lilia didn't notice their arrival in the drawing room at first, as she was deep in conversation with Mrs. Ross, who wanted to know more about Lilia's suffrage work. But after a few minutes Lilia sensed she was being watched, and she glanced across the room to where Paul stood. He was speaking to Mr. Ross, but his eyes were on her. Oddly, as soon as he saw her looking at him, he looked away. He hadn't said more than a few words to her all evening, and he had seemed uncomfortable in her presence. Was he offended by what she had said at dinner? He was used to her forthrightness by now, though perhaps he worried about the other guests. But he seemed more discomfited than offended.

Philip invited his guests to play the piano, a large, handsome upright at the far end of the drawing room. The Misses Ross were the first to respond and they played a tolerably well-executed duet. Miss Cavendish was next. Her bearing was regal as she sat on the bench and she played a Chopin étude by memory, the rippling arpeggios perfectly smooth and light. Even Lilia, who didn't play but who loved music, was impressed. When it was over, Miss Cavendish blushed charmingly in response to the applause from her audience and was easily persuaded to remain at the piano.

At the end of the next piece, Mrs. Ross asked Miss Cavendish to sing an Italian aria. "You sing beautifully, and I do so love the great arias."

"I will, but only if Canon Harris will sing with me," Miss Cavendish said, turning to Paul, who stood near the piano. "Your father tells me you have a fine voice, and I don't wish to monopolize the music all evening."

Everyone seemed to think this a wonderful idea, and Paul made no attempt to resist. He took a book of Italian arias from a nearby shelf and stood behind Miss Cavendish to turn the pages for her while they sang.

If ever two voices were meant to blend musically, theirs were—Paul's strong, rich tenor giving depth and support to Miss Cavendish's clear, sweet soprano. The singers seemed just as surprised and delighted by this discovery as their audience, and they needed no encouragement to continue.

Lilia was in danger of giving away a secret only her immediate family knew. Music affected her deeply, touching something in her that she couldn't identify or explain. Although it doubtless had a similar effect on others, she had worked so hard to beat down anything illogical or impractical in herself that her strong emotional response to beautiful music seemed uncontrollable by contrast.

It was only during the third aria, "Sebben, crudele," that she realized tears were running down her cheeks. Fortunately, nobody else seemed to notice.

When the aria was over, Lilia made a quick swipe at her eyes as Miss Cavendish began to play another Chopin étude. When Lilia looked up again, Paul was approaching her. He sat beside her on the sofa and held out her gloves.

"You left these in the dining room," he said, studying her face.

"Thank you. I'm not used to formal parties that require gloves indoors."

She took the gloves, but before she could put them on again, he put his hand on her bare forearm and said, "Are you all right?" It wasn't a light touch to get her attention, but a warm, lingering pressure.

A shiver went through her. "I'm fine. You've found out my susceptibility to music, that's all."

"Your secret is safe with me," he said gravely. "I'm glad you're susceptible to some forms of beauty."

She meant to make a flippant reply, but something in his eyes stopped her. Or perhaps it was the fact that his hand was moving down her arm to her wrist in what felt suspiciously like a caress. For a long moment, she held his gaze and was, inexplicably, afraid.

Fortunately, Mrs. Ross, who was sitting at Lilia's other side, chose that moment to ask her how she liked living in London, and as Lilia turned away from Paul, he withdrew his hand.

For the rest of the evening, Lilia stayed close to Mrs. Ross, as if the woman was her protector. She was relieved when the Rosses offered her a ride home in their motor car, and she accepted the offer quickly, before Paul could insist on accompanying her home himself.

6

If a man say, I love God, and hateth his brother, he is a liar: for he
that loveth not his brother whom he hath seen, how can he love God
whom he hath not seen?

—1 John 4:20

I put those candles on the altar myself last Sunday," said Canon Solmes.
"They couldn't have disappeared into thin air."

"If you're implying I took them, I'd like to know what you think I did
with them," replied Canon Johnson, who was normally mild-mannered—
when he wasn't being accused of theft.

Paul sighed and looked at the dean at the end of the long table, willing
him to intervene. Unfortunately, the dean appeared to be asleep, his wiz-
ened chin propped up by his clerical collar. This was becoming an all-
too-frequent occurrence at chapter meetings, which had ended on several
previous occasions with the four canons leaving the table as quietly as possible so as not to wake the old man.

"Since none of us has admitted to removing them from the altar,"

Thomas Cross said, "perhaps we could give one another the benefit of the doubt and consider possibilities other than theft."

If Paul hadn't disliked Cross so much, he would have been grateful for his attempt to smooth the ruffled feathers of the other two canons. As it was, Paul only chafed at what he perceived as Cross's air of superiority. Others didn't seem to see the sinister, predatory side of Cross. Perhaps they were deceived by his ability to exude warmth and compassion at will. Paul had to admit that the man was adept at getting what he wanted from people while simultaneously making them think he had done them a great favor.

Paul only half-listened to the rest of the meeting, his mind already on his next engagement, a meeting with the bishop at his palace. Shortly after Paul's visit to the penitentiary, he had asked for the bishop's advice regarding what could be done to improve the conditions of the inmates. The bishop had promised to consider the matter and had set up that day's meeting to discuss it further.

After a few minutes, Cross managed to pacify Canons Solmes and Johnson by promising to investigate the matter of the candles, and the meeting was over. All four canons glanced at the dean, who showed no sign of waking, and they quietly rose from their seats and filed out of the room. To Paul's annoyance, Cross fell into step with him as he left the chapter house.

"Ah, the mystery of the missing candles," said Cross, apparently in a friendly mood. "Every week there's a new problem of pressing importance to solve. But at least we're talking about something other than the Eastward position."

This was obviously a jab at Paul, who believed this to be a very serious matter indeed and had spent considerable time at the last chapter meeting arguing that the cathedral clergymen should adopt it. Facing the altar while celebrating Holy Communion honored an ancient and sacred tradition.

Facing the congregation instead, the current practice of the cathedral clergy, made no sense to Paul.

"If you knew more about church history," Paul said, unable to refrain from taking the bait, "you might realize its importance."

Cross laughed. "You amaze me, Harris. Have you been a medieval relic all your life? There's more to the church than history and tradition. What kind of message does it send to the congregation when the pastor turns his back on them during the most important part of the service?"

Paul didn't understand why Cross was still walking with him now that they had left the chapter house and the cathedral, but he didn't let his puzzlement end his combative mood. "I made it clear in our last meeting that when we celebrate the sacrament, we're in the role of worship leaders, not pastors."

"Yes, you made your views clear, but they hardly reflect reality. When was the last time you spoke with a parishioner about his experience of the service? Of course, if we're conducting services only to please ourselves, there's no need to find out what the parishioners think."

Paul had had enough. He stopped walking and faced his nemesis. "Cross, what do you want? Why are you following me?"

"I'm not following you. I thought you were following me."

"I have a meeting with the bishop."

"So do I."

The two men stared at each other.

Cross was the first to recover. "Well, it seems as though the bishop wishes to see us together. Perhaps he's going to confer some great honor upon you, and I'll be required to witness and pay homage."

"Let's go, then. I don't want to waste time standing with you in the street."

They walked the rest of the way, about half a mile, in silence. Paul's mind spun with the effort of trying to predict what the bishop wished to discuss with both him and Cross. Perhaps the dean had told him about the animosity between the two canons and the bishop intended to take disciplinary action. The canons were accountable to the dean, but as the man was elderly, the bishop often took over matters the dean found too difficult to manage. Paul and Cross didn't usually engage in public displays of hostility, but they had been arguing more openly at chapter meetings as of late.

At the palace, the two men were shown into the bishop's study at once. Paul had been in this room several times, but never with such an undesired companion. The study was spacious, but the dark green curtains and carpet and the rich brown bookshelves and chairs made it seem smaller. The bishop was sitting in the ancient black oak chair that Paul privately coveted. It didn't look particularly comfortable, but it was ornamented with intricate carvings befitting the dignity of a bishop.

At their entrance, Bishop Chisholm looked up and smiled. "Canon Cross and Canon Harris. Welcome." He looked exactly the way a bishop should—he was a distinguished, silver-haired gentleman in his late fifties whose lordly mien commanded respect.

They greeted him and sat in the two wingback chairs in front of his desk. The warmth of the bishop's greeting had reassured Paul a little, but he was still anxious.

"I'll get to the point at once," he said, to Paul's relief. "I've asked you both here today because of a talk I had with Canon Harris regarding the penitentiary at Whitechapel."

The topic of the meeting was what Paul had expected, but he couldn't understand why the bishop considered it necessary to involve Cross.

"I have visited several penitentiaries in and near London, and I am confident that most of them are doing very good work," Bishop Chisholm continued. "However, Canon Harris has informed me of the harsh conditions he witnessed at the Whitechapel House of Mercy, and I am convinced that reform is necessary. I have been informed that the Mother Superior of that institution has been associated with criminal activities and have arranged to have her removed.

"I would like the two of you to investigate a few other penitentiaries I have not had the opportunity to visit and suggest steps the church can take to reform them. I would also appreciate your involvement in implementing these steps."

Paul was stunned into silence. He had felt a momentary satisfaction at Cross's look of surprise when the bishop mentioned Paul's visit to the Whitechapel penitentiary, but that pleasure quickly dissipated. It was bad enough that he and Cross had to work together at the cathedral, but to work closely on a project that would require frequent, regular communication would be decidedly unpleasant. The bishop couldn't have punished them more severely had he taken the disciplinary action Paul had feared.

"I appreciate your investigation of this problem, my lord," Paul said finally, trying to hide his dismay, "but I don't understand why you've chosen the two of us in particular to work on this project."

"Since you were the first to bring the matter to my attention, and it is clearly something you feel strongly about, there was no question that I would offer the project to you. However, you have not had much experience with this type of work, and that is where Canon Cross's strengths can help. His work with the poor, as well as his involvement in prison and hospital reform, makes him the ideal partner for you. Your strengths complement each other." Bishop Chisholm turned to Cross. "What do you think, Canon Cross?"

A slow smile spread across Thomas Cross's face. "There's great wisdom in what you say, my lord. It would be my pleasure to work on this project and to help Canon Harris channel his new fervor for reform into useful and practical action. And to learn from him as well, of course."

Paul could not detect a shadow of sarcasm in Cross's tone. He could have murdered the man in cold blood right there in the bishop's study.

"Excellent!" the bishop replied. "I would like to meet with you both again in a fortnight to hear your plans for the project." He sat back in his chair, evidently pleased and apparently unaware of the animosity between the two younger men. Or perhaps he was well aware of it, and this project was his way of teaching them to work together more effectively.

The bishop turned the conversation to more general church matters, which Cross responded to at length while Paul sat mute and unhappy. He genuinely wanted to develop more awareness of social ills and try to alleviate them, but to have to do so in the company of a man who mocked him at every turn and had no respect for his ideals was intolerable. Surely it was better to have no social conscience at all than to try to develop one in an atmosphere that was inhospitable, even injurious, to its growth.

Paul felt relieved when the meeting was over, and anxious to be alone with his thoughts. But as he and Cross were shown out of the palace, it became apparent that his nemesis was going to be as difficult to rid himself of as a contagious disease.

Now that they were alone, Cross reverted to his usual sarcastic tone. "I say, Harris, what a shocking turn of events. I'm delighted to find that you must be my 'friend that sticketh closer than a brother.' Are you equally delighted?"

Paul ignored him and kept walking.

"I must ask, what in the world made you leave the safety of your study to deign to visit the Whitechapel House of Mercy?"

"It's no business of yours."

"Ah, but the bishop has made it my business, don't you think?"

Paul sighed. "I went there with a friend of mine. She was asked to visit the penitentiary by a former inmate, and I accompanied them."

"A friend?" Cross made the word sound vaguely immoral. "I'm surprised a friend of yours would move in the same circles as women of questionable character. Surely she's not one of them?"

"Don't be ridiculous. She merely wishes to improve the conditions of unfortunate women."

"Oh, one of the shrieking sisterhood, then? Those shrill, sour old biddies give me hives."

"She is none of those things. She's an intelligent young woman who has done more practical work to help people than you can ever hope to accomplish."

"I see," said Cross, observing Paul with new interest. "She doesn't sound like any friend of yours."

Paul ignored the insult, saying only, "You could learn a great deal from her."

"Perhaps I was mistaken, Harris. There's more in your head than vestments and incense. If you're a willing apprentice, I can teach you a great deal."

"I doubt there's anything you can teach me," Paul replied coldly. "Bishop Chisholm made it clear this is to be an equal partnership. We can divide the work so we needn't set eyes on each other more than is absolutely necessary."

Cross laughed. "I wouldn't dream of intruding upon your noble work more often than I must. Don't forget, though, that the bishop will want us to play nicely together. I know you wouldn't want to disappoint him."

Paul had reached the limit of his patience with Cross, and he turned on his heel and walked away. To his relief, Cross didn't follow.

Paul found himself heading towards Lilia's school, which she'd pointed out to him on one of their walks. He hadn't seen her since his father's dinner party three weeks earlier, partly because they were both busier than usual with their work. But he had also been avoiding her. The powerful attraction he had felt towards her in the cab was nothing compared to what he'd felt when he'd seen her in that blue dress at his father's party. The other women had worn more revealing, figure-enhancing gowns, but he had hardly noticed them. In her unusual dress, with its folds of soft drapery, Lilia had looked like a Greek goddess. He had tried to keep his distance, but when he'd seen her tears in response to the music, he had been undone. He knew his strange behavior that night had made her uncomfortable, but he hoped no real damage had been done to their friendship.

He paused in front of the redbrick building. It had been a house in its former life. It wasn't small, but it appeared so because of the two larger houses on either side of it. A white hand-painted sign proclaimed THE FERNHAM PREPARATORY SCHOOL FOR GIRLS. Paul frowned at that. It seemed Lady Fernham's influence extended to everything in Lilia's life.

Nobody answered his knock, so he tried the door. It was unlocked and he walked in, finding the front hall deserted. If it weren't for the unlocked door, he would have assumed the teachers had left for the day. Lessons would certainly be over by now.

He made his way down the main corridor and stopped at the first open doorway. The room was dominated by a massive table at the center, where Lilia sat with a stack of papers in front of her. She was wearing small round spectacles that made her look more like an actress playing the role of a schoolmistress than a real schoolmistress, and her dark hair was, as usual, coming loose from the knot at the nape of her neck.

The look of resignation that Lilia directed at the intruder from over the top of her spectacles quickly changed to pleasure when she saw him, and she sprang to her feet to greet him.

"Paul, it's been an age since I've seen you! How have you been?" She removed her glasses and gazed at him with bright eyes.

"I've been well," he replied, relieved by her warm greeting. Glancing at the painting on the wall behind her, he said, "I've never seen that Jeanne d'Arc before. I know only the Millais."

She turned to look at it. "It's by Harold Piffard. It belongs to Lady Fernham. She has an extensive art collection and allows me to borrow from it. The Mary Wollstonecraft is hers, too."

He moved closer to the Jeanne d'Arc painting. "She's too placid to be Jeanne, I think. But she looks a little like you, with that dark hair."

"Do you think so?"

He turned to look at Lilia again. Piffard's Jeanne did resemble Lilia, but only in a cold, superficial way. He didn't think an artist could capture Lilia's liveliness and energy.

"Only a little," he said.

Lilia returned to her seat and invited him to sit beside her. He did so, turning his chair to face hers.

"How are you settling in to your new teaching position?" he asked.

She wrinkled her nose. "It isn't quite what I expected."

"Tell me."

"It's certainly better than teaching at Ingleford. The parents here support my teaching methods, but the pupils need a good deal of prodding. I often lose patience with them."

"I suspect your complaint is common among schoolteachers everywhere."

"That may be, but I expected them to appreciate the diverse curriculum and the opportunities Miss Chapman and Harriet and I have worked so hard to give them."

"They certainly ought to appreciate that," he said, "but perhaps the diverse curriculum is more important to their parents than to them. Could that be it?"

"I think that's true for Alice and Lucy, Lady Fernham's daughters. They're surprisingly conventional for daughters of hers—she has such progressive ideas about women. My cleverest pupil, Amy, seemed to be interested in learning at first, but she won't apply herself. She's turning into a giddy, silly girl, and no amount of coaxing or even threatening on my part seems to do any good. I'm afraid she'll end up married to some dullard, wasting her intellect pandering to his every whim and spouting vacuous pleasantries."

"What if she marries a good man who appreciates her intelligence?" Paul asked, bemused. "I assume you'll allow the possibility of such a man's existence. Would she still spout the dreaded pleasantries?"

"You're mocking me. I shan't answer you seriously if you won't be serious."

"I'm perfectly serious."

"Very well. I can imagine such a man, but I can't endure the thought of an intelligent woman trapping herself in an institution I despise."

Lilia's vehemence took Paul by surprise. He had heard her speak negatively about marriage before, but never so strongly or specifically, and he had never paid much attention to it. He had assumed that a vague opposition to marriage, like untidy hair, was a requirement for all New Women.

"You exaggerate," he said. "I know husbands who respect their wives and make no attempt to force them into unthinking obedience. I doubt there are many brutes who wish their wives to fawn on them like dogs or slaves. Men don't want to be married to stupid or vacuous women."

"You're right," she shot back. "They want women intelligent enough to be *willing* slaves. What victory is there in conquest by force? It's far better to indoctrinate young girls with the belief that they're superior to men in their unique ability to sacrifice for others. Then when they're grown women, they can make sacrifices charmingly, as if born to do so."

"Self-sacrifice is admirable, regardless of one's sex." Feeling drained by the argument, he sighed. "Do you really see no way in which a man and woman can have a relationship of mutual love and respect?"

"That's an entirely different question. I do believe such a relationship can exist, just not within marriage."

"What do you mean?"

"Two intelligent people don't need an artificial, archaic formality such as marriage to sanction their commitment to each other." She suddenly looked uncomfortable. "If Amy—we were speaking of Amy—should choose such a free union with a man who respected her, I would heartily approve."

Paul stared at her, not trying to hide his shock. It was one thing to argue for equality between women and men, but it was quite another to advocate something as bizarre and immoral as a free union. People certainly did have such relationships—he had only to think of his own mother and James Anbrey—but a man and woman who lived openly together without being married were shunned by respectable society. Beyond that, marriage was a sacrament. To remove the ceremony in which a man and woman were mystically united by God as one flesh would strip the relationship of all beauty and meaning. What remained would be as cold and cerebral as a business partnership, albeit one that happened to include sexual relations.

"I don't expect you to agree with me," Lilia said. She looked at him as if she had been trying to explain an electric locomotive to a prehistoric cave-dweller and had only just realized how pointless it was.

Paul remained silent.

"Well," said Lilia in an unnaturally bright voice, springing to her feet and breathing a sigh of relief, "I'd forgotten how refreshing it is to debate with a worthy opponent. I have fewer opportunities for such things now that I'm teaching every day. You haven't seen the whole school yet, have you? I'll give you a tour, if you like."

Paul didn't feel refreshed, and he was suspicious of her changed tone. Had she been waiting for an opportunity to tell him her views on marriage and said more than she intended? Whatever her motives, he didn't want to return to the argument, so he murmured a vague assent and followed her out of the room.

The other schoolrooms looked much like Lilia's. Paul only half listened as she talked about lessons, students, and the school in general. By the time the tour ended back in her schoolroom, he was feeling more at ease. Lilia asked about his life, so he told her about his conversation with the bishop. She listened attentively, her eyes never leaving his face.

"Do you think Cross will try to interfere with your part of the work?" Lilia asked when he had finished.

"I don't know. He may not. After all, I don't believe he wishes to work with me any more than I wish to work with him. But he also seems to enjoy provoking and mocking me, so I'm not sure which impulse will win out."

"He sounds horrid. If I were you, I should be sorely tempted to box his ears."

"I think the bishop would frown upon cathedral clergymen coming to blows," said Paul wryly. "I can't say I'm not tempted sometimes, though."

"Well, perhaps the increased interaction with Cross will strengthen your character."

"That's what my friend Stephen thinks. I think it's more likely to drive me mad."

Lilia regarded him curiously. "You're very good at hiding your feelings, aren't you? I'm beginning to suspect you feel things as strongly as I do. Perhaps more so."

"Perhaps. It seems necessary to hide one's feelings in public."

"I envy that ability. I'd like to wrestle alone with my feelings instead of having the world observe the process."

"I can understand why you'd like that, but I think it's better not to learn how to hide one's feelings too well. It can be rather isolating."

She nodded, still studying his face.

"Despite Cross, I'm glad I can do something to change the penitentiary system," he continued. "I'm grateful to you for starting my education in that area."

"I'm glad, too," she said slowly. "Changes to the Whitechapel House of Mercy can't come too soon, and I haven't got the influence to do as much as you can."

Paul was puzzled by the hesitation in her voice. He had thought she would be delighted to hear that forces besides her own were marshaling for a cause she believed in. "There's something troubling you about this project," he said.

"Yes, I suppose there is. I'm just not sure how to explain it in a way that won't offend you."

"We agreed to be frank with each other. I can survive being offended." He didn't feel as confident as he sounded. After all, if she believed in free unions, she might have other beliefs he wasn't prepared to hear about.

"Very well," Lilia said. "I believe you'll suggest good ideas for penitentiary reform, but I don't like the fact that this project will be entirely controlled by the church. Even the word *penitentiary* is a problem. I'd like to see these women being offered help without being forced to regard themselves as sinners or even penitents."

"I agree with you," he said.

She looked startled. "You do?"

"While I have no objection to the church's funding the project, it ought to rely on people who have practical experience with these women, not clergymen like me who have no idea what it feels like to be desperate enough to resort to the most extreme options."

Lilia was silent for a moment. Then, meeting his eyes with undisguised admiration, she smiled and said, "I've changed my mind. I'm no longer concerned about the church's control in this case. Indeed, the bishop couldn't have done better in choosing you for this project. I only hope Cross has the sense to follow your lead."

He realized there had to be a connection between the way she was looking at him and the way his heart had begun to hammer against his chest. He could no longer think clearly.

"When is it your turn to deliver the sermon at the cathedral?" she asked. The abrupt change of topic brought him back to reality and cleared some of the fog from his head.

"Next Sunday. Why do you ask?"

"I'd like to attend, if you don't mind."

"I'd be delighted." *Delighted, but very confused*, he might have added. She had just expressed her opposition to two long-established traditions the church held dear—marriage and church influence in social reform—yet she wanted to hear him preach. The woman was unfathomable.

"As much as I hate to admit it, you're more open-minded than I am and I want to show you the same good faith," Lilia said. "Besides, after what you've told me about your work life, I'm far more interested in it now than I was before. Seraphic smiles and empty ceremony bore me. Ecclesiastical melodrama, on the other hand, piques my interest."

"I don't know if the melodrama will be evident during the Sunday service."

"That's all right, I'll use my imagination if necessary. And just so you know, I have no intention of being converted. I'm really just curious about your life."

"I promise not to try to convert you, then," he said, suppressing a smile.

"And if Cross is there, I can box his ears for you."

"That would be very entertaining indeed."

7

We desire . . . that we may be able to leave the house of God without that anxious longing for escape, which is the common consequence of common sermons.

—Anthony Trollope, *Barchester Towers*

Until the hawk-nosed canon with the nasal voice began to recite the litany, Lilia had paid close attention to the service. She enjoyed the music sung by the choir and the chanted psalm. But the priest's voice, combined with the formulaic words of the litany, left her cold, and she had to remind herself not to stare at the stained glass windows beside her or the wooden trusses on the ceiling, lest she give herself away as a tourist instead of an ordinary Sunday worshipper.

The verger had directed her to sit too close to the front of the cathedral. While her pew offered a good vantage point from which to observe Paul as he preached, she was worried about standing when she ought to be sitting, or sitting when she ought to be kneeling. Her childhood church had involved fewer changes of posture—indeed, she recalled a great deal of interminable standing, but perhaps the memory was based solely on the easily tired legs of a young girl.

Lilia shifted her attention to the stalls where the canons sat. Thomas Cross was easy to identify based on Paul's description of him as dark and pantherlike, though Paul had understandably neglected to mention Cross's stunning good looks. He and Paul sat facing each other on opposite sides of the chancel. This seating arrangement, as well as their clothing, created an almost comical image of good versus evil. Paul, with his fair hair and the white surplice he wore over his cassock, looked like an iconic Anglo-Saxon angel; Cross's dark coloring and black cassock suggested an equally powerful force on the side of evil. Lilia half expected them to rise up with swords in their hands and engage in supernatural combat, and she was absurdly disappointed when they didn't.

After the congregation recited the Creed, Paul took his place in the pulpit, an impressive dark wood structure carved with figures of animals and saints. Lilia wondered if the pulpit was high above the heads of the congregation for practical reasons, so the people could see the preacher and he them, or for theological ones, to indicate the preacher was closer to God than his flock.

Before he spoke, Paul swept his gaze slowly across the sanctuary as if to take special note of each individual there. Then he began to speak in a strong, thrilling tone Lilia had never heard him use before.

"What is the connection between church ceremonies and worship? What does it mean to worship God? And what does worship have to do with keeping the law, such as the law of circumcision, which St. Paul speaks of in today's epistle? Let us begin by considering the origin of the word *worship* and its earliest use in the scriptures. The Hebrew word *shachah* is usually translated as *worship*, but it literally means to bow down or prostrate oneself on the ground, usually before a superior."

After delving into the Hebrew and Greek translations of the word *worship* for a few minutes, Paul shifted his focus to its use in the Bible: "Let us consider the well-known Genesis story of Abraham about to sacrifice his beloved son, Isaac. Just before Abraham takes Isaac and binds him on the altar, he tells his companions, 'I and the lad will go yonder and worship.' This is an intentional, as opposed to customary, act of worship that involves sacrifice. Abraham places on the altar what he loves most and prepares to surrender his child to God. Worship, in this case, is an act symbolizing complete dedication.

"Is it any wonder, then, that the church places so much emphasis on ceremony and religious forms? Although using specific forms of liturgy, kneeling to pray, and bowing at the name of our Lord can be meaningless if the heart of the worshipper is not involved, these actions are not merely symbols of worship: in a very real way that is linked to ancient traditions and language, they *are* worship. As Dr. Newman said in his sermon on ceremonies of the church, 'The Bible then may be said to give us the spirit of religion; but the Church must provide the body in which that spirit is to be lodged.'"

Lilia was enthralled. Even if Paul were not an effective speaker, her love of ancient languages and history would have ensured her attentiveness. She had never heard such a scholarly sermon before. The hellfire-and-brimstone sermons of her youth seemed designed to terrify her instead of persuade her into belief. This sermon was comfortingly impersonal by comparison, more like a university lecture.

When Paul began to speak less about the meaning of the word *worship* and more about the Bible, her attention lapsed. She noticed that Thomas Cross's impassive expression had changed to a slight frown, which deepened when Paul quoted John Henry Newman. She glanced at the people in the pews around her. Only a few wore glazed expressions of boredom or confusion. She saw Grace Cavendish across the nave, where the wealthier parishioners sat, wearing a speedwell-blue hat perched at a fashionable angle on her golden head. She gazed up at Paul with the same rapt attention she had given him at his father's dinner party.

In consternation, Lilia realized she herself was in danger of looking at him in exactly the same way. It wasn't necessary to understand or even care about what Paul was saying in order to appreciate the eloquent way in which he said it. And except for noticing his resemblance to James Anbrey, Lilia had never given much thought to his physical appearance. Indeed, there was nothing remarkable about it—except when he smiled. And, she realized now, when he preached. It was as if the cathedral was his natural setting, the only place where a rare, powerful illumination could blaze out from inside him. The man and his setting were equally beautiful.

The unexpectedness of the transformation added to his allure. Lilia knew she was also a good public speaker, but her public persona was essentially the same as her private one. In contrast, Paul was quiet, even awkward in private, whereas in the pulpit he was in complete command of his material and his audience.

Paul concluded his sermon by saying, "St. Paul does not suggest, as some believe, that there is no meaning in outward signs and ceremonies. Instead, he urges us to ensure that those outward, visible signs be true reflections of inward, spiritual grace." After a pause that allowed his final words to echo in the ears of his congregation, Paul descended from the pulpit, the hawk-nosed canon rose and gave the blessing, and the service was over.

As the congregation filed out of the cathedral, Lilia lingered near the front door, hoping Paul would have a moment to speak with her. She gazed at the white marble baptismal font nearby, wondering irreverently what would happen if someone were to drink from it. She waited for a long time, watching Paul greet parishioners at the door as they left. When there were only a few people left in the queue, Lilia joined it.

"You came," he said with a smile, taking her hand. "I'm glad."

"I told you I would."

"What did you think of the service?"

"It was quite different from any church service I've attended before. Your sermon impressed me very much, although I have to admit you lost me at 'circumcision of the heart.'"

"I'm sorry about that. I was trying to connect my ideas about worship with the scripture readings for today, but it was probably rather forced."

Their conversation was interrupted by the arrival of Thomas Cross, the dark angel himself, at Paul's elbow. Paul had no choice but to introduce him to Lilia, and she immediately found herself the object of Cross's interested gaze.

"So you're the friend who has inspired Canon Harris's passion for reform," Cross said, looking amused. "You've accomplished what I've been working towards unsuccessfully for months."

A muscle tightened in Paul's jaw, but before he could speak, Lilia said, "You're mistaken, Canon Cross. I've done nothing but introduce Canon Harris to some people I know who wish to see changes in the penitentiary system. He needs no inspiration beyond his own mind and heart. And after hearing his sermon today, no doubt you, too, will be inspired to combine *your* passion for reform with the inward, spiritual grace that must accompany the actions of any Christian."

Cross stared at her, clearly shocked by her impertinence. She stared back with the merest hint of a smile. Cross then looked at Paul with raised eyebrows and turned away, shaking his head.

When Cross was out of earshot, Paul and Lilia burst out laughing like a pair of naughty children.

"I can't believe you said that," Paul told her. "You managed to insult him and preach to him in the same breath. I daresay he has never been spoken to in such a way by a woman."

"I shouldn't have done it," she said, knowing she didn't sound the least bit sorry.

"You shouldn't have, but I'm glad you did. I would hate to have missed seeing that look on his face. You could not have done better had you actually boxed his ears."

They were again interrupted, this time by Grace Cavendish, who must have had the same plan as Lilia to be at the end of the queue. She acknowledged Lilia with a coolly polite nod, then turned to Paul.

"What a wonderful sermon, Canon Harris," Grace said. "It's so important to be reminded how outward forms and ceremonies give shape and structure to one's faith."

Paul smiled. "Thank you."

"Could I trouble you to explain your reference to the Abraham and Isaac story?" Grace inquired. "I thought it was fascinating how you connected it to the word *worship*, but I don't remember exactly how you did it."

Paul glanced at Lilia, who had begun to move away. It was only too clear that Grace wanted Paul all to herself, and Lilia had no desire to fight for his attention. She also felt she had done enough damage at the cathedral for one Sunday. She raised her hand in farewell, and he returned the gesture before turning back to Grace.

Despite Paul's compelling public persona, Lilia decided she preferred his private self. The complicated, shy, emotional man she knew was more genuine than the one she had just seen in the pulpit. And despite all the beauty and eloquence she had encountered at the cathedral that day, she thought Paul could accomplish more by leaving the church and becoming more involved in reform work. For all his skill in speech, at the cathedral he merely perpetuated a dying tradition, rather like a museum guide pointing out the significance of historical artifacts. While one could admire those artifacts, they had little to do with the realities of modern life. And although Lilia loved the classical authors and ancient languages, they meant more to her as marks of equality with men—who, after all, had for centuries jealously guarded their Greeks and Romans from the prying eyes of women—than anything else. Her work for the women's movement was real and vibrant and would change every facet of women's lives. Paul was merely studying history; she was making it.

Lilia had no intention of expressing these views to Paul; they would only offend him and convince him of her arrogance. It was enough that he accepted her as his equal. No man would brook a woman's setting her work above his unless it was in a vague, Angel in the House sort of way. Although she knew Paul didn't believe all women should have complete equality with men, he respected her intelligence and her opinions, even when those opinions were diametrically opposed to his. And he was the only man she knew with whom she could let down her guard completely.

Lilia was glad to have worked out a rational explanation for Paul's importance in her life, but she knew she was being irrational about one thing: Paul was too generous with his smiles. After the cathedral service, he'd smiled at Grace as warmly as he'd smiled at her.

Even if Lilia's work was superior to Paul's, her character was surely inferior, she decided. For it had to be a sign of a weakness to begrudge such generosity.

∽

Later that afternoon, Ellen joined Harriet and Lilia for tea. Perched on the edge of the brown horsehair sofa in Harriet's main parlor, Lilia announced her decision to become a member of the Women's Social and Political Union.

Her friends didn't seem surprised. Lilia had been speaking of the WSPU in glowing terms for weeks. If she had a portrait of Mrs. Pankhurst, it would already be on the wall of her schoolroom. And she had spoken to several women in the organization's leadership who encouraged her to join the Union. But Lilia wanted her friends to become members, too.

The parlor was severely tidy, and Lilia never felt quite comfortable in it. Aside from the ubiquitous pipes on the walls, every object had a practical function: there was one square tea table on which only tea things were allowed and a bookshelf with Harriet's books arranged alphabetically by author.

"Does this mean you're leaving the NUWSS?" Harriet asked.

"Yes, I think so, though I know women who are members of both organizations."

"That's less often the case now. The WSPU's methods have become more aggressive lately, and that doesn't sit well with the NUWSS." Harriet paused. "It's not that I don't agree with Mrs. Pankhurst. I see the need for more direct action. But I must think of the school."

Lilia knew what Harriet meant. Their school was funded by NUWSS members. All their pupils were daughters of NUWSS members. If both she and Harriet joined the WSPU, they could lose both pupils and financial support.

"Lady Fernham likes the WSPU," Ellen put in quietly. "She heard Mrs. Pankhurst speak and found her ideas convincing. I don't think she'd mind if we all joined the WSPU."

"There!" said Lilia. "That ought to set your mind at rest, Harriet."

"Lady Fernham is only one of the school's patrons," the ever-cautious Harriet replied, "but yes, it does help to know that."

"I'm going to be part of a WSPU demonstration next week in Parliament Square," Lilia said. "We'll be protesting the prime minister's refusal to receive a small deputation of suffragettes. After the outpouring of support when we marched last week, it's hard to believe the government still refuses to hear us."

Harriet smiled. "Now the WSPU is 'we' and 'us,' is it?"

"I was speaking of all women who want the vote," Lilia said, a touch defensively. But then she smiled, too, and added, "Yes, I suppose I'm already identifying with the WSPU even though I haven't done anything for them yet. Will you consider joining, too?" She looked from Harriet to Ellen.

"I'll think about it," Harriet said. "But I'll talk to some of the school's patrons first, just to hear their opinions."

"I'll come," Ellen said, "but I hope I won't have to speak in public."

"You don't need to speak. Just act."

After the discussion, Harriet announced that she had a headache and went to her room to rest, but Ellen stayed to learn more about the planned demonstration.

When Ellen rose to leave half an hour later, she turned to Lilia with an earnest look and said, "I don't think I've ever told you how much I've changed since meeting you. Lady Fernham, in her kindness, took me out of the life that kept me trapped, but you've made me believe I can do something meaningful for the Cause. Before I met you, I was full of doubts and fears, thinking I was insignificant. Now, when I feel afraid, I think of your words from your St. Crispin's Day speech: 'Do not wait for others to act because you are afraid. Do what you can in your little corner of the world, and know that a great army of women acts with you.' Because of the courage you've given me, I now see my true worth."

Who could remain unmoved by such impassioned words? It was the longest speech Lilia had ever heard from her quiet friend. She reached for Ellen's hand and squeezed it. "Thank you," she said, "but don't forget that the courage you speak of comes from you. My role was only to make you aware of its existence."

Ellen had indeed changed. She no longer seemed fragile or mournful, though she was still soft-spoken. In light of her apparent failure to influence her pupils, Lilia was especially pleased to be a positive influence on Ellen.

That night, Lilia dreamed that she was leading an army of young women who stormed Parliament and slew the male MPs with jewel-encrusted swords. Standing on the bodies of the fallen men, her army proclaimed a new Parliament made up entirely of women.

8

I felt that the moment had come for a demonstration such as no
old-fashioned suffragist had ever attempted. I called upon the women
to follow me outside for a meeting of protest against the government.

—Emmeline Pankhurst, *My Own Story*

SEPTEMBER 1907

A fortnight after Lilia attended the cathedral service, Stephen Elliott
came to London to visit Paul. It had been a long time since Paul
had seen his friend, so despite a workload made heavier by the penitentiary
project, he set aside his duties for the afternoon. As they walked through
St. James's Park towards Westminster, Stephen revealed that he had
proposed to Rosamond, the village squire's daughter, and she had accepted
him.

Paul heard these tidings with pleasure. "I'm happy for you, Elliott. I only
hope she's worthy of you."

"Worthy of me!" Stephen sputtered. "I'll never be worthy of her, no
matter how hard I try. You haven't met her, Harris. You don't know how
beautiful she is, how pure and sweet, how forgiving . . ."

83

Paul smiled, only half listening to the litany of Rosamond's virtues that ensued.

"What of you, Harris?" Stephen pressed. "Am I to believe your heart remains free? Is there no lady in your life who interests you?"

Paul didn't know how to reply to this, and so said after consideration, "There is someone my father has hinted about, someone he wishes me to take notice of—a Miss Cavendish."

Stephen rolled his eyes. "Your father! Good heavens, Harris, I know you're a dutiful son, but surely you won't be ruled by your father in matters of the heart. I suppose this Miss Cavendish is an ugly spinster with money. Am I correct?"

"On the contrary, she's very pretty. As for the money, I don't really know, but her father has a prosperous business, so you may be right about that."

"She must not be very intelligent."

"You're wrong there, too. She is well-read and can converse upon a greater variety of subjects than the average woman."

Stephen studied his friend's face curiously. "And yet you remain unmoved by her?"

"I enjoy her company and find her charming. If that qualifies as being 'unmoved,' then I suppose I am."

"I can't understand you, Harris. If this Miss Cavendish is as beautiful, clever, and wealthy as you say, what are you waiting for? Has some other woman ensnared you?"

Paul was annoyed to feel heat rise to his face, as if he were a schoolboy. "I'm not in love with anyone, if that's what you mean. I do have a friend who means a great deal to me, but . . ."

"Why have you never mentioned this person? Tell me about her," Stephen ordered.

Paul knew perfectly well why he hadn't told Stephen about Lilia. He didn't speak of her to anyone associated with the church because he didn't expect them to understand his relationship with her. The church was not, as a rule, sympathetic to women's suffrage, and he didn't think even Stephen would understand what drew him to Lilia. For that matter, he wasn't sure he himself understood it.

Paul was spared having to answer by a disturbance in Parliament Square. They were only just approaching and couldn't see what was happening, but they heard the shouts and rumblings of an agitated crowd.

He quickened his pace, and Stephen did the same. As the two men entered the square, they saw a crowd gathered in front of the steps of one of the government buildings. Several police constables were there, too, dragging people away from the scene. No, dragging *women* away. Paul and Stephen passed a woman who was being pulled away by two constables, each holding one of her arms. She was struggling and shouting, "Votes for women!"

"It's those militant suffragettes causing trouble again," Stephen said with an exasperated look. "I used to consider them merely a nuisance, but now they're becoming a danger to themselves and others. Why do the police allow them to begin these demonstrations?"

A heavy feeling settled in Paul's stomach. He knew there were extremist suffrage groups, women who interrupted and heckled members of Parliament and chained themselves to railings. Their antics were invariably reported in the newspapers. He was glad Lilia was a member of the respectable NUWSS instead of one of these more militant groups. All the same, he felt uneasy as he and Stephen moved into the heart of the crowd.

A tight circle of people had formed around a prone figure at the bottom of the steps, preventing a clear view. Paul could tell she was a woman, for he could see part of her crumpled gray skirt and her delicate white hand looking like a dead bird on the ground. Looking at the faces of the people closest to her, he recognized Lady Fernham and Harriet, and his heart nearly stopped as he realized who the woman on the ground could be.

In a frenzy of terror, Paul pushed his way to the center of the crowd, looked down, and saw Lilia kneeling on the ground, cradling the head of Ellen Wells. Lilia held a blood-soaked cloth against Ellen's head. There was something ominous about Ellen's stillness and the angle of her neck.

Paul crouched down beside Lilia and put his hand gently on her shoulder. She looked at him blankly, her face white.

"Have you checked her pulse?" he asked.

She didn't seem to understand the question. "She needs a doctor" was all she said.

Paul reached for Ellen's wrist himself. There was no pulse.

Someone in the crowd was screaming hysterically. Paul stood up to find Stephen, who had also elbowed his way through the crowd, and after conferring briefly, they sprang into action. Paul directed members of the crowd who had remained calm to soothe those who had not, and Stephen tried to make a clear path for the police and ambulance men.

Paul returned to Lilia and Ellen as soon as he could, taking Ellen's limp hand in his. Although he knew it was likely too late to say the prayer for the sick, it didn't seem appropriate to say the prayer for the dead. He needed to pray, for his own sake as much as for anyone else's. And perhaps there was a chance Ellen could hear him.

"O Almighty God, and merciful Father, to whom alone belong the issues of life and death—" He stopped, realizing he had begun the prayer for a sick child, and started again. "Our Lord Jesus Christ, who hath left power to his Church to absolve all sinners who truly repent—" Once again he stopped. He knew these prayers well and didn't understand why he could remember them only in fragments. Perhaps it had something to do with the way Lilia was staring at him, as if she didn't know him.

He tried again. "O Father of mercies, and God of all comfort, our only help in time of need."

But now a police constable and the ambulance men had arrived, and Paul was in the way. He stepped aside and waited while the constable questioned bystanders, including Lilia. Paul didn't hear the questions or responses, but from where he stood, it looked as though the constable was making only cursory inquiries and not really listening to the answers.

He himself had many questions. What was Lilia doing at a demonstration run by militant suffragettes? Why were her friends there as well? Had they merely happened upon the scene and stayed to listen? How had Ellen been injured?

While he waited, Paul saw a banner on the ground bearing green, white, and purple bands. Without knowing why he did it, he picked it up and tucked it into the front of his cassock.

As the constable left and the ambulance men took Ellen's body away, Paul approached Lilia. Before he could say anything, Lady Fernham asked Lilia, "Would you like to come home with me?"

"No, I can't right now," Lilia replied coolly. "I'll come by tomorrow, though, to help with the funeral arrangements." She spoke as if she were discussing a trivial social matter, though her face was still very pale.

Paul cast a worried glance at her. She was in shock, of course. As a priest, he had seen many people's reactions to death, and it was always difficult to know how to comfort those who remained eerily calm like Lilia.

Stephen appeared at Paul's side, looking weary. "I say, Harris, what a wretched mess we walked into! How did that poor girl end up so badly hurt?" Stephen had many virtues, but tactfulness wasn't one of them. Perhaps he hadn't noticed Lilia nearby or didn't realize she was Ellen's friend.

"She was trying to save me," Lilia said bluntly.

Stephen and Paul looked at her.

"I was standing at the top of the steps, making a speech. The other speakers had already been threatened and pushed by men in the crowd, so I thought if I could stand there"—she pointed to a ledge jutting out from the top step—"it would be harder for anyone to get to me. Ellen came with me and barred the way to the ledge."

She paused, looking so stunned and lost that Paul took a step closer to her. "You needn't talk about this now," he said.

But she went on. "A man pushed Ellen down the steps. I saw him only out of the corner of my eye when I was speaking, but he came up behind her and gave her a violent shove."

Paul looked at the spot, sickened by the thought that anyone could push a woman down a full flight of stone steps merely for supporting a friend who was making a speech.

Stephen looked from Paul to Lilia and back again with a puzzled frown, and Paul made the necessary introductions, even referring to Lilia as a dear friend of his. But Stephen continued to look puzzled.

"Everything seems to be cleaned up here, so I'll go home now," Lilia said in an expressionless voice. She turned and walked away.

Paul had no intention of letting her out of his sight. He turned to Stephen and said in an undertone, "I'm going to see that she gets home safely."

Stephen nodded. "Go on."

Paul turned to follow Lilia, but she was moving so fast that it took him a few minutes to catch up with her. When he reached her, he said, "May I walk with you?"

"Do as you please."

They walked in silence. Paul didn't know if it would be better to try to break through her silence or wait until she was ready to speak. He chose the latter option, but his concern mounted with every step.

When they were a few blocks from her house, Lilia suddenly stopped and said, "I must go to the school before I go home. There are some books I need to look at before tomorrow's lessons."

"Perhaps you ought to cancel those," he ventured. "You've had a terrible shock, and it might be better to stay home."

"Nonsense. It will be far better for everyone if I carry on as usual." She turned and headed towards the school. Paul felt he had little choice but to go with her.

It was late afternoon, and the shadows of buildings and trees were lengthening around them. As Paul watched Lilia unlock the front door of the empty schoolhouse, her silence was echoed by a general hush in the neighborhood. Not a man, woman, or child—not even an animal—could be seen or heard from where he stood, as if he and Lilia were the only living creatures left in the world.

He followed her into the building and down the corridor to her schoolroom. The dying light coming from the windows added to the eerie atmosphere, but Lilia didn't bother to light a lamp, intent on a violent search of her desk drawers.

"What books are you looking for?" Paul asked. "Perhaps I can help."

"I'm not looking for books. I'm looking for my cigarettes. I usually hide a few in my desk." She continued to ransack the desk, her movements becoming increasingly frantic.

Paul couldn't stand it any longer. He went to her and put a restraining hand on her arm. "Lilia, please stop. Will you sit and talk to me?"

She didn't meet his eyes. "I don't want to sit or talk. Oh, God!" This exclamation was accompanied by a look of horror. She backed away, staring down at the front of her white blouse, which bore a dark stain. She touched it with her hand, then stretched out her hand in front of her.

"Her blood is on me," she said with a horrible, hollow laugh. "Why, Paul, we're in a play. 'Here's the smell of the blood still. All the perfumes of Arabia will not sweeten this little hand.' Now, what's your line?"

Paul stepped forward and took her firmly by the shoulders. "Lilia, look at me!"

Slowly she obeyed him.

"Ellen's death was not your fault," he said.

"It *was* my fault," she replied with sudden calm. "I convinced her to join the WSPU. She was afraid of what might happen if we made public protests." Her lower lip trembled. "Ellen said she didn't have the courage to speak. I said, 'You don't need to speak. Just act.' She acted, and she was killed for it."

His heart ached for her. "I see why you feel responsible," he said quietly, "but you didn't plan for her to get hurt. It was her choice to climb up there with you. And that man killed her. You did not."

"Still, I ought to have known . . . I ought to have been more careful with my words. She has always taken me too seriously."

Lilia's voice broke, and Paul took her in his arms. She began to weep, hiding her face against his neck. He was surprised by how slender and fragile her body felt. Her height and the sheer force of her personality created the illusion that she was bigger and stronger than she really was. Her hair smelled of the cinnamon-scented tobacco in the cigarettes she smoked.

When her sobs subsided, she didn't move away from him. Instead, her body relaxed against his, her head resting in the hollow between his neck and shoulder. She was perfectly still. After a moment, he pressed his lips to her forehead. She slowly raised her head to look at him, her eyes, huge and dark, framed by wet eyelashes. Those tempting lips of hers were dangerously close to his.

"I have a question about confession and absolution," she whispered.

He blinked. "Yes?"

"May I make a confession to you as a priest if the confession is . . . about you?"

"No," he said slowly, hoping she couldn't hear the sudden pounding of his heart. "You ought to confess to a different priest." Tightening his arms around her, he added, "Confess to me anyway . . . to the man, not the priest."

"I think I have the order of events wrong," she said softly, so close he felt her breath on his cheek. "I ought to commit the sin first, then confess."

He would have kissed her then, but he heard the front door of the schoolhouse open with a bang, and footsteps clattered noisily down the corridor towards Lilia's schoolroom.

Paul and Lilia sprang apart as if caught in a guilty act and a moment later, Harriet rushed in. She was carrying a lamp and light flooded the room as she entered.

"I was worried about you," Harriet said. "Nobody knew where you'd gone."

"I'm sorry," Lilia said. "I meant to go home but then stopped here to get my books for tomorrow. Paul came with me."

Harriet looked from Lilia to Paul, who tried to appear dignified even though his face was on fire. He wished Harriet hadn't brought the lamp.

"Surely you don't intend to teach tomorrow after what happened," Harriet said to Lilia.

"No. I was going to, but I've changed my mind."

"Are you hurt?" Harriet asked, looking at the bloodstain on Lilia's blouse.

"No."

"Let's go home," Harriet said. "Canon Harris, would you like to come with us?"

"No, thank you." Remembering the banner he had rescued, Paul reached into the front of his cassock and handed it to Lilia. "I thought you might wish to keep this."

"The WSPU colors." She took it and smoothed it between her fingers. "Thank you." It seemed as difficult for her to meet his eyes as it was for him to meet hers.

After the women left, Paul remained on the street in front of the schoolhouse for a while, stunned. How long had he been lying to himself about his true feelings? What he had told Stephen about not being in love with anyone was entirely untrue. He was utterly, hopelessly in love with Lilia.

9

In my return back through the passage, I heard the same words repeated twice over; and looking up, I saw it was a starling hung in a little cage. —"I can't get out—I can't get out," said the starling.

—Laurence Sterne, *A Sentimental Journey Through France and Italy*

The Parliament Square demonstration was on the front page of the *Daily Telegraph* and the *Times* the next day. The stories dwelled on the sensational details, dismissing the suffragettes as hysterical madwomen. Ellen's death was mentioned, but only briefly. The *Daily Telegraph* article claimed that if Ellen had "devoted her energies to finding a respectable husband, she wouldn't have fallen into the hands of unnatural women whose disordered minds could think of nothing but votes and equality with men."

Lilia was enraged by these comments, even though it had been clear from the dismissive way the police treated the suffragettes at the scene of Ellen's death that there would be no investigation. Despite Lilia's and Lady Fernham's insistence that a man had pushed Ellen to her death, nobody else admitted to seeing him, and the constable who had questioned Lilia made no pretense of believing her story. It seemed more convenient for the police—and society at large—to dismiss Ellen's death as an accident.

Mrs. Pankhurst went to Ellen's funeral and honored Lilia and Harriet with a visit afterwards.

"I know it's difficult to hear these offensive comments," Mrs. Pankhurst told Lilia, "especially when the loss of your friend is so recent. But don't despair. We can use the anti-suffragists' weapons against them."

"How can we?" asked Lilia, awed by the fiery little woman.

"You can start by speaking at the WSPU's next meeting. You can tell the true story of Miss Wells's death, and we'll ensure that the press is there to hear it."

"That's a good idea," Harriet put in. She too seemed awed by Mrs. Pankhurst and was smoothing her skirt in an uncharacteristically nervous manner. The day after Ellen's death, both Harriet and Lady Fernham had joined the WSPU.

"I'll do whatever you think will help," Lilia said. She was determined to work harder than ever for the Union, as a result of what she saw as her responsibility for Ellen's death, and especially as Mrs. Pankhurst herself supported her.

Lilia threw herself into a punishing schedule. It was difficult to accomplish all her goals, as teaching took up most of her daytime hours, though in the evenings, if she had no meetings or speaking engagements, she wrote articles for *Votes for Women*, the WSPU newspaper. She had little time to think about anything but her suffrage work, which was also a convenient excuse to avoid Paul. He left messages for Lilia at her house and even at the school when his attempts to see her were thwarted. After two weeks, he sent her a letter:

Dear Lilia,

Lately, I have been getting to know your maid Lizzie quite well. As pleasant as she is, I cannot help feeling frustrated, since my object has been to speak with you. Lizzie tells me you and Miss Firth are working very hard for the WSPU, which explains why you are never at home. Surely no work, even for the noble cause of women's rights, is so important that it requires you to exhaust yourself and imperil your health.

If you are avoiding me because of what happened in the schoolroom after Miss Wells died, please don't. I think we ought to talk about it. If I offended you in any way, I apologize.

Yours,

Paul

P.S. I never did hear the confession you spoke of in the schoolroom and would like to.

Lilia read this letter with mixed feelings. The first paragraph seemed condescending. Did he mean to be ironic by using the phrase "the noble cause of women's rights"? He didn't understand how important that cause was. And he seemed unnecessarily insistent, since it had been only two weeks since they had last seen each other. Longer periods without contact had elapsed in the past without mention. And she didn't want to think about what had happened—or almost happened—in the schoolroom.

Lilia set the letter aside for the moment. She didn't want to lose his friendship, but now that she knew without a doubt that their physical attraction was mutual, she saw how dangerous it was. Surely he must know, as she did, that there was no future for such a relationship. They lived in two different worlds that were more often than not hostile towards each other.

That evening, Lilia went to Lady Fernham's house for dinner. She had been there several times before, but this was her first opportunity to meet

Lord Fernham. The Fernhams' dining room was oppressively formal, dominated by a huge mahogany table and matching sideboard, and the wallpaper was a dizzying design of interlocking scarlet and black diamonds. Alice and Lucy, the Fernhams' daughters and Lilia's pupils, were both wearing red dresses with black trim, and they blended into the decor of the room so well that Lilia kept forgetting they were there.

Lord Fernham was a pale, thin man with a drooping moustache and strange glittery eyes. He greeted Lilia pleasantly enough, but he seemed preoccupied and said very little during dinner. Even Lady Fernham was quieter than usual, and Lilia wondered if they had had an argument. Or perhaps it was common for them to have little to say to each other.

Alice and Lucy took their cue from their parents and were completely silent until dinner was over, at which point they asked permission to show Lilia their new starling. Happy to escape from the uncomfortable silence, Lilia followed them upstairs, where they showed her the songbird and chattered happily about their new party frocks. Lilia admired the dresses, which were brought out for her inspection. She had little to say about the starling—she had always been troubled by the sight of caged birds—and after a few more minutes of conversation, she left the girls and headed back downstairs. She stopped just outside the drawing room when she heard angry voices coming from within.

"The least you can do is tell me what you're planning," Lord Fernham was saying. "I looked like a fool in the session yesterday when one of the other members jested about my wife's friends chaining themselves to railings. I had no idea what he was talking about."

"I wasn't aware I had to report all our activities to you," was Lady Fernham's cold reply. "Besides, I wasn't there myself, so I don't understand what you're so upset about."

"I've been patient with you and your causes, Marian, but this is too much.

Where will it end? I thought the Wells girl's death would make you realize the folly of your actions, but you continue to encourage your friends' foolish and even dangerous behavior. This Miss Brooke, I'm told, is one of the worst of them. Why don't you counsel her to be more moderate?"

"You know nothing about her or anyone else I associate with," Lady Fernham snapped. "You're merely worried about how you'll look to your colleagues in Parliament."

"Why shouldn't I be worried? It's clear enough they perceive me as a fool who allows his wife to control him. I won't have it any longer. I insist upon knowing in advance when and where these public meetings and demonstrations will occur."

"Why? So you can stop them? We had an agreement, John."

"Damn the agreement! I've lost so much credibility in Parliament that it no longer matters which cause I support. I can do nothing more for you and your causes. At this point, all I want is to try to repair the damage that has already been done."

Lilia had only a few seconds to withdraw behind a large potted fern before Lord Fernham stalked out of the room and up the stairs. Fortunately, he didn't see her, but she didn't know whether she should enter the drawing room or give Lady Fernham time to recover from the quarrel. She slowly emerged from behind the fern and hesitated in the doorway. Lady Fernham saw her and beckoned her inside. To Lilia's surprise, her friend looked calm, even relaxed, as she motioned for Lilia to sit down in a chair next to hers.

"Would you like a cigarette?" Lady Fernham asked, taking a silver cigarette case from a drawer in a small side table.

"Yes, please."

Lady Fernham handed Lilia the cigarette. "I apologize for that unpleasant conversation. No doubt it was loud enough for most of the household to hear."

"I did hear it, I'm afraid. Will he make your life very difficult now?" Lilia spoke quietly, worried that Lord Fernham would return, or worse, eavesdrop at the door as she'd been doing.

"Don't worry about him. We have these conversations all the time."

She lit Lilia's cigarette, then her own. Lilia didn't know what to say.

Lady Fernham sighed, put her cigarette to her lips, and inhaled deeply. Then she smiled and looked around the room. "I love smoking in the drawing room," she said. "It drives John mad. He tells me that a drawing room is meant for ladies, not cigarette smoke. In his mind, of course, the two can't coexist. It gives me great pleasure to smell the stale smoke in the draperies, in my clothes and my hair. I suppose it's childish, but smoking is one of my many little ways of rebelling."

Lilia nodded sympathetically.

Lady Fernham closed her eyes, looking older than her forty years. "John and I married for love, you know. He was a dashing young man, the brother of one of my childhood friends. He had such energy and ambition back then—you'd never know it to see him now—and he was madly in love with me. Although my parents approved of him, I was an independent young woman—like you in many ways, Lilia—and I would have none of his attempts to make love to me. I sent back his letters unopened, refused to dance with him at balls, and spoke as little as possible when I couldn't escape his presence at social gatherings.

"His persistence impressed me, though, as did his interest in women's rights. Would you believe there was a time when he was more of an advocate for women's suffrage than I was? I was quite a beauty in those days, and I enjoyed the power I believed I had over men. I wasted a good deal of time on coquetry. I'm glad you're not like that. You're more serious than I was, and you don't get caught up in the little vanities that enslave so many young women."

"If Lord Fernham believed in women's suffrage back then, what happened?" Lilia asked.

"I married him." Lady Fernham waved her cigarette in the air as if to blame the drawing room furnishings for her husband's transformation. "Once we were married, he modified his views to conform to what his peers and especially his superiors believed. His ambitions became focused on what he must do to rise in the political world.

"You may find this strange, but I still consider myself fortunate in my husband. He has given me far more freedom than most husbands allow their wives, and he has tolerated my involvement with the women's movement—indeed, he has supported the women's suffrage bills in Parliament, as you know, albeit only when it's been convenient for him."

Lady Fernham leaned forward, looking at Lilia intently. "I don't know if you realize how lucky you are. You're free. No man has a claim on you. No man has conquered and enslaved you mentally, physically, or spiritually. You're not free from all struggle and suffering, of course—you must feel lonely, you must have desires—but you haven't bound yourself to a man you'll come to despise.

"The fundamental truth is this—all men are cowards. I've never met a man who can hold to his convictions when other temptations come his way, whether they be greed, power, or lust. Perhaps men suspect that we are the stronger sex, and that's why they still hold out against our cries to be recognized equally under the law. When we get the vote, when we get equal pay for equal work, and when we are allowed into every profession, it will become clear how much stronger we really are.

"I'll say it again—all men are cowards. Even your young priest, Canon Harris. Indeed, clergymen are more cowardly than the rest of them because they have more to lose."

"I don't understand," Lilia said, startled. Though Lilia had sensed she didn't like him, Lady Fernham had tolerated Paul's presence in Lilia's life thus far without comment.

"Ambitious men will make whatever sacrifices are necessary to rise to the top of their profession. For a clergyman, the desire for position and power is combined with a faith that's always in danger of being shaken, especially in these modern times. Canon Harris may tell you he supports women's suffrage—indeed, he may even believe it—but the moment that belief interferes with his position in the church, he'll abandon it. And anything you do that interferes with his faith will make him resent you later."

"But you don't know him," Lilia began, then stopped in confusion.

A slight smile appeared on the older woman's face. "I know his type. But I hope I'm wrong about him, for your sake."

"He's just a friend," Lilia said.

"Is he?" Lady Fernham looked skeptical. She added in a softer tone, "I keep forgetting how young you are, my dear. Despite your intelligence and education, you know little about men. Even in the midst of that horrible scene when Ellen died, it was clear that the only person that young man saw was you."

"I'm sure he understands . . . that is, I don't think . . ." She stopped again.

"There's nothing to worry about, of course, if you have no feelings for him," her friend said. "But even the slightest attraction will cause no end of trouble."

The slightest attraction? Lilia, who never blushed, felt her face grow hot as she remembered what she'd said to Paul in the schoolroom and the kiss that had almost happened.

Her blush must have given her away, for Lady Fernham said quietly, "It's more than friendship, Lilia."

"I don't want it to be."

"Then you must end it. It's best for both of you."

Lilia was silent.

"Let us speak of him no more," Lady Fernham went on. "You can tell me what plans are afoot for the next demonstration. Oh, and I nearly forgot to tell you that your last speech effectively raised Ellen to the status of a martyr, according to the *Guardian*. Imagine, a speech by a suffragette being reported in a major newspaper and, I might add, commented on favorably! I saved a copy of the article for you—let me find it."

As Lady Fernham rose to rummage through a drawer in a nearby desk, Lilia was relieved the conversation had turned from Paul to a safer topic. But she continued to feel unsettled, and when she went home that night, what she had seen and heard that evening stayed with her. Lilia felt Lady Fernham's disappointment with her husband acutely, and it depressed her. Was he really an example of the best an intelligent woman could hope for in a life companion? She tried to dismiss Lady Fernham's words about men, specifically Paul, as biased by her unhappy marriage, but she couldn't. She had heard similar stories from other women, and she wasn't prepared to take the risk of trusting any man, even Paul, with her heart.

Before Lilia went to bed that night, she wrote a reply to Paul's letter:

Dear Paul,

I have indeed been working long hours and have had little time to think, much less see friends. The WSPU requires all of my energies, and I can think of nothing else right now. You might consider the possibility that a woman's work can be as all-consuming as a man's.

Please forget what happened in the schoolroom. You didn't offend me, but I regret the stupid things I said and did. My only explanation is that I wasn't in my right mind after witnessing Ellen's death. Let it pass.

Lilia

That night, she dreamed of violent clashes with faceless men and of women falling from rooftops and church spires. But she also dreamed of kissing Paul—and of doing other things with him, too. She awoke in hot, breathless confusion, and it wasn't until the gray light of dawn seeped into her room that she was able to fall asleep again.

10

Stretching my unreasoning arms
As men in dreams, who vainly interpose
'Twixt gods and their undoing, with a cry
I struggled to precipitate myself
Head-foremost to the rescue of my soul
In that white face . . .

—Elizabeth Barrett Browning, *Aurora Leigh*

OCTOBER 1907

Paul was having a terrible day. He had been restless and distracted during his morning prayers, which sounded empty and hollow to him, and the two hours he had set aside for work on his book were spent staring at a blank sheet of paper, writing a phrase or two, then striking them out. The afternoon was even worse. During his weekly meeting with Cross regarding the penitentiary project, his colleague, with unseemly relish, picked apart the report Paul had written about one of the penitentiaries he'd visited the previous week.

Paul had a new reason to be angry with Cross. A week earlier, Paul had been summoned to a private meeting with the bishop, who had cautioned him about his involvement with the women's suffrage movement. The conversation had taken Paul by surprise, as he hadn't thought anyone knew about his hovering at the margins of suffrage meetings. And anyway, that could hardly be termed "involvement." Paul had asked the bishop who had given him that information, but he'd been told only that it came in a letter from a credible source who wished to remain anonymous.

Paul had immediately suspected Cross, who could have easily investigated Paul's connection with Lilia after she'd insulted him at the cathedral. Cross likely considered her suffrage activities excellent fodder with which to blacken Paul's name. The bishop hadn't delivered his admonition harshly, but it had been an unmistakable warning. It was the first time the bishop had expressed displeasure with him.

After enduring thirty minutes of criticism on this day, Paul lost his patience and interrupted Cross. "Why must you thwart me at every turn? What have I done to you that justifies your writing a letter to the bishop to try to undermine me?"

Cross stared at him. "What are you talking about? I didn't write such a letter."

"Telling falsehoods is unbecoming of a clergyman, Cross."

"Be careful what you say, Harris. I could give you the same advice."

"I knew you wouldn't admit it. But what I do when I'm not working is no business of yours, and you had better stay out of it."

"I don't care what you do in your private life," Cross shot back, "though perhaps it would be a good idea to spend more time praying for a better temper. Then you might be able to take advice about your writing without flying into a rage. Not every word you write is divinely inspired, you know."

Paul stalked out of the room without replying.

Once alone and walking in a cool wind that helped clear his head, Paul became ashamed of his outburst. He had behaved childishly, no matter how justifiable his reason for being angry. At the same time, it had been a relief to give vent to his anger instead of letting it build up inside him as he usually did.

After several weeks of working with Cross on the penitentiary project, Paul was dismayed, though not entirely surprised, to realize no real progress had been made either with the project or in their ability to work together. They had split up the work in a predictable way: Cross took on most of the social and physical requirements of the work, though they both visited the penitentiaries, and Paul wrote the reports. It wasn't a satisfactory arrangement, as that day's meeting had made abundantly clear, but neither of them had discovered a better one.

Feeling unusually weary, Paul entered his house with the hope that Mrs. Rigby wouldn't wish to consult with him about household matters. He wanted to be alone in his study. Unfortunately, that respite was not to be, as he found Mrs. Rigby and Harriet Firth waiting for him in the front hall. Paul was surprised to see Harriet—he hadn't known that she knew where he lived—but he greeted her politely and invited her into the study.

"What can I do for you, Miss Firth?" Paul asked, sinking into the leather chair behind his desk.

Harriet ignored the chair Paul indicated and stood in front of his desk, looking more stern than usual.

"Forgive me for disturbing you, Canon Harris, but have you seen Lilia today?" she asked.

"No, I have not." He hadn't seen Lilia since the day Ellen Wells died, though not for lack of trying.

"She canceled her afternoon lessons and I haven't been able to find her. I must speak with her before the protest."

"What protest?"

"She didn't tell you?" She looked surprised. "Hundreds of WSPU members are going to Parliament Square this afternoon to protest the prime minister's refusal to receive a small deputation of women to discuss the suffrage bill. Many suffrage groups have worked together on this bill for nearly two years, and now it looks as though the government will kill it."

Paul was beginning to recognize the heavy feeling in the pit of his stomach whenever the WSPU was mentioned. It had been a month since Ellen's death, and he had hoped the incident would discourage the suffragettes from making public protests, though it clearly had not. And he still didn't understand why Lilia was suddenly so involved with the militant wing of the suffrage movement. Had she abandoned the more moderate, respectable NUWSS entirely?

"I overheard something today that I need to tell Lilia," Harriet went on, "but the protest is scheduled to begin in less than an hour—" She stopped abruptly and her face took on a grayish cast.

Alarmed, Paul rose and said, "Miss Firth, please sit down and rest for a moment. I'll call Mrs. Rigby to bring you some water."

She sat down, but shook her head. "I'm all right, really. I just need a moment."

The moment seemed to last forever, but eventually the color returned to Harriet's face.

"As I was walking to school this morning," she went on, "I passed two constables who were talking about the planned protest. They seemed to know too much about it, but what concerns me the most is something they said about bringing in reinforcements to, as they said, 'put those women in their place.' I have a bad feeling about this. I don't want Lilia to go."

Paul couldn't agree more. "If we leave now," he said, "we may be able to get to Parliament Square before the protest begins. We can take a cab."

"We'd better walk. The roads here and around the square will be clogged with traffic at this time of day. We'll get there faster on foot."

Paul hesitated. He was quite willing to walk—or even run—all the way to Parliament Square, but Harriet wouldn't be able to keep up with him and he didn't want to slow his pace for her.

As if she had read his mind, she said firmly, "I'm used to walking quickly and will have no difficulty."

Paul agreed, and the two of them set out immediately. Neither of them spoke as they walked, as if they were both trying to prepare themselves for whatever awaited them.

As they approached the square, Paul noticed that this crowd was larger and more diverse than that of a month ago, and at first he couldn't see Lilia or anyone else he recognized.

"I don't think we're too late," Harriet said with evident relief, but then she pointed to the east end of the square, where Lilia was ascending a makeshift platform with two other women. "Oh, I was wrong. We should have been here five minutes ago."

Paul and Harriet had reached the edge of the crowd, which was packed together tightly, making it impossible to move forward. Paul saw that one of the women with Lilia was Lady Fernham. The other was a small, dignified woman he didn't know.

Lilia began to speak. He wasn't close enough to hear what Lilia was saying, but her slim, upright figure communicated her usual confidence and determination.

What happened next was a nightmare. Only much later would Paul remember how strangely quiet the crowd was during those few minutes at the beginning of Lilia's speech. The momentary, eerie stillness of these people from every walk of life made what came later all the more shocking. The first person to break the calm was a man a few yards in front of Paul who cursed Lilia loudly, his crude words piercing the calm dignity of her speech. That curse seemed to release the inhibitions of the other members of the crowd. To Paul, it seemed as though they rose up as one united entity against the defenseless body of the woman he loved.

In reality, he saw very little at first because of the confusion and jostling of the people around him. The hostility of the crowd quickly escalated into a full-blown riot. The suffragettes were cursed at, spit upon, and shoved. Worst of all, Paul slowly realized that far from stopping the violence, the police were actually assaulting the women. One woman fell to the ground and covered her face after being hit with a truncheon, and two constables began kicking her. A gang of toughs who may have been plainclothes policemen dragged another woman away, down a side street. Another man was holding a woman's arms behind her while another grabbed her breasts.

"Go!" he ordered Harriet. "You're not safe here."

Without waiting to see if she obeyed him, he plunged forward into the sea of people, thinking only of reaching Lilia.

Paul had never witnessed a scene of such unprovoked violence, much less attacks against women, and he pushed through the crowd towards the platform where Lilia had been standing. He stopped to help up two women who had fallen and were in danger of being trampled, but there was little he could do in such a large, unruly crowd.

He finally saw Lilia standing about twenty yards away. For a long, agonizing moment, their eyes locked. All her earlier confidence had melted into confusion.

Then a large man in a dirty cloth cap struck Lilia hard in the back, knocking her down. Paul felt an echoing blow in his body, and his desperate attempts to reach her seemed as slow as if he were trying to run through water. He saw her struggle to stand up, but then the man who had knocked her down pushed her down again and kicked her in the stomach with sickening brutality.

Finally, Paul was at her side, and he sprang between her and her attacker. Paul was kicked and shoved as he got in the way, but at that point, two other men stepped in and pulled the attacker away. Paul gathered Lilia's motionless body into his arms, sure she must be dead. He checked her pulse. It was weak, but steady.

It seemed like a long time before Harriet and Lady Fernham reached them. Both women looked bedraggled, but uninjured.

"Is she alive?" Lady Fernham cried.

"Yes, but she's unconscious," Paul said. "We must send for a doctor."

"Let's take her home first," Harriet said.

"What if she has broken bones?" said Lady Fernham. "She shouldn't be moved."

"There are too many other injured people here," Harriet replied, glancing around the square. "It will take too long for a doctor to get to her if we stay here."

Paul followed Harriet's gaze. The square looked like a battlefield, with some women lying on the ground moaning in pain and others struggling to their feet and hobbling away, leaning on their uninjured comrades. Paul agreed with Harriet, and they were able to flag down an ambulance man who helped them take Lilia home.

Lady Fernham's Harley Street doctor was sent for, and Lizzie was nearly run off her feet as Lady Fernham ordered her about. Amid the general confusion, Paul never left Lilia's side. As soon as she was settled in her bedroom, he planted himself in a chair by her bed. He would not be moved, even when Lady Fernham told him Lilia was in good hands now and he was no longer needed.

When the doctor finally arrived, he examined Lilia and made several grunts that didn't seem to bode well for her. After what seemed like an interminable examination, he turned to Paul and Lady Fernham, the only other people in the room.

"This young woman has been treated roughly indeed," the doctor said. "I can better assess the damage when she awakens. We must wait to find out if her internal organs have been damaged. Send for me again as soon as she wakes or if you notice any change in her breathing. Her family must be notified, of course."

"I know her family," Paul said. "I'll send them a telegram."

When the doctor left, Lady Fernham again tried to dismiss Paul. "Canon Harris," she said imperiously, "there are enough of us here to sit with Lilia through the night. You needn't stay any longer."

Annoyance managed to penetrate the fog in Paul's brain, and he gave her an imperious look of his own—it was his best you-are-a-sinner look, one he reserved for special occasions. "*You* may leave," he said coldly. "I'll stay here until she wakes."

"That may take hours—perhaps even days. Surely you have duties to attend to."

"My duties can wait."

He returned his gaze to Lilia's face, which still looked frighteningly pale, framed by strands of dark, wavy hair. Lady Fernham turned on her heel and left the room. He suspected she would try to convince Harriet to make him leave, but unless they were intending to lift him bodily and carry him out of the house, he would not move. He took Lilia's hand in both of his, keeping two fingers on her pulse. It was reassuring to feel the rhythm of her heartbeat. Paul couldn't think about the possibility that she might die—not now, not before he had the chance to tell her that he loved her.

As the afternoon turned to evening and evening to night, Paul remained at Lilia's bedside. He turned his attention away from her only for the few minutes required to compose a telegram to her parents. He tried to word it in a way that would communicate the urgency of Lilia's condition without causing panic. He felt guilty for having failed her family in his promise to watch out for her.

When Lizzie came in with a tray bearing bread and cold mutton, he handed the message to her and asked her to send it immediately. Though he hadn't eaten all day, Paul couldn't touch the food.

Returning to his vigil, Paul fell into a stupor that was punctuated only by an occasional shooting pain in his left arm, where a blow from Lilia's attacker had landed, and by the comings and goings of Harriet and Lady Fernham. Once, from what seemed a great distance, he heard them whispering in a corner of the room: he heard his name mentioned, then the word *inappropriate* in Lady Fernham's critical tone. Harriet replied, "I don't know how to make him leave."

"Let him stay." The voice came from the bed, faint but clear.

Lady Fernham and Harriet rushed to the other side of the bed, and Paul took Lilia's hand again, thrilled to see that her eyes were open.

Harriet and Lady Fernham spoke at once. "How are you feeling?" "Can we get you anything?"

"Awful." Lilia took a deep breath, then grimaced. "It hurts to breathe. I'd like a glass of water, please."

Harriet rang for Lizzie.

Lady Fernham said, "Canon Harris, now that Lilia is awake, you may go."

Before he could argue, Lilia tightened her grip on his hand and said, "No. Stay with me, Paul."

This sealed Paul's victory over the forces of Lady Fernham. He watched over Lilia all night, glad to forgo sleep, food, and all other comforts for her sake.

11

Sometimes she went so far as to wish that she might find herself
some day in a difficult position, so that she should have the pleasure
of being as heroic as the occasion demanded.

—Henry James, *The Portrait of a Lady*

DECEMBER 1907

E mily! Lilia! Where have you been?" Mrs. Brooke exclaimed. "You've
been gone two hours, at least. Why didn't you tell me where you were
going?"

"We were just out for a walk," Lilia replied. "We didn't realize how much
time had passed. The sunshine was irresistible."

"Sunshine? What sunshine?" cried her mother, who always had trouble
seeing the sunshine for the clouds. "You're not even wearing a hat! It hasn't
even been a month since . . . since you—" But the long-suffering mother
couldn't continue, the horror of what had happened to her firstborn child
still too fresh in her mind.

Lilia refrained from pointing out that it had been more than a month—
almost six weeks, in fact—since the riot in Parliament Square. "I'm all

right—really, Mama," she said. "I feel almost as good as new. You've taken such good care of me."

"If only you would take better care of yourself. Now you've upset your sister, too."

Fourteen-year-old Emily did indeed look stricken, her dark eyes filling with tears. But it was clear to Lilia that Emily's distress was caused by her mother, not herself. She bit her tongue.

"I'd never do anything to hurt Lilia, Mama," Emily said in a choked voice.

"Of course you wouldn't, dear. She ought to have known better, that's all."

Lilia turned around silently, hung her coat on one of the pegs by the front door, and went upstairs to the bedroom she had been sharing with Emily. She was frustrated by the regular arguments she had been having with her mother since coming home to recover from the injuries she'd received during the Parliament Square riot. She knew her mother had been worried, but Lilia was accustomed to living on her own and found it difficult to be treated like a child again, as if she had no common sense. The only way to avoid arguments was not to respond at all, and though she knew her mother was upset by her silence, she would have been even more upset had Lilia said what she was thinking.

Lilia sighed and lay down on Emily's bed. It was the largest and most comfortable of the two beds in the room and Emily had insisted that Lilia use it during her stay in Ingleford. The room's furnishings had changed greatly from when Lilia was a child: although she and Emily shared this room for many years, the ten-year age difference between them meant its decor was dominated by Lilia's taste until she went to college. She had coexisted happily with a chaotic jumble of books, papers, specimens of interesting rocks and shells, and some objects the purpose of which was a mystery to everyone but herself.

Now, there were only a few books arranged neatly on a small bookcase, which also held two pretty gilt-edged jewelry boxes, a Chinese vase, and a purple velvet pincushion. The room was very feminine and very tidy.

A soft tap on the door interrupted Lilia's reverie. Emily came in bearing letters.

"Mama forgot to give these to you this morning. Three letters from London! Mama says your friends alone keep the post in business. No, don't get up! I'll bring them to you." She hurried to Lilia's side and handed her the letters.

"Thank you, Emmy."

Lilia sat up and glanced at the letters, recognizing the handwriting on each one instantly—one was from Mrs. Pankhurst, one from Harriet, and one from Paul. Taking up Harriet's letter first, she began to read, but then realized Emily was still standing there, looking worried.

"May I bring you more pillows?" Emily asked.

"No, I'm fine, dear, really. Here, sit with me." Lilia settled herself back against the pillows and reached out a hand to Emily, who squeezed in beside her.

"Wouldn't you rather be alone to read your letters?" Emily asked.

"No, you goose. I'd rather have you with me every minute of the day because you're such an angel. You've nursed your ill-tempered old sister back to health with far more patience than she deserves. I predict that when you grow up, you'll be a nurse like Florence Nightingale, or perhaps even a doctor."

"Lilia, don't tease me." Emily nestled closer and put her head on her sister's shoulder.

Lilia rested her cheek against her sister's golden-brown curls and said, "Would you like me to read the interesting parts of my letters to you?"

"Oh, yes, please. If you don't think your friends would mind, of course."

"I'm sure they wouldn't."

Harriet's letter was long and mainly contained news about the WSPU and public reaction to the riot in Parliament Square, neither of which Lilia could discuss with Emily. Afraid that Emily would follow in her sister's footsteps, Mrs. Brooke had insisted that Lilia promise never to discuss the WSPU, or even the women's movement in general, with Emily. That left very little to report.

"It's a long letter," observed Emily after a while. "Is it not very interesting?"

"Not very," Lilia lied. She went on, choosing her words carefully, "My friend Harriet is just telling me news of our friends and our work."

"Is she the one who wrote the letter in the *Guardian* about the riot?"

Lilia was startled. "How do you know about that?"

The letter had appeared in the *Guardian* a week after the riot. Harriet had described in detail what had happened that day, setting out the intentions of the WSPU for a peaceful protest and exposing the brutality of the police. She had found out that additional plainclothes policemen had been recruited from the East End and appeared to have been given orders to rough up the women before arresting them. Public reaction to the letter had been positive, with an outpouring of sympathy and support for the suffragettes.

"I heard Papa and Mama talking about it," Emily said, a bit sheepishly.

"Mama would have my head if she knew we were talking about it now."

"I know, but I don't understand why. I'm not a baby anymore, and I want to know about your work. It's important to you, so why can't I know?"

Lilia smoothed a wayward curl out of Emily's eyes. "When you're grown, I'll tell you everything you want to know. But for now, you'd better listen to Mama."

Lilia opened the letter from Mrs. Pankhurst. Direct communication from the busy Mrs. Pankhurst was always exciting.

"My goodness!" she exclaimed, already forgetting that she wasn't supposed to discuss the WSPU with Emily. "Mrs. Pankhurst has offered me a position as a paid organizer with the WSPU."

"A job? But you already have a job." When Lilia looked at her blankly, Emily added, "As a teacher."

"Oh. Yes."

After Lilia was injured in the riot, a temporary teacher had been hired to take her place at the Fernham Preparatory School for Girls. Though it had been only six weeks since Lilia had last been in the schoolroom, it felt to her like years.

Lilia set Mrs. Pankhurst's letter aside so she could read it more carefully when she was alone, but she was elated by the offer. As she was a relatively new member of the WSPU, it was a particular honor.

She opened Paul's letter with some trepidation. She had exchanged a few letters with him since the riot, careful notes about safe topics like her recovery and his work. She remembered little of his presence in Parliament Square during the riot, but she did remember how she had felt when she'd regained consciousness to see him at her bedside. She was afraid and in pain, and Paul was the only person she wanted with her. Now, her feelings towards him were more confused than ever.

This letter from Paul was similar to the others. She had set a formal, polite tone for their exchanges, and he hadn't deviated from it. He asked about her health and cautioned her not to resume her usual activities too soon. A few sentences about his work followed, and Lilia was about to put the letter aside when she stopped short at the last line.

"What's the matter?" Emily asked, apparently noticing Lilia's sudden stillness. "Who's the letter from?"

"It's from Paul," Lilia said slowly. "He's offering to come for a visit in a few days."

"Here? He's coming to Ingleford?" Emily jumped to her feet, forgetting the dignity befitting her fourteen years, and pirouetted around the room. "Aunt Bianca will be so happy!"

Lilia didn't know what to think about Paul's proposed visit. She missed him—missed especially the ease with which they had once talked and confided in each other—but she hadn't forgotten Lady Fernham's advice to end their friendship. At the same time, perhaps that would be too extreme. After all, their families would always be connected; it wasn't practical to cut off all communication with him.

But it was shocking that Paul would even consider visiting her. It was an established, if unspoken, belief among the Brookes and Anbreys that Paul would never come to Ingleford. His mother had never been able to convince him to visit. But now he was offering to come as if it were the most natural thing in the world—and to see her, Lilia. The visit seemed as marked and public a declaration of his feelings for her as if he had proclaimed them from the pulpit. Why couldn't he wait until she returned to London?

But perhaps she was overreacting. It was possible that Paul had decided to make peace with his mother and James and simply had no reason to avoid Ingleford any longer. Perhaps Lilia's presence was merely an additional incentive. And even if he were coming just to see her, was that so strange, considering her brush with death? Wouldn't any friend have made the trip after witnessing the horrible scene at the square? Perhaps—though, so far, none of her London friends had done so.

Lilia was so wrapped up in her thoughts that she hadn't noticed Emily leaving the room. A moment later, Emily and her mother burst in again in a flurry of excitement.

"Is it true?" cried Mrs. Brooke. "Is Paul really coming here?" She looked as if she hardly dared to believe the news.

"It appears to be true," Lilia replied. "You may read the letter if you like."

She held it out, and her mother eagerly made herself acquainted with the contents.

"How wonderful!" Mrs. Brooke exclaimed. "You must reply at once and tell him to come to dinner. The younger boys are still at school this week, and Harry won't be home, either, so we have plenty of room if he wishes to stay here for a few days. Now, what shall we have for dinner? A haunch of mutton, or perhaps a braised turkey—oh, and I must get Mrs. Seeley's recipe for Cabinet pudding, which is very nice—"

"Mama," Lilia interrupted, "you mustn't make plans without speaking to Aunt Bianca first. I'm certain Paul will want to see her, too, and if he stays more than a day, he'll surely stay with her and Uncle James." Lilia was certain of no such thing, but she felt it necessary to impress upon her mother the importance of allowing Bianca to make plans of her own with and for her son. "Besides, I doubt very much that he'll stay long. He's busy with his parish duties."

Mrs. Brooke gave her daughter a meaningful look. "Indeed. You must be honored that he's taking the time to visit you."

"I'm overcome by the honor of it," Lilia replied in a mock-courtly tone.

And she would be overcome—almost crushed—by the honor, if her mother continued to behave in this ridiculous manner. If the family intended to give Paul a reception fit for royalty, Lilia hardly needed to be present.

Lilia tried her best to ignore the whirlwind of activity in the house that afternoon, for her mother and Emily could speak of nothing but Paul's visit. Her mother's excitement was odd, as she had always been critical of Paul, particularly of his unwillingness to visit his mother. (It didn't matter that she criticized Bianca just as much for leaving her son behind in London when she'd come to Ingleford to live in unwedded bliss with James.) Lilia loved her mother, but she had never understood her, and the feeling was mutual.

But Lilia did feel compelled to intervene when Mrs. Brooke announced her intention to visit Bianca that very afternoon. She followed her mother to the door and asked, "Why are you going to visit her now?"

Mrs. Brooke paused in the process of stabbing her hat with a hatpin. "Why, to tell her about Paul's visit, of course."

"Please don't do that," Lilia said. "He has probably already written to her"—she devoutly hoped this was true—"and if he hasn't, it will hurt her feelings if the news comes from you instead of him."

"Good heavens, girl, I don't know what's the matter with you!" her mother exclaimed, opening the front door and stepping out. "Why in the world would it hurt her feelings to find out her son is coming here? She'll be overjoyed!"

Lilia sighed, frustrated by what seemed to be her mother's willful blindness.

"And here she is now, so you can tell her yourself!" her mother added in a defeated tone.

Bianca was indeed approaching the Brookes' front door, close enough to overhear Mrs. Brooke's last words.

"Tell me what?" she asked.

"I'm apparently not at liberty to say," Mrs. Brooke said with an injured look. "My daughter may tell you what she likes."

With this abrupt, enigmatic announcement, Mrs. Brooke removed her hat, turned around, and disappeared into the house.

"Please excuse my mother," Lilia said. "She's not herself today." She invited Bianca into the parlor.

"How are you feeling?" Bianca asked, watching Lilia lower herself slowly onto a straight-backed wooden chair. "James has instructed me to report his favorite patient's state of health in great detail."

Lilia smiled. "You may tell Uncle James that I'm very well and he can now devote his attention to the patients who really need his help. I still have headaches sometimes, but they're not very bad."

"What about your back?"

"Well," Lilia admitted, "I do have trouble sitting for long periods of time."

Bianca laughed. "You always did, you know. Now you have an excuse for being in constant motion! Honestly, though, are you in pain?"

"Not much anymore. It doesn't keep me awake at night as it used to," Lilia replied. She didn't like to talk about her injuries, but at the moment they were a useful diversion while she tried to think of a tactful way to introduce the subject of Paul's proposed visit.

Bianca brought Lilia's stalling tactic to an abrupt end by asking, "What is this news everyone seems so reluctant to share with me?"

"Oh, it's not that we're reluctant. It's just so very odd." Lilia hesitated. "I received a letter from Paul today. He says that he might pay a visit . . . here, in a few days . . . if it's all right with . . . us." The unspecified "us," which Lilia meant to include Bianca without actually admitting that Paul hadn't mentioned her, only added more awkwardness to an already uncomfortable moment.

Bianca was clearly shocked. "He's coming here?"

Fleetingly, Lilia toyed with the idea of sending Paul a strongly worded letter telling him not to make the visit. She didn't think she could patiently endure many more of the same expressions of surprise from her family and friends. Why hadn't he written to his mother first?

"Yes," Lilia replied. "Perhaps he doesn't realize I'm quite well now. I intend to return to London soon, anyway, so I'll see him there. I could write to him and tell him not to come."

"No, please, don't," Bianca said. "I'm glad he's willing to come here to see you. I should not like to see him discouraged from coming, not after all the times I've invited him."

Lilia was worried she had made the situation worse. "Of course. I'm sorry. It will be a good opportunity for everyone to see him."

Bianca studied her face for a moment, and the reason for Lilia's discomfort seemed to dawn on her. She patted Lilia's hand and said, "Don't worry about me, my dear. I think you know Paul has been angry with me since I moved here. Whether he chooses to see me or not has nothing to do with you. I'm glad—so very glad indeed—that the two of you have become good friends. Be happy, Lilia, that he cares enough to brave Ingleford for you."

Later that evening, when Lilia had a chance to be alone and think, she wrote her reply to Paul's letter.

Dear Paul,

Both of our mothers are happy to hear of your proposed trip to Ingleford. You are welcome to come, but it isn't necessary to do so for my sake. I'll see you in London when I return after Christmas.

If you still wish to come, my mother has urged me to invite you to dine at our house. However, I must remind you of the duty you owe your own mother. She is overconcerned about any discomfort you might feel on account of her, so I must urge you not to slight her by forgetting that Ingleford is her home now more than it is mine. Therefore, I insist that you visit her before coming to dine with us. You will displease me very much if you do not, and a displeased invalid (for an invalid you seem to think me still) is not pleasant company for anyone.

Your friend,

Lilia

Feeling wearier than she had in days, Lilia extinguished her candle and lay down in bed. It was only nine o'clock in the evening, but she decided to act the invalid after all and not stir until morning. But as soon as she closed her eyes, her mind awakened, whirling with thoughts about her future. It was time to think seriously about what she was doing with her life.

She lit the candle again, took out Mrs. Pankhurst's letter, and reread it. In addition to the offer of employment, Mrs. Pankhurst had written about her new plans for the WSPU. The riot had proven that it was now too dangerous to stage public protests and demonstrations. Instead of allowing women's bodies to be brutalized for merely speaking out in public, Mrs. Pankhurst argued, it was time to speak the language men understood: *There is something that governments care far more for than human life and that is the security of property, and so it is through property that we shall strike the enemy.*

Lilia was glad the WSPU would no longer hold public protests. Although her injuries were a badge of honor in her eyes, the riot had frightened her. She was excited about the new direction Mrs. Pankhurst wrote about, and she couldn't wait to get back to work.

12

We read, or talked, or quarrelled, as it chanced.

We were not lovers, nor even friends well-matched:

Say rather, scholars upon different tracks,

And thinkers disagreed; he, overfull

Of what is, and I, haply, overbold

For what might be.

—Elizabeth Barrett Browning, *Aurora Leigh*

As Paul gazed out the train window, he didn't see the barren, damp December landscape. Instead, he saw the sunshine and greenery of early summer and a group of children in makeshift armor charging down a hillside towards him. He remembered Lilia as Jeanne d'Arc leading her army, a fierce, slender girl with a wild mane of dark hair. But he also remembered coming upon a horrifying scene that evening in the Brookes' garden: his mother and James Anbrey in a lovers' embrace.

As the train approached Ingleford, Paul felt that a great ordeal was awaiting him—in fact, this day could bring *two* great ordeals. The first was his visit to his mother. She had agreed enthusiastically to meet him at the train station, but she hadn't responded to his injunction that she come alone. That meant James might be with her, a possibility Paul couldn't imagine himself managing very well. He had nothing to say to the man. In the event of James's presence, the only advantage of the visit would be its brevity. Paul would have only a few hours from the time he arrived in Ingleford until he was expected at the Brookes' house for dinner. Never had the unfashionably early dinnertime of five o'clock been more appealing.

Despite Paul's anxiety, a small, perverse part of him wanted James there. There were two reasons for this: he was hoping to find that James was his inferior in every way so he could gain more satisfaction from despising him, and he wanted to prove to Lilia that he could endure the most distasteful of situations for her sake. Although her insistence that he visit his mother had irritated him at first, he now looked upon it (not entirely tongue-in-cheek) as one of the necessary tests a knight must pass in order to gain his lady's favor. Therefore, the more unpleasant the test, the more pride he could take in passing it.

Though it did worry him a little that in all the medieval romances, there were always three tests. Even if he considered his attempt to save Lilia's life during the Parliament Square riot one of those tests, and the second his visit to his mother, that still left one unaccounted for.

The object of his trip to Ingleford—the imperious lady herself—could create his third ordeal. Lilia's letters since the riot had been formal and polite, but her last had been colder than the others and could hardly have been less encouraging than if she had told him not to come at all. She hadn't indicated the slightest desire to see him, which pained him a great deal. If he had missed her less, he may have been too discouraged to attempt this trip. Thoughts of her dominated his waking hours and his dreams, interfering with both his work and his peace of mind. He needed to hear from her own lips whether she loved him or not. Based on the intimate embrace they had shared in the schoolroom the day Ellen died, Paul thought he had reason to hope, but her letters and her avoidance of him since that day suggested otherwise. He didn't wish to prolong the agony of trying to guess what her feelings were, so here he was.

As the train slowly came to a halt at Ingleford station, Paul wrenched his thoughts away from Lilia and transferred them to the more immediate concern of who awaited him on the platform.

As soon as he disembarked, he scanned the small group of waiting people. His mother stood alone, apart from the others. It had been several months since they had seen each other, for she didn't get to London often, and when she caught sight of him her face lit up and she hurried forward to greet him.

Paul's relief at seeing her alone enabled him to return her warm embrace without effort.

"Paul, dear, you're more handsome every time I see you!" she exclaimed, beaming into his face. "But why are you dressed like that?"

He had expected this question, for he had decided to wear ordinary clothing instead of his cassock and clerical collar. His white shirt, black trousers, and black morning coat wouldn't have attracted attention from anyone who didn't know him, but it was the first time he had worn layman's clothing in public since his ordination. The decision had been not so much the result of thoughtful consideration as a general feeling that he didn't want to be on duty that day.

"I thought I'd dress like an ordinary man for a change," was his explanation to his mother.

"You overshot the mark, then," she replied. "You look far too fashionable for the simple rustics of Ingleford."

Paul wondered if she classed herself with the "simple rustics" of whom she spoke. She had once been very fashionable herself, but the dark green dress she wore now was faded and the collar looked as though it had been turned. In London, she would sooner have died than worn a dress that was more than a year out of fashion.

His mother took his arm as they left the train station. "We can walk to the house. It will take only a quarter of an hour. The Brookes don't live far from us, so you can walk there, too."

Paul didn't particularly want to see the house where his mother and James Anbrey lived, but he couldn't very well suggest to her that they walk around the village for two hours. He hoped his luck would remain with him and James would be away from home.

Paul only half listened to his mother's stream of small talk about the people she knew and her life in Ingleford. Most of the people she seemed to consider friends were James's patients, people who would have been her social inferiors in London. She spoke briefly of the Brookes, too, which caught Paul's attention, but she said nothing about Lilia.

When they arrived at the house, it was all Paul could do to hide his shock. It was tiny, not much bigger than a hovel, really, with a small front room that seemed to serve as parlor, drawing room, and dining room in one. What a difference from the large, elegant house in London she had shared with Philip and Paul! It seemed like utter poverty; he was sure his mother must have been suffering.

At least there was a maid-of-all-work, a thin girl with straw-colored hair who emerged from the kitchen to set a pot of tea and some sorry-looking sandwiches on the table in front of them. Fortunately, too, there was no sign of James, and Paul started to relax as his mother asked about his work.

Almost an hour passed pleasantly as they conversed upon superficial topics. The sandwiches were palatable and the tea was actually quite good. But Paul began to feel truly sorry for his mother. She was clearly trying to make the best of her unpleasant situation and although it had been her choice to live in such circumstances, Paul wondered whether he ought to offer to help. He had more money than he needed from the combination of his canonry and a generous allowance from his father.

"Mother," he said as soon as there was a pause in the conversation, "may

I send you some money when I get back to London? I have few expenses these days and I don't spend very much. Perhaps you could make use of it."

She colored deeply. "Thank you, Paul, but I don't need anything."

It was such an obvious lie that he could think of no response. An uncomfortable silence ensued.

"You'd better not speak of the riot when you're with the Brookes," Bianca said at last. "They're upset about Lilia's involvement with the suffragettes and they don't wish to speak of it. For my part, I think Lilia is a very brave young woman and they ought to be proud of her. You showed great courage, too, Paul, when you rescued her. The Brookes consider you a hero for saving her life."

"I didn't save her life, exactly," Paul said, embarrassed by the overstatement. "But I could hardly stand by and watch her being attacked without doing something." He still couldn't speak of the incident without emotion. He tried to hide his feelings, but his mother watched him closely.

She leaned forward, looking into his eyes, and asked, "Are you in love with her?"

It was his turn to color, and he looked away. It had been many years since he had shared his feelings, much less his secrets, with his mother. At the same time, he was desperate to tell someone how he felt, and desperate, too, for reassurance. Knowing Lilia as well as she did, perhaps his mother could offer that reassurance.

"Yes, I am," he replied, meeting her eyes again.

His mother smiled triumphantly. "I thought as much," she exclaimed, "especially when I found out you were coming here to see her! I'm very happy to hear it."

"You are?"

"Of course. Lilia is already like a daughter to me, and I think she's good for you. Besides, the Brookes and James and I have long hoped for this match."

"You have? I had no idea."

"We didn't want to say anything to either of you, lest you turn against the idea. These days, children tend to rebel against matches their parents try to make for them."

Paul was touched. He decided it was safe to pursue the reassurance he sought. "Mother, without asking you to betray any confidences, do you think Lilia shares my feelings?"

"I don't know for certain, dear. She's never said so to me, though I do know she admires you and values your friendship. That must count for something."

The conversation, which had taken a most delightful turn from Paul's point of view, was interrupted by the arrival of James, who appeared in the doorway without warning. Bianca jumped up from her chair when she saw him.

"Darling, you're home!" she said, embracing him without shame. He actually kissed her on the forehead in front of Paul, who felt as if a bucket of ice water had been thrown in his face.

"Mrs. Smith's list of aches and pains was shorter than usual today," James replied, "so I'm home early." He smiled at Paul and came forward to offer his hand. "Welcome."

Paul shook hands with James stiffly, withdrawing his own hand as quickly as possible. It amazed him that this man—the man who had taken his mother away and devastated his father—could walk into the room so boldly and greet Paul as if they were friends.

James pulled up a chair beside Bianca and regarded Paul with interest. He wore a shabby brown jacket and he needed a haircut. His hair, the same shade of gold as Paul's, curled over the collar of his coat.

"How was your trip?" James asked. "Was the train crowded?"

"Not in the first-class carriage," Paul said, meeting the other man's eyes. He wasn't going to be stared down by this self-satisfied rustic booby.

Unaware that he had silently been labeled a self-satisfied rustic booby, James merely nodded and looked away.

Bianca bit her lip, looking distressed. Then, in an artificially bright tone, she said, "In the fall it was so hot here—was it just as hot in London? Then there was that sudden drop in the temperature and it rained. It just poured like nothing I've ever seen before. The farmers' crops in this area were ruined, and the same people who had been complaining about the heat then started to complain about the cold . . ." Her voice trailed off. James took her hand and squeezed it.

Paul couldn't believe he was being forced to watch this unashamed display of physical affection. It was disgusting. Revolting. A fragment from *Hamlet* raced through his mind, something about Claudius paddling in Gertrude's neck with his fingers—no, his *damned* fingers. He stared at a patch of carpet across the room. Unlike most events he dreaded, this experience was worse in reality than in his imagination.

A seemingly endless silence ensued. Paul considered the possibility of simply getting up and leaving, but he didn't want to insult his mother. She had been genuinely happy to see him, and her straitened circumstances couldn't help but evoke his pity, despite the other emotions that clouded his vision.

His mother broke the silence. "Paul has been telling me about a project for penitentiary reform that the bishop has put him in charge of," she said to James.

James turned his gaze back to Paul, who couldn't tell if the interest in the older man's eyes was real or feigned. "Is that so?" James asked. "What are your duties in relation to this project?"

Bianca was looking at Paul pleadingly.

"There are actually two of us in charge of the project," Paul replied, making his best attempt to be civil. "We visit the penitentiaries in London and prepare reports on the conditions we find there."

"And what have you found? That is, if you're at liberty to discuss it."

"Most of them are tolerable, considering the little money available to them. I've seen deplorable conditions in a few of them: overcrowding, a terrible diet, and extreme punishments for minor offenses—or in some cases, for no offenses at all. One of the penitentiaries has been closed down as a result of our inquiries."

"There has been talk of establishing a similar institution here in Ingleford," James said. "Despite the small size of the village, there is unfortunately a demand for such a place. Several young women are in dire need of alternatives to the lives they've been living."

"Unfortunately, sin isn't confined to urban areas," Paul said ponderously. He knew he was being childish, but he couldn't stop.

James didn't seem to have heard him. "Perhaps you would consider speaking to the people on the planning committee the next time you're in Ingleford. They would benefit from your knowledge."

"Perhaps," Paul replied coldly, certain that the next time he would be in Ingleford would be after his death or never, whichever came first.

He didn't think he could survive another interminable silence and was just about to look at his pocket watch in hopes that it was time to leave, when, to the all-too-evident relief of everyone in the room, the front door burst open and Lilia walked in.

Paul's heart knocked wildly about in his chest when he saw her. Fortunately, she greeted Bianca and James first, which gave him a few seconds to recover. The last time he had seen her, she had been a small, crumpled figure on a bed, badly hurt and only semiconscious. But the tall, slender young woman he saw now brimmed with life, energy, and strength, her cheeks rosy from walking in the cold winter air. She was the most beautiful creature Paul had ever seen.

It astonished him to see how warmly she and James greeted each other. Paul knew that Lilia and his mother were fond of each other, but it hadn't occurred to him that James might be included in that affection. Though it was unsettling, he didn't have time to take it in, as Lilia next turned to look at him with a smile every bit as warm as the one she had given the others.

"I almost didn't recognize you in those clothes, Paul!" she exclaimed, looking him up and down. "What a shocking breach of your custom! Whatever do you mean by it?"

Still overwhelmed by her presence, he had no clever reply to make, so he repeated what he had told his mother.

"I've come to collect you a bit early," Lilia said. "I hope you don't mind. My mother is panicking because dinner will be ready sooner than expected, and she wants to be certain it will still be hot for you. I also thought you might need a guide to our house from here."

"Thank you," Paul said fervently. She had no idea what she had rescued him from.

It took only a few minutes to say the necessary farewells—a curt nod for James and a quick embrace for his mother—and Paul was released into the wintry air with Lilia by his side.

"Perhaps we ought to walk more slowly," he said as they started out at what seemed a breakneck speed.

"Why? Are you tired?" She gave him a sidelong glance.

"No, but I thought you might be."

"Do I look tired?"

"No," he said. "You look well." It was a possibly the most massive understatement of his life.

"So I am. I've almost completely recovered, so there's no need for you or anyone else to worry about me." She paused to gaze at him intently. "How very distinguished and handsome you look, Paul. I feel as though I'm escorting a mysterious nobleman to my parents' house. Your mother must have admired you excessively."

He didn't know how to reply. Thinking of his mother reminded him of the conversation he had had with her and James, and he was suddenly deeply ashamed of his behavior. His desire to cut James down to size had led him to behave like a spoiled, petty, jealous child. Didn't his mother have enough troubles without his causing her pain? Yes, she and James had wronged him and Philip, but Paul didn't need to fight Philip's battles. As for himself, he was an adult now and ought to be able to put past hurts to rest.

"Are you all right?" Lilia asked, slowing her pace. He became aware that she had been watching his face as he walked silently beside her.

"I'm fine. Forgive me. I was just thinking about the visit with my mother and . . ." He couldn't bring himself to use James's name, and his voice trailed off.

"Was it very difficult?" Lilia's voice was warmly sympathetic.

"Yes, it was."

"Well, I'm proud of you for going through with it." She took his arm, an innocuous gesture that would have meant nothing to him months ago. Now, the light touch of her hand on his arm lit him up like a wick in a candle.

"You shouldn't be. I behaved badly. Besides . . ." His tone was softer as he said, "*You* asked me to do it, and that was all the incentive I needed."

Lilia didn't respond, but she didn't seem displeased, either.

They turned a corner and entered a winding lane, and Lilia stopped and looked around furtively. Startled, Paul turned to face her. She searched her coat pockets and after a moment she produced a cigarette and a match.

"You don't mind, do you? I haven't had a cigarette in days."

Paul shook his head.

"Last week, my mother caught me smoking in the lane behind the house and had a fit. I had to listen to a long lecture about what the neighbors would say if they saw me and what could possibly possess me to take up such a 'nasty, dirty masculine habit.' I don't want to endure that again."

Paul watched her in silence, struck, as he always was, by her feminine, graceful way of indulging in this supposed nasty masculine habit. Seeming to misunderstand his interest, she offered him the cigarette, which he refused.

"I'm sorry, Paul, I'm already forgetting who you are," she said. "If you were wearing your priestly garb, I would never have made such an offer. Wearing these clothes, you'll have difficulty keeping me within the bounds of propriety."

Keeping her within the bounds of propriety was the furthest thing from his mind. Instead of saying so, he told her, "I think your decision to escort me to your parents' house was motivated by something other than concern about my ability to find it. Admit it, Lilia—you were desperate for an excuse to leave the house so you could smoke!"

She laughed. "I'll admit no such thing. Is it so difficult to believe that I could be motivated by genuine hospitality?"

"When a cigarette hangs in the balance, yes."

Lilia's warmth and friendliness banished the fears caused by the discouraging coldness of her letters. They had slipped back into their old, comfortable way of relating to each other, although there was something new, too, an undercurrent of excitement. Paul was very aware of this unspoken, thrilling tension, but he couldn't discern whether she felt it, too. He wanted to be alone with her, and when the Brookes' gray stone house appeared at the end of the lane, Paul was disappointed. He didn't want to make polite conversation with Lilia's family when he had so much to say to her privately. He didn't yet have the courage to express his feelings to her, but he believed he could muster it once her family was out of the way. If necessary, he would ask her to walk with him after dinner.

Paul was pleasantly surprised by the reception he received from the Brookes. Mr. Brooke was exactly the way Paul remembered him: a peaceable, easygoing man. Mrs. Brooke had aged a good deal in twelve years—raising six high-spirited children would naturally take its toll—but she was warm and welcoming. The youngest child, Emily, was the truly delightful discovery. A charming, pretty girl with perfect manners, she seemed awestruck by Paul, as if he were a royal visitor from an exotic land.

At the dinner table, Paul told Emily what he remembered about their first meeting when she was a toddler. When he explained that he had tried to save her from the French army, and that Lilia had informed him Emily was in fact the Dauphin of France, everyone laughed.

"Lilia always pressed Emily into service as some odd character or another," Mrs. Brooke said. "Emily played the role of a one-legged sea captain when she was about five or six. Lilia insisted that the poor child hop about the house on one leg for at least a week for the sake of authenticity!"

"Our little twig was always coming up with new roles for all her siblings to play," agreed Mr. Brooke. "The boys were more difficult to convince, but I was always impressed she could get them to mind her in the end."

Paul didn't hear anything beyond the words "little twig." Lilia's father clearly hadn't meant it as an insult, for he was smiling at her indulgently, and nobody else seemed to take offense, but Paul didn't like it. She didn't look in the least like a twig. In fact, sitting at the dinner table across from her, Paul was so struck by her beauty that he couldn't look directly at her. She was wearing a white blouse edged with lace, and her hair was tied back loosely with a ribbon like a young girl's.

"Is it true that you're going to become a bishop?" This question came from Emily, who was sitting beside Lilia.

"I don't know," Paul replied, coming out of his reverie. "Perhaps someday."

"People would call you 'my lord,' then, wouldn't they?"

"I suppose they would."

"I doubt that Paul wishes to be a bishop for the title," Lilia broke in, a hint of sharpness in her voice. "At least, not *merely* for the title."

"Oh, I didn't mean that," said Emily, looking alarmed.

"Of course you didn't, dear," Mrs. Brooke said. "Lilia misunderstood you. The title is an appropriate sign of respect for a leader of the church." She turned to Paul. "Based on what your mother tells me, you're likely to become dean of the cathedral when the old dean dies, and after that it's only a matter of time before you become a bishop."

Paul set down the forkful of braised turkey that had been on its way to his mouth. "I fear my mother's hopes have colored her perception of reality. I'm too young to be appointed to such positions in the church. And anyway, I'm happy with my canonry."

"Lilia has told me what a good preacher you are. She was exceedingly impressed with your sermon the day she visited the cathedral."

Mrs. Brooke beamed at him, but there was something unsettling about her look. As with Emily, he had the sense of being treated like visiting royalty, but Mrs. Brooke's gaze held something more, a delighted sense of a mission accomplished. Paul felt as though he had been cast in the lead role of a play without having seen the script. He glanced at Lilia, whose compressed lips indicated her displeasure. Throughout dinner, Lilia and her mother had closely resembled two unsynchronized pendulums: the happier Mrs. Brooke looked, the unhappier Lilia looked, and vice versa.

Mr. Brooke changed the subject, and Paul was relieved that he was no longer the focus of attention. He began to feel comfortable enough to enjoy Mr. Brooke's stories about his pupils. Even though Mr. Brooke was the headmaster at the village school, it was clear he wasn't the scholar that Lilia was. Paul felt a sense of affinity with her for this. He, too, had grown up with parents who didn't understand his insatiable thirst for knowledge. But Paul also noticed a dismissiveness in the way Lilia's parents spoke of her and to her. Their affection for her was evident, but they also seemed to consider her intellect an embarrassment, like a rare disease of which they must not speak. In contrast, Philip and Bianca had always praised Paul for even his most minor accomplishments. The realization made Paul admire Lilia's strength and intellect all the more.

When dinner was over, Lilia's parents announced that they were obliged to visit friends, and they were sorry they couldn't stay to speak with him further. Paul said he understood, unable to believe his good fortune. He wouldn't have to create an excuse to be alone with Lilia, after all.

As everyone rose from the table, Paul overheard Emily whisper to her mother, "Mama, must I go with you? I'd like to get to know Paul better."

Paul waited anxiously for Mrs. Brooke's answer, pretending to straighten his shirt cuffs so his eavesdropping wouldn't be detected.

"Yes, Emily, you must," her mother whispered back. "You will no doubt have other opportunities. Say farewell, now, and come along."

Emily turned sorrowfully to Paul and offered her hand. "You've done us a great honor by visiting us. I hope to see you again soon."

Charmed by her ladylike gesture and speech, he raised her hand to his lips and kissed it. Her face lit up.

As Mrs. Brooke ushered her husband and younger daughter out of the room, she said to Lilia in a loud voice, "We'll be back late, so don't stay up waiting for us. Cook will be out for the evening, too."

"Yes, Mama," Lilia said, the dark look on her face again contrasting with the brightness of her mother's.

It dawned on Paul that Lilia's parents were giving him their unspoken blessing to court their daughter. There was no other reasonable explanation for the way Mrs. Brooke had been beaming at him all evening and trying to make everything as agreeable to him as possible, or for the way everyone conveniently disappeared so he and Lilia could be alone. He was naturally pleased by this realization, but having the blessing of her parents meant nothing if Lilia objected. As she showed him into the drawing room—unlike the house his mother shared with James, this one had a separate drawing room, though the furnishings were old and the carpet worn—she seemed tense and unhappy.

Lilia sat in a chair by the window, motioning for him to sit across from her. His chair was separated from hers by a small table. Paul resented the table and wished she had chosen the sofa across the room so they could sit together. Lilia propped her cheek on her hand and gazed out the window. He studied her face awhile without speaking, cursing himself for his cowardice. The thought of expressing his love to her was terrifying when he was so unsure of her response.

"Lilia, are you unwell?" he asked finally.

She turned to look at him as if only now realizing he was there. "No, I'm fine. Forgive me, Paul. I'm just tired of being here. I'm grateful to my family for taking care of me, but my mother still treats me like a child. I miss my freedom."

He felt relieved that he wasn't the source of her unhappiness. "I can certainly understand that. I can't imagine staying with *my* mother for more than a day or two. I must say, though, your sister, Emily, is the most charming girl I've ever met. You must enjoy her company."

Lilia smiled. "Yes, of course. She'd be sorry to hear you call her a girl, though. She thinks of herself as a grown-up woman, and you've only made things worse with that act of gallantry in the dining room. No doubt she fancies herself madly in love with you."

Paul hesitated. If only Lilia would confess *herself* madly in love with him, he would be overjoyed.

"I'll have so much to do when I get back to London, I won't know where to begin," she continued. "Mrs. Pankhurst wrote to me about a new approach the WSPU will be taking to get the government's attention, and I'm very excited about it."

"I didn't realize you intended to remain with the WSPU."

She looked surprised. "Of course I will. What made you think I wouldn't?"

"The NUWSS is more respected. And safer."

"You must not know me if you think I'd find either of those reasons compelling."

He frowned. "I thought the riot might change your mind about speaking out in public."

"Really? Does that mean you approve of the efforts of the government and police to silence us?"

"Don't be ridiculous. That's not what I said."

"Isn't it what you meant? Most of the English public thinks that way. They'd be thrilled to see us cower and slink back to our domestic duties."

"You know that's not what I believe," Paul said, irritated by her superior tone.

"We have a new strategy to fight the enemy," she replied, her eyes glowing preternaturally, as if she could see through him to the New Jerusalem. "If we must be arrested and imprisoned, we'll be arrested for breaking the law, not for merely speaking in public. We're going to start destroying property. And I'm going to resign from my teaching position. Mrs. Pankhurst has offered me a paid position with the WSPU."

"Are you mad?" Paul exclaimed. "You would resign from a noble calling to expose yourself to ridicule and physical danger just to get the vote? I absolutely forbid you to do it."

Her eyebrows shot up. "You *forbid* me? You have no authority over me, Paul."

He was so upset, he barely heard her. "I can't understand why you would deliberately and repeatedly put yourself in harm's way just to get the vote. Is women's suffrage worth dying for? Are you aware how close you came to dying in Parliament Square?"

He had no idea how the conversation had spiraled out of control, but out of control it certainly was. All the emotions he had felt during the riot and his vigil at Lilia's bedside that night came back to him vividly. Tears stung his eyes and he rose from his chair and turned his back to her, struggling to regain his self-command.

But Lilia followed him and stood before him, taking his left hand in both of hers. In her usual, quicksilver way, she was as contrite now as she had been angry a moment before.

"I'm sorry," she said, looking up into his face. "I had forgotten you were there. I'm not as careless with my own life—or as ungrateful to you—as I must seem. I haven't even thanked you for jumping into the fray to rescue me."

"I'm sorry, too," he said, still shaken. "I know I have no authority over you. I shouldn't have spoken to you that way."

She was standing very close to him, and they moved into each other's arms. Paul was trembling, overwhelmed by the intensity of his emotions and the closeness of her body. The embrace lasted a long time, long enough for him to know he couldn't let her go—not now, not yet. He loosened his hold on her just enough to rest his cheek against hers. She made no attempt to move away, and he realized she was trembling just as much as he was.

Her perfect lips were too close and too tempting to resist. He kissed her gently, sensitive to the slightest reluctance on her part. There was none. In fact, she returned the kiss with a passionate eagerness that set his blood on fire. He lost all sense of time, intoxicated by the sweetness of her lips and the warmth of her body against his. Their tongues met as the kiss deepened, and her arms tightened around his waist.

Suddenly Lilia pulled away and retreated to the sofa across the room, as outwardly breathless and stunned as he felt. Her face was flushed and her hair fell in loose waves over her shoulders, the hair ribbon having come undone during their passionate embrace.

Paul followed her. Her response to his kiss had given him the confidence to speak, and he went down on one knee before her and took her hand.

"Lilia, I love you. You mean more to me than anything else in the world and I can't live without you. Will you be my wife?"

A look of alarm replaced the confusion on her face. "Paul, please get up," she said quietly.

He did as she bid him but didn't release her hand. Sitting beside her on the sofa, he fixed his eyes on her face, his heart pounding.

She took a deep breath. "You know how I feel about marriage."

"I hoped you might make an exception for me." He tried to smile but failed.

She was deadly serious. "Marriage is a degrading institution. I'd be making a travesty of my beliefs if I were to marry."

"Put aside your beliefs for a moment, then, and consider me as an individual instead of a sinister representative of Man. Do you love me?"

He searched her face. She wouldn't meet his eyes, though she allowed her hand to remain in his.

"You're asking me to do the impossible," she said. "How can I put aside my beliefs? How would you respond to someone who asked you to do the same?"

"I'm putting aside my belief that I ought to marry a woman who believes in God. Surely that means something to you."

"It means we'd be a terrible match."

"Lilia, I want to take care of you. As my wife, you would still be free to work for the women's suffrage movement, but you wouldn't have to struggle to support yourself. You could do as you wish, work as much or as little as you like."

"What if I wish to struggle?" she shot back, pulling her hand out of his grasp. "I don't want to be taken care of, and I don't want to dabble in the women's movement as if it were embroidery I might take up merely to pass the time. I'm committed to this fight; I'll be in it wholeheartedly, or not at all."

"I don't understand," he said. "You talk about the women's movement as if it were a religion. In fact, your religious fervor far outstrips mine. I see there's no room for me in your philosophy, but what about your heart?"

"It's a poor belief system that can't be lived out," she said. "My 'religious fervor,' as you call it, is part of my identity. I don't believe yours is the same. Is there anything at the center of your beautiful religious forms and ceremonies? Sometimes I think you don't really believe any of it."

This took his breath away. What basis did she have for such an accusation? Frustrated and angry, he rose to leave. But his lips still tingled with the sensation of hers against them, and he wasn't ready to give up yet. He sat down again and took a deep breath.

"Let's set aside the question of marriage for now," he said. "All I want to know is this—do you love me? Surely you can answer that question without reference to your abstract philosophies or political agendas."

Her face was inscrutable. "It isn't that simple," she said.

"For heaven's sake, Lilia, it *is* simple."

"I consider you a friend. A dear friend. No more." She still wouldn't meet his eyes.

"And do you kiss all your friends the way you just kissed me?"

"Of course not." She retrieved her hair ribbon from the floor and gathered her hair behind her head to retie it. "That was merely . . . sexual instinct." She seemed to be deliberately choosing the words she thought would most offend him.

"You're being disingenuous," he said. "I thought I could count on you of all people to be frank with me."

She finally looked into his eyes and said, "I haven't answered your questions fully because I didn't want to hurt you. Let me be absolutely clear: I don't love you, Paul, and I will not marry you."

Mortified, he felt the blood drain from his face. He stood up and left the room, half expecting her to follow him or call him back. Surely she hadn't really meant what she said!

But she didn't call him back, and he found his way to the front door to collect his coat and hat. Without bothering to put them on, he let himself out and walked away from the house, not knowing or caring where he was going. He had been insulted, apologized to, kissed, humiliated, and dismissed—all within half an hour—and it was a miracle that he made it to the station in time to catch the evening train back to London. The only thought in his numbed brain during the train ride was that he had failed the third test.

◌◞

Lilia's ordeal was far from over. She retired to bed early that evening, before her family returned home, and when Emily came into the room and whispered her name, she pretended to be asleep. In reality, she didn't sleep much that night. Her mind was far too disordered, her emotions too confused by what had she had experienced with Paul. She was sorry she had hurt him, but she had seen no other way out of the predicament in which he had placed her. Feeling trapped in her parents' house and by their expectations of her was nothing compared to the way she'd felt when Paul had asked her to marry him. Becoming a clergyman's wife would suffocate her as effectively as sealing her in a tomb.

But she had underestimated the attraction between them. From the moment she saw him in Ingleford, she'd wanted to touch him. Had his layman's clothing allowed her to imagine that he might be willing to free himself from the restrictions of his vocation?

Her response to his kiss had been frightening, too. The mere touch of his lips seemed to turn her body to liquid fire. And even worse than her physical response had been her mental weakness, even helplessness, as if her mind had melted along with her body. In that moment, she would have submitted to anything he wanted, even something as contemptible as marriage. Fortunately, she had turned from his arms and had managed to hide this pathetic self from Paul. The weakness was temporary, she told herself, but she remained anxious. She didn't know if Paul would try to wear out her resistance, but if he did, she had no idea how long she could hold out. And if she gave in and married him, she would be well and truly trapped. Giving in would also mean her convictions were not as firm as she'd always thought. As contemptible as marriage was to her, she would be even more contemptible in her own eyes if she didn't follow through on her long-held beliefs.

Lilia devoted most of the sleepless night to devising strategies to avoid putting herself in danger, should Paul prove persistent. Were he any other man—specifically, not a clergyman—she would have suggested a free union. But he subscribed to conventional morality and would most likely consider such an offer vulgar and immoral. If the offer happened not to shock him as much as she expected it would, and in the unlikely event he accepted, he would despise himself. And if she married him, she would despise herself. Either decision would make one of them miserable.

Lilia fell into a restless slumber and awakened at dawn, exhausted and even more confused than she had been the night before. Emily was still asleep, so Lilia dressed and tiptoed out of the room, hoping to go for a walk before anyone else stirred. But her mother was waiting for her in the kitchen, sitting at the table with her nightcap still on as if she, too, had been awake most of the night. Lilia's heart sank at the expectant look in her mother's eyes, and she realized she couldn't escape the inquisition.

"You're up early," Mrs. Brooke said, peering at her daughter intently.

"Yes. So are you."

"You were in bed when we came home last night. Naturally, I'm curious about what happened between you and Paul while we were gone."

"We talked. He left." Lilia knew her cryptic response would frustrate her mother, but she had no intention of saying more than she had to.

Mrs. Brooke looked more disappointed than frustrated. "So he didn't make you an offer, then?"

For the first time, Lilia understood her mother's puzzling behavior of late. How could she have been so blind? Her mother's excitement over Paul's visit, the extra work she had put into dinner, welcoming him so warmly—it was all because she was hoping he would marry Lilia. The many times Lilia had told her mother she had no intention of marrying were apparently irrelevant when there was a potential flesh-and-blood suitor present.

"He did 'make me an offer,' as you put it," Lilia said stiffly.

"He did? Oh, that's wonderful!" her mother exclaimed. "I was so certain he would—after all, anyone would be after seeing the way he was looking at you during dinner. But you look so gloomy and downcast, Lilia, I could have sworn . . ." Her voice trailed off. "You did accept him, didn't you?"

"No, I did not."

A stunned silence followed this admission. When Lilia's mother could find her voice again, she cried, unmindful of still-sleeping family members, "Have you gone mad, girl? Do you know what you've refused? Bianca told me Paul gets an allowance from Philip Harris. That, combined with his living, amounts to five thousand pounds a year!"

"I don't care," said Lilia. "The last thing I want is to be some idle gentlewoman looking for useless tasks to occupy my time."

"Would you rather be like me? Would you rather raise six children with barely enough money to keep them properly fed and clothed?" Mrs. Brooke's voice rose dramatically.

Lilia sighed. "Our family isn't poor, Mama. We just don't meet your standards for gentility."

"You have no idea what you're talking about. I wish we hadn't sent you to Girton. Your education has done nothing but put ridiculous theories in your head that have nothing to do with reality. Don't you realize marriage is your only chance to have a comfortable life?"

"If so, there's no problem. An uncomfortable life will suit me far better."

"Don't be impertinent, Lilia. You may be a grown woman, but I'm still your mother and I'm entitled to some respect." Mrs. Brooke's distress had reached its apex, and tears began to run down her cheeks.

"I'm sorry, Mama," Lilia said, "but I can take care of myself. I've been doing so ever since I left Girton, and there's no reason why I can't continue to make enough money to survive for the rest of my life."

"*Survive* is exactly the word! Your lodgings, the food you eat, your clothing—you can only just keep yourself alive." Mrs. Brooke sighed and wiped her tears away with the back of her hand. "But you've always been a stubborn girl, and if that's how you want to live, nobody can stop you. I just hope you realize you've turned down the best—and possibly the only—offer of marriage you'll ever receive."

Lilia didn't see the point of arguing that the quality or number of offers she might receive was immaterial, since she didn't intend to accept one. She felt utterly worn out by her mother's distress and looked longingly towards the front door.

"I'll never understand you," her mother continued. "I want only the best for you, and yet you seem determined to make your life as difficult as possible. Don't you become tired of struggling against all the injustice in the world? Don't you sometimes wish to be like everyone else? Don't you want to be loved—to be first in someone's eyes?"

In her exhausted state, Lilia weakened against this new, gentler approach. She stood, unhappy and mute, waiting for her mother to finish.

Mrs. Brooke rose, approached Lilia, and put a hand on her arm. "You do care for him, don't you?" she pressed. "I don't think I'm wrong about that."

Lilia couldn't respond, nor could she listen to another word. She whirled around and headed for the door, grabbing her coat on the way out.

It was a cold, frosty morning, but Lilia barely noticed the cold or the beauty of the frost sparkling on the tree branches along the lane. She walked quickly but without a fixed direction, thinking only of escape. It didn't take long for her to become tired and cold, yet she couldn't return to the house to face Emily and her father, both of whom were probably now listening to her mother's story of how Lilia had ensured that she would forever be an old maid. She didn't have the strength to return to such a scene or to explain herself all over again.

Eventually she found herself at James and Bianca's house. It was still early, but James was just leaving with his medical bag, about to begin his morning rounds.

"Uncle James, I'm sorry to disturb you," she said. Her lips were so cold it was an effort to move them to speak.

"What brings you here so early?" he said with a smile. As he looked at her more closely, his smile faded. "You're half-frozen, my dear. Come in."

He immediately led her into the house and within minutes she was sitting in front of the fire in the kitchen with a blanket wrapped around her and a hot cup of beef tea in her hand. James pulled up a chair next to hers and looked at her with concern.

"Thank you," she said. "I hope I haven't made you late."

"What's the matter, Lilia? What's happened?"

In any other situation, she would have told him the truth, as that was what everyone did with James. Even if they had no intention of confiding in him, his gentleness, warmth, and concern were irresistible to anyone feeling burdened by a problem. But he suddenly seemed strange to her, not her familiar Uncle James but Paul's natural father, whether Paul wished to acknowledge that fact or not. It was the first time Lilia had seen so much of Paul in James's face and it startled her. Even the way he had drawn up the chair next to hers was exactly the way Paul would do it. She was momentarily speechless.

As if he had read her mind, James said, "I'll fetch Bianca. You can talk to her." He stood up, patted Lilia's shoulder, and left the room.

Bianca entered the kitchen a few minutes later, looking disheveled, as if she had been rushing to dress. As she walked in, she pinned up a section of hair at the back of her head.

"Lilia," she said, taking the chair James had vacated, "what's the matter?"

"I'm so sorry to disturb you," Lilia said, taking a deep breath. "I've had an argument with Mama, and I couldn't stay in the house."

Lilia's having an argument with her mother wasn't an uncommon occurrence, so Bianca merely waited.

"She's angry with me because Paul proposed to me yesterday and I refused him."

"Paul proposed and you refused him?" Bianca repeated slowly, looking stunned. It was unclear whether her surprise was due to the proposal or Lilia's refusal of it.

Lilia cast an agonized look at her aunt. "Mama didn't even try to understand my position. I can't marry him. I don't . . . he wouldn't . . ." Unable to muster the strength to explain her decision to yet another person, Lilia fell silent.

"Of course you mustn't marry him if you don't love him," Bianca said gently. "You have only to think of my marriage to Philip Harris to know what a mistake that would be."

Her nerves strained to the breaking point, Lilia covered her face with her hands and burst into tears.

Bianca slipped an arm around Lilia's shoulders. "Don't worry, dear. I doubt there's any great harm done. You must do what you think is right and pay no attention to the expectations of anyone else."

Lilia felt like an overtired child. Fortunately, her aunt understood without being told that what she needed most was rest and silence. Bianca convinced Lilia to lie down on the sofa, and after ensuring that she was comfortable and warm, the older woman slipped out of the room. Less than five minutes later, Lilia fell into a mercifully deep sleep.

13

Does any one suppose that private prayer is necessarily candid—
necessarily goes to the roots of action? Private prayer is inaudible
speech, and speech is representative: who can represent himself just
as he is, even in his own reflections?

—George Eliot, *Middlemarch*

JUNE 1908

Paul was sitting in front of the drawing-room fire in Stephen's cozy
vicarage in Stretham. He hadn't seen his friend since Stephen's
Christmas wedding six months earlier, and Paul only now realized how
much he'd missed the opportunity to speak freely with someone he trusted.
Stephen's wife, Rosamond, a modest, sweet-faced brunette, had brought the
two men glasses of port and left them alone, despite Stephen's invitation for
her to join them.

"The two of you have much to talk about," she had said with a smile. "I'd
only be in the way."

As she left the room, Stephen's gaze lingered on her fondly.

"You're very fortunate in your wife," Paul said when she had left. "How
did you manage to convince her to marry you?"

149

Stephen laughed. "I don't know. I must have been her only prospect at the time. I express my gratitude to her constantly, and as far as I know, she hasn't repented of her decision."

"Why should she? The two of you are well suited. I'm glad she makes you happy."

Paul smiled. It had been difficult for him to attend Stephen's wedding so soon after his own proposal had been rejected, but he had not explained the story to Stephen. He was glad his friend knew nothing of what had happened in Ingleford.

Stephen gave him a searching look. "You look exhausted, old man. I know you want the deanship, but surely you'll obtain it without having to expend your energy on so many different parish activities."

"I mean to slow down soon, but if everything I'm doing brings me even one step closer to the deanship, it will be worth the effort."

The old dean was failing fast, and it was clear that his replacement had to be appointed soon. Paul had taken on additional duties at the cathedral in order to prove to the bishop—and the king himself, for the deanship was a Crown appointment—that he was the best man for the job.

"The old dean might surprise everyone and outlive both you and Cross," observed Stephen.

Paul smiled and shook his head. "I think not. That doesn't mean I have any bloodthirsty designs to hasten his end. I can't say the same for Cross."

"You're not serious."

"No, of course not." Paul took a sip of his port. "But he is making himself ridiculous with his transparent attempts to impress the bishop and other influential people. He claims he has even begun writing a book about the church fathers, which I won't believe until I see it. He's no scholar."

"I suppose Cross is trying to make up for his weaknesses, just as you are with all these societies you've joined."

Paul's eyes narrowed. There was something about Stephen's air of nonchalance that seemed a bit too artful. "Do you think Cross and I have an equal chance of being appointed to the deanship?"

"Do *you* think the two of you have an equal chance?"

"Only if the people who matter are unable to see past Cross's polished façade." Paul went on to list Cross's faults, giving examples of his rudeness, arrogance, disregard for church tradition, hypocrisy, and lack of intelligence, all of which would make Cross the worst dean in the history of the cathedral, in Paul's admittedly biased opinion.

Once Paul finished, Stephen was silent for a while, examining the reflections of the firelight on his now-empty glass. It was unusual for Stephen to be silent for any length of time; it made Paul nervous.

"You haven't answered my question," Paul prompted.

"I beg your pardon. What was the question?"

"Do you think Cross and I have an equal chance of being appointed dean?"

"I don't know." Stephen frowned. "But I can't help thinking that the bishop has been wrong to encourage this competition between you and Cross. It seems to me it would be better for everyone if an outsider were appointed to the deanship."

Paul felt betrayed. Stephen had never particularly liked Cross, and Paul had thought he would be able to count on his friend to support him in his hopes for the deanship.

"Don't mistake me, Harris," Stephen added. "There's no doubt in my mind that you'd be an excellent dean. You have intelligence, energy, and love for the church, and you work harder than anyone I know. But if the worst happens and Cross is appointed dean, would you continue at the cathedral as a canon?"

"No. I could never be his subordinate. Can you imagine how he would lord it over me?"

"And if you're appointed dean, do you think Cross would continue in his canonry?"

"Probably not."

"All I'm saying is, no matter who gets the deanship, the cathedral will likely lose a good canon in the bargain. If an outsider were appointed, on the other hand . . ." Stephen shrugged expressively.

"Even if that were to happen, I don't think Cross and I can continue to work together much longer."

"Do you suppose Cross thinks about you as much as you think about him?" was Stephen's next, startling question.

"What's gotten into you, Elliott? Why are you asking these strange questions?"

"Because you've said far more about him than you have about the deanship," his friend replied. "I've never seen you like this before. I'm concerned that you'll become so consumed by this competition with Cross that you'll lose yourself in it."

Paul raised his eyebrows and said dryly, "What am I profited, if I shall gain the deanship and lose my own soul?"

"Exactly."

"I don't think there's any danger of that happening. I probably am too concerned about Cross's efforts to undermine me, but I am no more inclined to stand in the way of his getting the deanship—assuming he obtains it honestly—than I am to stab the poor old dean in the heart. I would be disappointed, of course, but I would survive . . . with my soul intact."

"I'm glad to hear it."

Their conversation turned to the goings-on at Stephen's parish and the wider world of politics. But late that night, when Paul lay wakeful in bed, Stephen's concerns about his competition with Cross troubled him. Paul knew he had changed, and perhaps not for the better, but he felt increasingly confident about being appointed to the deanship and didn't seriously consider the possibility that Cross might be appointed instead. Paul believed that once the decision was finally made, for better or worse, he would be himself again and take an interest in other things. But for now, nothing mattered more than the deanship.

For the first time in his life, due to the pressures of the competition for the deanship, Paul had found himself forgetting social engagements, even promises he had made to dine with his father. A week after his return to London after visiting Stephen, Paul realized that it had been an entire month since he had seen his father, and he decided to make an impromptu visit to his office. He also needed to talk about a difficult conversation he had had earlier that day with the bishop.

It was late afternoon, but the clerk at Philip's office told him his father had gone home for the day. This was unusual. His father worked long hours and stayed at his office well into the evening most days.

Paul took a cab to his father's house, feeling worried as well as guilty for having neglected him. Once at the house, he was confronted with more strangeness when Kitty, the maid who had known him for years, hesitated at the sight of him.

"What's the matter, Kitty?" Paul asked. "Is my father unwell?"

"No," she said slowly. "He's in the library."

Paul headed towards the library, but she called after him, "He has a visitor. He said he wasn't to be interrupted by anyone, no matter what."

"Oh. That's fine. I'll wait."

He sat in the front hall, wondering why Kitty seemed so flustered and who his father's visitor might be. A quarter of an hour later, he heard the library door open, and a man he didn't recognize came into the front hall, accompanied by his father. At first they didn't notice him.

"As I said, I'll do my best, but I can't promise anything," the stranger was saying. His cheap-looking suit and flat vowels surprised Paul: a man like that couldn't be his father's business associate. Was he one of Philip's employees?

"That's all I ask," Philip said. "And keep it to yourself."

Paul rose from his seat, not wanting to eavesdrop, however unintentionally. The men looked startled by his sudden appearance.

"Paul, I didn't know you were here," Philip said. "Kitty ought to have told me."

"I'll go, then," the stranger said, his eyes shifting from Paul to Philip, and he left abruptly.

"Kitty said you were not to be interrupted."

"You may always interrupt me. Come to the library."

Paul followed, and as soon as he was sitting in one of the comfortable leather chairs in the library, he said, "Father, you don't look well. What's the matter?"

"I'm fine, just a little tired." Philip sat beside him and smiled, but the smile didn't reach his eyes.

"I was worried when I heard you were at home instead of the office."

"That's nothing to worry about. I've been conducting some business from the house lately, just as a matter of convenience. How are you, son? It's been some time since I saw you last."

"I know. I'm sorry. Everything has been fine, though this morning the bishop called me to the palace and we had a . . . challenging conversation."

"What happened?" his father said with a look of concern.

Paul wasn't sure where to begin. The conversation with the bishop had shaken him more than he wanted to admit. He had been anxious to begin with, because he knew the bishop was meeting privately with Thomas Cross, as well, and there had been murmurs among the cathedral clergy that the bishop was treating these meetings as unofficial interviews for the deanship.

"The meeting began well," Paul said. "The bishop expressed his approval of the changes I suggested to the Sunday services, and he praised me for the additional work I've taken on with the penitentiary and other charities."

He paused and ran a hand through his hair. His father was listening intently, unmoving, as he waited for Paul to finish.

"Just when I thought our conversation was over," he went on, "Bishop Chisholm asked me about the status of my faith. I didn't understand what he was asking, and I told him my beliefs are the same as ever. He catechized me almost as if I were a child, though not in a patronizing way. It was the questions he asked—simple questions about Christianity—that surprised me. I answered every question, of course, but I couldn't help wondering at his purpose. He even asked me what is meant by *sacrament*, which comes directly from the catechism."

Paul swallowed hard and stared at the bookshelf above his father's head. "By this time, I was concerned enough to ask if he had reason to doubt my faith. He said, 'Canon Harris, you have done everything correctly. All the outward and visible signs are there, but I am not certain your heart is where it should be with God.'"

Philip frowned.

"You can imagine how I felt, hearing this from him. Have I not dedicated my life to serving God and the church? If the bishop himself doesn't believe in my sincerity . . ." Paul's voice trailed off, and he stared miserably at his feet.

"He must have been testing you," his father said, "perhaps to find out how you would react to simple questions. I do that with my employees. Even a bishop is a man of business at heart."

"I don't know. He seemed to be sincerely questioning my faith. There must be something in what he says, even though I can't see it."

"Perhaps the bishop has heard of your former attachment to Miss Brooke. He might not recommend you for the deanship if he knew you had considered marrying a militant suffragette, especially one who is in the public eye as much as she is of late. You might consider telling the bishop that you no longer have any dealings with that movement."

Paul wondered when he would be able to hear Lilia's name without feeling a stab of pain. He hadn't wanted to tell his father about his unsuccessful proposal, but in the weeks following his trip to Ingleford, he hadn't been able to hide his misery.

He replied, "Few people know of my . . . attachment to her. Certainly not Bishop Chisholm."

But the bishop had known about Paul's involvement with the suffragettes as a result of that anonymous letter. For a moment, Paul wondered if his father could be right.

"It's something to think about." Philip sat back in his chair and sighed. "Paul, why don't you stay? It's been a long time since you've been to one of my musical evenings. Even if you don't wish to sing, everyone would be happy to see you again."

"I'd like to, Father, but I can't. My Thursday evenings are now dedicated to the lecture series at the cathedral."

"Not even to see Miss Cavendish? She's been asking about you." His father's voice was deceptively casual.

"Not even to see her," Paul said. The mention of Grace Cavendish and his father's musical evenings only brought up another painful memory. Though Lilia had attended only one of those evenings, he couldn't forget how she had looked in that stunning blue dress and how he hadn't been able to resist touching her.

He cleared his throat and added, "I've been thinking of taking a vow of celibacy."

"Have you, now?" Philip regarded him quizzically. "That seems sudden."

"Not really. It's been on my mind for a while." It had been on his mind for six months, to be exact.

To his credit, his father didn't try to talk him out of it. The conversation turned to other matters, and Paul took his leave soon afterwards.

He hadn't told his father everything about his conversation with Bishop Chisholm. One comment that rankled was about Paul's prayers: "Your public prayers are eloquent, Canon Harris," the bishop had said, "but I hope your private ones are not."

It was a strange thing to say. What did the eloquence of his private prayers matter, as long as he meant what he said? But that must have been the bishop's point. Perhaps Paul had honed his public speaking skills too much, so much so that his words no longer sounded sincere, but surely any priest could be accused of an artificiality of expression at times. Knowing the words from the *Book of Common Prayer* by memory was bound to lead to set phrases in one's prayers, private or public. And Paul was a High Churchman—did the bishop expect him to extemporize like a Methodist, or some other dissenting preacher? It was preposterous.

It also disturbed Paul that the bishop had echoed some of the doubts Lilia had expressed about Paul's faith, those words that had cut him so deeply when he'd proposed to her. How was it possible that similar criticism could come from two such different people with opposing beliefs? It seemed that perhaps there *was* something lacking in his faith, but he didn't know what it was. The only course of action, however unsatisfying, was to continue to insist on his commitment and to work harder. What proof could he give of his sincerity if others were determined to believe him insincere?

Paul found it difficult to concentrate on his work that week. The deanship seemed less certain than ever. He only hoped the bishop had questioned Cross as intensively as he had Paul. But Cross was better at hiding his true self than Paul was, and Paul had no doubt that his nemesis had passed the bishop's test with flying colors. He tried not to think about it and to stay out of Cross's path that week, knowing that if Cross's interview had gone well, he would be certain to gloat about it.

Later that week, a stranger came to see Paul at home. It was late afternoon, and he was in his study working on the book that he sometimes thought he would never finish. Mrs. Rigby interrupted him to announce that a Mr. John Hirst was there to see him. Paul had never heard of the man.

"What is his business with me?" Paul asked his housekeeper.

"He wouldn't say, Canon Harris, only that it was something urgent and private."

"Very well. Show him in."

The man who entered Paul's study was clearly poor, but he was respectable-looking. His heavily lined face, combined with his upright, strong frame, made it difficult to guess his age: he could have been anywhere from five-and-fifty to seventy. His black hair, streaked with gray, and his dark skin hinted at the possibility of foreign blood, but his eyes were light gray, a surprising contrast. He was wearing a coarse brown jacket, worn at the elbows.

Paul invited Mr. Hirst to sit down and asked, "What can I do for you?"

The man lowered himself heavily into a chair in front of Paul's desk and said, "You don't know me, Canon Harris, but I'm here to ask for your help with my son."

"I don't understand. Who is your son?"

"It's a long story, Canon Harris, and painful to tell. Could I tell you a little about my past first?"

Paul agreed, and the man began his story. He had worked as a blacksmith for many years in Sheffield. His eldest son, an uncommonly clever boy, was ashamed of his father's low position and wanted to go to university so he could become someone important. The boy criticized his father's rough manners and way of speaking, and instead of helping his father in the smithy, he would disappear with friends who lent him books. Young Tom would read anything he could get his hands on. He soon began to imitate the polished manners of his friends, at least in public. In private, he spoke harshly to his parents, berating them for not having the means to send him to university. Finally, Mr. Hirst, desperate to give his son what he wanted, stole money to pay for his son to attend university.

"I know it was wrong, Canon Harris," Mr. Hirst said sorrowfully, "but I didn't think about right and wrong then—I just wanted my son to be a gentleman. That's what he wanted, and I thought he'd be happy if I gave it to him."

"Did he know how you obtained the money?"

"No, not 'til years later. But nothing I could do would make him respect me. I was still just John Hirst the blacksmith, with no education and no fancy speech. He thanked me for the money, but didn't ask where I got it. He wasn't saying much at all to me by then.

"I'm sorry to say I didn't stop stealing. It got into my blood, I guess you could say. After a while I wasn't careful anymore, because I didn't think I'd get caught. When my son was at university, I was caught and arrested, then sent to prison. When I got out, none of my family would have anything to do with me.

"I've been working hard since then to make a respectable life for myself. I've been living in America for the last ten years. I'm here now because I want to make up with my son, and that's how I hope you can help. He won't agree to see me. All I want is to tell him I'm sorry for the embarrassment I've caused him."

"I'm afraid I still don't see how I can help you," Paul said. "I don't know any Tom Hirst."

"He hasn't used the name Tom Hirst in a long while. He took the name of some distant relations named Cross. You do know a Tom Cross, don't you? I was told you work with him."

Paul was speechless. Cross had told the cathedral clergy that his father had died when he was a youth. Paul knew that Cross was not above lying when it suited him, but this lie was all the more shocking when this father was sitting alive and well in a chair in Paul's study.

"Do you know him?" Mr. Hirst repeated.

"We work together."

"I'm proud of the boy for making something of his life. I know he doesn't want to see me, but there must be a way I could, to apologize and tell him how proud I am. No matter who his father is, every man wants to hear those words, don't you think?"

"Yes," Paul agreed. There seemed to be no harm in trying to help Mr. Hirst, if Paul could think of an appropriate way to do so. He seemed sincere, and it was certainly consistent with Cross's character to act as his father had described. He was a hypocrite, preaching love and kindness to everyone while disowning his own father, who had sacrificed so much for him. Certainly Mr. Hirst had acted wrongly in turning to theft to put his son through university, but the fact that he had told Paul the truth about his criminal activities made his story more convincing.

"Have you tried to write to your son, Mr. Hirst?"

"Many times. The letters are sent back to me unopened. If he would only hear me for five minutes, that's all I ask. He won't even allow me into the cathedral. Can you imagine, a son not letting his father go to church? If you asked him to speak to me, maybe—"

"I don't think that would work," Paul said, "but I do want to help you. Let me think for a moment."

"Thank you, Canon Harris. Anything you could do . . . anything at all. I'd be right grateful." The man bowed his head and passed his large, calloused hand over his eyes.

Paul sat back in his chair. Perhaps he should tell the man that Cross was no friend of his, that Paul would sooner put out his own eye than do anything to help Cross. But he wouldn't be helping Cross so much as his father, who was clearly in need of support and encouragement. And if arranging a meeting between Cross and his father would make Cross realize his own errors, surely that would be good for everyone involved. But how was such a meeting to be arranged if Cross was as resolutely set against seeing his father as Mr. Hirst claimed he was?

All at once, the answer came to Paul. Cross was going to be faced with his hypocrisy, and Paul would be there to see it. He knew the pleasurable anticipation he felt wasn't strictly right from a moral or Christian standpoint, but he was certain that the end—the improvement of Cross's character and peace of mind for his father—would justify the means.

14

Window-breaking, when Englishmen do it, is regarded as honest expression of political opinion. Window-breaking, when Englishwomen do it, is treated as a crime.

—Emmeline Pankhurst, *My Own Story*

Lilia felt safest when she was making speeches. Not physically safe—any public speech always held an element of danger—but emotionally so. It didn't matter if the speech was to a small group of WSPU members, a large group of strangers at a public hall, or even an impromptu speech on the street (though she was discouraged by the WSPU leadership from making speeches of that kind). Public speaking used her entire brain, so there was no room left to think of things she didn't want to think about.

Today's speech was different, as it was part of a memorial gathering for fallen suffragettes in Highgate Cemetery. After Ellen Wells died, Lady Fernham had insisted upon her being buried in the Fernham family plot. Then, about a month after the Parliament Square riot, two suffragettes died as a result of injuries sustained during the melee, and they too had been buried in the same plot. Lilia didn't know how Lady Fernham had convinced her husband to allow it, but by now the plot had become almost a shrine to WSPU members.

Lilia addressed the group of about twenty people from a step in front of Ellen's grave. A sculpture of an angel holding a sword stood before the grave; it was draped with banners bearing the green, white, and purple WSPU colors.

It wasn't her best speech. First, Lilia was very aware of Mary Braddock standing at the front of the group. Mary had been released from the Whitechapel House of Mercy a couple of months earlier and had joined the WSPU immediately upon her release, but she hadn't wanted to talk about Ellen. Lilia worried that Mary blamed her for Ellen's death.

Another distraction was a strange man standing at the back of the group. He was so tall that he towered above everyone else, though his relaxed posture made his height less imposing than it could have been. His clothing wasn't exactly that of a gentleman, but it wasn't that of a ruffian, either: he was wearing a rumpled sack suit and a slouch hat set low on his forehead. Still, it was unusual for a strange man to attend a WSPU gathering, especially a relatively private one such as this. He could be a detective or a police investigator trying to obtain information about the Union's next move. One couldn't be too careful.

As Lilia spoke of Ellen, she gazed into a vague middle distance, away from both Mary and the strange man. "Ellen Wells didn't think she was brave enough to do anything meaningful. She had no idea she would be our first martyr. Perhaps that's not what she wanted. I've asked myself over and over again whether I influenced her too much. She believed implicitly in whatever action I thought we ought to take."

Lilia paused, surprised by the ache in her throat. She had never allowed her emotions to get the better of her during a speech before. And until now,

Paul had been the only person to know that she felt guilty about Ellen's death.

"Sometimes people tell me I'm brave," she went on, her voice trembling slightly. "But it's not brave to do what comes naturally, and it's natural for me to rush in where angels fear to tread. It wasn't natural for Ellen. She was a quiet, gentle person. Standing at the top of those steps with me, she was afraid." She paused again, remembering her few minutes alone with Ellen before her speech. Lilia had held her hand and reassured her that all would be well.

"But she did what frightened her, and that's true courage," Lilia concluded. "I can only hope to be as brave as she was someday."

She stepped down to make way for the next speaker. Moving to stand beside Mary, she took a deep breath to prevent the tears that threatened to fall.

"Thank you, miss," Mary whispered. "Ellen would've loved that speech."

Mary's approval assuaged Lilia's worries, but she couldn't help but wonder what Paul would have thought. Although she hadn't spoken to him since his visit to Ingleford six months earlier, she missed talking with him. She even missed arguing with him.

Their lives were more separate than ever. If Bianca's letters were any indication, he would soon be appointed dean of the cathedral. And no dean, she suspected, could afford to be friends with a member of the WSPU.

When the speeches were over and the women had come forward to place mementos and flowers on the suffragettes' graves, the group began to disperse. The impressive gothic sculptures and arches at Highgate Cemetery made for a majestic, solemn atmosphere, and the women conversed in hushed tones as they began walking down the path that led to the main entrance. Lilia paused to replace a banner that had fallen from the stone angel's arm, then fanned herself with her handkerchief. It was a warm day, and her muslin blouse was wilting against her skin.

"Pardon me."

Lilia started. She hadn't heard the tall stranger approaching, and he spoke in the loud stage whisper of a person unaccustomed to being quiet. He had taken off his hat to reveal a thick head of chestnut hair and bright blue eyes. His handlebar moustache seemed designed to hide a perpetually amused look.

"I hope you'll forgive a stranger for introducing himself, Miss Brooke," he said, offering his hand, "but I was so impressed by your speech I had to talk to you. I'm Will Reed." He had an unusual accent, with short vowels and an upwards lilt that made his statements sound a bit like questions.

After a slight hesitation, she shook his hand and said, "Thank you."

"I'm always getting in trouble for my ignorance of your country's customs. I assure you I mean no offense."

"Are you from Australia?" she asked.

"New Zealand. Common mistake." He grinned, revealing very white teeth against tanned skin.

Lilia was instantly intrigued. "I've always wanted to meet someone from a place where women already have the vote."

"It is so. I'm proud of that."

She glanced ahead, to where the other women had already disappeared around a curve in the path. "Shall we walk?" she suggested. He seemed harmless enough, but she didn't want to take chances. "What brings you to England?"

He fell into step beside her. "I'm here for a few months on a business trip. Both business and pleasure, in fact. My family is in gold mining. My father hates to travel, but I love it, so he sends me all over the world to work out his deals."

"That sounds like a good arrangement for both of you."

"It is, though sometimes he gets impatient with my extended stays in places I like. He's already badgering me to leave for Scotland, and I've only been in London less than a week. I have a good excuse to stay longer, though, because Mrs. Sheppard wanted me to bring her a report about the women's suffrage movement here—"

"Do you mean Kate Sheppard?" Lilia interrupted. Kate Sheppard was the leader of the New Zealand women's suffrage movement.

"Yes."

"You know her?"

"I do." Will's grin widened. "She's a friend of my mother's. Everything I know about women's suffrage was learned at her knee."

"I have so many questions for her," Lilia said. "I wish I could meet her."

"I know I'm a poor substitute, but I'd be happy to tell you what I know. I'll take any questions I can't answer back to her when I return to New Zealand."

"That would be wonderful."

"Why don't we talk over dinner this evening? My hotel has an excellent restaurant."

Lilia hesitated.

"I've said the wrong thing again, haven't I?" He sighed. "I keep forgetting about British propriety. Again, I meant no offense."

"I care nothing for propriety," she said, then realized her words didn't come out quite as she had intended. "It's just that I don't know you, Mr. Reed, and WSPU members are sometimes targeted by investigators or anti-suffragists."

"So you think I might be a spy? Or that I don't really know Mrs. Sheppard?" He winked at her. "I'll prove it to you. I'll tell you everything I know about her."

"Very well," she said. Although she wasn't convinced, it did seem unlikely that a New Zealander would be recruited as a spy for British anti-suffragists.

She needn't have worried, either way. By the time Lilia and Will reached the front gates of the cemetery, she was convinced that he not only knew Kate Sheppard, but also that he was himself an ardent supporter of women's rights.

"What do you think made it easier for women to get the vote in New Zealand?" she asked.

"It's a very different place." He opened his arms as if to encompass his homeland with them. "There's no established hierarchy, as there is here. Temperance societies have more power in New Zealand, and most Temperance advocates are suffragists, too. And in a frontier society, there's less of a divide between women and men than there is between different races."

As they exited the cemetery, she barraged Will with inquiries, all of which he answered patiently. But after a while, he laughed and said, "It's my turn to ask questions now. You said in your speech that it was natural for you to take physical risks, but aren't you afraid sometimes?"

"Yes, of course. I was afraid during the Parliament Square riot, but everything happened so fast. One minute I was speaking to the crowd, and the next I was on the ground being beaten."

"My God. And it didn't make you want to quit, or at least take a less public role?"

"If anything, it made me all the more determined to fight. When the police and government sanction such violence against women, there's something truly wrong with the country."

"You're magnificent." He looked at her with such warmth and admiration that she began to feel uncomfortable.

Lilia stopped at the street corner. "I've taken enough of your time, Mr. Reed. Thank you for answering my questions."

"Tell me, Miss Brooke, do you believe in love at first sight?"

"Certainly not," she said, taking a step back. "Mr. Reed, you must not expect anything of that sort from me. I'm not interested in romance."

"No fear," he said lightly. "I didn't mean anything by it. You'll get used to my way of speaking soon enough. I'm rarely serious."

She gave him a suspicious look.

"You must know you're a stunner," he added. "Surely a man might be allowed to remind you of the obvious from time to time."

"No." She meant the word to apply to everything he said—even to the things he hadn't said. "I'm immune to flattery."

"I'll take that as a challenge." With another wink, he tipped his hat and walked away.

⟳

A week after the memorial gathering in Highgate Cemetery, Lilia was in a hansom cab with Mary Braddock. They had drawn the curtains, and Lilia couldn't see Mary's face clearly in the gloom.

"Are you certain you understand what we're about to do?" Lilia asked.

"Aye."

"And you still want to be part of this?"

"I've been wantin' to for a long time now, miss."

"I'm sorry we had to change the plan, but with Ada dropping out at the last minute, I was her only possible replacement." Ada had left the WSPU when her fiancé threatened to break off their engagement.

"You won't get in trouble with Mrs. Pankhurst, will you?"

As a paid organizer, Lilia was expected to avoid arrest whenever possible, but it was becoming increasingly important to her to do more than just organize the volunteers who did most of the dangerous work. And she didn't want to leave Mary alone during her very first militant act.

"I don't think so. She'll understand." Lilia lowered her voice, even though the cabdriver couldn't possibly have heard her. "Remember, I'll go first, as I'm more likely to be recognized. After you hear the glass breaking down the street, wait a few minutes, then throw your own stone."

"I will, miss. I've got a strong throwin' arm, and a right good aim, too."

"I believe you." Lilia smiled at Mary's barely contained exuberance. Unlike Ellen, Mary seemed to have no fear whatsoever and had taken to law-breaking as if she'd been born to do it. She'd had a difficult upbringing in the East End, and it was likely she'd had to break the law to survive in her youth, after all, though she was tight-lipped about her past. All Lilia knew was that Mary was only nineteen and had lived on the streets long before being sent to the Whitechapel House of Mercy two years earlier.

Lilia ordered the cabdriver to stop a few blocks from their destination, and she and Mary got out and bid each other goodbye as if they were merely friends parting after an evening visit. Then they turned and walked in opposite directions.

Lilia was careful to walk normally, as if there weren't two large stones in her pockets. The summer evening was barely cool enough to justify the light coat she was wearing, and she had had to purchase a new hat that was large enough to cover most of her face. Because she was taller than most women, and the public was beginning to recognize her as a vocal WSPU member, it was important not to arouse suspicion before she had achieved her object.

She paused to glance behind her. It was eight o'clock. Not many people were on the street and offices were closed for the day, so it was late enough that nobody would be inside the buildings. The object of this mission was to break windows, not to cause injury, in order to prove that the government cared more about property than about women's bodies.

Doubling back the way she had come, Lilia tried to walk at a steady pace, but her heart was pounding and it was difficult not to speed up. At the street corner where the cab had stopped, she paused again. She could see Mary's figure on the other side of the street, nearly a block away, just in the place they'd agreed upon.

She gave the building in front of her a quick glance, then, satisfied that the darkness inside meant there was nobody within, Lilia reached into her pocket and hurled the stone with all her might.

The sound of shattering glass broke the quiet of the evening. Lilia heard alarmed voices from down the street, then increasingly quick footsteps, but she didn't look. She began to walk away at the same steady pace, her heart beating even faster this time.

When she reached the street corner, two things happened at once: a police constable grabbed her by the arm, and from the other end of the block there was a loud crash, then the tinkling of shards of glass, as musical to Lilia's ears as a symphony.

15

The same order shall the Curate use with those betwixt whom he perceiveth malice and hatred to reign; not suffering them to be partakers of the Lord's Table, until he know them to be reconciled.

—The Book of Common Prayer

Sunday morning dawned bright and clear. Paul hummed to himself as he took the communion vessels from the sacristy and arranged them on the altar. He had already spoken to the verger to ensure that Mr. Hirst would be welcomed and ushered to a pew near the front of the cathedral. He had mentioned that a special visitor would be at the service, and instead of giving Mr. Hirst's name, which the verger could easily let slip in front of Thomas Cross, Paul simply gave the verger a physical description of the man. The element of surprise was crucial—if Cross had any idea his father was there, he would likely have time to plan some way of removing him from the service. Paul had learned that Cross would be preaching on the parable of the prodigal son, nearly too perfect a coincidence. Cross would unknowingly be preaching to himself, and his father's presence would reveal the disparity between his preaching and his practice.

A little while later, the service began, but there was no sign of Mr. Hirst. Paul watched the entrance so intently that he nearly missed his cue when it was time for him to read the gospel. As he turned his attention to the gospel of St. Luke, he read the parable of the prodigal son slowly and sonorously. It had always been one of Paul's favorite parables, with its vivid contrast between the presumption and recklessness of the younger son and the jealous arrogance of the elder, and the immense love and forgiveness of the father were represented with beautiful simplicity.

When Paul was finished, the words of the prodigal son when reunited with his father rang in his ears—"Father, I have sinned against heaven, and in thy sight, and am no more worthy to be called thy son"—and for a moment Paul imagined hearing Cross say those very words to his father. But such humility seemed beyond Cross's ability.

As the congregation began to recite the Nicene Creed and Paul began to lose hope that Mr. Hirst would appear, the man did. Because the congregation was standing, nobody but Paul seemed to notice the old man's entrance. Mr. Hirst looked more disheveled than he had when Paul had first met him—his hair looked as though it hadn't been combed in days and his jacket was wrinkled. He also seemed to be walking unsteadily, but Paul didn't have a clear enough view of him to be certain. Paul shifted his attention to Cross, who hadn't yet noticed the new arrival. But towards the end of the Creed, Paul saw Cross turn and whisper something to Canon Johnson, after which Johnson turned and disappeared into the vestry. A few minutes later, Johnson reappeared in the nave and spoke urgently to the verger. The verger shook his head and said something to make Johnson raise his eyebrows and turn to glance at Paul.

By this time, the recitation of the Creed had ended and Cross rose to take his place in the pulpit. He stood there for a long time in silence, looking down at his notes, then glanced at the canons' stalls. Johnson, who had returned to his stall, shook his head slightly. Cross made no move in reaction to this, but his face was set and grim. Finally, he began to speak.

The sermon started promisingly, with a few illustrations of the difficulties of family relationships, but Cross was looking over the heads of the congregation as if to avoid eye contact with anyone. He moved on to expound upon the parable, starting with the errors of the younger son, then moving on to those of the elder.

"We must surely see ourselves in one of these sons," Cross said. "Haven't we all chosen the route of the dissipated younger son or the proud elder son? Some of us have been both at different times in our lives."

An audible *Amen* was heard from the pew in which Mr. Hirst was sitting. A muscle in Cross's jaw twitched, but he went on.

"Most interpretations of this parable draw parallels between the loving, forgiving father and God. But we can also consider the father's role as one we ought to take as mature Christians. We must turn from our sinful behavior, whether it resembles that of the younger or the elder son, and offer love and forgiveness to others, as the father did."

"Hear, hear!" came a loud voice, again from Mr. Hirst's pew. To Paul's astonishment, Mr. Hirst stood up and pointed at Cross. "That'sh my son, everybody! Your old father is proud of you, Tommy!" He started to sway and prevented himself from falling only by grasping the back of the pew in front of him. "Love and forgivenesh indeed! That's exactly what I want from you, Tommy. Will you give me your forgivenesh?"

The man was clearly as drunk as it was possible to be while still standing upright.

For a long, painful moment, everyone froze. Nobody seemed to know what to do. Nothing like this had ever happened during a cathedral service.

The verger was particularly confused, looking at Paul from across the nave for guidance. After all, knowing that one of the canons wanted this man present would certainly complicate the standard procedure for dealing with disorderly parishioners.

Cross stood in stunned silence in the pulpit, clearly unable to continue.

This was far worse than anything Paul had imagined. Instead of the satisfaction he had expected to feel at the rare sight of Cross at a loss for words, he felt instantly and deeply ashamed of himself for having engineered the scene. He couldn't have known Mr. Hirst would arrive in his cups, but he had known that the man's presence would unnerve Cross. How had he allowed himself to sink so low? A sick feeling settled in the pit of Paul's stomach, but he didn't allow himself to consider the matter further at that moment.

He heard Cross hiss in an undertone, "Get him out of here!"

Though Cross's words were not directed to anyone in particular, Paul rose from his stall and made his way down the chancel steps towards Mr. Hirst, who had now left his pew, mumbling incoherently and stumbling forward in the direction of the pulpit.

Paul beckoned to the verger and between the two of them, they were able to turn Mr. Hirst around and guide him out of the cathedral amid his loud protests. As they made their way out, Paul felt rather than saw the shocked stares of the congregation, and he felt as responsible for the disaster as if he himself had disrupted the service in a drunken fit. He had never felt more exposed, more guilt-ridden, more sinful.

When Paul and the verger had ushered Mr. Hirst outside, the old man turned to Paul in a moment of clarity and said accusingly, "You said you'd help me."

Paul avoided the verger's eyes. "I'm trying to help you, Mr. Hirst, but you're not making it easy."

It took some time to extricate the name of Mr. Hirst's hotel from him, but when that was done, Paul called a cab, managed to get the man into it, and paid the driver to convey him there.

Before he and the verger returned to the cathedral, Paul said, "I'll be responsible for that man, but I must ask you not to tell anyone I instructed you to let him into the service today."

"Very well, Canon Harris," the man replied, with a knowing look that Paul didn't like.

Paul realized there would be enough cathedral gossip from this day's events to keep everyone talking for months. Never mind the cathedral—there was enough drama to interest even the local newspapers. He shuddered.

When Paul returned to the cathedral, he saw that Cross had disappeared and the precentor was leading the stunned-looking choir in a hymn. Only then did Paul remember that he was the scheduled celebrant for the Communion. Like an automaton, he put on the green chasuble worn for the occasion and took his place at the altar. Canon Johnson joined him to assist with the sacrament, and Paul began the exhortation: "Dearly beloved in the Lord, ye that mind to come to the holy Communion of the Body and Blood of our Savior Christ, must consider how Saint Paul exhorteth all persons diligently to try and examine themselves, before they presume to eat of that Bread, and drink of that Cup."

It was only when he reached the sentence about receiving the Communion unworthily that his voice faltered. He continued, with some difficulty, "For then we are guilty of the Body and Blood of Christ our Savior; we eat and drink our own damnation . . ."

Paul's heart raced and he found it difficult to breathe, let alone speak. In the silence that followed, he temporarily forgot where he was, as the heaviness of his guilt overwhelmed him.

How had he allowed his hatred of Cross to take over his soul? When had he ceased to struggle against it and to confess it as a sin? How had he been able to celebrate the Communion week after week, sharing the bread and wine with Cross, hearing and sometimes speaking these words that warned him not to do so unworthily? Had he thought the words were meant for the congregation only, that he, as a priest, had the luxury of hating another man with impunity? He had deceived himself to such a degree that he had been prepared to enjoy the spectacle of Cross's humiliation with the self-satisfied pride befitting the elder son in the parable.

The possibility that Cross could return from wherever he had gone and proceed with the service, that Paul might once again share the bread and wine with a man he had deeply wronged, finally prompted him to act. He turned to Johnson and said in an undertone, "I can't go on. Will you take over?"

Bewildered, the other man assented, and an awkward public moment ensued in which Paul removed his chasuble—it seemed to resist his actions and cling to him like a living thing—and thrust it at Johnson, then turned and walked out through the vestry and out of the cathedral without looking back.

When he arrived at his house, he went straight to his bedroom, shut the door, got down on his knees, and wept. Though he spoke no words, either aloud or silently, it was the most sincere prayer he had prayed in months.

That night, he dreamed he had contracted a mysterious disease that was converting all of his internal organs to black bile: he felt a poisonous, heavy, liquid sensation slowly move upwards through his body, choking the movement of his blood. He awoke, gasping for air, just as the black bile reached his head.

Just as Paul had predicted, cathedral gossip ran rampant in the aftermath of the Sunday service. Everyone was talking about Cross and his father. Although the cathedral clergy had tried to prevent the gossip from leaking into the world at large, the dramatic spectacle at the cathedral was indeed reported in the local newspapers. The incident wasn't likely to create a full-scale public scandal, but Cross's reputation was tainted. He had told everyone his father was dead and was now forced to admit that Mr. Hirst was his father. While some people were sympathetic—"If I had such a father, I wouldn't admit it, either!"—most believed that, being a clergyman, he ought to have told the truth from the beginning.

The following week, the old dean died, and Paul was offered the deanship.

When he received the letter of appointment, Paul told no one. After two days, he went to see the bishop, a conversation he dreaded but which went surprisingly well. He confessed fully to his part in the disturbance at the cathedral and came away feeling both forgiven and understood.

Still, there was one more difficult conversation he needed to have before he could tell his family and friends about his decision.

He found Cross in the chapter house, sitting at the large table used for meetings and looking through some papers. The two canons hadn't spoken more than a few words to each other since the day Cross's father visited the cathedral. Indeed, since that day, Cross had gone about his work silently, speaking little to anyone. Now, he looked up at Paul's entrance and said curtly, "What do you want?"

Cross's greeting, if it could be called that, wasn't unusual, but it didn't make what Paul had to say any easier.

"I need to speak with you," Paul said.

"What about?"

"It's about what happened when your father—"

"Look, Harris, do you really think I want to listen to your sermon on the subject? Are you here just to gloat? I've said all I'm going to say about it, and you can read anything else you want to know in the papers."

"That's not what I'm here for." Paul hesitated.

"What, then?"

Paul sat down at the table and stared at the wall opposite him. It was easier not to meet Cross's eyes. "Your father came to see me the week before he came to the cathedral service," he began.

"What are you talking about?"

"He found out I work with you and asked for my help arranging a reconciliation. He told me about the hardships he'd experienced in his past and about your ambitions being beyond his means. I felt sorry for him—"

"Why am I not surprised?" interposed Cross grimly.

"—and I suggested he attend the Sunday service. I had no idea he would arrive in a drunken state, nor did I expect him to create a disturbance. I was under the impression he wished so strongly to reconcile with you that he would do nothing untoward."

"So you were merely acting out of kindness to reconcile me with my father." Cross's voice dripped with sarcasm.

"You had told everyone your father was dead and you lied about your name. I thought that seeing your father in the congregation would . . . improve your character."

"So you are the person, then, to whom I owe my disgrace," Cross said coldly. "I suppose you orchestrated the attack on me last year, as well."

"What attack?"

Cross gave him a wary look. "You must have noticed my long absence from the cathedral."

"I thought you were ill."

"I was driven into the country against my will by a hansom cabdriver, then beaten and left for dead by at least two other men. Did you have anything to do with that?"

"What? Of course not. How could such a thing happen? Did you tell the police?"

"It doesn't matter now."

"But—"

"I don't want to talk about it."

Paul leaned forward and clasped his hands together on the table. "I don't like you, Cross, but I would never sanction a physical attack on another human being."

Cross shrugged and tossed some papers into a box.

"Regarding your father," Paul continued, clearing his throat. "I was wrong to become involved and wrong to interfere with your personal life, and I'm sorry."

Cross stared at him. "Well, well. An apology from Canon Harris, of all people. But perhaps you have reason to be magnanimous with the lower orders of clergy these days. Are the rumors that you've been offered the deanship correct? It certainly won't be offered to me now."

"I have, but that has nothing to do with this. Besides, I've declined the offer."

"Are you mad? Why? Is your father going to buy you a bishopric?"

Paul rose from the table. "There are many complicated reasons for my decision that I don't wish to discuss at the moment," he said.

"Suit yourself." Cross fell silent and stared down at the table.

After a pause, Paul said quietly, "I've paid for your father's passage back to America. He leaves next week." He turned to leave but hesitated at the door. "I don't know why you and I seem to bring out the worst in each other," he said, still facing the door. "I wish it could have been different."

He left the room before Cross could make another cutting remark.

The conversation had drained him emotionally, and Paul needed to talk to someone who would understand what he had done and why. As soon as his duties were done for the day, he went to see his father, who greeted Paul with his usual warmth, though Paul was again concerned by his haggard appearance.

Before he could ask after his father's health, Philip said eagerly, "I hope you've got good news for me."

They were in the library. Paul didn't take the chair his father offered, choosing instead to pace around the room. "I do have news, but it's not exactly good."

Philip's face fell. "After that ugly business with Cross's father, I was certain the deanship would be offered to you."

"It was, but I've declined it."

His father stared at him, his face going so gray that Paul rushed to his side. Taking his father's arm and guiding him into a chair, Paul said, "I'm so sorry, Father. I'll ring for a glass of water."

After summoning the maid, Paul drew up a chair beside his father's and watched him worriedly, consumed with remorse for shocking him with such an abrupt announcement.

When Philip had rested for a few minutes and drank some of the water, he waved away Paul's concern. "I'm surprised, of course, but I'm fine. Tell me what happened."

Paul explained his part in Mr. Hirst's appearance at the cathedral. "I can't describe how I felt when I couldn't continue with the Communion," he admitted, once the story was told. "How could I have gone on for months— years—hating Thomas Cross and preaching love to everyone else without seeing what a hypocrite I was? Can you imagine how I felt?"

"I think so," Philip said, "but I still don't understand why you declined the deanship."

"I wanted it for the wrong reasons. I became so caught up in my own ambitions and in competing with Cross that I didn't notice how tainted I was becoming."

Philip looked confused. "But you've realized your error and confessed to it. Surely it is overscrupulous to do more. What harm could it do to accept the deanship? Surely many men feel as you have and have gone on to do great things in the church."

"Perhaps, but *I* can't go on without taking some time to think about what I've allowed myself to become and to pray for guidance."

"And you can't do that as dean."

"No. I should tell you I've resigned my canonry, as well. I'll leave the cathedral at the end of the month."

"What will you do?"

"I don't know just yet, but the bishop has assured me he'll find me a living somewhere, at least temporarily."

Philip was silent, staring at the floor.

Paul didn't understand why his news was affecting his father so profoundly. Philip had certainly encouraged Paul's hopes for the deanship, but he had always thought his father wouldn't have minded what his vocation was, as long as he was happy.

At last, Philip said, "I'm sorry, Paul, but I really don't feel very well. I think I must lie down."

"Of course."

Paul helped his father rise from his chair and accompanied him to his room. In spite of Philip's protests, Paul sent for the doctor and waited at his father's side until the man arrived.

The doctor's diagnosis was that Philip was overworked and merely needed rest. Paul hoped that was all it was.

16

Sweated women in the slums, who could not eat; foolish women in the prisons, who would not eat; and wise men in the House of Commons dining cheerfully.

—Gertrude Colmore, *Suffragette Sally*

JULY 1908

The air in Lilia's jail cell was stifling and hot. She shifted uncomfortably on the wooden platform bed, her coarse prison uniform damp with perspiration. Her back was hurting, too: it had never been the same since the Parliament Square riot.

The door of her cell opened with a loud banging and clanking, and the familiar black bonnet and holland dress of a wardress appeared.

"Are you awake?" she said. "Come with me."

Lilia rose unsteadily, her legs not quite ready to hold her. "Where are you taking me?" she asked.

The wardress didn't answer, but led her to another room where she was given her own clothing.

"Am I being released? Why today?"

This question also went unanswered. She had been sentenced to a fort-night in Holloway Prison but had been there only five days. She wondered if her hunger strike had precipitated the early release. Why had they not tried to force-feed her? She was quite sure she could have lasted longer than five days without eating. She didn't even feel hungry now, only a little disoriented.

Or perhaps the trouble Lilia had caused was the reason for her early release. She had done everything she could to encourage her fellow prisoners: sung "The Women's Marseillaise," the WSPU anthem, as loudly as she dared through the night; rapped "no surrender" in Morse code on her cell wall, until women in the adjoining cells had repeated it; whispered encouragement to others in the prison yard when they were taken out for exercise. She'd been yanked away by a wardress and forbidden to exercise with the other prisoners after that, and in protest she'd broken the gas jet in her cell with her shoe.

Despite her many unanswered questions, she was relieved to remove the discolored prison uniform with the broad black arrows that marked her as a second-division prisoner. The suffragettes considered themselves political prisoners, a first-division category, but instead they were treated like common criminals. Conditions were even worse for working-class suffragettes like Mary, who were often put in the third division and made to act as servants for the others.

After Lilia changed into her own clothes, she was led to the large gateway near the entrance and placed in a queue of other prisoners to be released. Mary was there, too, and Lilia exchanged a smile with her as they waited. Two wardresses watched them closely, so they couldn't talk.

As soon as the main doors were unbolted, the queue of prisoners filed outside into blindingly bright daylight. It was a hot day, but the air outdoors was far less oppressive than in the prison.

Now that Lilia could see Mary clearly, she looked terrible. Her skin had a yellowish cast and she was staggering, almost unable to walk. Lilia went to her side immediately.

"What happened to your leg?"

"It was hurt when I was arrested. A constable bashed it with his truncheon. I asked for a doctor, but he didn't see me 'til yesterday. He said it was nothin', just a sprain, but it's not getting better."

"Let me help you get home."

Mary's eyes darted from side to side and she said, "No, I can't go home. Where are the others?"

"What others?"

"The ones who meet suffragettes when they get out of jail." The WSPU usually greeted its released members with a crowd of supporters and a special breakfast.

"They didn't know we'd be released early," Lilia said. "I have enough money for omnibus fare. Where would you like to go, if not home? Would you like to come home with me?"

"I don't want you in danger."

"Danger? What do you mean?"

"I want to go to St. John's," Mary said.

Still puzzled, Lilia said, "The cathedral?"

Mary nodded. "Canon Harris will help me."

Lilia stared at her. She didn't think Mary knew Paul apart from their one brief meeting at the Whitechapel House of Mercy. And she expected Mary not to trust clergymen, given her bad experiences with the chaplain at the penitentiary.

"Are you sure?" Lilia asked.

"Aye. He's helped me before. He's one of the good 'uns."

"Very well." Lilia slipped her arm around Mary's waist and said,

"Lean on me. If you can try to walk a half block or so, we'll get on the omnibus."

Once she'd settled Mary and herself into seats on the omnibus, Lilia wanted to ask about Mary's connection with Paul, but the girl looked so weak and ill that Lilia didn't want her to exert any undue energy to speak. Truth be told, she wasn't feeling well, either. Her head felt heavy and she was a bit dizzy.

She was nervous about seeing Paul for the first time since his trip to Ingleford. She especially didn't want him to see her in this disheveled, dirty state, with the unpleasant smell of the jail still in her hair and clothes. But she reminded herself it was Mary who needed help and who had chosen to seek him out, not herself. She was only there to see that Mary got to the cathedral, and then she could leave.

When Lilia and Mary arrived at the cathedral, they entered through the main doors and paused while their eyes adjusted to the dim light. Mary was a small woman, but Lilia was exerting all her remaining strength to keep her friend upright. They staggered to the nearest pew at the back of the sanctuary.

A portly little man approached them and said, "I'm sorry, but you can't sit here. The cathedral is being cleaned today."

Lilia was sorely tempted to give him a lecture on how to treat people in need. It was no wonder modern society had little use for the church, if this man was representative of its staff. But she bit back her retort, for Mary's sake, and merely said, "My friend needs help."

The man peered at Mary with bright, beady eyes. "Is she drunk? We don't want vagrants here."

"She's ill," Lilia snapped. "We must see Canon Harris."

The man gave her a suspicious look.

"If he's here, I insist you fetch him at once. I'm Miss Brooke, and he's a friend of mine. I can promise you he won't appreciate the way you're treating us."

Lilia's veiled threat seemed to work. The man shuffled away and a few minutes later, Paul strode down a side aisle towards them, his black cassock billowing out behind him.

He looked at her as if he didn't recognize her. "Lilia? What's the matter?"

"We've just been released from Holloway," Lilia said. "Mary wanted to come here. Her leg is injured and she's faint from hunger."

Paul looked at Mary. "There's a private room about ten feet away where you can rest. Can you walk?"

"I'll try," she said.

Paul and Lilia helped Mary to her feet and each took one of her arms, guiding her to the room he'd indicated. It wasn't much more than an alcove, with two chairs and a tiny side table; Lilia couldn't imagine what its usual function might be. But she and Paul helped Mary into a chair and he offered Lilia the other one.

Paul crouched down beside Mary and said, "Shall I send for Mrs. Rutledge?"

Lilia had no idea who Mrs. Rutledge was, but Mary clearly did. "Please," she replied with a nod.

"Very well. I'll bring you something to eat, as well." He stood and turned to leave, but then turned back to give Lilia a searching look. "May I bring you some food, too?"

Only then did she realize how desperately hungry she was. She felt as if a rat were gnawing at her insides. "That would be lovely. Thank you."

"Don't move," he said. "I'll be right back."

He returned with two glasses of water and a small loaf of bread. He set the bread on the side table, then handed one glass to Lilia and the other to Mary.

It was the most delicious, refreshing water Lilia had ever tasted, and it was difficult not to gulp it all down at once.

Paul turned to the table and broke off some of the bread, then handed a piece to each woman.

Mary ate her piece quickly, and Paul said, "You'd better slow down. You must gradually accustom your body to food again." He spoke and looked at Mary with such kindness and concern that Lilia felt herself softening. They had come to the right place, after all.

The room was very quiet. The only sounds were muffled echoes from other parts of the cathedral: doors being closed, soft-soled shoes shuffling down an aisle, the sweep of what must have been a broom. The peaceful atmosphere surrounded Lilia like an embrace, an indescribable relief after the jarring noises she had been subjected to day and night at Holloway. She looked at what was left of the loaf of bread on the side table. She wished Paul would eat some of it, too. She fancied that if they ate it together, as a sort of spiritual ritual, it would mend the breach in their friendship.

"Is that the bread you use for Communion?" she asked. "It probably wouldn't be wise to tell your superiors you shared it with heathens."

He smiled, his face lighting up in the way she remembered so well. She wondered if a person existed who could be immune to that smile.

"Not to worry," he said. "This bread hasn't been consecrated. Heathens in need are welcome to it."

A few minutes later, the little man who had been so inhospitable to Mary and Lilia appeared in the doorway. "Canon Harris, Mrs. Rutledge is waiting at the west entrance."

"Thank you." Paul looked at Mary. "How do you feel? A little better?"

"Aye, I think so." Her face had regained its color and as she rose from her chair, she seemed steadier on her feet. Paul offered her his arm.

Lilia rose and said, "I can help, too."

"No need, miss," Mary said. "Canon Harris knows what to do. I'll see you soon."

"Very well."

As Paul guided Mary to the doorway, he glanced at Lilia and said, "Will you wait for me? I won't be long."

"Certainly."

Lilia waited in the little room, feeling strangely bereft. People always needed her and wanted things from her, sometimes to the point of exasperation on her part. But now she was clearly not needed.

When Paul returned, he took the chair Mary had vacated.

"Mary is safe now," he said. "You needn't worry about her."

"I don't understand. Why didn't she want to go home?"

"Her uncle is home and out of prison again."

This information meant nothing to Lilia, and she gave him a baffled look.

"She lives with him," he explained. "He's opposed to her suffrage activities, but he spends a good deal of time in jail for various crimes. Mary is safe when he's in prison, but when she first joined the WSPU, he beat her so badly that she almost died."

Lilia felt the blood drain from her face. The water glass she was holding began to shake. Paul took it from her and set it on the table.

"I'm sorry," he said. "I thought you knew."

"Why didn't she tell me?" Lilia murmured. "I'm her friend." She tried to remember whether Mary had said anything about her private life, but the only conversations that came to her mind were about the WSPU.

"Perhaps she was ashamed. People often hide their private pain, even from friends."

"But she told you."

"I'm a priest. You might be surprised how much people are willing to tell me." He touched his clerical collar, adding, "Sometimes seeing this is enough to open the floodgates."

"But Mary had such a bad experience with the chaplain at the Whitechapel House of Mercy. I thought she'd avoid all clergymen after that."

He gave her a wry look. "Not everyone sees us as the enemy, present company excepted."

"I don't—" she began, but he smiled, and she realized she had taken his bait. She tossed her head and said briskly, "Who is this Mrs. Rutledge and where has she taken Mary?"

"Mrs. Rutledge oversees a house of refuge nearby. It's not a penitentiary, so you needn't give me that suspicious look. There is room for only four guests, so we use it for women and children who are in imminent danger. They can't stay long, unfortunately, but it offers a temporary place for them to recover from whatever violence they've experienced."

"And Mary has been there before."

"Yes." He hesitated, as if choosing his words carefully. "She sought me out at the cathedral after she was released from the Whitechapel House of Mercy. She remembered my visits there when I was working on the penitentiary project. That's all."

But it wasn't all, Lilia sensed. Paul had never been one to boast about his accomplishments.

"Did you establish this house of refuge?" she asked.

"Yes."

"I'm glad."

"It was so little, given what I wanted to do. Several women have gone from there back to the streets or to male relations who beat them. One has already died from her injuries." Paul's lips tightened and he looked away.

"I wish Mary would have told me," Lilia said, half to herself. "I could have tried to protect her—or kept her identity secret, at least." Glancing at Paul, she added, "You must hate the WSPU for making Mary's life even more difficult than it already is."

"No," he said firmly. "She has told me how the WSPU has given her a purpose she never had before. And seeing how powerless she is, like so many others in her position, has convinced me how important it is for women to have the vote."

Lilia was moved, and it was a moment before she could meet his eyes. When she did, she saw that he was looking at her intently, and she raised her hand in a half-conscious movement to smooth her hair. She had pinned it back as best she could in her cell that morning, without the benefit of a looking glass or brush, and it felt tangled and grimy. She wished he wouldn't look at her that way. Those clear green eyes seemed to miss nothing.

"Have you become a suffragist, then?" she said, trying to lighten the mood.

"I don't know. You be the judge."

It was a strange conversation. Lilia wondered how much of the strangeness was in her perception alone—perhaps her weakened state had made her think Paul still cared for her, at least as a friend. Or perhaps the strangeness lay in the setting—they had never been together like this in an almost-empty cathedral.

"Were you and Mary arrested together?" he asked.

"Yes. We were both released early, too. Mary was probably released today because of her leg, but I don't know why they released me. They didn't even try to force-feed me, though perhaps I wasn't on my hunger strike long enough for that. One of the wardresses told me she heard the governor say I'm more trouble in prison than out of it."

"That's certainly possible," Paul said, looking amused.

"My theory is that the prison officials and MPs are worried about the publicity I'll draw to the Cause. They know I'll write and speak about every-thing that happens to me, and I suppose that makes them nervous."

"I have a theory, too," he said, "but I don't think I can share it with you."

She gave him a quizzical look, but he didn't elaborate. The cathedral clock began to chime the hour, and he said, "I'm sorry, but I have a meeting. And you'll want to go home and rest. Will you let me hail a cab for you?"

She assented. As they made their way outside, Paul said, "I'll check on Mary tomorrow to make sure she's all right."

"I should like to see her, too. May I go with you?"

"I'm afraid not. Very few people know about the house of refuge, and if you were to be seen going there . . ."

"The secret would be out. I understand."

"I could call on you tomorrow evening, if you like, and tell you how Mary is."

"I'd appreciate that. Thank you."

Once in the cab, Lilia pulled back the curtain to wave to him, but he had already turned back towards the cathedral.

～

When Paul went to Lilia's house the following evening, Lizzie greeted him like a long-lost hero, and even Harriet was more cordial than she used to be. She was on her way out but told him she was sorry she couldn't stay to talk. It occurred to him only after she had left that she probably knew all the details of his failed proposal to Lilia and merely felt sorry for him.

When Lilia entered the parlor where he waited, Paul was relieved to see that she looked much better than she had the day before. He had been more alarmed by her appearance at the cathedral than he had let on. But though she was still too pale, her eyes were bright and she moved with her usual energy.

She surprised him by sitting beside him on the brown horsehair sofa, turning a little to face him so that her knee nearly touched his. She was so close he could smell the distinctive cinnamon-tobacco scent of her cigarettes.

"How is Mary?" she asked.

"She's better now that she's eating again, but the doctor went to see her this morning. It turns out her leg is broken and has been for some time."

"That's outrageous!" Lilia's eyes flashed with anger. "The injury occurred during her arrest and the prison doctor claimed it was just a sprain."

"She's being well cared for now and can stay at the house of refuge for at least a month. I've made sure of that."

"Thank you."

"I confess I was worried about you, too, yesterday. Are you feeling better?"

"Yes, much better—but yesterday we spoke only of me and Mary. I'd like to know about your life. I heard the old dean of the cathedral died, so does that mean the deanship is yours?"

He hesitated. He didn't feel like telling the whole painful story again, but she was looking at him with such interest that he ended up relating everything, from his first meeting with Mr. Hirst to his decision not to accept the deanship. Lilia's dark, expressive eyes never left his face.

When he had finished, she said, "It must have been difficult to decline the deanship when you wanted it so much."

"Yes." He felt uncomfortable and could say no more. Why had he confided in her? He had fallen into their old friendly intimacy without thinking.

She didn't seem to notice his discomfort. "And it must be difficult still, not knowing where you'll go or what you'll do next. It isn't like you not to have every step of your life planned out."

"That's an exaggeration," he said defensively. "I never thought I could plan everything."

"All right, then, *almost* everything," she replied with a twinkle in her eye.

"It isn't not knowing my next step that troubles me most," he went on, more thoughtful now. "It's how easily I deceived myself. Others saw through my false piety—the bishop certainly did, and so did you, when you talked about the emptiness at the core of my 'beautiful religious forms and ceremonies.'"

"Oh, don't remind me!" she exclaimed, surprising him with her vehemence. "I should never have said such a thing."

"I'm glad you did," he said, realizing the truth of his words only as he said them. "So few people tell me what they really think. I could always count on you to tell me the truth. I only wish I had taken your words more seriously at the time."

"You give me too much credit," she said quietly, looking away. "I didn't know what I was talking about. It was needlessly hurtful, and I'm sorry."

"I forgive you," he said.

"I do think you would have made a good dean, but I know you too well to believe your conscience would have let you rest had you accepted."

He felt absurdly, overwhelmingly relieved that she understood his decision, especially since his father hadn't.

Quietly, Lilia added, "I've missed talking to you. We were good friends once, weren't we?"

He felt something painful and dangerous unfurling in his heart, and he stood up abruptly. "It's late. I've stayed too long."

"It's not so very late," she said, looking startled. "You needn't go yet."

"Yes, I must." He turned to leave.

At that moment, Lizzie poked her head into the parlor and said, "I'm sorry, Miss Brooke, but Mr. Reed is here. I've told him you have a visitor, but he insists he'll only be a moment."

"Very well. Paul, don't go yet. I'll introduce you."

Before Paul could say anything, a very tall man burst into the parlor with a large bouquet of flowers, which he thrust into Lilia's hands, saying, "My poor dear girl, how are you?"

He was clearly a foreigner, and not a very well-mannered one at that, rushing at Lilia in such a way. And he hadn't even removed his hat.

But to Paul's surprise, Lilia behaved as if this was a normal occurrence, taking the flowers and asking Lizzie to put them in a vase. She said mildly, "Your hat, Mr. Reed. And I have another visitor."

The man only then seemed to notice Paul, and he blinked in astonishment at Paul's clerical collar. "I beg your pardon, sir . . . er, father." He swiftly removed his hat.

Lilia stepped in to introduce the intruder as Mr. Will Reed. "He's from New Zealand," she added, looking at Paul as though he ought to be delighted by this information.

Paul gave the other man a curt nod.

Mr. Reed looked more puzzled than the situation warranted. "I didn't know you were religious," he said to Lilia. "Or have you been driven to it by your time in prison?"

"Canon Harris is a family friend," Lilia said.

Not that again. Paul thought he deserved a better label than "family friend," though he supposed "rejected suitor" would have been worse.

Mr. Reed laughed. "I do apologize, Canon Harris. I'm always saying the wrong thing. Fortunately, Lilia is very forgiving."

"It's no problem," Paul said. But it was a problem. Also problems were Mr. Reed's familiar tone and his use of Lilia's Christian name.

"Are you really all right?" Mr. Reed asked Lilia. "When I found out you were released from prison and received no celebratory breakfast, I was shocked. How can the Union treat its best woman in such a way?" He pronounced the word *best* as if it were *beast*.

"I'm fine, truly. There's no need to make a fuss. And I was released unexpectedly, so the Union didn't know about it."

"Well, you look fine indeed. Better than fine." He winked at her in a way that made Paul feel that he, not Mr. Reed, was the intruder.

Surely Lilia must have been offended by this man's disrespectful manner and the liberties he was taking. But she didn't look offended.

"Women can vote in New Zealand," she said to Paul, as if this fully explained Will Reed's presence in her parlor. "Mr. Reed has been sharing his ideas with the WSPU based on the success women have achieved in his colony."

"If your families were friends," Mr. Reed said, swiftly changing the subject, "the two of you must have known each other as children."

"I was twelve when we met," Lilia said.

"Is that so?" Mr. Reed turned to Paul. "What was Lilia like as a girl? I must know."

Paul said stiffly, "Very much as she is now."

"What?" Lilia exclaimed, looking hurt. "Are you saying I haven't grown up?"

Paul looked at the vibrantly beautiful woman in front of him, then at Will Reed, who was gazing at her worshipfully. "I'm saying that a strong personality such as yours is often evident from a young age. I'm sorry, but I really must leave."

"Let me walk you out," Lilia said.

"Please don't trouble yourself." He spoke firmly, in his best clerical, the-meeting-is-now-ended tone. She took the hint and simply nodded.

Once outside on the street, breathing in the cool night air, Paul stared up at the sky.

"Fool!" he said aloud. If Will Reed was the sort of man Lilia found appealing, Paul had never had a chance with her. He turned on his heel and strode away.

17

He is not here; but far away

    The noise of life begins again,

    And ghastly thro' the drizzling rain

On the bald street breaks the blank day.

            —Alfred, Lord Tennyson, "In Memoriam"

AUGUST 1908

You do understand, Mr. Harris, that what I'm about to tell you regarding your father's will is merely a formality, given his financial situation at the time of his death?"

"Yes."

"Although your father's intentions can't be carried out, I thought you might wish to know what they were."

"Thank you. Please proceed."

Mr. Chiddington, in proper lawyerly fashion, began to explain in great detail what Philip Harris had intended to do with his money and assets before entering into a series of failed business deals that put him in debt. It didn't really matter, not so much because the money and assets no longer existed, but because Paul could not currently concentrate on details—any

196

details. He hadn't been able to think clearly since receiving the news three weeks earlier that his father had died of a heart attack during a business trip to France.

This foggy state of unreality had descended upon Paul from the moment the telegram had arrived from France. Nevertheless, he did everything that was expected of him as the head of the family—a ridiculous title, he thought, for someone who was the only member of Philip's immediate family, at least since Bianca's desertion. Paul notified the extended family of Philip's death and arranged to have his body brought back to England. The bishop had kindly offered to officiate at the funeral, so Paul conferred with him and gave him the information he needed to fill out the register. The bishop had also arranged for Paul to keep his residence and housekeeper until his mourning period ended.

Paul hadn't yet shed a tear or even felt particularly sad, and he wondered when he would feel human again. He had counseled enough bereaved parishioners to know that his sense of unreality was normal, but it was still unnerving. He couldn't believe he would never see or speak to his father again. He kept expecting Philip to walk into the room and laugh about the capital joke he had played on everyone.

What haunted Paul most was the possibility that his decision to decline the deanship had played a part in his father's death. Philip had made Paul's ambitions his own, and he certainly hadn't understood Paul's decision, as their last conversation made clear. He reminded himself of Philip's exhausted look during their last conversation, even before Paul mentioned the deanship, as well as the shifty visitor with whom Philip had closeted himself in the library. But it didn't matter how many times Paul told himself that his father's financial problems were probably the greater strain on his heart. Paul couldn't help reproaching himself for these things too: if he hadn't been so consumed by the deanship for so long, perhaps he would have noticed earlier that something was wrong and could have encouraged his father to confide in him.

After Mr. Chiddington left, Paul remained in his study and tried to work, but he kept forgetting what he was writing and staring blankly at the wall instead. He didn't notice until Mrs. Rigby knocked on his study door that the afternoon had turned to evening and the room had grown dark.

"Canon—er, Mr. Harris, your mother is here."

His mother? He had never invited Bianca to his house, and she would not arrive unannounced. When she came to London, they usually met in a neutral public place, a place that suited the formality of their relationship.

But when he went into the front hall, his mother was indeed there, looking sheepish and holding a suspiciously large carpetbag, suggesting her intention to stay longer than a few hours.

"Mother, what are you doing here?" He tried to make up for his unwelcoming tone of voice by embracing her, albeit stiffly.

"Paul, dear, how are you?" she asked, pulling away to look anxiously into his face. "I hope you don't mind. I was just so worried about you rattling about alone in your house that I had to see you."

"I'm fine. You needn't have worried."

"Would you mind very much if I stayed with you for a few days, just to assure myself you're all right?"

In fact, he did mind. His mother, with her penchant for dramatics and general intrusiveness, would only disorder his orderly existence. And her very presence seemed an insult to the memory of his father. Furthermore, he could think of several other people whom he would prefer as houseguests if he were desperate for company. But his mother was here now, and he couldn't very well turn her away without causing an unpleasant scene and feeling guilty about it later.

"As you wish," he said.

Paul asked Mrs. Rigby to prepare the spare room for his mother and went back into his study, ostensibly to give his mother time to settle in. In reality, he needed to steel himself for her visit.

Paul reemerged for dinner and sat down with Bianca at the table. Mrs. Rigby had worked a miracle, for Paul didn't eat at home often and there wasn't usually much food in the house. Somehow, his housekeeper had procured a pair of roast hens, mashed potatoes, stewed mushrooms, sprouts, and a lobster salad. Bianca exclaimed enthusiastically over the food, and Paul was grateful for it, too, realizing he hadn't eaten yet that day. But when Mrs. Rigby withdrew and the topic of their dinner was exhausted, an awkward silence fell between mother and son.

"I'm glad your housekeeper takes such good care of you," Bianca ventured after a few minutes. "I was worried you might not be eating. You never were a hearty eater, especially when you were troubled."

Her tone of concern grated on Paul's ears—it sounded contrived. He had eaten quite enough to keep himself alive for many years without his mother's help, and he resented her definitive statements about the effect of his mental state on his eating habits. He couldn't reply without sounding rude, so he remained silent.

"What have you been doing with your time since you resigned your canonry?" Bianca asked.

Paul had written to tell her about his resignation and that he wanted to explore other avenues of ministry. In fact, his last day at the cathedral had been the day of his father's death, though he hadn't known it until later.

"It's only been a few weeks," he told her. "Most of that time I've spent arranging Father's affairs, as well as his funeral and burial."

"Oh." She looked distressed. "Did all of that go well? I mean, was it a great deal of work for you?"

"Oh, yes, it went well," he said coldly. "As well as a funeral and burial can be expected to go."

"You know what I meant." Her eyes pleaded with him from across the table. "I wish I could have helped you with something . . . some of the arrangements, perhaps. I hated to think of you doing everything alone."

The only thing that would have been worse than arranging his father's funeral and burial alone would have been doing it with his mother. Even she wouldn't have the nerve to appear in public as the grieving widow of the husband she'd left for another man.

Desperate to change the subject, Paul asked, "How is James?" He was proud of himself for being able to utter the name of Bianca's lover so casually. It was the first time he had ever spoken it aloud. It seemed odd to use his Christian name, but what else could Paul call him—Mr. Anbrey? Father? The first was too formal and the second preposterous, if technically true.

Bianca's face instantly brightened. "He's well, thank you. The father of a new family that moved to Ingleford a few months ago was very ill with some sort of lung problem, and after James treated him, his condition improved dramatically. The family was very grateful to James, and they invite us for tea regularly now."

"I'm surprised he can do without you for a few days." Paul realized belatedly that he sounded mean-spirited, but it wasn't his intention.

"It was his idea for me to come. He thought I could perhaps be of some comfort to you."

Paul stared back at her dumbly. The beautiful middle-aged woman who sat across the table from him, with her fading red-gold hair and drab, grayish-green dress (at least she didn't pretend to be in mourning), was a stranger to him. The loquacious, affectionate mother he had known as a child couldn't be the same person as this awkward older woman who didn't seem to know how to talk to him. The gulf between them was too great to be bridged, though despite his resentment towards her, something inside him wanted to bridge it. But didn't she understand that she was the last person he wanted to see now?

To Paul's dismay, Bianca seemed to take his silence as encouragement, and she began to speak glowingly of Philip. "People always gravitated towards him, you know, because of his warmth. He loved meeting new people and learning about their lives and interests. And he was such a good businessman—shrewd, a good judge of character. That's why he did so well."

Paul didn't consider telling her that Philip hadn't done so well, after all. He merely gritted his teeth and tried to appear interested while Bianca retold the story of how she and Philip had met. Philip hadn't judged her for being an unmarried mother and Paul, just a year old when they met, had taken to him instantly. Paul had been a difficult baby, but he would let Philip hold him and calm him when even Bianca couldn't.

"And he loved teaching you things when you were little," Bianca went on. "He would answer your questions about everything, from where God lives to what causes rain. I sometimes grew impatient with you during that stage, but he didn't, and if he didn't know the answer, he would go to great lengths to find it out. He even wrote to an Oxford don once to get an answer—now, what was the question? I can't seem to remember—"

"I would rather not hear you speak of my father, if you please," Paul cut in.

Bianca looked startled. "But surely you wish to remember what a wonderful father he was to you."

"I can do that without your help. Besides, if you thought he was so wonderful, why did you leave him?"

"You know why I left. It had nothing to do with him and everything to do with me and James. I'm speaking of Philip as a father to you. I thought you'd want to know what he was like when you were very young, things you wouldn't remember."

"I don't want to hear those things from you."

Bianca's eyes filled with tears. "How can you be so cold and unfeeling? You aren't the only person affected by Philip's death. I was his wife, and a wife knows her husband better than anyone else. Nobody can possibly know what I'm feeling."

A shaft of ice went through Paul's heart. He had forgotten how irrational and cruel his mother could be, however unintentionally. The very accusation that he was cold and unfeeling when he had just lost the person he loved most in the world was the worst insult he could imagine. But now that she was upset, whatever he said would only make it worse.

Paul stood abruptly. "I'm going to retire early. Please let Mrs. Rigby know if you need anything."

Bianca reached out her hand to him, still tearful. "Paul, I know you and I don't always understand each other, but surely we can comfort each other . . . lean on each other during this sad time."

Paul ignored her hand and said, "I'm tired, Mother. We can talk more tomorrow."

The relief he felt once he was alone in his bedroom was fleeting, out-weighed almost immediately by anger. What exactly was so sad about this time for her? It was no secret that she had never loved Philip. Did she really expect Paul to comfort her when he was the one who most needed comfort? He was also troubled to realize that the anger he felt towards his mother for her past desertion was still as strong as it had been when he was just fifteen. He wasn't a child any longer. Why was it so difficult to forgive her?

Part of his life—his life at the cathedral—was over, and the next part hadn't yet begun. Even God seemed far away. Paul's past seemed full of mistakes, false longings, attempts to be someone he was not, and people who had disappointed or hurt him. Why should his future be any better? It stretched out ahead of him like an endless, desolate road in the wilderness.

18

If you promised, you might grieve
    For lost liberty again;
If I promised, I believe
    I should fret to break the chain:
Let us be the friends we were,
    Nothing more but nothing less;
Many thrive on frugal fare
    Who would perish of excess.

       —Christina Rossetti, "Promises Like Pie-Crust"

Lilia hesitated at the front door of Paul's house. She had written him a letter of condolence when she'd first heard of Philip's death, but she had been thinking about him a great deal since then and wanted to see for herself whether he was all right.

She knew he might not want to see her. She had made him uncomfortable during their last visit by telling him she missed him, and she wished she hadn't said it. But before her unfortunate comment, they had talked the way they once had, the rare kind of conversation that bypassed surface concerns to get to the heart of a matter. She wasn't so naïve as to think they could pretend his proposal hadn't happened, but the friendship they had built had to count for something. In any case, she was here now and he could refuse to see her if he chose—though she hoped he wouldn't.

When Paul's housekeeper showed Lilia into the drawing room, she was surprised to see Bianca, who gave a cry of delight and rose to embrace her.

"Lilia, how wonderful to see you! I was hoping I'd see you while I'm in London."

"Where is Paul?"

"He had to do something at the lawyer's office—sign some papers, I think. I expect him to return soon."

"How long have you been here?"

"Two days. I'm going back to Ingleford tomorrow. Shall I ring for tea?"

"Yes, please." Lilia wondered if Paul had invited his mother to stay with him or if she had invited herself. Knowing her aunt, the latter option was most likely. She sat in a wingback chair across from Bianca.

"I'm afraid I surprised Paul when I arrived," Bianca said, confirming Lilia's suspicion. "I couldn't bear the thought of him being alone at such a time."

"How is he?"

Bianca sighed. "I don't know. He's been so quiet. He disappears into his study all the time. Whenever I try to talk about Philip, he becomes angry with me. Everything I say is wrong, it seems. I want to comfort him, but I don't think he wants me here."

Lilia felt sorry for Bianca, but she was also surprised her aunt would expect Paul to speak of Philip with her. Given their family history, Lilia understood why he wouldn't.

"Perhaps he just needs more time," Lilia said. "He'll talk when he's ready."

"But it's so strange. Some men seem to have no feelings, or if they do, it's impossible to get at them, but Paul isn't like that. Since he was a child, he's always felt things so deeply—he is very like James that way. It can't be good for him to preserve this cold silence. Perhaps he feels nothing, but surely that's unnatural."

Sad, no doubt, Lilia thought. *He feels sad.*

The subject of their conversation walked in a few minutes later, and Lilia saw for herself the cold remoteness of which his mother had spoken. Paul took Lilia's hand briefly in greeting but didn't meet her eyes, and he seemed distracted as he sat down to join them for tea. He inquired politely about Lilia's health and her work, then asked his mother which train she had decided to take to Ingleford the next day. His pleasant manner didn't mask the tension between him and Bianca. Perhaps he had forgotten Bianca's tendency to become garrulous and insensitive when she was uncomfortable, but Lilia saw through these mannerisms to her genuine love for her son. Paul clearly did not, and the more Bianca talked, the more visibly tense he became.

"How is Mr. Chiddington? I haven't seen him in years," Bianca said to Paul, adding for Lilia's benefit, "He's the family lawyer. A very good one, too."

Lilia saw a muscle tighten in Paul's jaw, but all he said was, "He is well."

"Why, Paul, I've just had a wonderful idea," Bianca proclaimed. "Now that you have no ties to the cathedral and no responsibilities yet anywhere else, why don't you take a trip somewhere, perhaps to the Continent? It would be a refreshing change for you, wouldn't it? Your father must have left you enough money to be comfortable without having to work for a while."

"That's not possible," Paul said curtly. He ran a hand through his hair, which was already disheveled, and stared at the far end of the room.

"Why not?" Bianca asked, clearly disappointed that he didn't think her idea as wonderful as she did.

Lilia interposed then, trying to spare Paul the necessity of replying when he obviously didn't want to. "Aunt Bianca, have you been to the Continent?"

Bianca kept looking at her son, resisting Lilia's attempted derailment, but he neither returned her gaze nor spoke. Finally, she turned to Lilia and said, "When I was still with Philip, he often took me with him on his business trips. I visited France and Italy with him a number of times. He did so love France—it's rather apt he should die there."

"I'm surprised you remember," Paul said to his mother in the coldest tone Lilia had ever heard him use.

"Remember what?" Bianca asked, surprised.

"What my father loved."

"I remember a great deal," she said quietly.

"What you don't seem to remember is that you left him for another man, so you would oblige me if you wouldn't act the part of the loving, bereaved wife in my presence."

Bianca's face fell with shock and hurt.

"Paul, I don't think that's the impression your mother meant to give," Lilia said, compelled to defend Bianca against this unprovoked attack. "She lived with your father for many years, so she would know his likes and dislikes."

Paul turned on Lilia, his tone changing from ice to fire. "What makes you think you have a right to interfere? And why is it that you're both so adept at interfering when you're not wanted and disappearing when you are?"

Without waiting for a response, he rose and stalked out of the room. Bianca and Lilia exchanged a stunned look, but Lilia was quicker to recover. She wasn't hurt by his words, as he was clearly upset and not himself, and she could see some truth in what he'd said.

"You see how it is," Bianca said as she started to cry. "He doesn't want me here. I should go at once. It would be a relief to him."

"No, don't do that," Lilia said, torn between sympathy and frustration. Frustration was winning, for Bianca's tendency towards self-pity could be grating. "Regardless of what he says, he does need you."

"What am I to do?"

"I don't know, exactly. Just try to be patient with him, and don't speak of Philip."

"I don't understand that," Bianca said, sniffling into her handkerchief.

Lilia sensed there was nothing she could say to help her aunt understand. In any case, she was more worried about Paul, who seemed utterly alone in a prison of his own making.

"I'm going to try to talk to him," Lilia decided aloud.

"Would you? I'd appreciate that, for you see I can say nothing right. Perhaps you can make him understand that I do care about him."

As Lilia rose from her chair and went in search of Paul, she had no intention of trying to make him understand anything. She hoped only to understand him better and to offer comfort, if she could.

From the front hallway she saw that his study door was closed. Lilia knocked and tried the handle. It wasn't locked, so she opened the door slowly, saying, "Paul, may I come in?"

He was sitting at his desk behind piles of papers. As she entered the room, he looked at her as if he had forgotten she was in his house.

She closed the door behind her and went to stand in front of his desk. "You seem to have quite a lot of work to do," she said after a moment of silence, and looked at the papers. "Are those from the lawyer?"

He nodded. "My father's affairs were not exactly in order when he died," he said. "Look at this." He handed her a letter from the top of a pile.

She sat down in the nearest chair and perused the letter. It took her a few minutes to understand, because of the convoluted legal language, but she slowly gathered that Philip's business had been in dire financial straits. He had left a great deal of debt.

Looking up, she said, "Did you know of these troubles before your father died?"

"He didn't say a word to me about any of this. You won't tell my mother, will you? I don't want her to have reason to criticize him."

"I won't tell her. Will selling his house pay off the debt?"

208   CLARISSA HARWOOD

"No. I just learned today in my meeting with the lawyer how extensive the debt is. Even if everything he owned free and clear is sold, it won't make up more than half the debt. I have some money saved that I could put towards it, but even so . . ." His voice trailed off.

Lilia could only imagine how much this news must pain him. "Paul, I'm so sorry."

"If I had paid more attention to him, perhaps he would have told me his troubles," he continued, "but I was so ridiculously focused on the deanship that I ignored everyone around me. While my father was struggling with his business, falling further into debt, with nobody to talk to, I was consumed with visions of my own greatness—puerile shadows of the magnificent church leader I thought I could become." His voice broke, and he averted his gaze.

Without hesitation, Lilia rose and went to his side. She put her hand on his shoulder and said, "Don't be so cruel to yourself, Paul. I can't bear it."

Still seated, he turned to her blindly, slipping his arms around her waist and burying his face against her. Lilia stroked his hair as he began to weep. She had never touched his hair before. It was soft and thick, and there were strands of darker gold beneath the lighter ones.

When he stopped crying, he made no move to release her, his face still hidden against her breast. Lilia rested her cheek on top of his head and stroked his back. The intimacy of their posture felt oddly natural.

After a while, he pulled back and took out his handkerchief to wipe his eyes. Then he stood up and, taking her hand, led her around his desk to the two chairs in front of it.

"Will you stay a little longer?" he asked as he sat in one chair, and drew the other close to his.

"Of course." She sat, and he took both of her hands, his elbows on his knees, bowing his head as if in prayer. She noticed that the sun must have set, for the room was growing dim.

He looked up and said, "I'm sorry I lost my temper in the drawing room. I shouldn't have said what I did about your interfering."

"Don't give it another thought. You were quite right about me."

"I don't know about that. I needed you today, and you didn't disappear."

"That's true." She searched his face. "Paul, I don't believe your decision to decline the deanship had any part in your father's death. He loved you and would have supported any vocation you followed. Even someone who knew him as little as I did could see that."

Paul raised his hand to her face, gently brushing away a tear she hadn't known was there. "Sweet Lilia," he said softly. "Do you always weep when you console others?"

She shook her head dumbly, shocked by the thrill that went through her when his fingers touched her face.

"You know," he said, gripping her forearm lightly, "it always surprises me how small and delicate your bones are. When I'm not touching you, I assume you're made of iron. Unbending and unbreakable."

"You make me sound like a machine," she whispered.

"As I said, I think it only when I'm not touching you."

They exchanged a long look. A very long look. Lilia realized she was holding her breath, and she forced herself to take in some air, but her blood pounded in her head and she couldn't look away. Their faces were mere inches apart, and the danger was upon her before she could avoid it. She leaned closer, aware only of wanting him.

Paul didn't move, but she heard his breathing quicken.

She knew she shouldn't take advantage of his vulnerable emotional state. But a kind of madness possessed her and she pressed her lips against his. He went still for a few seconds, but then he returned the kiss, gently at first, then passionately. His hand moved to the back of her neck, under her hair, caressing her bare skin and making her tingle all over.

Their tongues met, tentative and exploring. His hand moved from her neck to her collarbone, skimming lightly over the thin silk of her blouse, then down to her breast. When his thumb brushed her nipple, she drew in her breath and pressed closer.

Paul pulled away as abruptly as if she had set him on fire. He yanked his chair to a safer distance and dropped his head into his hands.

"I'm sorry," she said, trembling. "I meant only to comfort you. As a friend."

It sounded as though he said, "Damn you," but it wasn't like him to use such language and his voice was muffled, so she couldn't be sure.

He took a deep breath and raised his head to look at her. "There are some things I understand better than you do. If you try to be my friend, you'll only torture me. Either that, or we'll become lovers and I'll have to leave the ministry. Either way, I'll eventually come to hate you, as well as myself. Is that what you want?"

"Of course not."

"Then you have two choices: marry me, or leave me alone."

"If those are my choices," she said slowly, "I'll leave you alone."

"Coward."

He spoke the word softly, but it hit her with the force of a hammer blow. Lilia had been called many names, but never that.

"Did you hear me?" Paul said. His eyes had taken on a strange, feverish glow. "I said you're a coward. You love me—it shows in your eyes and the way you touch me and the tone of your voice. Do you deny it?"

"No," she whispered.

"And still you choose to walk away?"

"Yes."

"Go, then."

She was trembling so violently that it was difficult to stand up. She smoothed her skirt, avoiding his eyes, and said, "I don't want to part in anger."

"I'm not angry." His voice was, indeed, admirably calm. "I've finally discovered the one battle you won't fight, though I think it's one of the few worth fighting. Goodbye, Lilia."

"Goodbye, Paul." She turned and left the room.

Bianca was still in the dining room. Lilia stammered an awkward farewell, ignoring her aunt's questions, and fled.

When she was at home and calm enough to think about what Paul had said, she was struck by how wrong he was about her not fighting this battle. She felt as weak and bruised as an unarmed foot soldier on the losing side of a war.

19

Thou art indeed just, Lord, if I contend

With thee; but, sir, so what I plead is just.

Why do sinners' ways prosper? and why must

Disappointment all I endeavour end?

      —Gerard Manley Hopkins, "Thou Art Indeed Just, Lord"

SEPTEMBER 1908

Paul's least favorite part of his new post as vicar of Ingleford was standing at the church door after the Sunday service, greeting parishioners as they filed out. If the greetings had been perfunctory and polite, as they had been at the cathedral, he wouldn't have minded, but his rural parishioners were in the habit of engaging in long, rambling monologues about everything from the weather to the daily activities of their distant cousins. Even worse, others made no scruple to criticize his High Church practices.

Mr. and Mrs. Bedner, parents of four unruly children, greeted him pleasantly enough. But as Mrs. Bedner paused in the open doorway to separate two of her squabbling sons, Mr. Bedner said, "Those candles on the altar are an eyesore, Vicar. Could you remove them?"

Paul suppressed a sigh. How could candles offend these people? It wasn't as if he were using incense or the Eastward position.

"We like things simple," Mr. Bedner added, as if reading his mind. "It's just a small step from candles on the altar to smells and bells."

"Indeed" was all Paul could manage.

Old Mrs. Brown must have heard the exchange, for she shuffled past him shaking her head and muttering, "No popery."

The criticisms weren't a complete surprise to him. When he had accepted the post, the bishop had warned him that the previous vicar had been so Low Church as to be almost Puritan, so Paul would need to change some of his own practices to avoid shocking his new parish. Paul was willing to compromise, but the parishioners didn't seem to be. Even the small changes he had made—such as the candles on the altar—were suspicious, dangerous, and, to some, downright heretical.

Ingleford was the last place Paul had wanted to go. He had no desire to live in the same village as James and his mother or Lilia's family, but it turned out to be the only position immediately available. Given the difficulties of his father's financial affairs, Paul couldn't afford to be choosy. Besides, the post was temporary. Mr. Russell, the previous vicar, had taken a year's leave of absence to recover his health. Paul's mother told him the villagers believed Mr. Russell's health had broken down on account of his shrewish wife. Bianca didn't seem to see the irony in her enjoyment of village gossip. Perhaps she had forgotten how it felt to be the subject of it.

Paul gazed longingly at the bright blue sky from the church doorway. It had rained that morning, but the sky was now clear, leaving a perfect autumn day. At least most of the parishioners had left, and he wouldn't have to stay at the church much longer. Being solely responsible for the spiritual life and activities of an entire parish was more draining on his energy than the more limited duties of a cathedral canon. He had suspected as much before arriving, but the reality took some getting used to.

"Good morning, Parson," Timothy Gill said, shaking Paul's hand heartily. "Fine sermon."

"Thank you," Paul replied, wondering if he would ever get used to his new title. It was a relief to see Timothy's friendly face. He was a good-natured carpenter who seemed content to take the good and the bad in everything, including vicars.

"The roof seems to be holding up," Timothy said.

Paul's first Sunday service in Ingleford three weeks earlier had been dramatically interrupted by a thunderstorm, followed by water pouring from a leak in the church roof directly upon the purple-feathered hat of the squire's wife. Her shriek had drowned out the organ and the ensuing commotion had made it impossible to continue the service. Paul had seen nothing for it but to join the congregation as they'd gathered containers to catch the water.

Timothy had attempted to fix the leak, but when it rained again during the sermon that morning, Paul was certain he had seen a trickle of water running down the back wall.

"It's certainly better," Paul said, not wanting to contradict the other man outright, "but I'd like you to check it again tomorrow. Until I preach a sermon on Noah's ark and the flood, which I have no intention of doing soon, I prefer not to receive aid from the elements."

Paul closed up the now-empty church, looking forward to his walk home. The little house he had rented was a pleasant half-mile walk down a wooded lane.

But his freedom was not yet to be realized. The village squire, Mr. Nesbit, appeared to be inspecting the church grounds and, upon Paul's approach, said, "Mr. Harris, may I have a word?"

Paul hastily reassembled his public face. "Certainly."

"You're doing a fine job," Nesbit began. "I know this parish is nothing like what you're used to, and I appreciate your patience with us."

"Thank you. It is indeed very different."

He wasn't deceived by the compliment. Nesbit was a consummate politician, always genial and smooth on the surface, but he was good friends with Mr. Russell and was as resistant to change as the other parishioners, even if he expressed that resistance more subtly.

"If I might ask for further patience on your part," Nesbit went on, "the way you celebrate the Eucharist is . . . well, a little distracting."

"How so?"

"Elevating the elements above your head. Kneeling in front of the altar. I have no doubt you have good reason for such spiritual calisthenics, but would you consider restraining yourself a bit? As a High Churchman, I'm sure you desire that calm, meditative state of mind for all parishioners during such an important part of the service. But your actions make such a state of mind difficult for some of us."

"I see," Paul said wearily, nearing the limit of his patience with parishioner complaints. "I appreciate your concern and will certainly consider what you've said."

"Thank you, Vicar. I do apologize for the stubbornness of your new flock. It must be trying for an intelligent young man such as yourself."

"Not at all."

When Nesbit was finally gone, Paul felt an ache at his temples that he knew would spread and tighten around his head like a metal vise if he didn't rest soon.

"You look as though you could use some amusement. Care to join me in the graveyard?"

Paul turned to see Edward Brooke waving at him from the small cemetery beside the church.

Edward, a sculptor, was three-and-twenty, the second of Lilia's four brothers and the only one who currently lived in Ingleford. Paul remembered little of Edward from their brief meeting as children, but, as Edward himself had pointed out, he was quieter than his boisterous brothers and people tended not to remember him when the others were present.

If anyone but Edward had interfered with his long-awaited freedom, Paul would have found an excuse to get away. But Edward's warm, friendly demeanor had put Paul at ease from the moment they'd met, and, despite thinking it prudent not to cultivate close relationships with Lilia's family members, he was in need of a friend. It also helped that Edward looked nothing like his older sister, having inherited their mother's short stature and golden-brown hair.

Paul went to where Edward stood near the entrance to the graveyard and said, "I'm more than ready for amusement, not to mention curious about how I'll find it here."

"You'll see." Edward grinned. "Mrs. Hill was unhappy with the angel I carved on her husband's gravestone—she thought it looked like a cupid. She's insisted I change it to avoid the danger of pagan associations, but unfortunately, the alterations I've just made have turned it into something else entirely. Could you look at it? I'm hoping what I think it resembles is not what anyone else thinks."

Paul assented to Edward's request and they made their way to Mr. Hill's gravestone, the largest and grandest in the cemetery. The carving stood out prominently against the black marble, and Paul stopped short.

"Oh, I see." Paul frowned and tried to imagine an angel instead of what he actually saw.

"What does it look like to you?"

"Well . . ."

"No need to be polite. Tell me the truth."

"It looks like a walrus," Paul admitted, wincing.

Edward gave a groan of anguish. "That's what I thought. Mrs. Hill will have my head for this."

"Surely not."

"You don't understand. When Mr. Hill was alive, he bore a very strong resemblance to a walrus. It's a well-known fact among the villagers."

Paul laughed, the first time he had done so since his father's death. He felt surprised, pleased, and guilty all at the same time.

"That *is* a problem," he said to Edward.

"What am I to do now?" the other man demanded, though he too was smiling.

"Would it work to carve two angels? The right side of the walrus"— Paul suppressed a chuckle and pointed at the carving—"that long line there, couldn't it be the beginning of another angel's cloak, or perhaps a trumpet?"

"Perhaps." Edward squinted at the carving and sighed. "I'll have to think about it. I'm on my way to my parents' house for lunch. Would you like to join us? They won't mind."

But Paul's headache was worsening and he knew lunch with Lilia's family would be too much for him, so he politely excused himself.

He walked at a leisurely pace down the lane to his house, marveling at the silence, which was punctuated by an occasional birdsong. Having lived his whole life in the city, Paul had thought he might have trouble adjusting to country life, but he loved the quiet and fresh air.

Paul's house was a modest gray stone Tudor-style cottage. It needed some repairs, but the mullioned windows and the way it was nestled in a clearing in a little wood had charmed him. It was also a safe distance from his mother's house and that of Lilia's parents. His mother was delighted that he had moved to Ingleford, but since their last uncomfortable visit in London, they had come to an unspoken agreement: she would not mention Philip, and Paul would not speak disrespectfully or unkindly of James.

A large gray cat sat on his doorstep. Paul nearly tripped over it, as it was exactly the same shade of gray as the stones.

"Go away," he said to it. "I don't like cats. Find a home where someone will appreciate you."

Paul had never had pets, and the cat didn't seem to understand that he didn't want it. When the cat had first appeared, he had asked his neighbors if it belonged to them, but nobody seemed to know anything about it. It had continued to appear on his doorstep every day since with an expectant look on its face.

The cat didn't move, its green eyes narrowing into slits. Paul fancied that it looked smug. He stepped over it, as he always did, let himself into the house, and found that Mrs. Mills, the village woman he had hired to clean and cook for him, had already left.

There were disadvantages to the peace and quiet. His new duties kept his mind fully occupied during the day, but as soon as he was at home alone, his last encounter with Lilia would come back to him in vivid detail—that passionate kiss, the warmth and softness of her body, her inability to deny that she loved him. It gave him a spark of hope, despite her decision to leave him alone. Sometimes he even toyed with the idea of leaving the ministry for her, but even if he wasn't sure what form his future would take, he couldn't imagine giving up his calling. Nor could he see himself in a free union, even for Lilia. Thus, he tried his best not to dwell on the memory of those matchless lips against his, for such thoughts only weakened his resolve not to seek her out.

The following week, Paul returned to London. He had to see Mr. Chiddington to take care of some lingering problems with his father's estate. After leaving the lawyer's office, he hesitated on the street corner, his resolve not to see Lilia nearly forgotten. He knew the WSPU office was only a few blocks away. Perhaps he could walk that way, and if Lilia happened to be coming or going, they would meet as if by accident. But after a few minutes of indecision, he talked himself out of it. He still had errands to do in London and could decide later.

His last errand was a visit to Mary Braddock. He had entrusted Canon Johnson with overseeing the house of refuge, but Mary had recently been deemed well enough to go home. She had written to assure him that she was safe and feeling better, but he wanted to judge for himself.

Mary lived in an East End tenement, and Paul found her alone in the tiny front room, its yellowed wallpaper peeling and stained. Mary herself looked well, with color in her cheeks and her leg propped up on a cushioned stool. She was glad to see him, and told him that her leg was healing well. She could even walk on it and would demonstrate, if he wished.

"That won't be necessary," he hastened to say. "Why not stay off your feet as long as you can? You won't do yourself any favors by risking reinjury to that leg."

"I want to get back to work for the WSPU."

"Do they have more sedentary work you can do? Office work, perhaps?"

"I'm not an office girl. I can't type or even write well. What I'm good at is breakin' things."

He tried to hide a smile. "Perhaps you can discover a new skill. Leave the physical activities to women who are stronger."

"That's exactly what Miss Brooke said not an hour ago," she said.

"Miss Brooke? She was here?" Paul looked around the room as if Lilia would materialize merely by his speaking her name.

"Aye. She left just before you came."

Paul was seized by an undignified desire to run out into the street, hoping for a glimpse of Lilia. But he managed to stay where he was.

"I wrote to her yesterday, when I got here," Mary said, "and she came as soon as she could. I knew she would, even though I told her not to bother. Mr. Reed came with her."

Paul felt a sudden chill even though the room was overwarm. He had hoped never to hear that man's name again.

"Have you met Mr. Reed?" Mary asked.

"Yes," Paul replied grimly.

"He calls himself the Union's errand boy—he does odd jobs for us, fixin' broken chairs and carryin' heavy boxes, even though he's got heaps of money. Not that he said so, of course, but one of the other girls told me he stays at the Savoy Hotel."

"I see." Paul hoped that his flat tone would discourage Mary from going on about Will Reed, but she didn't seem to notice.

"It's too bad men can't be WSPU members. He's been workin' ever so hard for us. Well, not for us so much as for Miss Brooke. I made a bet with Alice Marks that Mr. Reed will ask Miss Brooke to marry him before the month is out."

Paul frowned.

Misunderstanding the reason for Paul's expression, Mary said, "I know bets aren't strictly right, Mr. Harris, but it's not gamblin', really. It's just in fun."

"Do you think Miss Brooke will accept him?" Paul regretted the question as soon as he asked it. If Lilia was willing to torture him, it didn't follow that he must also torture himself.

"Not likely. She always says she'll never marry, and I'm sure she wouldn't move to New Zealand. Maybe he would stay here, though. She likes him, that's certain, but he might not want to be her third love."

"What do you mean?"

"Miss Brooke doesn't love anyone as much as she loves the WSPU. Mrs. Pankhurst is second in her heart. Mr. Reed will have to take third place." Mary grinned at her own cleverness.

Paul suspected Mary was right, but he was supremely tired of the painful subjects of Lilia, marriage, and Will Reed. "Tell me about your home life," he said. "Are you safe here?"

"Aye, no need to worry about him." Mary never spoke her uncle's name. "He's been arrested for assaulting a constable and won't be out of prison for a long time. You must think my family loves jail, for all the time we spend there."

Paul assured Mary he thought nothing of the sort and was only happy that, for the time being at least, she was safe from her uncle's violence. He promised to check on her the next time he was in London, then left hastily, before she could reintroduce the subject of Will Reed.

By the time he was on the train back to Ingleford, Paul had convinced himself that his talk with Mary had been exactly what he needed. He also had a plan: every time his mind drifted to Lilia, he would think of Will Reed, too. Surely that ice water would cool his feverish longings. But when he was forced to put the plan into practice almost immediately, all it did was leave him in despair.

20

"How that man could talk. He electrified large meetings. He had faith—don't you see?—he had the faith. He could get himself to believe anything—anything. He would have been a splendid leader of an extreme party."

"What party?" I asked.

"Any party," answered the other. "He was an—an—extremist."

—Joseph Conrad, *Heart of Darkness*

September had been a difficult month for the WSPU. Lilia had met with a new MP, Robert Wilton, who was sympathetic to women's suffrage. As a result of their meeting, he put forward a petition in the House of Commons to support a women's suffrage amendment to the Reform Act. Unfortunately, his petition was defeated, and Lilia was hard-pressed to hide her discouragement. She couldn't help wondering how much longer she and her colleagues would be able to fight for the vote when they made so little headway.

There was one bit of exciting news: Mrs. Pankhurst was planning to leave for a lecture tour in America in a month and had appointed Lilia her deputy. Lilia was thrilled with the promotion, but some women who had been WSPU members longer were not. There were already divisions within the ranks regarding the hierarchical organization of the Union, but Mrs. Pankhurst had never pretended it was a democracy and didn't trouble to justify her decisions to promote some and demote others. While Lilia didn't agree in theory with Mrs. Pankhurst's methods, she considered them minor annoyances that were worth overlooking in light of the older woman's excellent leadership. In order to get the results they wanted, it was necessary for WSPU members to set aside petty disagreements and focus on their common goals. Thus, Lilia tried to bear the new chilliness from her colleagues patiently, but it wasn't easy.

She went to a luncheon party one afternoon given by Lady Fernham, hoping for a respite from her work troubles. But as the guests, all WSPU members, assembled in Lady Fernham's drawing room, their conversation naturally drifted to the Cause. Miss Selwyn, a senior member who had cherished hopes of being Mrs. Pankhurst's deputy, seemed particularly insistent upon introducing controversial subjects. Although she was a hard worker, she always objected loudly to new ideas unless they were her own. She also held surprisingly conservative views for a militant suffragette. Lilia thought Miss Selwyn would be happier in the NUWSS.

"I think we ought to talk about Mary Braddock," Miss Selwyn announced, perching on the edge of an overstuffed chair. "She ought to be censured for the orchid house business."

Two weeks earlier, Mary had broken into the orchid house at Kew Gardens and destroyed some of the valuable plants. This act had not been approved by Mrs. Pankhurst, but it was consistent with the WSPU's practice of destroying property. Mary had escaped without being caught by the police and she proudly admitted her actions to WSPU members.

"Not now," Lilia said. "Mrs. Pankhurst isn't here. Let's save it for our next meeting at Clement's Inn." She took a cigarette from her case and began to search through her skirt pockets for a match.

"Surely you don't need Mrs. Pankhurst to make a decision for you, now that you're her deputy." Miss Selwyn gave Lilia a pointed look. "You must see that Mary and the other hotheads have drawn the wrong sort of publicity to the Cause."

Nettled, Lilia retorted, "Mary is a loyal soldier in our ranks who isn't appreciated as she deserves."

"I expected you to come to her defense, Miss Brooke, being an extremist yourself, but I wonder if Mrs. Pankhurst would agree."

"Miss Brooke and Mrs. Pankhurst are in agreement on all important matters," Lady Fernham put in, reaching over to light Lilia's cigarette. "Naturally, some individual members of the Union will act in ways not perfectly in accordance with our mandate."

"Yes, but they shouldn't get away with it," insisted Miss Selwyn. "Isn't our fight more important than any individual? Shouldn't we at least present a united front to the public?"

"That's the ideal," Lilia said, "but in reality, we can't always do it. And if you had seen Mary as I did the last time she was released from prison, you would have sympathized with her plight. Her leg was broken during her arrest and not properly treated. The prison doctor claimed it was only a sprain."

"I'm sorry for Mary," Miss Selwyn said, "but we can't control what happens in prison."

"Miss Selwyn," Harriet interjected from across the room, "surely you know that working-class women are treated badly in prison, far worse than middle-class ones. Miss Brooke and I are both concerned about what we've witnessed, and I daresay you would be, too."

Waving her hand, Miss Selwyn said, "Oh yes, that's a kind way of pointing out that I haven't put my own life in jeopardy as the rest of you have. I also know that loyalty to Miss Brooke—in this group, at least—is unwavering, so I'll keep quiet."

Lilia's friends tried to defend her, but after an uncomfortable silence and Lady Fernham's unsuccessful attempts to change the subject, Lilia excused herself and—for the first time ever—hid in the lavatory. She was haunted by Paul's accusation that she was a coward. He must have known it would rankle. Was she now becoming a coward in matters of work as well as love?

The lavatory was modern and as attractively decorated as a bedroom, so it was a pleasant place to hide. At odds with the pink floral wallpaper was a painting on the wall of a ship in a storm. The way the ship teetered on the edge of a wave represented perfectly Lilia's own state of mind, and she stared at it as if hypnotized.

When she left the lavatory, Harriet was waiting for her in the corridor.

"Did Miss Selwyn upset you?" Harriet asked.

"Not really. She has a right to believe what she likes about me."

"Don't worry about her. She has an odd way of criticizing people to their faces and praising them behind their backs. She did the same with you: after you left the room she started to speak of all the good things you've done for the WSPU. Even she agreed that nobody can keep up our spirits the way you can."

In a low voice, Lilia asked, "Where am I to turn when I lose *my* spirits?"

"Why, you may turn to us, your friends, of course," Harriet exclaimed in surprise. "All I meant is we believe in you. Whatever is the matter? Something has been troubling you all afternoon, I can tell." Harriet laid her hand on Lilia's arm.

"Forgive me," Lilia said with a sigh. "I don't know what's wrong except I feel cross and out of sorts today. Perhaps I'm losing hope that we'll get the vote, though I didn't want to admit it in front of the others. This morning I reread John Stuart Mill's *The Subjection of Women*. He published it almost forty years ago, but we're still repeating his arguments for establishing equality between the sexes over and over again. What has changed since then? When will people listen to us?"

"They will. Don't lose heart."

Lilia was too dispirited to reply. She returned to the drawing room and tried to be cordial, but she left the party early. She refused Harriet's offer to walk home with her because she thought she needed to be alone, but once she was on the street, she felt an immense loneliness. She had been staying busy and fighting with all her strength to keep the hollow, empty feeling at bay, but it caught up to her now with a vengeance. She told herself it was ridiculous to feel lonely when friends and colleagues were around her all the time. She also told herself there was no point thinking about Paul when any relationship between them was impossible. But she did feel lonely, and she did miss Paul. Perhaps it was time to visit her family. Ingleford was a small village and it would be easy to encounter him there as if by accident.

When she reached the street where she lived, she saw Will striding towards her. When he saw her, he sprang forward and lifted her off her feet, enveloping her in a bear hug.

"Will, you barbarian! Put me down this instant!" Lilia cried. "What are you doing here?"

He obeyed, setting her down lightly and grinning at her. "I was at your house, looking for you. Haven't you noticed my absence?"

"What absence?"

"Come, now. We haven't seen each other for at least a week. Tell me you've missed me."

"I haven't missed you a bit," she said with a smile.

"Liar."

Lilia couldn't help liking Will. She found his open, relaxed, flexible temperament particularly refreshing, largely because it was so different from Paul's. She never had to worry about offending Will or having to sort out his complex emotional state—indeed, Will's emotional state seemed to range only from mild to extreme happiness. In fact, Will reminded her of a large, lovable dog, who needed only a pat on the head to please him. He would have disliked this comparison, but Lilia thought it apt.

"What's the matter?" he asked.

"Nothing. Why do you ask?"

"You seem different. More serious than usual."

"I must be serious. My work is important, and it requires a great deal of energy."

"You needn't convince me of that. But don't you ever want to relax and enjoy yourself?"

"Of course. I just haven't got time."

He turned and took both of her hands in his. "Lilia, let me show you how to have fun. Give me this evening to prove to you that pleasure can be as good for you as work."

She hesitated.

"Let me take you to dinner at my hotel," he pressed. "I've been asking for weeks now, and you haven't given me a good reason for refusing. It's time you said yes."

"I don't think—"

"Good. *Don't* think. Come with me."

Still she hesitated.

Will argued, "Surely you're not worried about your reputation. Is all your talk about being a modern woman just talk, after all?"

She knew he was playing a game with her and that she shouldn't take his bait. He liked to challenge her, to push her to prove she wasn't conventional, to put her theories into practice. As silly and childish as the game was, she wanted to win. She would prove that she could do as she liked, and to Hell with anyone who tried to stop her. She agreed to join him for dinner.

Will's hotel, the Savoy, was the grandest hotel in London. Lilia had never been inside, but she knew she would have to change into her best dress. Will waited while Lilia stopped at her house to put on the blue silk gown that Lizzie kept rolling her eyes at. But Lilia didn't wear it often, so it still looked new. What was the point of getting rid of a perfectly good dress, even if it was out of fashion?

But when Lilia and Will entered the luxurious dining room of the hotel and she saw what the other women were wearing, she wished she had suggested a different restaurant. The other women wore elaborate beaded and lace-trimmed gowns and even more elaborate hats. One woman's hat was enormous, a sweep of ostrich feathers in a swirl of tulle.

Will must have sensed Lilia's hesitation, for he looked down at her and said in an undertone, "Welcome to the circus. We'll watch the plumage go by from the safety of a corner table."

She laughed, and it no longer mattered that her dress wasn't new or fashionable.

It seemed to Lilia that the maître d'hôtel treated Will with more deference than he did his other guests, despite the fact that Will's rumpled brown sack coat couldn't possibly meet the dress code requirements. It made her wonder for the first time how wealthy he really was. She knew he had money, but he was so casual and relaxed, very different from her conception of a wealthy person. She couldn't even imagine him dressed in a frock coat like the other men in the dining room. He always looked as though he had come from a hunting expedition or a ramble over a mountain range.

The food was delicious. Lilia had just taken her first bite of dessert, a special creation of the chef's that was called pêche Melba after the Australian singer Nellie Melba, when she noticed Will looking at her with unusual seriousness. Thus far he had been a delightful dinner companion, telling her stories that he thought would amuse her and being his usual lighthearted, charming self.

"You're the most beautiful woman here," he said.

"Will, that's simply not true," she protested. "Look at the blond woman in the red dress over there. She's lovely."

His eyes didn't leave her face. "I saw her. She's all right, but the two of you aren't even in the same category."

She chose not to ask him to explain the classification system he had in mind. "Are there any desserts named after famous New Zealanders?" she asked, hoping to distract him.

"Not to my knowledge." He said no more about her appearance, but he remained serious as they finished their dessert and rose to leave.

Once out of the dining room, Will said, "Would you like to come up to my room? It has a stunning view of the river."

Lilia was not so naïve as to think the invitation was only to see the view. She felt a strange combination of emotions: confusion, curiosity, anxiety, recklessness. And the wine she'd had at dinner didn't help. She rarely drank and she felt fuzzy-headed.

"Why not?" she said with a smile.

Will hadn't exaggerated about the view. His suite of rooms had both east- and south-facing windows, and when he turned out the lights, the city below them came alive. Lilia went to the south window and looked down at the river shimmering with the reflection of light from the lamps on Waterloo Bridge. Then she moved to the east window, where the spire and dome of St. John's Cathedral glowed in the darkness.

Some of the fog in her brain cleared and she began to have second thoughts. What was she doing? She had been playing a child's game with Will, after all.

From behind her, Will placed his hands on her shoulders, and she turned to face him.

"What is it, my dear girl?" he said. "It's not like you to be so quiet."

"It's nothing," she said.

She knew he was going to kiss her. And she was going to let him. Perhaps a kiss from one man was very like a kiss from another.

Will's moustache tickled her skin. It wasn't an unpleasant sensation. He was good at kissing, good enough that she wondered how many other women he'd kissed. But she felt no fire, no tingling, nothing but a scientific sort of curiosity and annoyance with herself for analyzing the moment in such detail.

As she returned the kiss, she willed herself to stop thinking.

But when she felt his hands beginning to unfasten the hooks at the back of her dress, she pulled away. "I can't do this."

"Why not?" he asked.

"I can't explain it."

"Is there someone else? Do I have a rival? I'll kill the bastard," he said cheerfully.

She didn't reply.

"All right, you don't have to tell me." He took her hands in his. "But you should know I've fallen in love with you."

"Oh, Will." She sighed. "I told you not to do that."

"I know, but I couldn't help myself. Will you travel around the world with me? Think of the adventures we'd have. Don't you love me, even a little?"

"No. I'm sorry. Traveling with you does sound wonderful, but I can't."

"Will you marry me, then? You won't have to move to New Zealand. We can make our home here."

"You know I don't want to marry."

"And you won't even share my bed tonight?"

"No." She stepped away, out of his reach. "I'm not the right woman for you. I hope you'll find someone who will love you as you deserve."

He didn't press her, but although he tried to resume his lighthearted manner, she could tell he was hurt. He went down to the lobby with her and hailed a cab. Just before she stepped in, he took her hand and said, "If you change your mind, you know where to find me. But I won't stay in England much longer." His eyes were sad.

"I'm sorry, but I won't change my mind," she said.

In the cab on the way home, Lilia berated herself for her reckless behavior. Until that evening, she had been so careful to keep Will at arm's length. What had possessed her to go to his hotel? It wasn't as if she had been overcome with passion for him. She had been flattered by his attention, and he had proven to her that she wasn't immune to it after all.

The evening with Will had proved something else to her, too. Loath as she was to admit it, there was only one man in the world whose touch she craved. She was starting to realize that, no matter how much time she spent apart from Paul, she couldn't stop thinking about him or wanting him. But she wasn't ready to give in. She would hold on to her resolve—or, from Paul's perspective, her cowardice—as long as she could.

21

No one can say of the modern English girl that she is tender, loving, retiring, or domestic. . . . Love indeed is the last thing she thinks of, and the least of the dangers besetting her. . . . But the Girl of the Period/does not marry easily. Men are afraid of her; and with reason. They may amuse themselves with her for an evening, but they do not readily take her for life.

—Eliza Lynn Linton, "The Girl of the Period" (1883)

Three days after Lilia's evening at the Savoy with Will, Mrs. Pankhurst came to her house for a talk. It was an unusual occasion. Normally, if the Union leader wanted a meeting with Lilia, it would take place at the WSPU office at Clement's Inn or, less frequently, at Mrs. Pankhurst's own house. Thus, Lilia was a little nervous. Not many people could make her nervous, but her leader was one of them.

"I'll get right to the point," Mrs. Pankhurst said as soon as Lizzie had brought the tea and left them alone in the parlor. "Now that you're my deputy, you'll be subjected to more public scrutiny than usual, and I won't be here to advise you."

"Yes, I understand."

"First, let me say that I admire your courage in advocating for reforms that few others dare to speak about. I refer, of course, to your advocacy of contraception and free unions. I don't wish to dampen your enthusiasm, Miss Brooke, but I must urge you to be more diplomatic and to keep your more extreme views private."

"Very well." But Lilia was puzzled. She thought she had been careful not to mention those particular beliefs in front of audiences who wouldn't be open to her views.

Mrs. Pankhurst took a sip of tea. "You ought to know I agree with you on both subjects, but speaking of them in public will only close the ears of the people from whom we most need support."

Lilia nodded blankly.

"It's also very important to keep your private life as blameless as possible." Mrs. Pankhurst set down her teacup. "I ought to have spoken to you about this sooner, but I don't like to interfere in anyone's personal business."

Now Lilia was very nervous indeed. She waited for an explanation, or a condemnation, gripping her hands together in her lap.

"You and Mr. Reed have been spending quite a lot of time together. He makes no secret of his interest in you, and I've already cautioned him several times to behave with more decorum."

Lilia bit her lip, then said, "Why didn't you tell me this sooner?"

"I saw no reason to trouble you. Your own behavior has been beyond reproach. That is, until recently."

Dear God. Why did Lilia feel as though she were about to be lectured by her mother? What had happened to the progressive, modern Mrs. Pankhurst who advocated equal rights for women?

"Some acquaintances of mine saw you at the Savoy Hotel with Mr. Reed."

So that's how it was? Even Mrs. Pankhurst was bowing to conventional morality. Lilia was disappointed in both Mrs. Pankhurst and herself.

"Please understand me, Miss Brooke," the other woman said with energy, compelling Lilia to meet her eyes. "I have no problem with your actions personally, but you must think of the way they reflect on the WSPU. While I'm in America, you will essentially *be* the WSPU."

"But we're already censured for unsexing ourselves," Lilia protested. "For being unwomanly and immoral. I was called a 'female hooligan' the other day because of our militant activities." She picked up her teacup.

"Yes, I can see why you might be confused. I'll explain it by telling you about my marriage." Mrs. Pankhurst was a widow, and although she rarely spoke of her private life, she had made no secret of her happy nineteen-year marriage to an older man. "When we fell in love, I suggested a free union, but he refused."

Lilia's teacup paused on its way to her lips.

"He shared my ideals and my belief that marriage was an unnecessary, outdated institution, and in theory he agreed with free unions. But he was sobered by the experiences of friends of his who had shared a free union and were nearly destroyed by society's condemnation. He also quite rightly pointed out that I would be severely hampered in my public work if we were not properly married.

"Miss Brooke, if you love Mr. Reed, I suggest you marry him. For all his exuberance and sometimes indiscreet behavior, I believe he's a good man. He won't stand in the way of your work for the WSPU, and he has been a great help to the Union, financially as well as practically. He may be a help to you, too."

"I'll think about it," Lilia said. She looked down at the teacup she had forgotten she was holding. As she set it down on the table, the cup wobbled, rattling loudly in its saucer.

"It's your decision, of course."

After Mrs. Pankhurst left, Lilia leaned back in her chair and closed her eyes. She wondered if anyone besides Mrs. Pankhurst's acquaintants had seen her at the Savoy with Will. There was no knowing who else might have recognized her. If any of the anti-suffragists knew about her indiscretion, they could use the story to damage her reputation. And if anyone knew she had actually gone to Will's room, they could make enough trouble that she might have to resign from the WSPU leadership, perhaps from the WSPU entirely. But she shrank from dwelling upon such a possibility. It was too upsetting.

When Harriet returned home from teaching lessons that day, Lilia was still in the parlor.

"What's happened?" Harriet inquired as she walked in. "You look as though you've seen a ghost." She reached for the teapot and, finding it cold, rang for Lizzie.

"Not a ghost—Mrs. Pankhurst."

"Oh? Then why do you look so grim?"

Lilia related her conversation with Mrs. Pankhurst, pausing only when Lizzie came into the room to replace the cold tea with a fresh pot.

Harriet hadn't known about Lilia's evening at the Savoy, and she looked baffled. As soon as Lizzie had left them alone again, she said, "Why on earth would you go to Mr. Reed's hotel with him?"

"I don't know, Harriet. It was stupid of me. I did kiss him, but I didn't stay. I knew as soon as I went to his room that it was a mistake."

"The minute I met that man, I thought he'd cause some sort of trouble."

Harriet was one of the few WSPU members who hadn't been charmed by Will. She was a serious woman, and his lack of seriousness made her suspicious. Though he spoke English, it might as well have been Chinese for all Harriet's inability to understand what he said.

"I don't know what to do," Lilia said.

"You must do something. I assume you're not in love with Mr. Reed."

"I'm not. But perhaps marrying him wouldn't be so bad. He said we could live in England, so I wouldn't have to move to New Zealand with him."

Harriet looked skeptical. "I understand Mrs. Pankhurst's point about your reputation, but I'm surprised she would suggest you marry Mr. Reed. He has no sense of decorum. Even if you marry him, he'll undoubtedly do and say things that will embarrass you, if not actually damage your credibility and that of the Union."

"I don't think he's as bad as all that, but you do have a point."

"If respectability is what you're looking for, why not marry Paul Harris instead?"

This idea had occurred to Lilia, too, but she didn't reply at once. Instead, she rose to inspect the pipes on the wall, as if seeing them for the first time. Her favorite was a silver-blue opium pipe with metal filigree rosettes, and she stared at it as if it would give her the answer she sought.

"I don't think it would work," she said finally. "He doesn't live in London anymore."

"Ingleford isn't so far away. You could arrange something."

"He doesn't support the WSPU. If I were still with the NUWSS, it might work, but he doesn't approve of militant action."

"I admit that's a problem. Lilia, do stop staring at that pipe, or I'll start to worry about your sanity."

Lilia returned to her seat across from Harriet and they discussed Lilia's dilemma for a while longer, considering different possibilities. There were serious drawbacks to all of them, and nothing was decided.

Lilia lay awake in bed that night, her mind spinning with her attempts to find a way out of her difficulty. She tried to think of what would be best for the WSPU, not herself. But what seemed best for the WSPU was that she resign and allow someone like Miss Selwyn to take her place, someone who never made mistakes in public, who never expressed extreme views, and who never kissed the wrong man. But Lilia couldn't be that selfless, even in her imagination.

By the time the sun began to rise in the cool, damp early morning, she had a plan. It wasn't the perfect plan, but it was the best one she could think of. She had written it all down, so many pages that her hand was in pain. Putting her plan into practice was harrowing enough that she had to do it that day—otherwise, she would lose her nerve. She made a hasty toilet, left a note for Harriet, and went to the train station just in time to catch the early train to Ingleford.

Paul wasn't at the church when Lilia arrived. The sexton told her he was expected back in half an hour, so she chose to wait. At first she stood in front of the church, but the chatter of the old man, who had held his post for forty years and had a story to go with every one of them, only made her more anxious. At least he didn't recognize her as "that Brooke girl," which was the way most of the villagers referred to her. She excused herself and retreated to the graveyard, where she read the epitaphs. Thinking of death suited her mood and calmed her a little.

After what seemed an interminably long time, Paul finally appeared. He found her at the grave of John Beresford, who, the inscription assured her, was *At Home with the Lord.*

"Lilia, what are you doing here? Are you visiting your family?" He looked surprised and cautiously pleased to see her.

"I must speak with you. I'm sorry to arrive unexpectedly, but I didn't have time to write first. Do you have a few minutes?"

"Yes. Would you like to talk in the church?"

"I'd rather not." She suppressed a shudder. That church held too many bad memories for her. "It's nice weather—why don't we walk?"

He agreed, and they made their way down the wide carriage drive in front of the church. Lilia instinctively turned away from the main road and the village, towards a footpath that skirted a field.

"Why aren't you wearing your cassock?" she asked. He was wearing his clerical collar with a black shirt, coat, and trousers. His black armband wasn't obtrusive because of his dark clothing, but it gave her pause, reminding her how recently his father had died.

"I still wear it on Sundays, but it turns out not to be very practical for rural life," he replied. "I decided to make a change after helping the villagers capture an escaped sheep."

Imagining Paul chasing a sheep momentarily distracted her from her anxiety, and she smiled. "I can't imagine you doing anything so undignified."

"I assure you I was thoroughly and publicly undignified. You would have enjoyed it."

"Do you like living here?"

"I like some things about it, but the experience has been a challenge so far."

There was a brief silence. She knew he was waiting for her to state her purpose, but she couldn't yet bring herself to do it. The task loomed too large, despite the many different ways she had practiced saying what she had to say.

"What's the matter, Lilia?" he said, looking at her with concern. He reached out to touch her arm, but she evaded him.

"Please, let's keep walking," she said in a low voice. "I'll tell you in a moment."

He made no further attempt to touch her or to speak. The footpath ended and they had to choose whether to turn left, into a small wood, or right, onto a side road that led back to the village. Lilia hesitated, then turned left. Paul followed her through the underbrush at the edge of the wood.

Once they were on even ground, walking side by side on a path through the trees, Lilia took a deep breath. "I have something to ask you, but first I must tell you that Mrs. Pankhurst has appointed me her deputy while she's in America on a lecture tour. It's a great honor."

"Congratulations," he said, his voice expressionless.

This was much more difficult than she had imagined. In a halting voice, she continued, "I recently did something foolish that jeopardizes my new position. I assume you remember Mr. Will Reed."

Paul frowned. "Yes."

Lilia resolved not to look at him again until she had finished her story. "He spends quite a bit of time at the WSPU office, and we've become friends. The other day, he invited me to go to dinner with him at his hotel. I had dinner with him and . . . I also went up to his room afterwards."

Paul stopped walking. When she turned to look at him, his face was white. Had it really been necessary to tell him everything? Her natural frankness had worked against her once again.

"Why are you telling me this?" he asked, his voice hollow.

"Please, let me finish. Nothing happened at the hotel. I let him kiss me, but I didn't stay long. I regret going to his room, but I can't explain why I did it, because I don't understand it myself. Some of Mrs. Pankhurst's acquaintances saw me at the hotel, and she's found it necessary to caution me about my behavior. I hadn't thought it mattered what I do in my private life, because WSPU members are already accused of being vulgar and immoral, but Mrs. Pankhurst convinced me that I must do something to salvage my reputation."

Lilia's words were coming out in a rush, and she felt she wasn't explaining the situation very well. She placed her hand on the trunk of a tree to steady herself. "Will has asked me to marry him. I refused, but Mrs. Pankhurst urged me to reconsider. She thinks I ought to marry him as soon as possible to avoid further damage to my reputation, but . . . I'd rather marry you."

There. No matter what his response, she had said everything she came to say and she was relieved the words were out. At the same time, her face was burning, and she was afraid to look at him, afraid to see what was in his eyes, afraid he would say no, afraid he would say yes.

He said nothing.

"You may speak now," she said, staring at the ground.

"What do you expect me to say?" His voice was low. "I wasn't prepared for this."

"I know. I'm sorry it's so sudden, but I'm sure you can understand that something must be done soon."

"You say you would rather marry me than Mr. Reed. Why?"

"I haven't got feelings for him beyond friendship. You're the only man I could possibly . . . endure a lifetime with."

"I'm flattered."

"Paul, I'm being honest with you. You know I never wanted to marry. But now, when there's so much at stake—" She turned to him and reached out as if to take his hand, then thought better of it. "I've never wanted anything more than to be a leader of the WSPU. To lose this wonderful opportunity—admittedly, by my own recklessness—would be devastating."

"So you wish to sacrifice both yourself and me to the Cause."

"I don't see it that way."

"Are you not proposing to use me to create a façade of respectability for yourself so you can continue to do what you want to do?"

She blinked. "It isn't necessary to put my request in such harsh terms, but I suppose you have the right to view it that way."

"What of my reputation? Have you thought of that?"

She had not. "If you mean that an agnostic militant suffragette is hardly the ideal wife for a clergyman, I won't argue the point. But you were willing to marry me before this, and I was no less militant or agnostic then."

"It's not just that. Surely you're not so naïve as to think a hasty marriage will be good for either of our reputations. You know what people will think."

"Yes," she shot back, "but by the time nine months have passed, they'll know they were wrong."

"Dear God!" It was a frustrated exclamation, but could also have been a prayer. He sighed, then went on earnestly, "Lilia, you're asking me to consider marriage as a business proposition, but to me, it's a sacrament. There is no beauty or sacredness, not even affection, in the bond you speak of."

"If I saw beauty or sacredness in marriage, I wouldn't have stood opposed to it for so long," she replied, "but I do see a place in it for affection. That's why I don't want to marry Will. You know I care for you. I told you so the last time we were together."

"Did you? In a vague way, perhaps. But you also told me you'd rather leave me alone than marry me."

"I'd rather marry you than lose everything for which I've worked so hard."

He gave her an exasperated look. "Again, I'm flattered. And if I'd known all it took to convince you to marry me was to enlist Mrs. Pankhurst's support, I wouldn't have wasted so much time on that first proposal."

"It will be better than you think," she said, uncomfortably aware that she sounded desperate. "I've considered all the details, and I think we could come to an agreement that would be acceptable to both of us. I've written down my conditions." She opened her handbag and fished out the document she'd spent most of the night writing. "Of course, you may add some of your own."

"Oh, Lilia." He fell silent, ignoring the papers she was holding out and looking at her with something akin to pity.

"You may take a few days to think about it, if you wish," she added graciously.

"That won't be necessary. I can't marry you under these circumstances. I'm sorry."

He turned and strode away, leaving her alone among the trees.

22

Some of the "New Women" writers will some day start an idea
that men and women should be allowed to see each other asleep
before proposing or accepting. But I suppose the New Woman won't
condescend in future to accept; she will do the proposing herself. And
a nice job she will make of it, too!

—Bram Stoker, *Dracula*

Paul walked back to the church in a daze, hardly believing what had just
transpired. When he had first seen Lilia in the graveyard, his heart
had raced in the old, familiar way, and he hadn't been able to suppress his
happiness. But his talk with Mary about Will Reed had put a damper on
his spirits, and seeing Lilia so soon afterwards made him think there was
trouble and the New Zealander was the cause of it. Which, in a way, he was.

Paul couldn't understand why Lilia had gone to Will's hotel room. He
had long ago accepted that she spoke of things no respectable, well-bred
woman would speak of, but to act as she had done was incomprehensible.
And perhaps she hadn't told the whole truth about what had happened in
that hotel room. Will didn't seem like a gentleman, and if a woman willingly
went to his room, surely he would expect her to go to bed with him. But

Paul had no experience with these types of situations. He also preferred not to think about what might have happened in that room.

As stunned as he was by Lilia's actions, Paul was more concerned about the damage to her reputation. He didn't want to see her publicly humiliated. He knew her, and for all her bravado and willingness to shock people, she also had a sweet, vulnerable side. And he loved her, despite—or perhaps because of—all her contradictions. The woman he loved was finally willing to marry him, but not under the circumstances he had hoped for.

Was that the answer? Since he did love her, no matter how unusual the circumstances, wasn't it his duty to try to offer her the respectability she wanted? There was no guarantee that marrying him would make her immune to public talk or disgrace. If her behavior with Will became public knowledge, even a hint of scandal could drag Paul and his good name down with her.

But none of these considerations mattered to Paul as much as the calculating, businesslike nature of Lilia's proposal. It had given him the strength to refuse her and walk away. Had she shown any of the vulnerability that had moved him in the past, had she told him she loved him, had she touched him—even just to take his hand—had she said anything at all about wanting to be with him, his resistance would have crumbled.

Instead, to see the ominously thick sheaf of papers she had produced from her handbag, to hear her speak of a mutually acceptable agreement, and, worst of all, to find that she could be his wife only because he was the only man she could "endure" a lifetime with—good heavens! If any proposal were designed to elicit a flat refusal, this was it. And if Lilia's attempt was representative of what women were capable of, Paul fervently hoped the task would remain in men's hands.

At the same time, he had sensed her anxiety and he could imagine how humbling it must have been to seek him out with her request. It showed how much she wanted to keep that leadership position, to be willing to set aside her beliefs about marriage for it. But that was part of the problem: the only time he had seen true passion in her eyes during their conversation was when she'd spoken of the WSPU. She'd shown no passion for him, only for her work. Mary's claim about the man who married Lilia having to take third place in her heart seemed only too true. And Paul wanted the primary passion of the woman he loved to be for him.

Paul wrestled with his thoughts all day and through the night. Sometimes he decided he must marry Lilia; other times he thought himself ridiculous for even considering it. By morning, he had come to no resolution.

Later that day, he received another unexpected visit, this time from Harriet Firth. He was at the church when she arrived, having just finished meeting with a young couple he was to marry the following week. The meeting had done nothing to help him forget Lilia and her proposal, and he was staring at the wall in the small office adjoining the vestry when Harriet appeared in the doorway.

"Good afternoon, Mr. Harris. May I speak with you?"

"Certainly, Miss Firth," he said, rising to his feet as she entered the room. "What brings you here?"

She sat down in the chair across from his desk and he returned to his seat, hoping that this second impromptu meeting in as many days wouldn't throw his life into further disorder.

"I'm sorry to trouble you at work," she said, "but I think my errand is important enough to warrant the disruption. I understand Lilia was here yesterday."

"Yes, she was." He was on his guard, not wanting to share personal details with Harriet, who he sensed had never approved of his presence in Lilia's life.

"Lilia told me about your conversation," Harriet said. "She didn't want to, but I ferreted the truth out of her, because I was worried. I know you probably don't wish to speak of this with me, but I think you should know Lilia is writing a letter to Mr. Reed that I hope she won't send."

"Lilia is entitled to write to whomever she wishes, for whatever reason, without my—or anyone else's—interference," Paul said coldly. When, he wondered, would people stop talking to him about Will Reed?

"Yes, of course that's true," Harriet said, raising her chin and meeting his eyes. "But I don't want to see her throw her life away because of one foolish mistake. She is devastated to think that her actions may have hurt the WSPU. Lilia is my friend, and I intend to interfere, as you put it. If she marries Mr. Reed, I have no doubt she'll regret her decision for the rest of her life."

"How well do you know the man?"

"Not well. I don't particularly like him, but my opposition isn't based on my personal opinion of him so much as on Lilia's lack of feelings for him. She doesn't love him, Mr. Harris, and I don't see the point of her binding herself to a man who will take her away to New Zealand, far from the work and the people she loves."

"He can't force her to go if she doesn't wish to," Paul interposed. "And given Lilia's longstanding opposition to marriage, surely it would suit her to live apart from her husband, even on different sides of the world."

"You may be correct. It may all work out for the best and my fears may be groundless. But are you willing to risk losing her?" Harriet's eyes seemed to bore into his.

Paul stood up. "Miss Firth, I refuse to be pressured into marriage for the sake of the WSPU."

"I understand." She rose also, but before turning away she added, "I came here because I thought you'd wish to know what Lilia is contemplating. I know her proposal must not have been attractive to you. She's confused and probably wouldn't be a good wife at first, perhaps not for a long time. But I believe she loves you and that the two of you could be happy together eventually."

Paul was taken aback. If Lilia had spoken these words herself the day before, she would have had a good chance of success with him. Oddly, though, the fact that they came from Harriet gave them greater weight. She was a sensible woman who knew Lilia and could coolly assess what needed to be done in a situation that neither Paul nor Lilia could be objective about. In short, she inspired confidence.

"Has she told you she loves me?" he asked.

"Not in so many words, but I believe she does." Harriet nodded with a grim expression that was at odds with her message. "Thank you for listening to me, Mr. Harris. By the bye, I'd appreciate it if you don't mention this conversation to Lilia. She wouldn't be pleased to know I came here on her behalf."

He agreed to keep their conversation to himself.

She left, and Paul stared after her as if he had received a mystical visitation. Harriet couldn't have known whether her attempt at persuasion would be successful, but his mind had been teetering back and forth with such regularity that it took only a light tap to tip the balance. When Paul left his office, his mind was made up. He wasn't the sort of man who questioned a decision once he had settled on a course of action, so he wrote to Lilia as soon as he got home.

Dear Lilia,

I have given more thought to your offer and if it still stands, I will accept it. I suppose I ought to have a look at your conditions: will you send the document to me by the earliest post? If you wish, I can also make arrangements for a special license so we can marry without having to wait for the banns to be read.

Paul

He disliked the tone of his letter. It was as businesslike and emotionless as her proposal had been, as if she had set the tone for all of their subsequent exchanges. But he didn't know if she had already put her other plan into action or even if she had reconsidered her initial offer to him, so he thought it best to maintain a neutral tone until he heard from her again.

Two days later, he received her reply, along with the ominous document. Her letter was brief.

Dear Paul,

Thank you for your letter and for the suggestion about the license. I would definitely prefer that to having to wait for the banns. Wherever you would like to be married is fine with me: simply let me know when you've made the arrangements. If you would also please sign the document, it would set my mind at rest.

Lilia

When Paul read her letter, he shook his head. They might be two lawyers corresponding about a longstanding court case instead of lovers arranging their wedding. He supposed he had better get used to such interactions, a thought confirmed when he read the document that accompanied the letter. It must have taken hours to write; he was amazed by her uncharacteristic attention to detail. But as he continued to read, his detached, lawyerly attitude dissipated.

Lilia's conditions encompassed everything from where she would live (in London with Harriet during the week, and with Paul in Ingleford on the weekends) to which domestic duties she would be willing to perform (she was willing to cook on the weekends if he wished it, but he ought to speak to her family about whether it was advisable). Most of the document was about her work for the WSPU, which could be summed up as a request for complete freedom to perform her duties without any interference from him.

The document was an offense to his sensibilities and a monument to Lilia's arrogance and presumption. Anyone reading it would assume that she was doing him an enormous favor by marrying him and that he ought to be grateful for every concession she made. She even represented spending weekends with him as an act of charity. How exactly did she think *he* would benefit from this marriage, which was rapidly looking as though it would be no real marriage at all?

He skimmed over her work-related conditions, but another clause relating to the wedding ceremony stopped him short:

I don't care who performs the ceremony, but the officiating clergyman must remove the injunction for the wife to obey the husband. Although the wedding ceremony is not as sacred to me as it is to you, I can't promise something I have no intention of carrying out. Everything else in the vows may stand.

Paul knew of no clergyman who would be willing to do this except himself, and he couldn't very well be the officiant at his own wedding. Surely she didn't think he would try to force her to obey him. Knowing her, it was more likely that she wanted to make a public protest against the wording of the vows.

He thought there was nothing in the document that could surprise him more than these lines, until he read the following:

If you want children, I ask that we wait a year. Children will limit my ability to work, and I require at least a year of freedom before such a restriction is imposed upon me.

If he wanted children? What could she possibly mean? Marriage inevitably resulted in children. Was she suggesting that they abstain from sexual relations for the entire first year of their marriage? Did she think it was even possible, given their history? Hadn't she noticed that they couldn't be within a few feet of each other without feeling an irresistible physical attraction? It didn't help that the language of her document repeatedly represented him (and now their hypothetical children) as a limitation on her freedom. He flung the document across the room in anger, scattering the pages everywhere.

But after he had calmed down a little, he thought again how strange it was for her to work out the details of any matter in such careful fashion. Lilia was all about ideas, and she usually let the details work themselves out, if others didn't step in to do it.

There was only one explanation for this excruciatingly specific document: she was terrified. Her fear of marriage had prompted her to impose as many conditions on him as she could think of. And she was making it as difficult for him to marry her as she could in order to save her pride. Satisfied that he had figured out her motives, Paul felt less anger and more pity. He sent the document back to her unsigned, accompanied by the following note:

Dear Lilia,

I cannot sign your document. By leaving it unsigned, I do not reject your conditions, but as we are going to be married we must learn to trust each other. I give you my word that you may have whatever reasonable freedoms you desire, but they will come as a result of discussion between us, not by your imposing them upon me.

I will do everything I can to please you without doing violence to myself in the process. Don't forget—you have known me since I was fifteen, and if I were a monster, you would know it by now.

Paul

Lilia didn't reply, but when Paul sent another note a day later asking if she would be ready to marry him in Ingleford on Thursday of the following week, she agreed. Thus, the date and time were fixed, and with so little time left, it turned out that they didn't see each other again until their wedding day.

23

I have observed . . . that the clergy carry off all the nicest girls. You will see some of the finest, who have money of their own too, marry quite commonplace parsons. But the reason is obvious. It is their faith in the superior moral probity of Churchmen which weighs with them.

—Sarah Grand, *The Heavenly Twins*

OCTOBER 1908

Paul was as anxious as Lilia to keep the wedding quiet, given that he was still in mourning for his father. This fact made it easier to explain to his mother that he and Lilia desired no fanfare or merrymaking. His mother and Lilia's family were pleased, if surprised, by news of the impending marriage, and nobody asked uncomfortable questions.

Paul did have to endure the chaffing of Stephen Elliott, whom he had prevailed upon to come to Ingleford to perform the ceremony. Stephen arrived the day before the wedding, and he and Paul spent the evening talking and drinking port in front of Paul's drawing room fire. Paul had been uncomfortable asking Stephen to omit the "obey" clause from Lilia's vows, but after his initial shock, Stephen seemed merely amused.

"I thought you'd forgotten all about the infamous Miss Brooke," he said. "Well, you're marrying an unconventional woman, so you'll have to expect an unconventional marriage, won't you?"

Paul was surprised that Stephen took the unusual request in stride. He had expected more resistance from his friend, not only to changing the vows, but to the marriage in general.

"It did occur to me," Stephen went on, "that the marriage may not be legal if I change the vows."

"I hadn't thought of that."

"Would Miss Brooke object to my saying them as they are, and she could repeat only what she agrees with?"

Lilia was still in London and would be arriving just before the wedding the next morning. "I don't know," Paul replied. "I'll ask her tomorrow before the ceremony. If she objects, we may need to risk the legal problem."

Stephen grinned. "You've been well and truly caught, old man. Most married men learn quickly enough to obey their wives, not the other way 'round, but you're better prepared than most."

"How quickly did *you* learn it?"

"Within a week, my friend. Within a week."

Paul offered his friend more port, but Stephen said, "I'd better not. The last thing you need at your wedding is a drunken officiant. You ought to stop too."

Paul hesitated with the bottle poised over his own empty glass. He was a sporadic drinker who could go for months without anything but wine at the Eucharist. But, given the state of his nerves, the port was tempting.

"You're right." He set down the bottle.

Stephen said, "I trust you won't mention my tampering with the vows to any of our colleagues or my superiors."

"I won't."

"I wouldn't do this for anyone but you, Harris."

"I'm grateful," Paul said. "You're not obliged to do it."

Stephen's face became serious. "Yes, I am."

"What do you mean?"

"When I first met Miss Brooke the day Ellen Wells died in Parliament Square, I was concerned by your association with her. You didn't seem to realize that a relationship with her could damage your career." Stephen looked away for a moment, clearly uncomfortable.

Paul began to wish he had poured them both another glass of port.

"I wrote a letter to the bishop," Stephen continued. "I thought a warning coming from him would be more effective than one coming from me."

"It was you!" Paul exclaimed, shocked. He hadn't thought about that letter in months, but he remembered how upset he had been when the bishop admonished him about his involvement with women's suffrage. "I thought Cross wrote that letter."

"I'm not surprised. Although my motives were pure, or so I thought at the time, my actions were not those of a friend. I'm sorry. Changing the wedding vows is the least I can do to make up for the trouble I caused."

Paul was silent. He couldn't believe his closest friend had betrayed him in such a way.

"That letter must have caused a great deal of trouble for you," Stephen said, staring at the floor.

"Yes." He glanced at his friend's bent head. "When the bishop told me about it, I thought I'd lost my chance for the deanship. And I was unjust to Cross because I was so certain he wrote it."

"I'll do whatever you like to make it right. I'll speak to the bishop, and Cross, too, if you wish." Stephen looked up. "I really am sorry, Paul."

"I forgive you," Paul said. "There's no need to speak to anyone. My life is very different now."

"You're kinder to me than I deserve." Stephen brightened. "I say, old man, we're far too solemn, considering it's the night before your wedding. Let's speak of more pleasant things."

Paul agreed, but privately he thought solemnity was perfectly appropriate for the eve of a wedding. Especially this one.

The next morning, Paul and Stephen went to the church an hour before the ceremony was scheduled to begin. Edward Brooke, who had agreed to be Paul's attendant, arrived soon afterwards. Stephen and Edward, both easygoing and good-natured, were the perfect companions for Paul, who needed to be distracted from worrying about the many things that could go wrong.

Lilia arrived at the church with her parents and sister shortly before the ceremony. When Paul saw her, what was left of his anxiety dissipated, and a warm feeling spread through his chest. She was wearing a simple pearl gray dress with a matching hat, and her hair was pinned in a becoming mass of curls at the nape of her neck. As Paul greeted her, he was aware of her family watching them curiously, and he felt too awkward to speak. He merely squeezed her hand, which even through her gloves felt ice-cold. She gave him a tiny smile in response. Whatever she was feeling within passed outwardly as the reticence and modesty appropriate for a bride, but Paul wasn't fooled.

His mother and James arrived then, and as the two families greeted each other, Paul took a few minutes to speak privately with his bride.

"How are you?" he whispered.

"I'm fine." She returned his gaze steadily, but her eyes revealed nothing.

"Are you certain you want to do this?"

"I haven't changed my mind. Have you?"

"No," he said quickly, relieved. With that settled, he briefly explained the potential legal problem Stephen had raised about the vows and asked what her preference was.

She thought for a moment, then said, "He may say the complete vows, but I'll leave out the 'obey' clause when I repeat them."

Paul relayed this information to Stephen, and the ceremony began.

The small, simple ceremony didn't suit Paul. He was a High Churchman and he loved elaborate ceremonies. He would have liked more guests and more attendants, in a bigger church, with music, prayers, and scripture readings, and he would have liked his bride to wear a white dress and veil—though at least she wasn't wearing black, as he had feared she might.

Since so few details of the wedding were as he wished, Paul wasn't prepared for the way he felt when he said his vows. He was overwhelmed by the sacredness of the moment and struggled to keep his emotions in check. Lilia said her vows in a clear, steady voice, though her face was pale and her hand still cold when he slipped the ring onto her finger.

After the ceremony, the two families went to the Brookes' house, as Lilia's mother had insisted on preparing the wedding breakfast. As if mindful that this breakfast was the closest thing to revelry allowed them, the small group was abuzz with gay chatter and laughter. Nobody mentioned Lilia's omission from the vows, perhaps because they knew her so well that it hadn't surprised them.

But it ought to have surprised them how quiet she was during the breakfast. As if to make up for Lilia's reticence, her family surrounded Paul with warm congratulations. Emily was too shy to say anything, but she kissed him on the cheek, and Edward clapped him on the shoulder, welcoming him as a fourth brother. The older generation gave him obvious but well-intentioned advice. Mr. Brooke shook Paul's hand and assured him that life with Lilia would never be dull. James also shook Paul's hand and told him to be kind to Lilia. And his mother, who had sniffled into her handkerchief throughout the ceremony, imprisoned his neck in a stranglehold and burst into happy tears all over again. Paul endured it with good humor.

After a couple of hours, when topics of conversation had dwindled and Paul had complimented Mrs. Brooke on her excellent cooking, he asked Lilia if she was ready to leave. She seemed only too happy to do so, especially when her mother said, "You mustn't expect much of Lilia in the kitchen, Paul. I'm afraid she's hopeless, despite my best efforts."

Paul didn't know how to reply, so he said nothing, but outside on the walk home, he said to Lilia, "The cooking doesn't matter to me, you know. I have a housekeeper, Mrs. Mills, who comes in every afternoon to cook and clean: she can stay on, if you wish. Or you can hire a live-in cook."

"Since I won't be here during the week, I don't think a live-in cook will be necessary, unless you want one for yourself," she replied. She added dryly, "It will set my mother's mind at ease to know there's no danger of my poisoning you."

"I hope I'll never make you wish to do such a thing," he said with a smile. She had taken his arm as they walked, which was a pleasant reminder of the early days of their friendship.

He was worried she wouldn't like his cottage. Perhaps she would find it too small or otherwise inappropriate for her needs. He felt ridiculously anxious to please her, to make her happy that she had married him, despite the strange circumstances and his knowledge that she would likely not have married him under different ones. Despite her brief flash of humor, she was not herself, and he had no idea what she was feeling—perhaps regret.

The gray cat was lying belly-upwards in the sun on the front step when they arrived at the house. Lilia bent to pet it and asked, "Is that your cat?"

"No, and I can't seem to convince it to go away. It's here every day."

The cat seemed to realize it had found an ally, for it rubbed itself against Lilia's skirt and looked up at her appealingly.

"Well, you may not think it's your cat, but it seems to have decided otherwise," she said.

Paul smiled, but he stepped over the cat and ushered Lilia into the house, firmly closing the door before the animal could dart inside.

He took her on a tour of the cottage. She said nothing as they went through the ground-floor rooms—the small parlor, his study, the dining room, the kitchen—and she remained silent as they went upstairs.

"You may do anything you like with the house," Paul said as they ascended. "If anything is not to your taste, please change it." He stopped at the top of the stairs and turned to look at her.

She gazed at him doubtfully. "I don't think you'll want to give me free rein with your house—"

"Our house," he interposed.

"Our house," she repeated slowly, as if she was learning a new language. "But you've seen some of my rooms in the past, and you're far too tidy to tolerate my clutter. For your sake, I'll try to keep the disorder to a minimum."

"I'm not worried about that. It is a small house, though, and perhaps you'll find it cramped. We'll move, of course, when my year here is finished."

She said gravely, "I don't think the house is too small. I've never lived in grand style, you know, and I won't be here during the week, anyway."

He showed her the bedrooms quickly. He had moved out of the larger bedroom so she could have it and had taken the smaller one across the hall as his own. He hoped she would understand that he wasn't ready to discuss their sleeping arrangements just yet.

Either she didn't understand or she was taking advantage of his discomfort, for she glanced from one bedroom to the other, then gave him a direct, challenging look.

"Does this mean we won't be sleeping together?" she asked.

Paul felt himself blushing to the roots of his hair. He thought he saw a tiny, mocking smile at the corner of her mouth, but he didn't look long enough to be certain. After making it clear in her document that she didn't want children, why would she expect to share a bed? Was she toying with him?

"Let's talk downstairs," he said.

They went down to the parlor and sat in the two large armchairs by the fireplace. There was a time when he could have spoken frankly with Lilia about almost anything, but this wasn't the Lilia he knew. She was so remote and sardonic that it was difficult to discuss redecorating the rooms in the house, much less their sleeping arrangements. She bore little resemblance to the woman who had kissed him passionately only a few months earlier.

He took a moment to search for the right words before beginning. "Lilia, you wrote in your document that you don't want children for at least a year."

"Oh." She looked more surprised than she had a right to. "Yes, but I didn't mean . . ."

"What *did* you mean?"

She was silent for a long moment, looking down at her lap and twisting her wedding ring. "I thought we could use some sort of contraceptive device."

"I won't do that," he said curtly. He had thought she fought for contraception only on behalf of poor women who couldn't afford children. He had never imagined she might have a personal interest in it.

She shrugged. "I merely thought you had the right to expect something from me, since the benefits of our arrangement seem mostly to be mine."

Her speech made Paul's blood run cold, her tone and choice of words echoing those of the document he had come to hate. She seemed oblivious to the fact that they were now married and he wanted to shake her.

He pressed the heel of his hand against his forehead. "I don't think I ought to assume all the privileges of a husband until we are used to the idea of being married. Everything has happened very quickly."

"Aside from the obvious, what privileges have you chosen not to assume?"

"Nothing specific. I want you to be comfortable, to act as you would if we were not married . . . within certain limits, of course."

"What limits?"

He sighed. "Must I spell everything out?"

"Yes, you must," she retorted. "I need to know exactly what you expect of me now, as well as what you'll expect of me when you choose to assume your rights—"

"I said 'privileges,' not rights."

"It's all one to me. I don't want to hear your expectations couched in courtly language to make them more palatable to me." She rose from her chair and went to stand at the window.

"Why must you view me as the enemy?" he said to her back, struggling to keep his temper. "I'm not trying to trick you into a false sense of security in order to burden you with ridiculous demands."

"They won't seem ridiculous to you."

"For heaven's sake, Lilia!" he exclaimed. "Why are you so determined to destroy any chance of happiness between us?"

She turned to face him and the cool, sardonic façade was gone. "I'm not. I just don't know how to . . . do this."

His anger forgotten, he rose and went to her, putting his hands gently on her shoulders and looking down into her face. "I don't know, either," he said quietly. "I'm sorry."

She took a deep, shuddering breath. "I'm sorry, too."

Paul pulled her into his arms and held her tightly. It was the right thing to do. She slipped her arms around his waist and hid her face in his neck.

He could feel the hard thudding of her heart, or perhaps it was his own—he couldn't tell. It was better that they didn't speak, better just to hold each other. But he was worried. What had happened to his peaceful life? If their first day as husband and wife was like this, how could they survive months, much less years, together?

After a while, she pulled away and said, "I'd like to finish our conversation."

It was the last thing he wanted to do, but Paul nodded and they sat down again.

She said, "What did you mean when you said I may act as if we're not married?"

"I meant you may do as you wish. Live with Miss Firth during the week, work for the WSPU—do everything you did before. Just spend the weekends with me. The only limit I can think of is that you would not be free to encourage the attentions of other men."

"Do you think I would do that?" she asked quietly.

"I don't know what you would do."

"My behavior with Will Reed has shocked you."

"It has done," he admitted.

She gave him a puzzled look. "Is there nothing you want from me besides refusing the attentions of other men?"

"I have no conditions, only a request. Since you'll be here on weekends, I'd like you to attend the Sunday service. Just as you've found it necessary to protect your reputation in public, I'd like my parishioners to know that my wife exists and at least appears to support me. You need only be present. I don't ask that you actually pay attention to my sermons. That would be expecting you to do more than half the congregation does already."

"Very well. That's not too much to ask." She looked at him curiously. "Do you preach the same sort of sermons that you preached at the cathedral?"

"I used to, but I've been told by several parishioners that they can make neither head nor tail of anything I say, so I'm trying to change my style."

"You must not let them change you too much." She smiled, and he saw the old Lilia in that smile, the one he had fallen in love with. It gave him hope.

"Would you like to take a trip with me tomorrow?" he asked. "Perhaps to the coast? Or we could go to Cambridge and visit your alma mater." Though not a proper honeymoon, exactly, he had assumed she would stay with him for a few days after the wedding.

"Tomorrow?" She looked surprised. "I can't. I must go back to London. I have an important meeting with Mrs. Pankhurst."

He tried not to look as disappointed as he felt. "I didn't think you'd leave so soon."

"I have a great deal of work to do this week. Mrs. Pankhurst leaves for America soon, and I need to be up to date on her plans for the WSPU."

"I see."

"I'll return next Saturday," she said, sounding a little like a mother trying to placate an unhappy child.

"Of course." He was emotionally drained by the conversation and by the demands of the day, and he excused himself to be alone for a while in his study. He tried to read, but even that seemed too taxing, so he lay down on the sofa.

As he lay there, he thought of his father. Philip wouldn't have wanted him to marry Lilia under these circumstances. The marriage could so easily become a mirror of his parents' unhappy one. Throughout his childhood, Paul had seen the light die in his father's eyes every time Bianca turned away from him, no doubt thinking of the man she really loved. Lilia's work would capture her attention, instead, but it would become a barrier between them all the same.

Paul awoke with a start to a dark room. At first, he was too disoriented to remember he was in his study. When he lit the lamp and squinted at the small clock on his desk, he was astonished to find that it was nearly ten o'clock. He had slept soundly for more than six hours.

He opened his study door quietly, assuming Lilia had gone to bed. The lamp was lit in the dining room and there were papers all over the table, but she wasn't there.

He picked up a paper. It was a schedule of WSPU meetings. Another paper was filled with rough notes for either a speech or an article about the treatment of suffragettes in prison.

Glancing around the room, he saw more papers on the floor, as well as a pair of blue slippers lying helter-skelter. He picked up the slippers and followed the trail of papers into the parlor.

Only one lamp was lit in the parlor, and Lilia was asleep on the sofa, a pencil in one hand and papers strewn all around her. She had changed into her nightgown and wrapper, and one bare foot was stretched out past the sofa's edge.

Paul whispered her name, but she didn't stir, and he drew closer, mesmerized by the sight of her. Her white nightgown was prettier than the dress she'd worn for the wedding, with a froth of soft lace at the low neckline and wrists. Her hair was down too, spilling over her shoulders in loose dark waves. A knot of longing wedged itself in his throat and he found it difficult to breathe.

If he kissed her, would she push him away? In that moment he was willing to accept anything she wanted—even whatever strange ideas she had about contraceptive devices—if she would let him take her to bed.

He reached out to touch her hair, then lifted a strand to his lips. With the back of one finger he stroked her cheek. She shifted slightly, turning her face away.

He left the room to find a blanket. When he came back, he draped it over her, making sure to cover her bare foot. Her breathing remained deep and even, and he left her in peace.

24

Every injustice that has ever been fastened upon women in a
Christian country has been "authorized by the Bible" and riveted and
perpetuated by the pulpit.

—Helen H. Gardener, *Men, Women and Gods*

Lilia waved from the window as her train pulled out of the station.
Paul stood on the platform, one hand raised in farewell. He looked
somber in his all-black clothing, and she wished she had kissed him goodbye, though such behavior in public, even from a properly married couple,
would have shocked the good citizens of Ingleford.

She sat back and closed her eyes, feeling both relieved and guilty. Paul
had no idea how much she hated Ingleford. If he were still a canon at the
cathedral and they could live together in London, life would be easier for
them both. In a village where everyone knew everyone and differences of
any kind were suspicious, Paul would be judged for marrying her just as her
family had always been judged for her unconventional behavior.

Paul also had no idea how difficult it had been for her to agree to his request that she attend church, but it was the only thing he'd asked of her, so she couldn't refuse. From his perspective it surely seemed reasonable, but that church had been the bane of Lilia's existence throughout her childhood. She couldn't count the times she had been told that little girls who asked impertinent questions or talked when they ought to be silent would go to Hell. When she'd thought of God since, if she thought of Him at all, she could picture only a cruel tyrant.

She stared out the window as the train chugged serenely through the landscape of gently rolling hills, neat hedgerows, and trees in the process of shedding their leaves in preparation for winter. A pain in her hand made her look down, and she realized she had been twisting her wedding ring until it chafed. She raised her hand to look at it more closely. She would have preferred a plain gold wedding band, but Paul had chosen a more elaborate ring. It was pretty and delicate, studded with tiny diamonds and sapphires.

He had thought of everything and made all the arrangements in such a short time, and she was grateful he had made it so easy for her. But the burden of gratefulness weighed heavily on her. He had bound himself to her for the rest of his life simply because she had asked him to. She knew her document had upset him, but she had hoped it would push him to express his own expectations clearly. He was such a romantic, he probably didn't even know he *had* expectations. But she had seen the disappointment in his eyes when she'd told him she would have to return to London, and she knew it was only the beginning of his displeasure.

She ought to have married someone else. Perhaps an older man, someone who was calm, patient, and preferably not in love with her, someone who wouldn't be hurt by her neglect of him. Although others could be fooled into thinking Paul was as calm and patient as he appeared in public, Lilia knew better. He was a highly strung, sensitive man who could be pushed too far, and she suspected he was already near his limit with her.

That morning, she had awakened in the parlor to find her slippers set out neatly by the sofa and her papers in orderly piles on a side table. She hadn't meant to fall asleep there. She had tried to prepare for her meeting in London while she'd waited for Paul to emerge from his study, but when he didn't come out after a few hours, she'd gone upstairs to bed. However, sleep had eluded her, so she'd returned to her paperwork downstairs.

His actions had been sweet, but she wished he had pushed the papers aside, awakened her, and made passionate love to her instead. He wasn't the only one disappointed by his spouse's expectations. She had been looking forward to the intimacy of sexual relations with him, even thinking it might help smooth out their other difficulties, so she had been stunned when Paul refused to even discuss contraception. Of course, in public, nearly everyone was opposed to it, but she had assumed that in private he would be willing to satisfy their sexual desires without risking pregnancy every time. Did he really think abstinence was the only option? But he was Anglo-Catholic, so perhaps she ought to have expected it.

She was worried that Paul's objection to contraception masked a more serious difficulty. She remembered how shocked he had been when she'd told him she had gone to Will's hotel room. Perhaps her willingness to go that far was as bad in Paul's eyes as actually giving herself to Will. Had Paul's passion for her lessened because he now thought her immoral? She hoped not; such an attitude on his part would kill her feelings for him.

It was a great relief to arrive in London, where no negative familial or religious associations awaited her. She would be working at the WSPU office in the morning and going to Mrs. Pankhurst's house for their meeting in the afternoon, and her only true immediate concern was that Will might be at the WSPU office. She didn't want to see the hurt in his eyes or to have to explain her marriage to him. It was difficult enough to explain it to herself.

The office was a hive of activity when she arrived, but to her relief, Will wasn't there. It was a large room, though not large enough for the Union's needs, crowded with desks and chairs and a long table at one end where meetings were held. An editor and typist were rushing to finish the latest issue of *Votes for Women*, which Lilia needed to read and approve before it could be released. Harriet was participating in a discussion at the long table with other organizers about a planned deputation to the prime minister in a fortnight. Lilia managed to join the discussion and read bits of the newsletter at the same time, but when a third task was required of her—Miss Selwyn wanted to discuss a new plan to attract publicity for the Cause—Lilia turned from her other tasks to give the proposed plan her full attention.

Miss Selwyn was accompanied by two young women who wore the feverishly excited look of new members. There wasn't enough room for everyone to sit down, so they stood in a corner of the office where Lilia could see and be seen by the others in case anyone else needed her.

"I think it's time to destroy more significant property," Miss Selwyn said. "Breaking windows and setting fire to letterboxes is all very well, but the public is starting to expect it. We need to do something different, and I have the perfect idea."

"Go on," Lilia said.

"There's an empty church in Lewisham. It's scheduled for significant repairs next month, so the congregation has been moved temporarily to a different building. I think we ought to set fire to it."

Lilia blinked. "A church?"

"Yes. It's a way of damaging property and making a statement about male privilege at the same time. What institution has oppressed women more over the centuries than the church?"

"But a church . . . isn't like other property."

"How so?"

Lilia wasn't sure how to explain the distinction, given that it was more a vague sense she had absorbed from Paul than her own. After a few seconds, she thought of a better objection.

"Some of our members are Christians," she said. "It will offend them."

"When did you start worrying about offending people?" challenged Miss Selwyn.

When did you become an extremist? Lilia was tempted to retort. But instead she said, "It's not the right time. Let's wait and see what comes of the deputation to the prime minister. If we go too far, the support we've gained will be lost."

"I fail to see how setting fire to an empty church is going too far," Miss Selwyn persisted. "We're merely continuing what we've been doing: harming no living creature, only property."

"I can't allow it," Lilia said.

Miss Selwyn frowned. "Let me write down my plan. You may reconsider when you see the details."

"No, I won't. As I said, wait until after the deputation. Then we'll talk about it again."

Before Miss Selwyn could respond, the editor of *Votes for Women* began waving frantically at Lilia from the other side of the room, calling out, "Mrs. Harris, could you look at this when you've got a moment?"

It was the first time anyone had called Lilia by her married name, and she felt as surprised as Miss Selwyn looked.

"Oh, yes, I heard from Miss Firth that you married," Miss Selwyn said, recovering. "Congratulations."

"Thank you."

"And is it true your husband is a clergyman?"

"Yes."

"If I'd remembered that," Miss Selwyn said serenely, "I wouldn't have troubled you with my plan."

"My marriage has nothing to do with my opposition to your plan," Lilia said, despite knowing full well that nobody, including herself, would believe this.

"Ah."

There was something in the other woman's eyes that made Lilia suspicious. Surely it was no coincidence that the day after her wedding, her least-favorite colleague wanted her approval to damage a church.

Miss Selwyn left with a haughty flounce, her minions trailing after her, and Lilia went to attend to the editor's concerns.

Several Union members insisted on taking Lilia out for luncheon at a nearby Aerated Bread Company shop, where she was subjected to good-natured raillery about her marriage. None except Harriet had met Paul, so they were full of curiosity about the man who had managed to convince confirmed spinster Miss Brooke to be his wife. Lilia answered the barrage of questions as briefly and honestly as she could.

Was he rich? No. Good-looking? Yes. A supporter of women's suffrage? Yes.

Was she madly in love with him?

Lilia sent Harriet a panicked look from across the table.

"Of course she is," Harriet declared.

"When I heard you were married, I was certain it must be to Mr. Reed," one of the women said, "especially when neither of you came to the office yesterday."

"Poor Mr. Reed," another woman said. "Now we know he wasn't there because you broke his heart."

"That's enough of this silliness," Harriet interposed. "One would think we were a group of vapid society ladies instead of serious working women."

Lilia gave her friend a grateful look.

Once Lilia and Harriet were alone in the office after lunch, Harriet asked how things really were between the newlyweds.

"Difficult," Lilia replied. "I hope we'll do better when I see him this weekend."

Later, during her meeting with Mrs. Pankhurst, Lilia found out about a problem with the WSPU in Norwich. Mrs. Teller, the local WSPU leader, was losing her focus on women's suffrage because of her strong political sympathies. The wife of a Liberal candidate, she was associating the WSPU with the Liberal party instead of keeping it separate from party politics, which was an important WSPU mandate. Mrs. Pankhurst asked Lilia to go to Norwich for a few days to speak with Mrs. Teller and try to smooth out the difficulties.

Mrs. Pankhurst was all business throughout their discussion, and Lilia wondered if her leader even knew about her marriage. But at their parting, Mrs. Pankhurst said with a twinkle in her eye, "I hear congratulations are in order."

"Yes. Thank you."

"You work fast, my dear. I had no idea you could conjure up a respectable husband in such a short time. I do hope you'll be happy."

"I've known him for years," Lilia replied. "His parents and mine are good friends." Then, hearing the defensiveness in her voice, she added, "I appreciate the advice you gave me on the subject of marriage."

"I'm glad. And since you've chosen a man you know and trust instead of the unpredictable Mr. Reed, so much the better."

Despite her misgivings about her marriage, Lilia thought so, too.

25

I intended to reason. This passion is detrimental to me; for you do not reflect that *you* are the cause of its excess.

—Mary Shelley, *Frankenstein*

NOVEMBER 1908

Lilia's trip to Norwich was successful in the main, but also exhausting, taking several days longer than expected. Mrs. Teller was suspicious of Mrs. Pankhurst's new deputy and reluctant to rein in her political sympathies, but Lilia was persistent. She used all her powers of persuasion to convince the older woman of the importance of upholding the WSPU mandate. Mrs. Teller gave in grudgingly, but there was still more work to be done mending the rift between Mrs. Teller and her Norwich colleagues. In this, Lilia was not as successful.

By Friday, it was evident that Lilia would not be able to return to Ingleford at the weekend, so she wrote to Paul:

I'm sorry to have to renege on my promise to you, but something urgent has arisen. The WSPU needs me right now and I can't refuse to fulfill my duties when Mrs. Pankhurst has shown so much confidence in me. I hope you understand. I'll come to Ingleford as soon as I possibly can.

She was a little surprised that Paul didn't reply, but perhaps he simply didn't know where to send a letter, because she was traveling. He probably assumed he'd see her soon enough.

But events seemed to conspire against them once again. When Lilia was set to leave Norwich, Mrs. Teller suddenly resigned, throwing the local WSPU into a state of confusion. It took a few more days for Lilia to appoint a new leader and help her understand her duties. And then, once that was settled, there was a mechanical difficulty with her train that led to another day's delay.

When Lilia finally reached the train station in London, she decided on impulse to take the next train to Ingleford instead of going to her London house. It was a Saturday, and she was anxious to make up for missing the previous weekend with Paul. She slept most of the way there, already feeling the strain of too much traveling, but as the train pulled into the station, she felt a spark of excitement. As much as she hated Ingleford, she was looking forward to seeing Paul. His becoming her husband had temporarily obscured the fact that she was fond of him.

Since she hadn't written to tell him she was coming, nobody met her at the train station. She decided to walk to the house and, after arranging for her trunk to be sent on later, she started out, shivering a little in the chilly autumn twilight, but glad for the chance to stretch her legs.

When she arrived at the cottage, the gray cat was sitting on the doorstep, its fur puffed up against the cold. She bent down to pet it, wondering if she ought to knock at the door or enter unannounced. Paul would likely scold her if she acted like a guest, so she let herself in. As she opened the door, the cat darted inside before she could stop it.

She left her carpetbag at the door and waited for her eyes to adjust to the dim light inside. At first she thought Paul wasn't home, but as she walked through the parlor she saw a sliver of light underneath his study door. The cat brushed against her skirt, purring, and she scooped it up in her arms, then knocked.

"Come in," he said.

She entered, still carrying the cat. He was working at his desk, and he looked up at her blankly, then frowned.

"I don't want that cat in the house," was all he said.

Taken aback by this poor excuse for a greeting, she left the room and took the cat outside, then stood in the parlor, unsure what to do. Before she had made up her mind, Paul emerged from his study, looking a little less stern, though still not particularly happy to see her.

"Have you eaten dinner?" he asked.

"No. Have you?"

"No. Mrs. Mills prepared a meal for me about an hour ago. When she left, I forgot about it; I was busy writing my sermon for tomorrow. If you're hungry, we can eat together now."

"Yes, I'd like that."

"Come to think of it, there may not be enough for both of us."

"I don't need very much."

Despite Paul's warning, there was plenty of food. In fact, judging from how little they both ate, there was too much. And the food was the least of Lilia's concerns. Paul's cold, distant manner made her uncomfortable. He was obviously angry with her, presumably for staying away as long as she had, and she didn't relish the idea of talking about it, especially since he looked so forbidding. However, the lengthening silence between them was becoming unendurable.

"I'm sorry I was away for so long," she said, nudging a chunk of potato with her fork from one side of her plate to the other. "I meant to return last weekend, but my new position requires more of my energy than I anticipated. I suppose one must expect to have extraordinary demands on one's time when taking on new duties."

"Is one of your new duties burning down churches?" he asked in a conversational tone.

"What?" She dropped her fork, which clattered loudly on her plate.

"Surely you know how quickly London news reaches Ingleford."

She stared at him.

He rose and left the room, returning a few seconds later to hand her the previous day's issue of the *Times*. A headline near the bottom of the front page read: FIRE AT ALL SAINTS' CHURCH IN LEWISHAM.

"Hellfire and damnation!" she exclaimed.

"Indeed." He returned to his seat, looking at her with an inscrutable expression.

She read the article, though she had a good idea what it would say. Arson was suspected. A copy of *Votes for Women* and two WSPU pamphlets had been found at the scene. Nobody was hurt, but the roof collapsed, essentially destroying the inside of the church.

"Paul, I had nothing to do with this," she said. "One of the WSPU members suggested this plan, but I refused to approve it. I'd never agree to such a thing."

"Why not? It's consistent with the other property damage the WSPU has done."

"But a church isn't merely property," she said, thinking how odd it was to repeat the same argument with Paul that she'd had with Miss Selwyn. "It's sacred . . . consecrated space. Isn't that what you think?"

"Does it matter what I think?"

"I understand that you're angry," she replied, automatically slipping into the calm, persuasive tone she had used with Mrs. Teller and her colleagues in Norwich. "I'm sorry this happened, and I promise the people who did this will be censured."

"I'm not angry," he said.

It was such a blatant lie that she was momentarily speechless.

"Based on what I know of the WSPU," he went on, "setting fire to an empty church is perfectly understandable behavior."

"But surely you don't approve of it?"

"Burning down a church isn't something I would do, obviously, but we're not speaking of me."

She didn't know how to read his expression. It was true that he spoke reasonably, even calmly, but his eyes were cold.

"I'm sorry, nevertheless," she said. "This event is bound to make your life more difficult because of your connection with me."

"You needn't apologize. When we entered into this agreement, you made it clear where your priorities lie. I accepted that agreement, so you have no obligation to explain yourself when you're acting in accordance with it."

He was far angrier than she had realized. His polite words formed a wall of ice around him that she had no idea how to break through. She would have known better what to do if he had shouted at her, or even struck her.

"Paul, we ought to talk—"

"Not now." He stood up. "I haven't finished writing my sermon and don't want to be disturbed. Do you intend to go to morning service tomorrow or will you be returning to London?"

"I'll attend the service. There's nothing I can do in London until Monday, so I'll stay here until then . . . if you don't mind." She was annoyed with herself for asking permission to stay in what was supposed to be her house as well as his, but he certainly wasn't exerting himself to make her feel at home.

"Very well." He left the room, and a moment later she heard the decisive click of his study door.

She was desperate for a cigarette. But when she took one from her case and sat down in the parlor to light it, she remembered Lady Fernham telling her how much Lord Fernham hated it when she smoked in the drawing room. While Lady Fernham had gleefully defied his wishes, Lilia had no intention of doing the same with Paul. She put on her coat and went outside.

The cat was still there. Lilia lit her cigarette and sat on the front step as the animal huddled close to her for warmth. She scratched its head, listening to its loud, rumbling purr. Snow began to fall, gentle flakes eddying and whirling, then dissolving in the gathering darkness. Watching the snow calmed her a little and helped her not to worry about what was happening in London with the WSPU. Harriet had recently left her teaching position to become a WSPU organizer and in Lilia's absence she would step in, to admonish Miss Selwyn or to answer questions from the police or the press, should anything arise before Monday.

From the front step, she could see Paul's study window, a square of light muted by the drawn curtains. Was he really writing his sermon or was that only an excuse to avoid her? Why wouldn't he talk to her? He had been angry with her before, but he had never shut her out completely. If her family had seen the newspaper article, they were surely upset with her, too, but Bianca and James might not be, and she longed for the comfort of their company. But they were Paul's parents, and she couldn't confide in them about her disastrous marriage.

There was nothing for it but to smoke another cigarette and stay outside with the cat until her face and hands were numb with cold.

∾

Lilia had a fitful sleep that night, and she awoke the next morning later than she had intended. After quickly washing and dressing, she went downstairs to find a note from Paul on the dining room table informing her that he had already left for church. She wondered if he expected her not to go. As much as she would have liked to avoid the curious stares of half the village, she gritted her teeth and set out. She would show him she could keep her word, even if it killed her.

Lilia arrived only a few minutes before the service began, and she slipped into her family's pew next to Edward, who, with their mother, sat like bookends on either side of Emily. Her father didn't attend church except on special occasions. Both Edward and Emily looked happy to see her, but her mother merely nodded solemnly. Mrs. Brooke believed it was indecorous to express emotion in church, so she could have been either dismayed or overjoyed to see Lilia; there was no way of knowing which.

Mrs. Stott in the pew in front of them turned around to look at Lilia, then whispered something to her husband. He glanced back at Lilia, too, unsmiling. Though she was relieved she could sit with her family, Lilia felt exposed, on display. Not knowing who knew about the Lewisham church fire made everything worse. It seemed as though everyone was giving her critical looks. Was it all in her mind?

The Jackson family sat across the aisle. When she was ten, Lilia had led her siblings through their garden in an imaginary raid on a pirate ship. Mr. Jackson had appeared on the Brookes' doorstep the next day, his face as purple as the beetroot that would now never grow in his garden because it had been trampled upon by "young barbarians."

Mrs. Barton sat near the front of the church. She had sternly told an adolescent Lilia that she was no longer welcome to associate with Mrs. Barton's daughter, Susan, because Lilia had put improper ideas into Susan's head. Lilia never found out what the supposedly improper ideas were, but she had mourned the loss of that friendship for months.

Everywhere she looked, she saw people from her past who now seemed united against her, a gossiping, nitpicking, judgmental mass of humanity. But she couldn't understand her anxiety. She was a courageous public speaker, used to facing larger and more hostile crowds. She had been heckled, jostled, even beaten. Why did she feel so cowed and panic-stricken by a small gathering of rural parishioners?

When Paul took his place at the front of the church, his presence only added to Lilia's unease. He looked handsome and priestly in his black cassock and clerical collar, but he didn't acknowledge her presence. Would it be inappropriate for him to smile at her? Was he still angry with her? But wasn't it un-Christian of him to remain so? Couldn't he tell she was suffering, having to be in this church for his sake? He was the reason she couldn't leave—or, even better, laugh in the faces of these narrow-minded hypocrites. She was the vicar's wife and had to act accordingly, despite the fact that these people surely found the idea of her as said vicar's wife highly amusing. Or they would, if they had a sense of humor.

Lilia was so caught up in trying to sort out her thoughts and calm herself that she was only half-aware of the service. The music, usually the best part of any church service for her, grated on her nerves. Didn't the others notice that Mrs. Plumstead was playing the harmonium too loudly and couldn't keep proper time?

Even when Paul began to deliver his sermon, Lilia was unable to pay close attention, hearing only fragments of phrases. It wasn't like the eloquent sermon of his that she heard at the cathedral last year. Just as this church was darker, smaller, and more austere than the cathedral, Paul himself seemed diminished, a muted version of his former self. His voice was still resonant and strong, but there was something missing.

He was preaching on a passage from Hosea, one of the minor prophets. What was the point of choosing something obscure that these people could never relate to? At the cathedral, it would be different: people there would expect a more scholarly, esoteric sermon. Here, it was as if he were speaking a different language from most of his listeners.

And then, slowly, as if watching a ship emerge from thick fog, Lilia understood that the sermon was for her, and only for her. This realization came about as Paul read the passage on which his sermon was based:

> *Then said the Lord unto me, Go yet, love a woman beloved of her friend, yet an adulteress . . . So I bought her to me for fifteen pieces of silver, and for an homer of barley, and an half homer of barley: And I said unto her, Thou shalt abide for me many days; thou shalt not play the harlot, and thou shalt not be for another man.*

Lilia didn't know much about the story, but she knew enough to find it distasteful. God instructed the prophet Hosea to marry a prostitute, Gomer. When she proved unfaithful, God told Hosea to take her back. Paul treated the story as a spiritual allegory, as no doubt most clergymen did. Hosea was God, and Gomer, the nation of Israel. The Bible had harsh words for Gomer, whose children were told to turn her out of the house and whose husband promised to "hedge up her way with thorns, and make a wall, that she shall not find her paths." Despite this, the congregation was given to understand that Hosea—and by implication, God—was loving and compassionate.

It was one of the strangest stories in the Bible, and there was only one reason Lilia could think of why Paul would choose to make it the focus of his sermon—to humiliate her. He had found it necessary to tell her on their wedding day not to encourage the attentions of other men. Surely this indicated his belief that she was, if not a prostitute, at least potentially adulterous. His shock when she told him she'd gone to Will's hotel room and his decision not to share her bed seemed to point to the same belief. It seemed that he viewed marrying her as a kind of Christian duty, stooping to raise the fallen woman.

But how could he do something so despicable as to write a sermon with the intention of shaming her publicly? In all the years she had known him, she had never seen him act with deliberate malice. There was the Thomas Cross incident, but Paul hadn't gone this far to hurt his enemy. Did he consider Lilia an enemy, too? She was ready to believe he did.

Her whole body began to shake. No doubt he would wish for her to help him create an impression of wedded bliss for his parishioners, but she couldn't even contemplate standing with Paul at the entrance to the church when the service was over. She closed her eyes and tried to breathe evenly, counting to one hundred once, twice—she didn't know how many times— until Paul had stopped speaking and the harmonium assaulted her ears again for the final hymn.

As the congregation rose to sing, Lilia turned to her brother. "Edward," she whispered urgently, "I must go. I don't feel well."

"I'll come with you," he said, looking alarmed.

"No, that's not necessary. I just need some air."

"Are you certain you don't want me to come along? You look pale."

The kindness in her brother's eyes nearly brought her to tears, but she shook her head and stumbled out of the pew, down the aisle, and out of the church. Once outside, she gathered up her skirt and broke into a run, not caring if anyone saw her. She ran all the way to the house as if pursued.

At the house, she leaned on the back of the nearest chair, gasping for breath and starting to feel foolish. Her hair had come loose from its knot at the nape of her neck, and she took off her hat and tried to twist her hair back into place, without much success. She placed her hand on her chest and, still breathing hard, went up the stairs to the room Paul had assigned to her and began to pack her things. She was free to go, wherever and whenever she wished. She was no longer in a panic, but she moved quickly, wanting to be out of the house by the time Paul returned.

Her wish was not to be realized. As Lilia made her way downstairs with her carpetbag, she heard the front door open, and a moment later Paul met her at the foot of the stairs. He was still wearing his surplice and cassock and his hair was disheveled as if he, too, had been running.

"Lilia, what's the matter? Edward told me you were unwell, so I came home as quickly as I could." He looked and sounded like the old Paul, the one who cared about her, not the cold stranger of the day before or the malicious priest she believed she had seen only minutes earlier.

But Lilia was too upset to care which version of him stood before her now. "I think you know what's the matter," she said.

"I don't."

"Are you so blind to your own behavior?"

"I don't know what you mean. You're going to have to tell me."

"How dare you?" she exclaimed, her voice shaking with fury. "Do you want me to repeat your sermon back to you, to hear your own condemnation of me from my lips?"

He looked stunned. "When did I condemn you?"

"Are you saying you didn't mean to imply that you're the longsuffering prophet with the adulterous wife?"

"Are you mad? Of course not."

"Don't lie to me."

"Why would I do such a thing, Lilia?"

"Only you know. Perhaps it's your way of hedging up my way with thorns."

"I don't choose the readings for the service. They're prescribed for me by the lectionary."

"There were other readings you could have based your sermon on. Don't patronize me!"

"I'm not—" He stopped, looking at her carpetbag, and said quietly, "Oh, I see."

"What?"

"You're looking for a reason to run away again."

She shook her head, incredulous. "I needn't look for one. You've done everything you can to drive me away. And to add insult to injury, you're trying to make me believe it's all in my mind."

"How long will you be away this time?" he asked, giving her a strange, challenging look.

"I'm not coming back, Paul. I *will* go mad if I stay with you under these conditions."

His lips tightened and he looked away.

"I don't blame you, not entirely," she said in a calmer tone. "I know I've made your life difficult. It was idiotic of me to think my reputation would be saved by marrying you when we don't even live together. This arrangement isn't working, and I wish I'd never suggested it."

He neither moved nor spoke.

She left.

26

The mind is its own place, and in itself
Can make a Heav'n of Hell, a Hell of Heav'n

—John Milton, *Paradise Lost*

The damp, sour air in the small room was suffocating. The woman on the bed groaned in pain, sweat glistening on her face, running into her damp hair and soaking the pillow.

"When will the doctor be here? I sent for him almost an hour ago," her husband said, looking at Paul accusingly, as if he were personally responsible for the delay.

"Soon," Paul said, hoping his voice sounded soothing. "I'm certain he'll be here soon." He hoped he spoke the truth. Frankly, he was as anxious for James Anbrey's arrival as anyone else, if only because it meant he could leave the room in order to get a breath of fresh air.

Paul had read the service for the sick from the *Book of Common Prayer*, but it was rare for him to bear the full responsibility for an ailing parishioner, especially one as ill as Jane Perry. By the time Paul was called to the bedside of someone so ill, James was usually already there, and Paul would read the service and leave. Once the patient's spiritual health was taken care of, he felt no responsibility for his or her physical health. But he had dropped by the Perrys' house for a routine visit and Mrs. Perry had taken ill suddenly, so he was staying until James arrived.

Fortunately, James did arrive a few minutes later, dripping wet from the icy rain shower that had been dousing the village all afternoon. Removing his coat at the door of the one-room cottage, James strode to the bedside of his patient without acknowledging anyone else, not Paul or Mr. Perry or even the Perry's frightened young daughter, Dora.

Paul had been in sickrooms with James often enough to be familiar with the other man's methods. James had eyes only for his patient at first, but as soon as he had made the sufferer as comfortable as possible, he would notice the others. He took Mrs. Perry's wrist and felt her pulse, then asked a few questions about the location and intensity of her pain.

After some gentle prodding, both physical and verbal, James turned to Mr. Perry and said quietly, "It will take time to determine what is the matter with your wife. I'm going to give her something to dull the pain a bit."

"It was so sudden, Doctor Anbrey," Mr. Perry said. "One minute she was standing there washing dishes and the next, she was on the floor screaming."

James reached out to put his hand briefly on Mr. Perry's shoulder, then began to search through his medical bag.

Paul rose from his chair on the other side of the bed, deciding it was time for him to leave, but Mrs. Perry cried out, "Mr. Harris, you're not leaving, are you?"

"Not if you wish me to stay," Paul replied.

"Please stay. Could you read the service again, the part about putting away the sins of those who truly repent?"

"Yes, of course." Paul sat down again. James caught his eye and smiled as if Paul were the patient and in need of encouragement.

As James administered the drug, Paul read the prayer, thankful for the prayer book and its measured, beautiful language, and for the fact that he needn't find his own words or attempt to create the false impression that he felt the comfort he was attempting to impart. Sometimes he did feel it, but today wasn't one of those times.

Even after he read the prayer, it was clear that Paul and his prayer book would be needed for a while longer. He wasn't used to spending so much time in the company of James, though Paul was more comfortable working with him than speaking to him in social situations. Working alongside James, Paul could view him merely as a physician, and a good one, at that. He exuded quiet competence and compassion, making both patients and their loved ones believe he would move heaven and earth to help them if he could. As Mrs. Perry dropped off to sleep, Paul listened as James spoke to Mr. Perry as he would to an old friend. Little Dora Perry had climbed into James's lap and was playing with his stethoscope, distracted from her fears about her mother. It was the perfect tableau for a painting: the good doctor surrounded by his grateful patients.

But Paul had no desire to be part of this scene and he was glad when he was no longer needed. He was a little uneasy when James decided to leave with him. James promised Mr. Perry to return later that evening to check on his wife, then fell into step with Paul in the lane outside the cottage. It was no longer raining, and the air was sharp and chill.

Paul thought it best to speak first, to keep the conversation professional. "Do you know what's the matter with Mrs. Perry?"

"No," James replied. "It may be her appendix, but I can't be certain at this point. Pain of this type is difficult to diagnose."

Paul couldn't think of anything else to say, and they walked in silence for a while.

"Your mother and I have been talking about you and Lilia," James said.
This seemed ominous.

"We haven't seen much of either of you since the wedding," the doctor
went on, "and we were hoping you could dine with us sometime soon. When
will Lilia return to Ingleford?"

"I don't know," Paul replied. "She's very busy with her work."

"Perhaps you could come for supper on your own this week, then, and
when she returns, you can both come."

"Perhaps. I'll have to check my engagements for the week." Paul hadn't
made any formal visits to his mother and James before the wedding and he
didn't see any reason to start now. James's inquiries smacked of more than
just friendly interest, and Paul's unease intensified.

"Is everything well between the two of you?" James asked.

Paul didn't know how to answer this question. If he said everything was
fine, it would be an outright lie, but if he told the truth, it would lead to
more questions. Finally, he settled on the vague, "Our living situation is a
challenge, but we're trying to adjust."

This was also a lie. He and Lilia hadn't communicated with each other in
the week since she had left him.

"Edward told me Lilia was upset in church last Sunday," James said,
undeterred.

Not for the first time, Paul wished he didn't live in a small village where
everyone knew everyone else's business. It had been bad enough when the
villagers heard the news of the Lewisham church fire: their responses ranged
from jests about the destructive tendencies of his wife to unsolicited advice
about how he ought to control her. But parishioners' comments were the
least of his worries: Bishop Chisholm had sent him a letter asking to meet
at his earliest convenience in London. By now the bishop would know that
Paul had married the WSPU deputy leader, whom some people considered

directly responsible for the church fire. It would be perfectly reasonable from the bishop's perspective to refuse to recommend Paul for another living.

James continued, "I don't know how much Lilia has told you about her past experiences with that church, but she had a hard time of it as a child. Mr. Russell was always chiding her about something and threatening her with eternal punishment."

"How do you know that?"

"She told me," James replied simply. "I also witnessed some of it in the early days, when your mother and I still attended church. I think Lilia confided in me and your mother because we experienced similar criticism from the vicar and scorn from parishioners. Lilia's parents meant well, but they were largely oblivious to the way she was treated. Your mother and I bore it better—we were adults and had each other—but Lilia was only a child.

"I'm saying this," James went on, "only because it might help you understand that it's bound to be more difficult for Lilia to attend church, especially this church, than it would be for anyone else. If you're patient with her, she may—"

"Thank you," Paul interrupted. "I'll think about that." He didn't wish to add to the troubles he already had by saying something he might regret.

They had reached a fork in the road and James looked as though he would go to the right.

"I'm late for an appointment," Paul said hurriedly, starting to turn left.

"Paul, wait." James's voice was firm, and Paul was startled enough to turn and face him. "I'm worried about Lilia. She's strong in some ways, but fragile in others. She needs to be treated gently."

Paul felt his composure beginning to crack. Who did this man think he was, speaking of Lilia as if he knew her better than Paul did?

"I'm not saying this to cause you pain," James added. He looked at Paul with the same warmth and concern he had shown to the Perry family. "I care about both of you and want you to be happy."

Paul could withstand no more of this. He was acutely sensitive to any attempt on James's part to take on a fatherly role. Paul had managed to keep him at a distance thus far and there had been no danger of his doing so. But James was intruding now, prying into affairs that had nothing to do with him.

Not trusting himself to speak, Paul simply walked away.

By the time he reached his house, Paul was exhausted with the effort of keeping himself together. He had no appointment, despite what he had told James, and he went upstairs to the room Lilia had slept in for only two nights, but which he thought of as hers. He sat on the bed and stared numbly at the wall. The room was bare, almost sterile, as if it had never been inhabited. He had believed Lilia when she'd told him that she wasn't coming back. He had no idea why he had been so angry with her that weekend; it had taken him several days even to admit to himself that he had been angry. It was true that having to wait to see her for more than a fortnight after the wedding had been difficult, but his disappointment had been mixed with anticipation.

When she had appeared unexpectedly that day at the door of his study, holding that stupid cat and looking beautiful and alive and happy, something had snapped inside him, something he had no control over. At the time, he had felt justified in treating her coldly, while another part of him, a weaker part, stood by and watched in mortified silence.

Paul lay down on the bed and studied the ceiling. Stretching out his arm, he ran his hand over the bedclothes, then turned over to bury his face in the sheets. They smelled faintly of Lilia's cinnamon-scented cigarettes.

He didn't know what to think about his sermon that had upset her so much. Beyond that, he was genuinely shocked that she believed him capable of such an act of condemnation. He had had no conscious intention of

288 ❧ CLARISSA HARWOOD

applying the Hosea story to his own marriage—he was no prophet, and Lilia was no prostitute. He could only just begin to understand her behavior now that James had told him about Lilia's experiences with the church as a child.

Yes, she had overreacted, but he considered himself primarily responsible for the events of the disastrous weekend. Not only had he treated her coldly, but in her eyes he had publicly labeled her a prostitute. He was her husband and his role was to protect her, to defend her against the criticism of others, but he had turned out to be her harshest critic. He knew to the core of his being that he loved her enough to give up his life for her. Why, then, had he behaved as he did?

Paul couldn't answer this question, so he continued to live his life in a fog, doing what was expected of him, plodding along without thinking beyond the next day, caught in a vicious cycle of his own making that prevented him from seeking out his wife. The embarrassment of knowing his marriage had failed before it was even a month old, knowing he had killed it and not understanding why, kept him silent and miserable.

He remained this way for another week, despite the increasing attempts of his and Lilia's families to talk to him about his marriage. It was relatively easy to manage Lilia's parents: her mother was obviously unsympathetic to her daughter's unconventional ways and felt sorry for Paul, and her father seemed to see no trouble anywhere unless someone informed him very distinctly that there was some.

Bianca was more difficult to brush off. She seemed to think that Paul had deliberately driven Lilia away.

"I hope you haven't demanded too much of her," she said at one point. "You do tend to expect a great deal from people, you know."

Paul didn't think it was unreasonable to expect his wife to spend two days a week with him, but he chose not to defend himself.

A few days later, Paul was visiting Mr. Thompson, an old widower whom

Paul admired for his quiet wisdom. Mr. Thompson had a wide range of interests and had written several books on subjects as various as theology, botany, and shipbuilding. In the course of their discussion, of the church and of Mr. Thompson's late wife, the burden of silence about Paul's marriage became too much for him.

"I wouldn't be the man I am without my Flora," Mr. Thompson said. "We were together for sixty years, and when I reread the books I wrote, I see her influence in every line."

"You must miss her very much," Paul said.

"I do, but she's been gone ten years now, and the pain has lessened while the joy has increased—not only the joy of remembering her, but also the knowledge that my own death is coming. I'll see her again soon."

Paul hoped, selfishly, that Mr. Thompson wouldn't die soon. Despite his eighty-odd years, his mind was sharper and more active than that of most forty-year-olds, and Paul didn't want to be deprived of his company or his wisdom.

"I hope you'll have many happy years with your wife also, Mr. Harris. How is she?"

Paul had been asked this simple question countless times during the past two weeks, but he couldn't give Mr. Thompson the polite, evasive answer he had given everyone else.

He bowed his head and said quietly, "She left me."

There was a pause. Then Mr. Thompson said, "I'm sorry to hear that. Why did she leave?"

Paul had been keeping the secret long enough that now, in the presence of someone he hadn't known very long but whom he trusted instinctively, the story poured out of him in a torrent of words. He told the old man everything, from how the marriage had come about to what had happened the day Lilia left.

When Paul had finished, the old man sat with him in silence for a while.

Paul began to worry that he had said too much, not about himself, but about Lilia. Surely her beliefs and behavior would be shocking to a man as old as Mr. Thompson, and Paul hadn't spared her any more than he had spared himself in telling his story.

"Well, you've certainly found yourself a very unusual wife," Mr. Thompson said finally, sounding bemused rather than critical.

"Found her and lost her," Paul said.

"Why are you so quick to lose heart? You say you love her. Then you must fight for her and for your marriage. Yes, it has begun badly, but you needn't despair. Why, if I had given up hope when Flora and I had difficulties—and believe me, we had many—we would never have had all those happy years together."

Paul thought what had happened between him and Lilia was beyond anything that could be termed mere "difficulties," but he only said, "I don't know what to do."

"What do you want to do?"

"I want to see her and tell her I'm sorry for the way I acted . . . and I want to ask her to come back."

"What prevents you from doing so?"

"I don't understand why I behaved as I did," Paul said slowly, "and I can't promise her it won't happen again."

"Well, there's hope if you're willing to change."

"I am willing."

"May I say a prayer for you?"

None of his parishioners had ever offered to pray for him before, and he was deeply touched. "Yes, of course."

Paul bowed his head, and the old man said a prayer: "Our Father, we ask Your blessing upon Mr. Harris. Bring light into his darkness, and lead him into Your truth. Amen."

Something profound happened during that simple, brief prayer, something Paul could never fully understand or explain. He felt himself go back to the moment Lilia left him and enter deeply into the pain of it.

There was only one other time he had felt that kind of anguish: when his mother had left him and Philip to live with James. That ache of abandonment he had felt as a fifteen-year-old boy came back to him—it was sharp, too raw for tears, too searing for words, and it enveloped him now as if it was happening all over again.

He had been alone in his room, reading Thomas à Kempis's *The Imitation of Christ*. He remembered Philip knocking on his bedroom door, announcing that Bianca was leaving, and then abruptly walking away. Paul had left the book open on his desk and gone to the window to watch his mother get into a hansom cab. She had left a note, which he hadn't found until much later, but she hadn't said good-bye that day.

Now, something told Paul it was safe to enter fully into that pain in a way that he couldn't have done as a boy. He was led by an invisible hand through this agonizing darkness, and just when he thought it might crush him, he was aware of the darkness lifting and a sense of comfort and peace.

Paul looked up. He was alone. Mr. Thompson had left the room, but muffled sounds in the next room indicated he was nearby. For a while longer, Paul remained where he was, in a state of acute awareness. He wasn't praying, but he felt what he recognized as the presence of God in a far more intense way than he ever had before. His physical senses were suspended, giving way to a spiritual sense that was far more real. When Mr. Thompson returned to the room, he sat down across from Paul again, looking at him kindly but saying nothing.

"Thank you," Paul said, knowing his words were inadequate, but finding no better ones.

It was enough.

The sense of peace stayed with Paul for the rest of the week. Even when he boarded the train for London on his first day free from work, that peace buoyed him, despite his concerns about the difficult conversations awaiting him.

He went to see Bishop Chisholm first. When he sat down in the bishop's receiving room at the palace, he hardly knew how to begin. He would have to admit that he not only had ignored the bishop's advice to end his association with the women's suffrage movement, but also had married the WSPU deputy leader.

The bishop, apparently tired of waiting for Paul to begin, said, "I heard rumors that you married a militant suffragette, but I didn't realize until recently that the woman you married is the notorious Miss Brooke." His tone was measured, but not severe.

"I apologize for not telling you sooner," Paul said.

"You know my opinion of the militant suffragettes, so I won't pain you by repeating it," the bishop said. "I will say I was shocked by the Lewisham church fire. I assume you knew nothing about it, but I wonder at your wife allowing such a thing to happen under her leadership."

"She knew about the plan but refused to approve it. The people involved went ahead without her knowledge."

"I have no quarrel with the women who want the vote. As far as I am concerned, they may have it, but I can make no public statements of support. You must understand that."

Paul did understand, because it was his own position, too. But he also knew that private support wouldn't help women get the vote. He had married Lilia, hoping, like a coward, that he could agree with her views in theory but avoid acting on them.

"You must know your marriage makes it difficult for me to recommend you for a permanent living," Bishop Chisholm said.

"Yes." Paul was caught between wanting to defend Lilia and working to avoid further damage to his career.

"Is there any chance your wife would be willing to take a less public role, or transfer her allegiance to one of the non-militant Christian suffrage societies?"

"No, I don't think she would." Then Paul surprised himself by adding, "And I wouldn't want her to compromise her beliefs."

The bishop shook his head and said, "That makes things very difficult indeed."

He had no idea how difficult, given that Paul was hurting his own chances of preferment because of a wife who had already left him.

"Do not mistake me," Bishop Chisholm continued. "I am pleased with the work you have done in Ingleford. Your perseverance with a difficult parish is a credit to you. Whatever my doubts about your marriage, I haven't forgotten what you are capable of."

"I appreciate that very much."

It was good to hear the bishop's affirmation of his work, and Paul felt cautiously hopeful about his future prospects of a better living, but it saddened him to realize that in the eyes of the bishop, his wife was a detriment to him. Lilia had to be aware that many people would think the same, which made it all the more important to tell her how he felt about her.

As soon as he left the bishop's palace, he went to the WSPU office at Clement's Inn to see Lilia. He had never been inside. For a moment, he stood looking up at the five-story brick building and screwing up his courage while office workers and newsboys rushed past him.

There was a reception desk just inside the building, but nobody was behind it, so he went up the first flight of stairs and into a large, open room filled with people and activity. Women hurried past him with bundles of papers. One woman at a nearby desk was typing furiously. Another was talking on the telephone and taking notes at the same time. There were WSPU posters and notice boards bearing newspaper clippings on the walls. Announcements and banners were piled on a table. At the other end of the long room, a cluster of women sat around a large table and Lilia stood before them, gesturing energetically as she spoke. He was too far away to hear what she was saying, but he knew those gestures went with her most persuasive speeches.

A bespectacled woman stopped in front of him, glancing at his clerical collar. "May I help you, sir?"

"Yes. I'd like to speak to . . . er, Miss Brooke."

"Do you mean Mrs. Harris?"

"Yes." He was absurdly gratified to hear that Lilia was using his name.

"Whom shall I say is asking for her?"

"Paul Harris. Her husband."

"Oh!" She peered at him more closely over the top of her glasses. "Yes, of course. I'll fetch her."

The bespectacled woman went to Lilia, whispered something, and pointed across the room to where Paul stood. Lilia turned and met his eyes, only a momentary stillness indicating she had seen him. She turned to speak to the women at the table, then began to walk towards him.

She was interrupted a few times by others who clearly needed advice or answers to questions. They buzzed to and fro around her like worker bees around their queen, and Paul was struck by both how much they depended on her and how completely in command she was.

When she finally stood before him, she kept a careful three feet between them.

"What do you want?" she said. She looked weary, with dark circles under her eyes, but she was still far and away the most beautiful woman he knew.

The typist's fingers went still as she watched Paul and Lilia with curious eyes. Two other women at a nearby desk smiled knowingly and whispered to each other.

"Can we speak somewhere privately?" he asked.

She glanced across the room. "I'm very busy."

"It won't take long." When she hesitated, he added, "Please."

She looked at him warily. Then, as if deciding that talking to him was the quickest way to get rid of him, she nodded and led the way back downstairs to the reception desk, which was still unmanned. There were two chairs at the desk, but it was clear she had no intention of sitting.

An office vestibule wasn't the ideal setting for the conversation Paul wanted to have, but at least for the moment it was private.

"I want to apologize," he said. "I behaved badly the last time you came to Ingleford."

She waved her hand wearily. "There's no need for that."

"Yes, there is. I don't blame you for thinking I was trying to drive you away, nor do I blame you for not wanting to come back. I was wrong in everything I did that weekend—treating you coldly, refusing to communicate with you, acting as if you were a criminal. The sermon, too—"

"It doesn't matter now."

"It *does* matter," he insisted, taking a step towards her. "I didn't see it before, but I understand now what that sermon must have done to you, what it must have made you think. I'm so sorry."

"Paul, we both said things we shouldn't have. I don't want to revisit our last conversation." She sighed. "Don't you see this marriage is bringing out the worst in both of us? We want different things, and I can't fulfill my obligations as your wife without doing violence to myself. We should never have married, and it's best that we stay away from each other."

"I can't accept that," he said firmly. "What you think I expect of you is not true—not anymore. You need never attend another church service if you don't want to. I don't expect regular visits from you, either, but I hope you'll want to see me sometimes. I've started to understand myself better in the past little while, and though I can't promise never to hurt you again, I *will* do better."

She made no reply, her face averted and eyes downcast. Paul took another step towards her. They were close enough that he could easily take her in his arms, but he knew that if he tried, she would likely resist.

"One more word," he said, "and I'll go. Will you please look at me?"

She slowly raised her eyes to his. Her eyes glittered with what could be anger or unshed tears—he couldn't tell which.

Paul went on, his voice trembling with intensity, "I love you, Lilia. Don't forget what good friends we once were . . . or how it felt when we kissed. I don't care how other people think a wife or husband ought to behave. And if you don't want me as your husband, let me be your lover. I'm sorry I wouldn't discuss . . . certain things with you before, but I'm willing now. I'll wait for whatever you can give me, whenever you can give it."

Their eyes remained locked during a motionless, fragile silence.

"I'll think about it," she whispered. Then she turned and went quickly up the stairs.

27

Let him kiss me with the kisses of his mouth: for thy love is better than wine.

—The Song of Solomon 1:2

DECEMBER 1908

I don't like it," Lilia said.

"You needn't like it," Harriet replied. "You knew when you became Mrs. Pankhurst's deputy that you couldn't act as freely as you did before."

"Yes, but I didn't realize I'd be protected to such an extent. You know me, Harriet. I don't like being coddled."

"If you call this coddling, you may be in the wrong position."

Lilia sighed and stared across the desk at her friend. It was early evening and they were alone in the WSPU office. Everyone else had gone home for the day, but they had stayed to work out the details of their deputation to the prime minister. The plans had been delayed after the Lewisham church fire, and now that there was a general election, it would be delayed even longer.

"You refuse bodyguards and insist on accompanying the deputation," Harriet went on. "I don't know what else you want. Mrs. Pankhurst has bodyguards; she understands the need for them."

"I'm not as well known as she is. I don't need bodyguards."

Harriet said, "You can't do everything as our leader that you did when you were only a member."

"I just want to help implement the plans I make. It's only fair."

"You need a break. Why don't you go to Ingleford for a while? It's the perfect time. We can't do much when the government isn't in."

"Do you really think that's a good idea?" Lilia said. She had told Harriet about her disastrous trip to Ingleford and Paul's subsequent apology, but her friend hadn't advised her one way or the other. It had been two weeks since Paul had come to see her in London.

"What can it hurt?" Harriet replied. "If Mr. Harris is true to his word, things will be better. If not, you won't have lost anything."

"I suppose I ought to have expected his coldness to me, given the church fire." Lilia smoothed the papers on the desk in front of her.

"It seemed to me he was more upset about your broken promise to see him that weekend than about the church fire."

"He's a priest. Naturally he'd be upset about anyone in my organization setting fire to a church."

"I'm not so sure. He'd probably set fire to his own church if it made you pay attention to him."

"Harriet, don't ever let him hear you say such a thing! You're hopelessly sacrilegious."

"Don't worry, I won't offend your reverend husband. I can't believe I ever thought it necessary to try to convince him—" Harriet broke off, looking mortified.

"Convince him of what?"

"Oh, nothing. I was just running off at the mouth."

"No," Lilia said firmly, "you were about to say something and I want to know what it was."

Harriet sighed. "It doesn't matter now. When you asked Mr. Harris to marry you and he refused, and then you started writing that letter to Mr. Reed . . . well, I was worried you were about to make a terrible mistake. Everything was happening quickly and I didn't want you to legally bind yourself to that . . . adventurer." Harriet uttered the word as if it were a curse.

Lilia stared at her friend in silence.

"I went to Ingleford the next day," Harriet went on. "I thought it was only fair to tell Mr. Harris what you were contemplating. I asked him to reconsider your proposal."

"Oh, Harriet. How could you?" Lilia felt a mixture of conflicting emotions: humiliation at the thought of her friend having to convince Paul to marry her, anxiety about his needing to be convinced, and gratitude that Harriet cared so much about her.

"I knew if you were going to marry anyone, it must be him."

"What did he say?"

"Oh, he put up a bit of a fight, but it was merely to save face. The man is mad with love for you, you know." Harriet looked uncharacteristically anxious. "You will forgive me, won't you?"

"Of course I forgive you." Lilia bit her lip. "I never could have married Will."

"No. And I wondered if all of your talk about fixing the damage to your reputation was protesting a little too much. Do you know what I mean? I think deep down you really wanted to marry Mr. Harris. You just didn't want to admit it."

Lilia smiled at her friend. "You're a wise woman, Harriet."

She had been shaken by Paul's visit to her, as much as she pretended not to be. His apology had seemed sincere, and she hadn't expected him to give her complete freedom to visit him only when she wished—and to avoid church services. And when he'd said, "let me be your lover," in that impassioned tone, it had been nearly impossible to steel herself against him. It was what she had always wanted.

But she was his wife, and the world wouldn't let her forget she was the wrong wife for him. Her own mother wouldn't let her forget it, if the regular letters Lilia received were any indication.

Why did you marry if you didn't mean to live with your husband? Mrs. Brooke had written in one. *Why do you insist upon doing illegal, violent things that you know will make his career difficult? Why don't you come home and be a wife to him? What has he done to deserve your neglect?*

As always, Lilia's first impulse in response to such chidings was to do the opposite of what her mother wanted. But she didn't want Paul to suffer. Despite her misgivings about the marriage and the uncomfortable sense that she was being weak, she decided to give him another chance.

Not wishing to take him by surprise as she had the last time, she wrote to ask if she might visit the following Monday. That day of the week seemed the safest. There would be no pressure from anyone, including her family, to attend church, and Paul would likely be more relaxed because it was his usual day off. Paul's response was brief but warm—*I would love that*—so she was set to take the Monday morning train.

A couple of days before her trip, Lilia visited Lady Fernham. Although she worried that she was being overly optimistic, it seemed wise to gain some knowledge of contraceptive devices before going to Ingleford, and Lady Fernham was the only person she felt she could turn to for advice. Lady Fernham had always been frank about matters most people considered too private to mention. But when Lilia tried to broach the subject, she surprised herself by having an attack of shyness.

"You want my advice about marriage?" Lady Fernham exclaimed in surprise. "Surely I'm the last person you ought to take advice from, unless you want it to be a bad one."

"Not about marriage, exactly. More about how to . . . prevent pregnancy. I thought you might know."

"Ah, I see."

Lady Fernham swiftly and discreetly dispatched her maid to purchase what she called a French irrigator. The device looked surprisingly like an ornament a respectable matron might keep on the mantel in her drawing room, but Lilia didn't inspect it too closely. She still felt unaccountably shy in the presence of Lady Fernham, who asked no questions and behaved as if such a purchase were the most natural thing in the world.

When Lilia arrived in Ingleford that Monday morning, Paul met her at the train station, looking subdued, but hopeful. He insisted on carrying her carpetbag and they walked to the house together. They said little aside from making brief, superficial observations about the weather and their families. Lilia was on her guard, sensitive to the slightest indication that he wouldn't keep his word about his expectations of her. He seemed to sense this, for he was quieter than usual. She was relieved when they reached the house and could focus on something other than each other.

As Paul opened the front door for her and followed her inside, he said, "I think Agamemnon has missed you."

"Who?" she asked, puzzled. Her question was answered by the arrival from the parlor of the gray cat, who sidled up to her with an unmistakably smug look.

"I couldn't get rid of him," Paul explained. "After a while, I began to admire his persistence, and when I gave him a name, he knew he'd won. He looks like an Agamemnon, don't you think?"

"Indeed," Lilia said, trying to conceal a smile.

"I thought he'd be useful in the house to catch mice. And now that it's winter, I didn't want to see him out in the cold."

She reached down to pet the cat, who rewarded her with his usual loud purr.

"Would you like to dine at your parents' house today?" Paul asked her. "They invited us as soon as they knew you were coming, but I haven't given them an answer."

Lilia hesitated, weighing the critical attitude of her mother against the long-delayed pleasure of conversing with her sister. "I think I'd like to go, if you would."

"Yes, of course."

Paul took Lilia's carpetbag upstairs. He was followed closely by the cat and less closely by Lilia herself. Leaving the bag in her bedroom, Paul paused on the landing and said, "You can find me in the study when you're ready to leave."

He went down the stairs, once again shadowed by the cat, and Lilia couldn't help laughing. "That cat is very fond of you. Are you certain Agamemnon is the right name for him? He seems rather docile."

Paul turned around, looking grave. "He can be ferocious when he chooses. You'll see that, hopefully, while you're here."

She smiled and went into her bedroom, closing the door behind her. The cat had lessened the initial tension between her and Paul, and after she had changed into a dark blue silk blouse and tidied her hair, she went downstairs, feeling more relaxed.

Though Paul's study door was wide open, she hesitated at the threshold. But she was reassured by the admiring look in his eyes.

"I forgot to mention you can bring your papers in here if you need to work," he said.

Only then did she notice the sofa that used to be in his study was gone. In its place was a second desk and chair.

"It's yours," he said in answer to her questioning look. "You ought to have your own space where you can work. Is it acceptable? You can have the desk moved closer to the window if you wish."

"It's perfect," she said warmly. "Thank you, Paul."

They set out to walk to her parents' house in a silence that was more comfortable than their walk from the train station had been.

Lilia was pleased to find that Edward and the Anbreys were dining with her parents and Emily that evening, as well. In addition to being happy to see them, she was convinced that with more people present, it was less likely that her mother would try to take her aside to lecture her about the proper behavior of a wife. Everyone seemed happy to see her, so dinner passed comfortably enough, with the usual boisterous talk around the table.

Her mother and Bianca dominated the conversation, as they usually did. That day, her mother had received a letter from Harry, Lilia's eldest brother, with the news that he had just been appointed captain of a ship. Lilia predicted her mother would refer to him for months to come as "my son Harry, the navy captain." Although Lilia was happy for her brother, she couldn't help feeling a familiar twinge of envy. He had always been her parents' favorite.

But she soon realized her family's focus on Harry was a blessing in disguise. It meant nobody would ask her questions about the rarity of her visits to Paul. It also allowed her to spend time alone with Emily. After dinner, the two sisters withdrew to the window seat in the drawing room for a private conversation, and Emily plied Lilia with questions about her work in London. Lilia obliged as best she could, though as always, she didn't discuss the WSPU's more extreme militant activities.

After telling Emily about her work, Lilia ventured to ask about the squire's son, Theodore Nesbit. At the dinner table, Edward had remarked upon Mr. Nesbit's more frequent attendance at church services of late. Emily blushed at this, alerting Lilia to the possibility of a romance.

"Does Mr. Nesbit speak to you often?" Lilia asked her sister.

"Not really," Emily said sheepishly. "He's a friend of Edward's, and sometimes he talks to both of us after morning service. I just happen to be there—that's all."

Lilia was quite certain Mr. Nesbit didn't speak to Emily just because she "happened" to be there, and it struck fear into her heart. Emily was a lovely girl, and if their parents intended to protect her from the world, they had better think of a way to protect her from men, as well. Didn't they realize it would take no more contact than Emily had already had with Mr. Nesbit to create a romantic attachment? Such an attachment might not lead to tragedy, if Mr. Nesbit was an honorable young man, but Lilia didn't want her sister's heart broken.

Lilia hadn't yet responded to Emily, but the younger girl seemed to understand something of what Lilia was thinking. Emily took her sister's hand and said, "Don't worry, Lilia. I do think Mr. Nesbit is handsome and kind, but I'm only fifteen. I don't think seriously of anyone." Then, seeing Lilia's face, Emily added, "I've told you the truth and you mustn't doubt me—really!"

Lilia squeezed Emily's hand. "Very well, but be careful. I don't want you to lose your heart. There are few men in the world who are worthy of you, and it's too much to expect that one of them could live right here in the village."

The other members of the family entered the drawing room and sat down together. Lilia's parents and Bianca began a conversation at one end of the room, and James, Paul, and Edward sat together at the other end. Nobody intruded upon Lilia and Emily in their private nook.

"It can't be so terrible to lose one's heart to the right person," Emily said. "When did you know you were in love with Paul?"

Lilia hadn't expected this question, and she said nothing at first, floundering for an appropriate response. Eventually she stammered, "I . . . I don't know."

"I admire him excessively," Emily went on, not seeming to notice Lilia's discomfort. "He's had a hard time here. You know how the villagers are, so suspicious of anything or anyone who's different, and just because Paul doesn't do everything the way Mr. Russell did, they criticize him. I've heard people say shockingly rude things to him after church services, but he always responds graciously. If anyone criticized me that way, I'd be tempted to strike them!"

Lilia laughed. "Emily, you wouldn't strike anyone if your life depended on it."

"You know what I mean. You're lucky to be married to such a noble-hearted man. And the way he looks at you . . . well, I hope someday a man will look at me like that. It's horrid that you have to be in London so often. You must miss him terribly."

Sweet, silly Emily. Her romantic imagination couldn't help but blind her to the complexities of Lilia and Paul's relationship. Emily was the only member of the family who didn't seem suspicious of the separate lives Lilia and Paul led. Even at dinner, Lilia had seen the older generation— her mother, Bianca, and James in particular—observing her and Paul with sober, questioning eyes.

Lilia said slowly, "Yes, I do. I do miss him."

Emily and Lilia continued their conversation for a while longer, then went to join their parents and Bianca. Lilia paid little attention to the general conversation because she was observing Paul—unobtrusively, she hoped. It was especially interesting to watch him with James. Although she couldn't hear what they were saying, she had never seen Paul look so relaxed in the company of his natural father. The two of them even laughed at something Edward said, looking suspiciously like friends.

Paul also seemed more comfortable than he used to be with Lilia's family. In the past, he had always worn a polite mask with them, but his eyes had told Lilia the real story—he was merely enduring their noisy chatter and hoping to escape to his precious solitude as soon as possible. Now, he actually seemed to enjoy their company.

Lilia would have been content to observe Paul all evening. She was still on her guard and she felt safer watching him from a distance. But a little later, he approached her as she was sitting with her parents and said, "Lilia, will you come and look at the book James brought for us?"

She rose and went with him.

On a small desk at the other end of the drawing room lay a huge, dusty volume of Horace's Odes, the *Carminum*. Fascinated, Lilia pounced on it at once, carefully opening the front cover, which looked as if it might crumble under her hands.

"Where did you find this, Uncle James?" she demanded, sitting down at the desk. "It looks as old as Horace himself!"

"I was looking through a box of books from my school days," James said, "and there it was. My schoolmaster gave it to me. He may have intended it as a gift, but, unfortunately, I considered it a punishment. I never could make head or tail of Horace, I must admit. I thought you and Paul, being scholars, would appreciate it more."

Lilia motioned for Paul to join her, and he pulled up a chair next to hers.

"It's been a long time since I've read Horace," Paul said. "This takes me back to my days at Eton."

"Yes, it does the same for me—*my* days at Eton, vicariously experienced through you, that is. Listen to the beauty of these words. Nobody writes like Horace: *Intermissa, Venus, diu rursus bella moves? Parce precor, precor.*"

"Yes, indeed. I always loved Horace, though I did struggle with translating some of his works."

"I never struggled," Lilia said, glancing mischievously at Paul, who hesitated only a second before taking the bait.

"Tell me how you would translate this one, then," he challenged her, and they immediately began to argue about it.

Lilia was in her element. She loved to compete with Paul in this way, and they quickly reverted to their childhood attempts to outdo each other in cleverness. But this time, there was an added sense of excitement, an undercurrent she couldn't ignore. They were sitting so close that her shoulder pressed against his arm. She noticed that James and Edward had left them to join the others.

They argued their way through several odes. Eventually, Paul turned to one near the beginning of the volume, "Vitas hinnuelo."

"I'm reluctant to discuss this one with you, because it's one of my favorites," he said, "and you will, no doubt, try to demolish my translation, but go ahead. Do your worst."

Lilia complied, finding no particular difficulty in the first two stanzas. The ode was simple, the words of a lover pursuing a young girl named Chloe, whom he compared to a fawn, and assuring her he would do her no harm. The last stanza was more difficult, and Lilia had to slow down a little as she translated.

"I think the last stanza goes something like this: 'However, I do not pursue you to crush you like the savage tiger or Gaetulian lion. Leave your mother at last: you are ripe to . . . follow, or perhaps comply with . . . a man.'"

"Well done," said Paul in a schoolmasterly tone that was softened by a hint of a smile, "though I've seen a different translation of the last line: 'you are ripe for a lover's kisses.'"

"Nonsense!" said Lilia. "There isn't anything about kisses in the Latin."

"Nevertheless, I think it's a more poetic translation. Wouldn't you consider sacrificing some accuracy in translation in order to retain the beauty of the language? I didn't know you were such a purist." He nudged her arm with his elbow and gave her a sidelong glance.

Perhaps it was just the mention of kisses, but it seemed to Lilia that his eyes were focused on her lips, and she began to have trouble thinking clearly. It helped to remember they weren't alone, though the others seemed to have forgotten them and were conversing gaily at the far end of the room.

Lilia said, a little breathlessly, "I think the words 'you are ripe to comply with a man' are poetic enough."

"I don't like 'comply with,' or even 'follow.' *Sequi* could mean 'pursue' instead."

"No, I don't think so. Horace uses *persequor* earlier in the ode to refer to the lover's pursuit of Chloe, so if he meant 'pursue' in the last line, he wouldn't have chosen *sequi*."

"Perhaps. I like the ambiguity of *sequi*, though. It raises the possibility that Chloe could pursue her lover as well as be pursued by him."

"But—" Lilia began, then stopped, disconcerted by the disparity between his calm, academic tone and the intense, hot look in his eyes. She tried again. "Don't you think 'comply with' is more consistent with Chloe's role throughout the ode?"

"It may be, but I prefer to think of Chloe as active, not merely the passive recipient of her lover's pursuit."

Lilia gave him a look that she hoped was a better answer than anything she could express in words. Could he tell she was trembling?

"Shall we go home?" he whispered.

"Yes."

Their families seemed a little startled by Paul and Lilia's sudden decision to leave, but they made no protests. Lilia couldn't put her boots, coat, and hat on fast enough. After saying quick farewells, they burst out of the house.

Paul took Lilia's hand and they hurried down the front walk towards the tree-lined lane. It was a clear, cold winter evening, and the sky was lit by millions of stars.

As soon as they entered the lane, Paul stopped, turning to face her, and pulled her into his arms. She leaned into him and raised her face to his. He kissed her hungrily, his mouth delicious and warm and thrilling. She wanted to weep with the relief of finally being able to touch him, of being held in his arms and kissed long and passionately. It seemed incredible that she had been able to stay away from him for so long.

"That conversation about Horace's Odes nearly destroyed me," he said when they paused for breath.

"Me, too."

"I almost kissed you in your parents' drawing room, in front of everyone."

"I wanted you to," she said.

They kissed again, a long, deep kiss, but the layers of winter clothing they were wearing began to feel like a torment. Lilia murmured against his lips, "Let's go home."

They resumed their rapid pace, and by the time they reached the house they were breathless with frustration and laughter. Agamemnon was waiting for them on the front step. When they went in, he shot past them into the dim interior of the house. Paul threw off his coat and hat and went to light the parlor lamp as Lilia removed her outer clothing.

They met at the bottom of the stairs.

"Finally," she said with a sigh, slipping her arms around his waist.

His mouth came down on hers again, and his hands went to her hair, pulling the pins from it until it fell in loose waves over her shoulders. Then he unbuttoned her blouse and stroked her breasts through the thin silk of her chemise, making her gasp with pleasure. Her hands moved down his back to grip his bottom.

He drew in his breath, then took her by the shoulders and held her away from him, looking serious. "Lilia, we haven't talked—"

"Yes, we have. We talk too much, in fact." She moved back into his arms and teased him with her lips a hairsbreadth from his.

"Forgive me," he whispered back. "I've been a fool."

She took his hand, led him upstairs to her bedroom, and showed him exactly how much of a fool he had been.

28

I have led her home, my love, my only friend.

There is none like her, none.

—Alfred, Lord Tennyson, *Maud*

Paul awoke the next morning to bright daylight and—incredibly—Lilia asleep in bed beside him. Her cheeks were flushed and her hair fell across the pillow and over her bare shoulders in a profusion of waves. She looked utterly irresistible, and Paul drank in the sight of her as if it he would never have another chance. He tried to breathe as quietly as possible, as if even that might awaken her and make her disappear. Twenty-four hours earlier, he wouldn't have believed he'd be sharing her bed. The best he had hoped for was to get through the day without an argument.

Hearing the hall clock chime seven, he reluctantly slipped out of bed and started to dress. He had a full day of work ahead and couldn't be late for his first meeting, but it was a struggle to tear himself away from Lilia.

He went downstairs to make tea and brought up a tray for her. When he set the tray on the bedside table, she murmured something incoherent and opened her eyes.

"Good morning, my love," he said, sitting beside her on the edge of the bed.

"Good morning. Oh, you're dressed," she said, gazing at his partly buttoned shirt. The disappointment in her voice was flattering.

"I have a vestry meeting in an hour."

She sat up and pushed the bedclothes aside. She was remarkably unself-conscious about her nakedness, which caught Paul off guard. He hadn't seen her body last night in the darkness, and now he couldn't look away.

"Must you go at once?" she asked, stretching her arms above her head.

"Not if you're going to do that," he said, reaching out to stroke her breast.

"Mmm." She closed her eyes and shivered. "Don't go. Kiss me instead."

"You siren." He leaned over to kiss the hollow at the base of her neck. "I gave you many kisses last night. Surely you've had enough."

"I'll never have enough."

He was powerless to resist this appeal, and they made love again. He felt a little shy about being naked in front of her in the light of day, but she made it clear that she found his body as attractive as he found hers, and he soon forgot his inhibitions.

He was late for his meeting.

Lilia surprised him by appearing at his office at the church that afternoon, just before he began his parish visits. She was soberly and modestly dressed in a black serge gown with a white collar and cuffs, looking for all the world like a proper vicar's wife.

"What are you doing here?" he asked, his heart jolting at the sight of her as if it had been months instead of hours since he saw her last.

"I was wondering what you're doing this afternoon."

"I must visit my parishioners."

"May I come with you?"

He stared at her. "Are you serious?"

She looked hurt. "Of course I'm serious. If you don't want me to come—"

"I do want you to come," he said, taking her hand. "I'm only surprised you want to. You'll likely find it dull. Or difficult. People will ask questions and be curious about you."

"Why do you think I want to go? You've had to answer those questions alone long enough."

"Lilia . . ." He wanted to say so many things, but he kissed her hand instead. So far their strategy of not talking was working well. There would be time for talking later.

It turned out that not many parishioners asked questions, at least not difficult ones. A few people made pointed comments about how nice it was to finally meet the vicar's wife, but Lilia was unfailingly gracious and polite, assuring them the pleasure was *entirely* hers.

As pleased as Paul was by Lilia's willingness to accompany him and her good behavior with his parishioners, he wondered if she was playing a role. Did she think he wanted her to be the perfect vicar's wife?

He saw a glimpse of the real Lilia during one visit to a mother and her adult daughter who were beset by poverty and recurring illnesses. These women had always been reticent with him, and he sensed they would be more comfortable talking to another woman. His instincts were correct, for they responded so well to Lilia's presence that he left them alone together. When he came back to collect her, they were conversing in low tones and her face was animated and sympathetic. Both women embraced her when she and Paul took their leave.

∽

Lilia stayed in Ingleford for two weeks and it was the most idyllic fortnight of Paul's life. Whenever he wasn't working, they spent nearly every spare minute in bed. He even gave Mrs. Mills an unexpected holiday, as her comings and goings quickly became inconvenient, and he and Lilia subsisted on bread and cheese and tea, much of which they consumed in bed. They spent hours exploring each other's bodies, learning what sort of touching the other liked and didn't like, avoiding all serious topics of conversation and speaking only the silly talk of lovers.

That first day, he brought up the subject of contraception, but she said she'd taken care of it. He didn't know what that meant. But she would say no more, and he was quickly distracted by her caresses.

One night, as they lay in bed after a particularly vigorous session of lovemaking, she said, "I hope I'm not tiring you out."

"Do I seem tired to you?"

"Not in the least. I just hope you're not humoring me." She smiled. "Perhaps there are other things you'd rather do."

He propped himself up on his elbow and looked down at her. "Lilia, I'd be an idiot if there was anything else I'd rather do. You're every man's dream in bed."

"I very much doubt that." But her smile faded as she said, "I'm glad you're happy, Paul, but I want to be yours only, not every man's."

Stricken, he said, "I didn't mean to suggest—"

She pressed her fingers lightly against his lips. "I know." Her fingers traced the line of his jaw, then moved down to rest against his bare chest. "I just want you to know you're the only lover I ever wanted."

Deeply moved, he caught her hand and kissed it. "I love you," he whispered.

"And I love you."

Tears came to his eyes. It was the first time she had ever told him directly that she loved him. "Do you?"

"Of course. Why do you think I was so afraid to marry you?"

"Oh, that was the sign, was it?" he said, laughing. "If you had meekly accepted my first proposal, would it have meant you didn't love me?"

"Something like that."

Paul returned home after a long day of meetings and parish visits to find Lilia at her desk in the study, perusing a letter. She rose to embrace him, but she seemed troubled, and he held her away from him so he could look into her eyes.

"What's the matter, my love?" he asked.

"It's a letter from Harriet."

"Tell me." He took her hand and led her to his desk, then sat and drew her down onto his lap.

"It will mean talking about something serious."

"It was bound to happen eventually. I can bear it if you can." But he wasn't as certain as he sounded.

"Very well." She slipped her arms around his neck. "You know the WSPU suspends militant activity when there's an election."

"Yes. That's why I've had the pleasure of your company for a whole fort-night."

"The trouble is that our members who were in prison before the election are still being tortured."

"Force-feedings?"

"Yes, and other brutal treatment. Walton Gaol is the worst."

"In Liverpool?"

"Yes." She shifted in his arms. "Mary Braddock is there, along with several others. They were arrested more than a month ago, but while they were on remand, they weren't allowed to communicate with any of their friends. They started a hunger strike and were force fed. Then they broke the windows of their cells. The result was even more brutal treatment . . ." Her voice trembled, and Paul tightened his arms around her.

"How did Harriet find out about this?" he asked.

"Mary told our Liverpool members who were at the police court for her trial, and they telephoned Harriet at the WSPU office." Lilia released herself from Paul's embrace and began to pace about the room. "The government and prison officials continue to ignore the fact that our members are political prisoners, and they continue to treat our working-class members like common criminals. I must do something."

"What can you do when the government isn't in?" Paul asked.

"We could lead a deputation to the governor of the prison. We can focus on his responsibility, not the government's, in this case."

Lilia stood in the middle of the room, biting her lip. Paul rose and put his hands on her shoulders.

"You must go back to London tomorrow," he said.

"Yes." There was a question in her eyes.

"I understand," he assured her. "This is important, and I won't stand in your way. I'll be here waiting for you."

"It may be a long time."

"I know. As long as you're not directly in danger, I can bear it. As Mrs. Pankhurst's deputy, you must stay safe." Paul was glad she was in a leadership position for this very reason.

She didn't reply.

He didn't press her, but he was worried.

That night, they made love slowly, lingering over every touch.

29

No coward soul is mine. —Emily Brontë

JANUARY 1909

Lilia met the eyes of the maid in the looking glass. "Go on, Lizzie. What are you waiting for?"

"I can't, Mrs. Harris." Lizzie stood frozen, holding the scissors in one hand and a lock of Lilia's hair in the other. "You have such beautiful hair."

"Oh, for the love of—" Lilia snatched the scissors out of the maid's hand and chopped off a thick section of hair just above her shoulder. "Now that I've started the process, surely you can finish it."

Lizzie took the scissors with an air of resignation and began cutting.

"Keep it a little uneven at the bottom," Lilia directed. "I don't want to look fashionable in any way."

"There's no danger of that," the maid replied grimly.

Despite her outward confidence, Lilia felt a pang as the last lock fell

317

away, remembering Paul telling her how much he loved her hair, winding his hands in it and stroking it as they lay in bed together. It was difficult to believe that only a week had passed since she had returned to London. But she must not think of him now. She had work to do, and he had no part in it.

"That's perfect," she said, peering out from under the long, uneven fringe Lizzie had cut across her forehead. "Now for the bleach."

"No, Mrs. Harris. Please don't make me do that."

As Lilia began to expostulate with Lizzie for the second time, Harriet walked into the room. Both women appealed to her to settle the conflict.

"I agree with Lizzie," Harriet said. "There's no need to go that far. Your appearance will be disguised enough with the shorter hair, spectacles, and different clothing. Besides, trying to bleach hair as dark as yours will likely turn it green or some other revolting color, and then you'll only draw attention to yourself."

Lilia banished Lizzie and Harriet from her room, reserving judgment until she had tried on the entire costume. When it was complete, she left the room to examine herself in the cheval glass at the end of the corridor.

"Good God," said Harriet from behind her. "It's almost too effective."

Lilia's shorter hair curled into an unkempt mop around her head, and the black-rimmed stage spectacles hid her eyes. The heavy brown coat and tweed hat were as unfashionable as garments could possibly be.

Lilia turned around to face Harriet and Lizzie. "Pleased to make your acquaintance," she said, flattening her voice and making an awkward curtsy. "I'm Joan Burns."

Harriet made a sound that was half-snort, half-laugh. "Joan Burns? You can't be serious."

"Nobody but you will get the joke. Trust me."

Lizzie shook her head and walked away.

"Honestly, Lilia, I don't understand why you're doing this," Harriet said.

"Someone must."

"Yes, but let it be someone with no ties, someone with no husband or family. Someone like me."

"You forget your poor health. Besides, is a spinster's life worth less than mine? What I'm doing is for all women, regardless of marital status or social class."

"You needn't prove your courage or your willingness to suffer, Lilia."

"You misunderstand me," she said, surprised.

Harriet turned to leave. "I understand you well enough. I understand that you're choosing to do something reckless, risking not only your husband's peace of mind but Mrs. Pankhurst's disapproval."

"Why do you think Joan Burns was born? She has no husband. She isn't a leader of the WSPU. She's just a common foot soldier. Lilia Harris will merely go into abeyance temporarily while Joan Burns does her work."

"You're playacting. You can't be all things to all people."

Harriet walked away, leaving Lilia puzzled and hurt. She and Harriet rarely argued, which may have surprised anyone who knew how strong-willed they both were. But they were of one mind on every political and social issue, so there was no reason to disagree.

Nobody seemed to understand that in addition to protecting Harriet's fragile state of health, Lilia was protecting Paul from the shame of his wife's being arrested and likely serving a prison term. She could never carry out her plan as Lilia Harris, only as Joan Burns, spinster and working woman. Perhaps it was cowardly not to inform Mrs. Pankhurst, but becoming Joan Burns would protect the WSPU, as well. Someone had to call attention to the brutal treatment of the working-class suffragettes in Walton Gaol, and Lilia believed she was the only person physically healthy and influential enough to do it. If nobody saw through her disguise and she was arrested and treated as badly as the others, she could prove that Lilia Harris and Joan Burns would never have been treated equally.

She did feel guilty for not telling Paul everything, but she knew he wouldn't approve. Why upset him if her actions came to nothing? There would be time to make it up to him later. No matter what she did, she was letting someone down. The conflict had torn her in two, and from that division, Joan Burns was born.

∽

Lilia stared at the walls of her tiny cell and shivered in the coarse brown serge gown of a third-division prisoner. So far, everything had gone according to plan. As Joan Burns, she had led the deputation to the governor's house. Her disguise had fooled even the other WSPU members, though they were all from the Liverpool chapter and didn't know her. She didn't want anyone else to be censured by Mrs. Pankhurst for militant action during an election, so she had arranged with the other organizers that she would be the only person arrested. All she had done at the governor's house was demand that the current suffragette prisoners be released and drop a few stones over the hedge of his garden.

Her sentence was a month in Walton Gaol. It was a much longer sentence for doing much less damage than the one she had received as Lilia Brooke for window-breaking. Without conscious intent, Lilia entered so fully into the persona of Joan Burns that even when handled roughly, she didn't fight back. Lilia Brooke had fought with all her might; Joan Burns resisted, but only passively. There had been only a cursory medical examination for Joan Burns and no special privileges, such as Lilia Brooke had received. The only similarity between them so far was that she had been on a hunger strike for five days and nobody had yet tried to force-feed her.

Now that she was in prison, she no longer pushed thoughts of Paul aside. Deprived of physical comforts and food, she fed instead on memories of their fortnight together. Their first attempt at lovemaking had been too awkward and desperate to be truly satisfying, but after that, it had been everything Lilia had hoped it would be. Once Paul allowed his natural sensuality to overcome his inhibitions, he was a good lover, considerate and passionate. She couldn't stop touching him, fascinated by his smooth, lean muscles and the golden hair on his chest—and other interesting places.

She missed him terribly and sometimes wondered if she had made a mistake in leading the deputation herself. Perhaps she could have found someone in the Liverpool WSPU who was willing to do it, with similar results. And what if Paul didn't forgive her for the steps she had taken to protect him? He might not be able to look past the fact that she had deceived him.

A strangled scream from a nearby cell broke into her thoughts, freezing her blood. She knew what the sounds meant: the scuffle of feet and voices and clattering of tools used for the evil business. She rapped on the wall the code for "No Surrender," but the noises from the next cell were loud enough to drown it out.

The scream was succeeded by a faint piteous sobbing, worse to hear than the scream had been. Was it Mary Braddock or Alice Marks? They had both been in jail for more than six weeks and Lilia knew their cells were near hers.

A moment later, the prison doctor and four wardresses entered Lilia's cell. What followed was something she knew enough about from other women's stories, and she was prepared for the pain. What she wasn't prepared for was the experience of being methodically overcome by physical force. The doctor, an older man, set about his task with grim determination, not meeting her eyes but merely giving orders to the wardresses.

They told her to lie down on her plank bed, and she obeyed. But when the wardresses held her limbs down and the doctor ordered her to open her mouth, she could no longer be passive. Clenching her teeth as tightly as she could, she began to struggle against her restraints.

The doctor cursed her and pried her mouth open with a steel gag. She felt it cutting into her gums and began to choke as the blood ran down into her throat. He paid no attention, taking a tube that seemed impossibly wide and pushing it down her throat. Her throat felt torn, and as the tube went down there was a searing pain in her chest.

The food was poured quickly into the tube, and Lilia began to choke again, writhing and struggling beneath her attackers. She was sick almost at once, her body involuntarily doubling up as she vomited, but the doctor leaned on her knees and a wardress pulled her head back. She nearly lost consciousness.

It seemed like forever before the doctor removed the tube and stepped back, looking down with disgust at the vomit on his sleeve. He only met her eyes for a second, and Lilia saw utter contempt on his face. Then, unbelievably, he slapped her. It wasn't a violent slap, not the sort meant to cause physical harm. He merely wanted to show how much he despised her.

As her torturers left, Lilia collapsed on the bed, shaking uncontrollably. But she didn't make a sound, and she didn't cry. Neither Joan Burns nor Lilia Harris—and especially not Lilia Brooke—would cry over this, at least not where others might hear.

Words were scrawled on her cell wall from previous prisoners, mostly quotations from the Bible or from Mrs. Pankhurst's speeches. Her eyes now fell upon one she hadn't noticed before, adapted from Thoreau's *On the Duty of Civil Disobedience*: "Under a Government which imprisons any unjustly, the true place for a just *woman* is also a prison."

Lilia lost track of time. She had at first used her twice-daily force-feedings to mark how many days had elapsed. But as she became weaker, she was forced to use all her strength just to recover from each session of torture. She tried to judge how much more her body could withstand. She sometimes worried that she couldn't remember clearly what was happening, and she needed to remember the details of her treatment in order to reveal the truth once she was released.

She read the words on her cell wall over and over again. They gave her comfort, even the Bible verses. After one force-feeding she meditated upon "Deeds, not Words," the WSPU motto. After another, when she couldn't rise from the floor for some time, she found parts of the twenty-third Psalm scrawled low on the wall: "Though I walk through the valley of the shadow of death, Thou art with me." Who was with her? Was God with her? Was there a God? She prayed, but didn't know to whom she prayed. She felt Paul's presence with her more than the presence of a god, so she prayed to him. *Help me bear this. Don't be angry. Be my support and my strength instead.*

She could have revealed her true identity. Sometimes when a wardress removed Lilia's spectacles before the force-feeding, the doctor would look at her as if he suspected she wasn't who she said she was. No doubt they would release her, or at least treat her more kindly, if they knew she was Mrs. Pankhurst's deputy, a lady with influence. But Lilia Harris was there, too, in spirit. She was protecting Joan Burns, comforting her and saying, *I will help you. The world will know what you are suffering. Don't be afraid.*

One day, a different doctor came, a younger doctor with a sneer and cruel eyes. "I don't know what Doctor Gilbert was complaining about," he bragged. "It's a simple procedure, like stuffing a turkey."

The preparations for her torture began as usual, but this doctor used a

324 ⠢ CLARISSA HARWOOD

smaller tube and ignored her clenched teeth, shoving it into her nostril instead. The pain made her cry out involuntarily and struggle to free herself, but it was no use. She could only cough, and she did so over and over again to try to prevent the tube from going in deeper. But it did go deeper, until she felt a sharp pain in her chest, and at once the doctor poured the food into the tube.

Something was wrong. She was suffocating. She kicked out at the doctor, freeing one of her feet and connecting with his leg. Momentarily distracted, he ordered the wardresses to hold her. One of them was crying even as she obeyed. Lilia couldn't breathe, coughing and choking so violently that they released her and she fell against the wall. She continued to cough uncontrollably, and a dark-brown liquid came out of her mouth.

After a while she was placed on the plank bed by someone with gentle hands and heard a new male voice speaking, but she couldn't sort the sounds into words. She knew only that her chest was examined and she was injected with something, and that she was too weak to resist.

She dreamed about blood. She was covered in it, and it filled up her tiny cell like Alice's tears in Wonderland, or the blood-red sea plagued by God in Exodus. She thought she would drown in it. She awoke to a sharp, stabbing sensation in her lower abdomen, then a rush of blood that she knew was not caused by the force-feeding. But her brief moment of clarity was lost in the intensity of the pain, and she knew no more for a long time.

When she awoke much later, she was no longer in the cell, but in a bed in an unfamiliar room with people she didn't know. It was quiet, and light was filtering through the windows. She cried then, and a woman's arms went around her, comforting her with words in a strange dialect. But she tried not to cry, for crying would bring on a coughing fit, and the coughing fit would bring on more pain.

More than anything, she wanted to be with Paul, but she knew she had hurt him. In her feverish state she couldn't remember what exactly she had done, but she knew it was bad and he might not forgive her.

30

Those who dare to rebel in every age . . . make life possible for those whom temperament compels to submit. It is the rebels who extend the boundary of right little by little, narrowing the confines of wrong, and crowding it out of existence

—Sarah Grand, *The Heavenly Twins*

FEBRUARY 1909

After more than a month without seeing Lilia, Paul was frantic. She had told him not to worry about her—a useless injunction—and that if anything went wrong, he could write to Harriet for information. And nothing had seemed wrong—at first. Lilia sent him two letters every week, claiming to be fine, just busy with her plans. The letters were brief, but they were warm and loving, which comforted him.

But after a while, he began to notice something odd about them. She never answered the questions he asked in the letters he sent to her. He knew she wouldn't say anything specific about her plans for the WSPU, but she didn't even reply to simple questions, nor did she respond to anything he told her about his life. He became suspicious enough to write to Harriet, but her reply was even more troubling: she said nothing about Lilia, only

325

that the WSPU was trying to have the Walton Gaol prisoners released as soon as possible. He decided to go to London, intending to surprise Lilia at the WSPU office.

Lilia wasn't there, but Harriet was. There were only a few other WSPU members in the office, and Harriet ushered Paul to the large table used for meetings, well away from the others.

She looked exhausted, and her face was an unhealthy grayish color. Paul was alarmed enough to temporarily forget his worry for Lilia, and he insisted on getting her a glass of water. Once he had brought it and she had taken a sip, a little color returned to her face.

"I know you're here to see Lilia, but she's not here," Harriet said.

"I see she's not in the office. Is she at the house?"

"No." Harriet pressed her lips together. "She's in Liverpool, in Walton Gaol."

He shook his head. "That's impossible. She's been sending me letters from London. I received the last one only two days ago."

"I sent those."

"They were in her hand."

"She wrote them all before she went to Liverpool. She post-dated them, sealed them, and gave me instructions to post them at regular intervals."

Paul stared at her. "Why would she deceive me to such an extent?"

Harriet sighed. "She knew you'd be worried. She wanted to protect you before she enacted her plan, and she also didn't want to shame you, so she took a different name and disguised herself as a working-class woman."

"Dear God." He pressed his fist against his mouth. "She led the deputation to the prison governor's house, didn't she?"

Harriet nodded grimly.

Perhaps Lilia did want to protect him, but he knew there were other reasons for her behavior. She liked to lead her troops, she liked to act on her plans instead of sending volunteers to carry them out, and her oft-voiced concern about the treatment of working-class suffragette prisoners would be enough to make her act as she had.

"How long has she been in jail?"

"Three weeks." Harriet took another sip of water.

"Has anyone tried to visit her? Is she on a hunger strike? Do you know how she's being treated?"

"She hasn't been allowed visitors, but she sent me one letter, which I received today." Harriet reached into her skirt pocket and pulled out a paper. She hesitated before giving it to him, and he had to restrain himself from snatching it out of her hand.

> Dear Harriet,
> I am being treated as we expected, but don't worry. It is only pain, and I will endure it for the greater good.
> Joan Burns

"The greater good!" Paul repeated in frustration. He read the letter multiple times, then looked up. "What does 'as we expected' mean?"

"I can't be certain, but... forcible feeding, presumably."

He frowned, studying Harriet's face intently. Was she trying to protect him, too? Taking a deep breath, he looked at the letter again. "Joan Burns. At least she hasn't lost her sense of humor."

Harriet smiled grimly. "She said I'd be the only one to get the joke."

"The first time I saw her, she was a twelve-year-old Jeanne d'Arc leading her army of brothers through a field. It's not something I can ever forget."

"I'm sorry about this. It was my plan from the first to lead the deputation to the governor's house, but she insisted on taking my place. And I can't go to Liverpool myself because—"

"Because while Lilia is being Joan Burns, someone must lead the London WSPU." He spoke gently. "You are above reproach in this, Miss Firth."

For the first time since he'd known her, Harriet looked like she was going to cry. But after a few seconds of silent struggle, she managed to resume her businesslike mien.

"Would you like the name and address of the WSPU organizer in Liverpool?" she asked.

"Yes, thank you. I'll take the next train there."

Harriet wrote down the information and handed it to him. "Unless Lilia is in grave danger, I know she'd prefer not to have her true identity known."

"I suppose that makes me Mr. Burns."

∽

Paul's train arrived in Liverpool early that evening, and he decided to go first to the house of the local WSPU organizer, Mrs. Feeney, who would have the most recent news of suffragette prisoners. The long day of travel and his worry about Lilia had strained Paul's nerves almost to the breaking point. He forgot about being Mr. Burns and used his real name when identifying himself to the maid who answered the door of the imposing four-story mansion.

He was left standing in the front foyer, a strange omission for a household as grand as this one, watching servants rushing to and fro. He seemed to have arrived in the middle of some commotion.

Eventually a well-upholstered, middle-aged matron came to greet him. "I'm so sorry to keep you waiting, Mr. Harris. I'm amazed you received my telegram so quickly. I'm Mrs. Feeney."

"I didn't receive your telegram," he said, alarmed. "What was it about?"

"Your wife is here. She was released from Walton Gaol unexpectedly this morning. The prison officials sent her here in a cab."

"Thank God! Will you take me to her?"

"The doctor is with her now, but . . . come with me."

Paul followed Mrs. Feeney to an upstairs sitting room, where she frustrated him by playing the hostess instead of giving him the information he wanted or, better yet, taking him to Lilia. Waving off her offers of food, drink, and a place to rest, Paul said, "Where is my wife? I must see her."

Mrs. Feeney hesitated, then said, "She's very ill. I believe she was released suddenly because the prison authorities didn't want . . ." She didn't finish, but Paul sensed the rest. *Her death on their hands.*

"I must see her," he repeated.

Mrs. Feeney rose and knocked lightly at the door of the adjoining room, then opened it and motioned Paul inside.

Paul entered the room, steeling himself for the worst. Lilia was in bed, her face as white as the pillows she was propped up against, and her eyes were closed. The doctor, a ginger-haired man about Paul's age, was listening to her heart through a stethoscope.

"I'm Paul Harris, her husband," he explained in a whisper, in response to the doctor's quizzical look.

He had to take a deep breath to calm himself before he could look at Lilia more closely. Her breathing was labored and noisy, and there was a patch of dried blood underneath one nostril. She was terrifyingly thin. Her height tended to camouflage any gains or losses in her weight, so it was particularly alarming to Paul that he could see a difference even though the bedclothes covered most of her body.

He sat in the chair beside the bed and took her hand. She opened her eyes and looked at him as if she didn't recognize him. Then she tried to speak, but she coughed instead, a horrible wracking cough that seemed to go on forever. She collapsed back against the pillows.

The doctor straightened up and beckoned Paul to join him in the far corner of the room.

"What's the matter with my wife?" Paul asked him anxiously.

"She has pleuropneumonia and a fever of 102 degrees. She also has numerous injuries."

"Injuries?"

The doctor hesitated, as if attempting to assess how much truth Paul was capable of hearing. "Your wife has been forcibly fed numerous times. Forcible feeding often causes lacerations to the throat when the tube goes down, especially if the patient struggles. In your wife's case, she seems to have been forcibly fed through both the mouth and the nose, and the mucous membranes have been torn. The pneumonia, I suspect, was caused by her being accidentally force-fed into the lungs."

"Will she recover?" Paul asked hoarsely.

"It's too soon to tell, but I think so, as long as her fever breaks. She's young and her overall health appears to be good."

"Thank you." Paul turned to go back to Lilia, but the doctor stopped him.

"Just a moment, Mr. Harris. I am sympathetic to the suffragettes, but I don't think young married women ought to be risking imprisonment and putting themselves in danger as your wife has done, especially in her condition."

He stared at the doctor in confusion. "What condition?"

The doctor looked uncomfortable. "I can't be certain, but I believe your wife was pregnant."

Paul took a step back, his legs suddenly feeling too weak to support his weight.

The doctor took his arm to steady him and guided him to a nearby chair. "I'm sorry."

Lilia was going to have his child and she hadn't told him. Even worse, she'd engaged in her usual dangerous activities, had been arrested and gone on a hunger strike in jail, all despite her delicate condition. Paul was stupefied.

"You said she *was* pregnant," Paul managed to choke out. "Is the baby—"

"I'm sorry," the doctor repeated. "It would have been early in the pregnancy. Her miscarriage is likely what precipitated her release from jail. A wardress found her in a pool of blood on the floor of her cell and assumed she'd been beaten. The prison officials don't want a scandal, so they let her go before she could be treated more brutally."

Paul stared at him blankly.

"Why don't you lie down and rest for a while?" the doctor suggested. "Your wife is being well cared for, and I'll send for you if there's any change in her condition."

Paul lay down in the adjoining room, but his mind was spinning. Had she known she was pregnant? Was that the reason for all the deception, not to protect him but to prevent him from knowing she was risking their child's life as well as her own? No. She wouldn't have started a hunger strike if she'd known.

But how could she be so thoughtless? Hadn't it occurred to her what her actions would do to him and to their relationship? He couldn't go on like this, never knowing what life-threatening situation she would throw herself into next. Perhaps he wouldn't have to, if she died. Guilt, anger, fear, and sadness took turns wrenching his insides.

Paul spent a long night at Lilia's bedside. He didn't allow himself to think. He prayed from time to time, but his prayers were brief and fragmentary. He remembered his similar vigil at her bedside after the Parliament Square riot. This time, he was her husband and didn't have to fight for the right to be with her, but this time there was also more at stake. His throat ached with tears, but he wouldn't let them fall.

31

The pride keeps up,

Until the heart breaks under it

—Elizabeth Barrett Browning, *Aurora Leigh*

Lilia survived the night, but she still had a high fever, and Paul made arrangements to stay longer. He wrote to the vicar of a neighboring parish for help with his duties in Ingleford. He also wrote a difficult letter to Lilia's family, trying not to worry them. He sent for some of his clothing, too, since he had boarded the train from London hastily and without luggage.

On the third day Lilia's fever broke. The first words she spoke to Paul were, "Will you forgive me?"

He looked up, bleary-eyed from lack of sleep. "I will, if you recover."

"And if I don't?"

"I won't forgive you."

"That's not very Christian of you." She began to cough, and he handed her the glass of water on her bedside table.

"I'm not a good Christian." He watched her drink. It seemed to pain her to swallow. "You shouldn't speak. It will hurt your throat."

"I prayed in the jail cell, you know. I didn't know what to say, or if anyone was listening, so I prayed to you."

The full significance of her words took a moment to sink in, but all he said after a brief silence was, "That's very bad theology."

"I can't imagine God. It was easier to imagine the best person I know."

He smiled wearily and reached out to stroke her cheek.

"It didn't count, anyway," she said. "I've never thought much of people who pray only when they're in distress."

"It counts. Now stop talking and rest."

Mrs. Feeney had a sofa moved into Lilia's room so Paul could sleep there without disturbing her. Now that she was out of danger, he could leave her for short periods without worrying, and he got into the habit of walking the streets of Liverpool. At first, he walked aimlessly, noticing nothing of his surroundings. But one evening, he began to pay attention. The industrial city didn't show itself to advantage in the gray winter light, especially near the docks, but at least the air was mild. Dock workers exchanged what sounded like friendly insults as they headed to a nearby pub, but their dialect was incomprehensible to Paul. Even late in the day, the street traffic was noisy, and he was relieved to find himself in front of a church, Our Lady and Saint Nicholas.

A small choir was singing inside, and Paul went in and sat at the back of the sanctuary, not wanting to draw attention to himself. Though he wasn't wearing his clerical collar, there was still a chance someone he knew could be there. But the small group of congregants was clustered near the front and nobody paid him any attention.

Evensong was under way and the dimly lit church was a haven of peace. Although he saw no censer, the church smelled faintly of incense. Along with the simple beauty of the choral music, the scent was a balm to his Anglo-Catholic soul.

He paid no further attention to the details of the church or the service, as he was so wrapped up in his worries about Lilia. But the longer he stayed, the calmer he felt. It wasn't just peace; though he had never been there before, it was a sense of homecoming.

He was startled by one of the prayers spoken by the officiating priest: "God save the suffragettes in Walton Gaol, help us with Thy love and strength to guard them, spare those who suffer for conscience's sake. Hear us when we pray to Thee."

He had heard of suffragettes interrupting church services to shout out prayers for their members in jail, but he had never been in a church where the prayers were included in the service as a matter of course. This, too, was balm to his soul.

After the service, Paul remained in his pew, letting the stillness wash over him. He didn't realize how long he had been there until he heard footsteps and looked up to see that he was alone in the church with the priest who had conducted the service.

"I'm sorry to disturb you," the young priest said. "I'm Mr. Delaney, the curate. May I help you somehow?"

You already have, Paul thought. "No, forgive me for staying so long," he said aloud. "You must wish to lock up the church for the night."

"Not at all. Stay as long as you like."

But Paul rose to leave, and Mr. Delaney walked him out. On the way, Paul asked about the church and its history, curious about the hints of Anglo-Catholicism he saw everywhere.

"I'm fairly new to the church," his companion said, "but I was born and raised in Liverpool. You may know this is the most Catholic city in England, mainly because of the Irish immigrants. Most of our Anglican churches are

High Church, and we're higher than most. In fact, our vicar will be leaving at the end of the summer because he converted to Roman Catholicism."

"Do you have a replacement yet?"

"No." The young priest looked at Paul curiously.

Before the other man could ask the reason for his interest, Paul said, "I was impressed by your prayer for the suffragettes. Is that common practice here?"

"Lately it is. You may have heard of the terrible treatment of these women at Walton Gaol, and we're trying to do what we can to help. It's not much, but . . ." Mr. Delaney raised both hands in a gesture that was both helpless and hopeful.

"My wife is a suffragette and . . . was imprisoned there. So I appreciate that prayer."

"I'm sorry. How is she?"

"Not very well, just now, but the doctor thinks she'll recover fully."

"If you wish to tell me her name, we can include it in the prayers this week."

Paul merely said he would think about it, unsure what name Lilia would want him to use. But he thanked the man warmly and left.

∽

One night Lilia said, "Are you very angry with me?"

"I don't know." He was lying on the sofa across the room, but couldn't fall asleep.

"I had no idea I was pregnant. Do you believe me?"

"Yes, I do."

"I would never have started the hunger strike if I'd known. Before I was arrested, I was so caught up in planning my disguise and the deputation that I didn't notice anything else. I kept forgetting to eat and sleep. I wouldn't have noticed any changes."

He was silent.

"I was using a contraceptive device when I was with you in Ingleford, too, but obviously it didn't work." She paused. "Will you come here, please?"

He left the sofa and sat in the chair by her bed, glad she couldn't see his face in the darkness.

"Will you hold my hand?" she whispered.

He took her hand and pressed it to his lips.

"I'm so sorry, Paul," she said. "I don't know how to explain why I did what I did. I thought I could avoid hurting you by becoming a different person, just for a short time. Joan Burns could give herself completely to the WSPU, and Lilia Harris could give herself completely to you. It was stupid and selfish of me, but I swear I would never knowingly jeopardize the life of our child."

"Yet you've put your own life in jeopardy countless times."

"That's different."

"Not as different as you might think. Not to me." His voice broke and he dropped her hand, leaning his forehead against the side of her bed.

He felt her hand on his hair. "Paul, darling, please don't cry. I do understand. I thought I was protecting you, but I only hurt us both. I promise I'll never do anything like that again."

But he couldn't help it, and she stroked his hair as he wept, then urged him to lie down in bed with her. He did so, careful not to hold her too tightly. He fell asleep with her in his arms.

∾

The hall that the Liverpool WSPU had rented was too small for the number of people assembled there, nearly one hundred in a room meant for sixty. With tables squeezed in, too, the room was crowded, hot, and stuffy. Paul had been invited to sit with Lilia on the dais, but he declined, choosing instead to join Mary Braddock and Harriet at a table near the front of the room. Lady Fernham sat nearby.

The purpose of the meeting, which included a breakfast as well as speeches, was to honor Lilia's work for the WSPU and welcome her back after her ordeal in Walton Gaol. The WSPU often held such meetings for members who had recently been released from prison, but in Lilia's case, the meeting had had to be postponed until she was well enough to attend.

Paul kept a close eye on Lilia, worried the crowd and the heat of the room might be too much for her. She was still fragile and thin, far from fully recovered, but it had been three weeks since her release from jail and she was well enough to return to Ingleford with Paul the next day. She sat with Mrs. Feeney and Mrs. Pankhurst, who had recently returned from her trip to America.

Mrs. Pankhurst opened the meeting. Paul had never seen her up close and was impressed by the energy and eloquence of the tiny woman with fire in her eyes. Aside from her height, she was, Paul suspected, a mirror of what his wife would be like in twenty years' time.

"Mrs. Harris has an enviable combination of intelligence, courage, and sympathy," Mrs. Pankhurst said, "which has served her well in her short time in leadership. She has averted crises and lessened the friction among some of our members. She has also drawn the attention of important public figures to the Cause. We of the Women's Social and Political Union are very fortunate to have this young woman on our side—indeed, she would be a formidable enemy!" Several audience members laughed.

As the speeches continued, Paul was amazed by the number of people who stood up to speak about Lilia. One after another, both women and men described what Lilia had done for the Cause and sometimes for them personally. One man, a member of Parliament, spoke about the increasing number of his colleagues who supported women's suffrage because of Lilia's letters and meetings with them. A young girl gave a halting, heartfelt speech about the way Lilia had helped her leave her employer, who had abused her, and found her paid work with the WSPU.

Even Mary made a short speech, despite her weakened state from her long prison term and her discomfort with public speaking. She ended by saying, "Mrs. Harris spoke for me when I didn't know what to say, and she acted for me when I didn't know what to do. But she also taught me to speak and act for myself."

Finally, it was Lilia's turn. The audience burst into spontaneous applause as soon as she stood to speak, and as she waited for the applause to die down, Paul could see she was struggling not to cry.

"Thank you," she began. "For once in my life, I think I'm speechless. I'm overwhelmed by your kind words." She paused and took a deep breath. "I am proud to be a member of the WSPU, but I couldn't have done anything without your support. I must single out a few people for special mention. Mrs. Pankhurst, you've been my inspiration, and you've taught me how to behave with dignity as well as forcefulness. And my dear friends, Lady Fernham, Miss Harriet Firth, and Miss Mary Braddock—words can't express the debt I owe each of you for your loyalty and encouragement.

"Finally, I must also thank my husband, Mr. Paul Harris. Anyone who knows me well will imagine the enormous patience and longsuffering required of any man who could have the nerve to marry me, and I am amazed by his seemingly endless reserves of both. He has supported my work even when it was against his best interests to do so."

The audience burst into applause once again. Several people turned to smile at Paul. Lilia raised her hand for silence.

"I have one more thing to say. My husband has made great sacrifices because of my work. I could list them all, but I wish to respect his privacy.

Suffice it to say he has given up what the best of married men take for granted: a wife who devotes herself to his comfort, a wife who is an equal partner in his household, and even merely a wife who lives with him. In short, he has given up a normal married life. I want to give him that, and I can do so only by resigning from the WSPU."

There was a collective gasp from the crowd.

Even before her words had fully sunk in, Paul was on his feet. In his strongest, most confident public voice, he said, "I cannot accept your resignation."

The room went silent.

His eyes locked with Lilia's. It was the longest public silence he had ever experienced.

Finally, Mrs. Pankhurst rose and said, "I think we ought to allow Mr. and Mrs. Harris a private conversation on this matter."

The audience began to talk amongst themselves as Lilia left the podium and Paul moved toward her. Aware of the stares of interested onlookers, Paul took Lilia's hand and led her out of the room and into an empty corridor.

Before she could speak, he said, "You must not do this."

"I want to be with you," she said. "It's not good for us to live apart."

"I agree things should change, but not at such a cost to you. We can compromise. Think of the way you've changed these people's lives and inspired them. You can't give that up. The WSPU is so much a part of you, I can't imagine who you would be without it."

"I would be your friend and your lover . . . and your wife," she said, tears running down her cheeks.

Paul took her in his arms. "You are all of those things. But I won't let you resign from the WSPU."

"What, do you forbid me?" She laughed through her tears.

"Yes, I forbid you."

"That sort of language didn't work when you first proposed to me, remember?"

"Very well, let me try again. Will you reconsider your decision to resign?"

"That's better." She dried her tears, kissed him, and led him back into the hall.

Epilogue

JUNE 1909

As the London train pulled into Liverpool station, Lilia raised her head from Paul's shoulder and said, "Let's get off the train and walk for a while. My legs are stiff."

"If you wish." He smiled and tucked a stray curl behind her ear. "You look like a wild duckling with that hair."

To fix Joan Burns's disastrous haircut, the hairdresser had had to cut it even shorter. Lilia used a pomade to smooth her curls, but it was a constant battle. She would be glad when it grew long again.

When they were on the street, Lilia took Paul's arm and said, "I want to see the church."

"It's a longish walk from here. Are you certain?"

"I've had three months to laze about, and I'm in perfectly good health now. Don't worry." She tired more quickly than she used to, but in most ways, she had recovered from her ordeal in Walton Gaol.

"I'm not worried. I just don't want the train to leave for Scotland without us, and a honeymoon trip to Liverpool wasn't my plan."

"Nor mine. An eight-months-delayed honeymoon is quite long enough. But I can't wait to see the church."

"Very well."

They walked to the church Paul had told her so much about, the church where, in the autumn, he would be vicar. It was open and airy, just as he had described it, with gray stone arches and walnut wood pews. It wasn't as elaborate as a cathedral, but it seemed to her nearly large and ornate enough to be one. The church was empty, save a few people milling about, and Paul gave her a tour, explaining the scenes depicted on the stained-glass windows and the significance of the carvings on the altarpiece and pulpit. As he talked, his face lit up in a way it hadn't done since he was a canon at the cathedral. Although she was interested in the church's Anglo-Catholic practices and tradition of supporting women's rights, she was more interested in watching him.

"I'm sorry," he said after a while. "I must be boring you."

"Not in the least. But we ought to leave if we hope to catch our train."

On their way back, Paul said, "Lilia, are you sure you want come back to Liverpool? After all the suffering you experienced at Walton Gaol—"

"As long as I stay out of jail, I'll be fine."

"Do you think you'll be able to do that?"

"Very amusing. I promised you I wouldn't do anything illegal or dangerous, and I intend to keep that promise, even when I join the Liverpool WSPU."

"Good. But it's more important to me that you tell me your plans, whatever they are, so we can discuss them together."

"Agreed. In any case, I want to focus on writing my book first."

Lilia had begun work on a book to expose the disparity between her experience in Holloway Prison as Lilia Brooke and in Walton Gaol as Joan Burns. Robert Wilton, an MP who was one of her supporters, had tried to open a public inquiry about her treatment at Walton Gaol, with no success. Her letter to Harriet—the only letter she was allowed to write while in jail—was used against her. She had written *it is only pain* in an attempt to assuage her friend's concerns, but the Home Secretary claimed it would be hopeless to bring forward a complaint with such a letter on record.

"I want to read your book when it's finished," Paul said.

She hesitated. "I don't intend to leave anything out, and some of the details will upset you."

"Let me make that choice. You know how I feel about being protected." He pressed her hand gently where it rested on his arm.

"Very well."

As they walked, two men passed them, conversing loudly.

"Did you understand anything they said?" Paul asked when they had gone by.

"Not a word." She laughed. "We're going to have to learn a new language."

He pointed out a squat red brick building with a TO LET sign. "That's a former rooming house. After we move here, I'd like you to look at it. I was thinking it could make a good house of refuge for women and children who need help."

She smiled. "That's a good idea."

When they were once again sitting beside each other in their compartment and the train began to pull out of the station, Lilia took off her hat and sat back with a contented sigh. "It feels so indulgent to take a trip with you. A whole fortnight together with no work to do. I wonder how we'll fill our time."

He gave her sidelong glance. "I have a few ideas."

"Do you?" she said with feigned innocence. "Do your ideas involve teaching me how to be the perfect vicar's wife?"

He looked alarmed. "Lilia, promise me something."

"What?"

"That you will never, ever try to be the perfect vicar's wife."

She promised.

Author's Note

The New Woman was as easily recognizable to the late Victorian and Edwardian public as the Angel in the House. Intellectual, sexually open, and independent, the New Woman was often represented in fiction of the period wearing rational dress and with familiar props, such as a cigarette and a bicycle, indicating her dangerously masculine and mobile habits.

The term *suffragette* was initially used in a derogatory way to refer to the women involved in the militant suffragette movement, but members of the Women's Social and Political Union (WSPU) decided to appropriate it for themselves. More conservative, nonmilitant women's suffrage groups, such as the National Union of Women's Suffrage Societies (NUWSS), preferred the term *suffragist*.

All the characters in this novel are fictional except for Emmeline Pankhurst, the founder of the WSPU. Her autobiography, *My Own Story*, sparked my interest in the WSPU, and her conversation with Lilia about marriage is consistent with her history. She did indeed suggest a free union to Richard Pankhurst, but he convinced her to marry him, instead, so her public work would be taken seriously. Her high profile and intimidating presence ensured her relatively good treatment in prison, and she was never actually force-fed, though prison officials did attempt it (she frightened them away).

Although I've taken the liberty of compressing the timeline of women's suffrage in England, the demonstrations, hunger strikes, forcible feeding, and militant activities referred to in the novel are based on actual events that happened during the first decade of the twentieth century. It was common for women as young as Lilia to rise quickly in the ranks of the WSPU. Her deputation to the governor of Walton Gaol and her brutal treatment in that prison are based on the actions of Lady Constance Lytton, who disguised herself as a working-class woman to draw attention to the preferential treatment she received under her own name during her previous prison terms. Her story, published as *Prison and Prisoners*, is well worth reading for its own sake.

Clergy in the Church of England responded in diverse ways to the women's suffrage movement. Many church leaders supported the conservative, nonmilitant NUWSS, but only a few supported militant groups such as the WSPU. Randall Davidson, the Archbishop of Canterbury, supported women's suffrage until the militants began to use violent tactics. One notable supporter was the Bishop of Kensington, who wrote in the *Daily Graphic*, "The present outbursts of militancy are mainly due to the persistent disregard of the claims of women." Among the suffragettes there were similarly wide-ranging attitudes towards the church. Some did indeed set fire to and even bomb churches to make a point about male privilege (most of these incidents occurred in 1913 and 1914, later than the scope of this novel), but others, including Constance Lytton, drew on their faith to sustain them during their hunger strikes and forcible feeding in prison.

The first British women gained the right to vote in 1918 (they had to be over thirty and meet a property qualification). By 1928, all British women over twenty-one could vote, finally achieving the same voting rights as men. Lilia would have lived to see the victory for which she had fought so hard.

Acknowledgments

Twenty years ago a scene from an unwritten novel popped into my head. It was a confrontation in a meadow between a quiet boy who didn't know how to play, and a fiery girl pretending to be Jeanne d'Arc, leading her army of brothers. That scene haunted me for many years before I finally gave in and started writing Paul and Lilia's story.

It's impossible to mention everyone who has made me a better writer during those twenty years, but I do want to thank the people who have directly influenced this novel:

Jannay Thiessen, Joyce Pitzel, and Christine Thorpe, who valiantly read to the end of a long early draft and still believed in my writing.

Abby Murphy, beta reader extraordinaire, whose brilliant suggestions shone light into my dark editing cave. My other wonderful beta readers, Kay Henden, Diane McIntyre Rose, and Kay Grimanis, whose comments helped smooth the rough edges and made my final draft sparkle.

Jennifer Delamere, who did double duty as beta reader and travel companion. Thanks for suggesting the Houses of Parliament tour and waiting patiently while I bought every suffragette-themed item in the gift shop, then waited again while I stood in the middle of Parliament Square and stared at steps.

The London Writers Society critique groups, who have helped me hone my craft, even the members who made me cry.

Central Home Church for being a supportive, non-churchy community, especially Jennifer Hryniw for repeatedly embarrassing me with praise for this book.

My amazing agent, Laura Crockett, who creates order out of chaos and whose enthusiasm for this novel has never wavered: we are living proof that when a new author and a new agent take a chance on each other, magic can happen! And to Uwe Stender and the whole TriadaUS team, you're a model of what a literary agency should be.

Katie McGuire, my insightful editor and fellow grammar nerd, for your patience with my many questions and comments and for understanding my vision. And to the clever and creative design team at Pegasus, thanks for the beautiful cover.

My husband Michael, who was always on Lilia's side, even when I wasn't. You knew and loved this book before anyone else did, and I couldn't have persisted without you.